THE HORSE CHANGER

'Messala Corvinus said it best of the opportunist, Quintus Dellius: "He was the Horse Changer of our civil war." In the course of a year, Dellius served Dolabella, then Cassius, and finally Mark Antony…'

Seneca the Elder

From *Suasoriae* 1.7 (trans. C. Smith)

Also by Craig Smith:

The Whisper of Leaves
Cold Rain
Every Dark Place

The Painted Messiah
The Blood Lance

THE HORSE CHANGER

CRAIG SMITH

MYRMIDON

MYRMIDON
Rotterdam House
116 Quayside
Newcastle upon Tyne
NE1 3DY

www.myrmidonbooks.com

First published in the United Kingdom by Myrmidon 2015

A catalogue record for this book is available from the British Library.

ISBN 978-1-910183-13-7

Set in 11/14pt Sabon by Reality Premedia Services, Pvt. Ltd

Printed in the UK by CPI Group (UK) Ltd, Croydon, CR0 4YY

1 3 5 7 9 10 8 6 4 2

Charles Blaney, Don Jennermann, and Frederick Williams:

hoi didaskaloi – the (beautiful) teachers.

I was fifteen when Charles Blaney enticed me to open the *Iliad*, eighteen when Don Jennermann assigned all the extant tragedies of ancient Greece, and thirty-six when Rick Williams walked with me through Plato's *Symposium* at the pace of six lines a day.

We like to say that our teachers make a difference in our lives, but the truth is only a select few have that kind of impact. I have pursued any number of intellectual passions in my life, but I always come back to the abiding mysteries of antiquity for consolation. For that I have three men to thank. First they were teachers then they were friends, constant and true.

CRAIG SMITH lives with his wife, Martha, in Lucerne, Switzerland. A former university professor, he holds a doctorate in philosophy form the University of Southern Illinois.

The Painted Messiah and *The Blood Lance*, the first of his novels to chronicle the exploits of T.K. Malloy, received international acclaim and have been translated across the globe in twelve languages.

In 2011, his novel *Cold Rain* was one of five titles shortlisted for the CWA Ian Fleming Steel Dagger for Best Thriller.

CONTENTS

I
VIRTUOUS TEMPERAMENT

Tuscany: 49 BC

I was sixteen when Julius Caesar crossed the Rubicon and rode into Italy at the head of Legio XIII. I knew several of the young men in Tuscany who joined his auxiliaries and begged my father's permission to enlist as well. He refused.

I was old enough, or so I thought, but my father possessed a farmer's slow reckoning of time. He said I would be of more use to Caesar if I finished my education. I protested that Caesar needed me now, but my father assured me a man like Caesar would always have another battle waiting.

In the three years that followed, Caesar chased the senate out of Italy, routed the legions of Pompey Magnus in Spain and Greece, secured Egypt and sailed to Pontus on the Black Sea, where he defeated an enemy force on the very day he arrived, uttering in the aftermath of that battle the immortal words, 'I came, I saw, I conquered.' Then, when the last of the senate's forces rallied in Numidia, Caesar sailed his wearied legions to Africa and, after a series of desperate battles, brought our great Civil War to its conclusion.

In the history of Rome, there had never been three more glorious years of war, or any general the equal of Julius Caesar. And all the while I sat in Tuscany adding summons and learning to parse Greek sentences.

Rome: 46 BC

When word came of Caesar's victory in Africa, my wise father kissed my head and sent me to Rome with his blessing. I was nineteen. My eyes were good in those days, my feet swift, my hands strong. I had a heart brimming with ambition. Like a few thousand other young men of my stripe, I had learned from my early childhood onwards to fight with a sword and hunt with a spear. I could box and wrestle with some skill and even had modest talents in archery. As for the art of horsemanship, I was unrivalled in all of Tuscany.

I was handsome in my youth, taller than most, with powerful shoulders and dusty brown locks. At seventy years of age, I still have broad shoulders and most of my height; the beautiful locks, however, have gone the way of all that is mortal. Judah, my secretary, smirks as I dictate this. It is always the same with young men: they can imagine any fate for themselves except old age and baldness. I was no different.

In Rome, I spent each morning for nearly a week in the vestibule of the house of Cornelius Dolabella. I had never met Dolabella, but my father enjoyed a long friendship with his great uncle, who was one of the lords of our province and the grand patriarch of the Cornelii. He had therefore instructed me to approach Dolabella before speaking to any other patrician. This seemed good advice. Dolabella, as everyone knew, was then a rising star in Caesar's party, which happened to be the only viable political faction left in Rome. Dolabella was twenty-eight years old; in the old days that would have made him too young for command and certainly too young for a position of any importance in the government. In the world Julius Caesar had fashioned, Dolabella was a general of the legions. In fact, he had already been promised a consulship in another year or two.

To my thinking, no man could match Caesar's accomplishments, and even with all my ambition I never imagined myself overtaking his glory, not if I had three lifetimes. But I thought I could hope for what Dolabella had accomplished. I decided all I had to do was observe his manner and conduct myself exactly as he did. Of course, I came to this dubious conclusion before I had ever set eyes on the man.

<hr />

On the sixth morning I visited Dolabella's house, the steward pointed to me; there were several of us waiting in the vestibule. I followed with some trepidation as he brought me through a splendid atrium then led me back through the house to the great man's office.

Dolabella was at his desk but had turned away that he might vomit into a bucket, the latest of several profuse offerings, from what I could gather. A servant held the bucket for him and then wiped his lips with a damp cloth after he had finished. Dolabella's secretary stood to the other side of his dominus, serenely indifferent to the stench in the room and of course the suffering of his master. When Dolabella finally sat upright again, or as upright as his misery allowed, he looked at me with a curiously indulgent smile. 'Come in, come in, young man. Don't be bashful. Step forward, let me have a better look at you.'

'Quintus Dellius, from Tuscany,' his secretary remarked. There was a warning tone in this, but Dolabella seemed not to notice.

'From Tuscany. A country boy. I like that!'

The secretary interceded at once: 'He carries a letter from your great uncle, Dominus.'

'Oh.' A moment of disappointment followed, and I naturally assumed my cause was lost. A sly smile followed, if only to see how I would react. 'I thought you were breakfast.' When I did not respond to this, he added, 'Pity it isn't so.' His wet eyes rolled back as if he were about to faint; then he spun suddenly toward his bucket, but it was only for the sake of a few awful dry heaves. When he sat up again, Dolabella looked at me with vacant eyes, then at his secretary. The secretary, divining the problem, whispered, 'Quintus Dellius from Tuscany.'

When Dolabella repeated this information, I found myself wondering at his sanity. 'What is your business, Dellius?' he asked cheerfully. 'Selling horses or wine? I'll wager it's one or the other from a Tuscan eques.'

'I have brought a letter of introduction from your uncle, Excellency.'

'Yes, yes, of course you have. How is the old bandit? Well, I hope?'

'Quite well, Excellency.'

'And he encourages me to give you all my business, I expect?'

'The letter is addressed to you, Excellency. I cannot guess what he encourages you to do.'

'Come then. Bring it forward. You don't expect me to walk in my condition, do you?' This was apparently a joke, but I hardly dared get too close, for the stench emanating from that bucket was nearly enough to inspire my own vomiting. Oblivious to the odour, Dolabella waited in his chair until I had stepped up to the very edge of his desk. Only then did he reach out and take the thing.

I had in fact stolen a glimpse of the letter before it had been rolled up and sealed. It provided a glowing estimation of my potential, not false in any particular but neither was it very critical. Fifty years on, I still recall two of the choicest phrases: '...a promising public career ahead of him...' and the capstone of the piece '...a young man of virtuous temperament...'

Dolabella broke the wax seal holding the letter and unrolled it. As he did this, he leaned to one side of his chair for the sake of an eye-watering fart. I glanced at the secretary, but he showed no reaction, not even to wince at the stench of it. As he read, I looked closely at Dolabella's features; he was not nearly the beauty his stone portraits made him out to be. He had luxuriously curly hair as advertised, but that was the end of it. His body was too thick for his height, his face too puffy. And he was soft, as if he sat perpetually at his desk or too often rode in a litter.

Scanning the contents of the letter quickly, Dolabella scowled. Then he threw that precious scroll of mine into his bucket of vomit. 'So Quintus Dellius comes begging an appointment in the officers' corps of Caesar's army after the fighting is finished. Is that how it goes, lad?'

'Certainly there must be a fight left somewhere, Excellency,' I answered. My father's bland assurances sounded quite stupid when I repeated them to a general of the legions.

Dolabella studied me suspiciously. Perhaps he thought I was making a jest; perhaps he was only curious at the degree of naiveté I possessed. His eyes swam over me in a way I did not like. I suspected it even then, but I was very soon to have confirmation that Dolabella was a sensualist without respect for custom or gender. In fact, he seduced whatever creature he fancied and did not care if he borrowed a senator's wife for an evening of debauchery or used a citizen of Rome as a woman. I was certainly handsome enough to tempt him, but I doubt that is why he ultimately decided to give me a position. I expect the advertisement of my 'virtuous temperament' appealed to Dolabella's keen sense of humour.

Dolabella gestured to his secretary, who leaned forward and whispered something. He nodded and looked at me again. 'I'm going to arrange an officer's training position for you with the German cavalry supporting Legio V. When that has finished, you will join my personal Guard. I am doing this for the sake of the friendship of our two families, but remember this well—on your life, Quintus Dellius! If you disappoint me in even the smallest detail, I will see that you...'

Before he could finish his threat, Dolabella spun toward his bucket again. As he was still heaving and gagging, I offered my sincerest assurances that I would not disappoint him. Whether he heard me or not, I cannot say. The secretary shooed me from his master's presence before Dolabella came away from his bucket.

—————

Legio V had served in Caesar's African campaign. Its cohorts, at that moment, were still in transit back to southern Gaul. I was therefore instructed to wait in Rome until I received orders to report to the Camp of Mars, fully equipped and ready to travel.

Anticipating this sort of delay, my father had arranged for a Tuscan family then living in Rome to provide me with lodging in exchange for several large casks of Tuscan wine from our estate. A servant and I had brought these by mule and wagon. The servant had sold the remainder of our cargo in the market place and refilled our wagon with non-perishable goods from a list my father provided him. At that point he returned to our estate, taking my riding horse with him.

The people I stayed with were second or third cousins on my mother's side, an elderly couple with grown children, all of whom had married and were living somewhere beyond Rome. My father had brought me to their house for a week when I put on my toga virilis, but that had occurred some five years earlier. I barely recalled the house and did not remember the family until I was standing in their presence again. No matter. They treated me as one of their own. The house, which was located in the very heart of Subura, was a fine old building, though it had seen better days. The neighbourhood was reputedly the worst in all of Rome, with every sort of vice on offer at discount rates. To be honest, such was my excitement at being in Rome, I hardly noticed the quarter's squalor.

Perhaps a week after my interview with Dolabella I got an invitation to a party at his house. The note, written over Dolabella's signature, promised an intimate gathering of the literati 'with a few dancers and musicians performing, if only to make the evening more bearable'.

I naturally assumed that by literati Dolabella meant poets and writers, not those fellows who paint graffiti on every building in the city; as for the dancers and musicians I had no idea they would perform without clothing. Of course I had heard about Roman decadence, but I enjoyed a rather sheltered view of it, at least up until the night I attended Dolabella's party.

I arrived in a toga and looked the perfect fool. This was Dolabella's aim, I'm sure. Dolabella's idea of an intimate gathering was to jam as many people as possible into his house. The property was overflowing with persons from every stratum of society. He mixed the dregs with the most illustrious family names, but only the young and beautiful. No greybeards at his party, nor any fellow who even looked like he had fallen on hard times. The only thing everyone had in common was perversion. Or the willingness to observe it at close quarters.

I had not been at the party long when I heard the very strangest rumour, preposterous actually, that Dolabella had filled a dozen large jars with coins. A veritable fortune, by all estimates. He proposed to award the entire contents of these to the patrician matron who could tally the highest count of male lovers before the conclusion of the last hour of the night. The contest did not begin at once, but four contestants were reportedly committed to the game and had begun making appointments. There were other matrons about, most of them without their husbands. They were obviously tempted by the prize as well. They only needed to get up their courage.

Until the main event began, which I never believed was anything more than a bad joke, we had other distractions. Most notable were the naked musicians and dancers who passed through the crowd; these were often pinched as they went by; some were even kissed. Boy to boy, girl to girl, even boy to girl. It made very little difference to that crowd, I can tell you. Pretty got a kiss, and everyone was pretty.

Gathered around Dolabella was a clutch of young boys dressed in skimpy tunics, the sort very young girls wear. These fellows had painted themselves as fashionable ladies do, darkened eyes, painted lips, and rouge upon the cheeks. If their hair was not naturally long they wore wigs of the very highest quality. I thought it must be some kind of party gag or a running joke that made no sense to an outsider, but in fact Dolabella treated them as his personal harem. Touch one of them and he would growl like a chained dog. Attempt to lure one of his she-males away and the fight was on.

Food passed by to be grabbed as one desired and of course one's cup was simply not permitted to remain empty. After the dancers came an interlude of ribald poetry, then a series of acrobatic trysts featuring two, three, and even four players on a couch. At midnight the party favours were let loose, brothel whores brought in by the cohort. These were ready to kneel on request, but they were only there to tease. After their ministrations had begun in earnest, Dolabella called for the matrons to begin the contest, seven in all. These came for the men already inspired, and I must say many of these ladies were quite lovely creatures at the start of the evening, young, well-tended, and expensively dressed. By dawn they resembled jackals quarrelling over scraps of rotten meat. Strangest of all was the solitary slave who followed each woman around the room, witnessing and then recording her accomplishments.

Early in the evening I had found safe haven with the other country rubes, also costumed in togas, but they were eventually dragged off to one couch or another by one of the contestants. I refused every offer. Truth is I was still an innocent. For my first, I did not care to play my part in some impossible tally of lovers. But disinterest was not always enough. Refuse an offer and the next one got quite physical, even nasty. I have since learned no fury compares to a highborn lady's outrage at being rejected once she has committed to playing the harlot for an evening.

I was not the only man to refuse their enticements, but for most of the men I expect a refusal was given for the pure pleasure of watching them go mad with frustration. A dozen large jars were filled with coins, all for the winner and none for second best.

I saw two young lords refuse one of the more attractive matrons early in the contest and admired their restraint. When these same fellows retreated quietly to the shadows, I followed them. I imagined some political intrigue from such serious men, at least until I could see why they stood so closely together. After that, I can promise you, I learned to be less curious.

Late in the evening I finally lost my innocence. This to a dark-haired lovely who only played for the joy of it. I was swaying from drink and laughing at her as she tried to undo my toga. I recall thinking she had confused me with one of Dolabella's statues. I was also fairly sure she would never get my toga unwound, but she informed me she was married to a senator; she knew well the intimate secrets of that dowdy costume. When I found myself with my toga around my feet, it was too late to resist, and besides I had an erection Priapus himself might have envied. We finished matters where we stood and, as she walked away without so much as a kiss goodbye, Dolabella began clapping his hands. After that, his harem joined the applause, and then the whole room. At long last no virgins remained under Dolabella's roof.

Now I must confess the full truth, for I have promised myself to hold nothing back in my history: I found the experience so exhilarating I tried to lose my innocence thrice more before the dawn and this time with any female who would have me. But some things we can only lose once. Eh, Judah?

It was summer, the season for war, but the wars were finished. Even restless Caesar was at his ease, dividing his time between the couches of Servilia Caepionis, Queen Cleopatra of Egypt, who was then visiting Rome with her consort brother, and Caesar's patient, long-suffering wife Calpurnia.

At the second of Dolabella's parties I went dressed more appropriately in a fine tunic cut in the Greek style. It was trimmed with gold thread and bore a line of gentrified purple to distinguish me from the pretty street boys Dolabella set about the room. It was a handsome tunic, I can tell you, so much so that I was hardly through the front gate before a sweet songbird knelt before me and proceeded to introduce me to the Egyptian arts. When she had properly fixed my attention, she pulled my tunic over my head and walked away with it. I never did see that tunic again or the girl either, for that matter.

Of course, I did not only attend Dolabella's orgies. I also spent several nights losing at dice. During the daytime I gambled on chariot races at the Circus Maximus and impromptu wrestling matches at the baths. A perfect artist with a horse, I knew the best team in a race at a glance. I could read a man's fighting talents nearly as well. I soon learned, however, that the finest horses in the world cannot win a race if their driver holds them back and no one is victorious in a wrestling match if there is more money to be made by losing it. Easy money? There is no such thing in Rome.

I was soon feasting on scraps and caging drinks at taverns where a man could get knifed for the sake of his fine tunic, which I had fortunately already lost. One night a young beauty persuaded me to borrow a sum of money on her behalf. All I had to do was sign my name and the matter was settled. If I didn't, she was headed to a brothel to pay off the debt her father owed. There is no fool to compare with a nineteen-year-old boy, especially where a presumably innocent young beauty is concerned. With her cupid-bow lips and limpid eyes, how could I possibly allow that sweet creature to become public fodder? It was unthinkable. I signed and got a sweet kiss on my cheek for a thank you.

The debt collector came to the house early next morning for the money. I was still sleeping it off and didn't recall signing anything. Not at first, at any rate. Then I saw my name, my province, my father's name, and where I lived in Rome. Yes, it seemed I had agreed to pay something. But such a figure as that? I couldn't believe it. The patriarch of the family protecting me bought me out of my debt without a word to my father, who would have ordered me back to

Tuscany at once. It was a handsome sum, I can tell you, and I promised to pay it back as soon as I could, though in fact it took some years before I possessed an amount sufficient to close the account. By then I had to repay the heirs. Civil wars are especially cruel in that respect.

By chance I saw that same girl some nights later at a different tavern and learned from my companion in debauchery she was the finest fellatrix in all of Rome; he could attest to this from personal experience. 'For two *asses* and a wink,' he whispered, 'you'll remember those pretty lips for the rest of your life.'

A wiser man would have laughed at his own folly and promised himself to take more care next time. Young Caesar that I was, I went to claim my just desserts. I got them, too. Three of her bully boys with clubs answered my demands. The boon companion watching my back? He was nowhere to be seen. But he was right about one thing. I never forgot those sweet lying lips and the kiss of faux gratitude she had given me.

After that, I swore I would change. In the end I only changed my haunts. I had not even recovered from my bruises when I heard a retired legionary of Pompey Magnus's army cursing Queen Caesar, the catamite. One-on-one, it was about as fair as a fight in the streets will ever be, but I fought as boys are taught to do. He fought to win. I spent the night on paving stones, properly kicked into submission and lucky I hadn't been stabbed in the bargain.

Next morning I went home late, only to learn I should have mustered on the Camp of Mars an hour before.

The family slave helped me gather my belongings. After I gave a hasty farewell to the master of the house and his wife, the slave and I ran through the city, though I must confess I had to stop and vomit three or four times along the way.

At the meeting point on that great field I put on the uniform of a young cadet, starting with short leather trousers under a long leather cuirass, military grade sandals, and a bronze helmet that never quite fit properly no matter how I padded it. A cavalry centurion received me irritably and sent me into the line, where I stood with several other young men of redoubtable virtue. The centurion looked me over with more contempt than he offered the rest. He smelled the stink of my breath. He touched the lumps under both eyes and my cut lip. He poked a bruise on my arm and watched me wince. Finally, he asked my name. Getting it, he said to me, 'You're a perfect disgrace, Quintus Dellius!'

I dropped my chin, imagining I was about to be washed out even before our training began. 'Look at me, when I give you a compliment, lad!' I met his gaze, though I expect I was blinking stupidly. 'You're in Caesar's army now. Off duty we drink like Bacchus, brawl like the mad furies, and ride whatever sassy mare swings her tail. On the march we're the scourge of the earth, the greatest army that ever fought under the standards of Rome! You've had your time off now and put it to good use, if I'm any judge of it. Unlike your mates here, who come with their clean faces and combed hair. Now it's all business for the next three or four months, nothing but work and pain, and you're the only one in the whole lot who's got a memory of good times to hold him over.' He turned on all of us now. 'You'll ride and you'll march, lads; you'll dig holes and then fill them up again; you'll build walls and you'll tear them down. You will fight day and night, bleeding as you do, until you earn a night like our Quintus Dellius just enjoyed. And when you get it, by Dis! you had better come back stinking of vomit and bruised from fistfights, like our friend here. How else will the guard of the watch know you're Caesar's men and not the pretties that used to dance with Pompey Magnus?'

He went on, as men like that do. He promised us a career of unending exhaustion if we didn't get killed outright. 'Live through it though, and this I promise you, lads: nothing will ever be sweeter than the memory of fighting for Julius Caesar.'

I forget the fellow's name. He left us after delivering us in Narbonne; I'm not even sure he bothered to give it. Which is a shame. That centurion was the only man I ever met who paid interest on his promises.

Narbonne, Southern Gaul: Summer, 46 BC

Three weeks and six hundred miles passed before we arrived in Narbonne, the winter camp of Legio V, called the *Alaudae*—the Larks. Legio V was composed of non-citizen legionaries, all recruited in Gaul but in every other respect like any legionary camp. The men were back from war and had their freedom for the most part. Some helped with the training of recruits, including the cadets; others left camp to live with their families or common law wives just beyond the fortified perimeter.

Narbonne was safe country without any threat close at hand, but it was also perfectly located so that the Larks might respond quickly to uprisings in the more northerly provinces of Gaul and of course the troublesome Iberian Peninsula. The cavalry attached to the legion was composed of recruits from several of the Germanic tribes, then as now considered the most ferocious fighters on earth. These wild creatures, given Roman discipline, were an especially dangerous group.

The cadets would eventually become junior tribunes in the auxiliaries and, possessing that exalted status, run errands for senior tribunes of the cavalry. After a bit more time we could expect to serve as second-in-command for scouting squads. Until then, we were handed over to a training centurion, who treated us to misery piled upon misery.

The first rule we learned was the most sacred rule of camp life: no one, not even Caesar, rides inside the camp. The next twenty or thirty rules we learned more slowly, usually with the help of our training centurion's *vitis*, a kind of swagger stick centurions use to dole out correction and punishment. This centurion, like the last, offered us no name by which to address him, or at least none I can remember; nor had he any affection for the whole lot of us. It did not seem fair in our perpetual exhaustion to be also hated, but there is good reason for it. Untried soldiers are dangerous to the whole army. Until they are blooded and proven true, they're about as useful as virgins or unbroken horses.

By late October I had some feel for my duties. I knew the trumpet blasts and flag signals by heart. I had also distinguished myself as the best rider among all the recruits. That got me the right to train against the Germans. These men loved nothing so much as spilling Roman gentry on the grass, but pain is a fine teacher, and I was soon the equal of all but the very best lancers.

For the most part our training centurion wearied us with routine. This included cleaning the tack, grooming the horses, and mucking the stables, all work that slaves will do if there are no cadets available. As the season began to come to an end and the distant mountains grew white, the camp prefect started sending us out on scouting patrols, sometimes with infantry in support and sometimes with the entire legion on the move, for even in winter Caesar's legions knew to stay fit for the sudden order to march.

II
FIRST BLOOD

Narbonne, Southern Gaul: November, 46 BC

Think of a summer storm arriving after a long hot afternoon of blue skies. First there is a low rumble of thunder and bit of haze on the horizon. Soon enough there is something in the air, intimations of a change one can almost smell; then suddenly the world is swallowed whole in a deluge. That is how Julius Caesar came to Narbonne. After his long summer holiday in Rome we suddenly got word he was laying siege to Marseille, a hundred miles east of Narbonne. In fact, it was old news. On the very day we learned of it Caesar and his general staff came leading their horses through the gate of our camp. This was just at sunset, and no one was really sure at first if it was only another camp rumour or fact. We knew soon enough. Orders came to pack for a march: we were to leave at midnight. Caesar, as I quickly learned first hand, loved nothing better than to take off in the middle of the night and march until past sunset next day.

Hispania Ulterior (Andalusia): Autumn, 46 BC

Gnaeus and Sextus Pompey, the sons of Pompey Magnus, had fought against Caesar with their father. After Pompey's assassination in Egypt, his sons joined Cato in Africa. In the wake of Caesar's African victory, Cato killed himself, but Pompey's sons made their way into the Iberian Peninsula, where the Pompey name still resonated. By late summer the two brothers had brought several of Caesar's legions under their own standards. Those who resisted the prospect of deserting Caesar took shelter in the fortified city of Oculbo, thirty miles east of Cordoba. The commander at Oculbo was Caesar's nephew, Quintus Pedius.

Caesar had begun planning a spring campaign in Spain as soon as word came that Pompey's sons had surfaced. Caesar advertised it in Rome as a 'mopping up' operation. Once he learned that his nephew had come under siege from two Pompeian legions, Caesar knew he must act at once or lose all of Spain before winter's end. Despite the lateness of the season and the uncertainty of the autumn sea he sent two legions along the coast via a fleet of ships. Before these troops had even mustered, Caesar took a carriage north along the Via Cassia. Changing horses every ten miles, he and a handful of officers acting as his cavalry escort averaged a hundred miles per day. After picking up Legio X in northern Italy, Caesar changed to horseback.

In Marseille he had hoped to find fresh recruits,

ships, and all the supplies he would need for the coming campaign. Instead, Caesar discovered the city leaders, friends last time they met, had ordered the gates closed against him. Not daring to leave a hostile force at his back, Caesar appointed elements of Legio X to form a blockade of the port. He then assigned other cohorts from that same legion to lay siege to the city. The force was insufficient for victory, but it assured containment until his fleet arrived and could finish the job. Caesar then moved in advance of the remaining cohorts of Legio X, which came more slowly and would ultimately transport Legio V's baggage train.

Caesar arrived in Narbonne just two weeks after leaving Rome. Within two more weeks he hit Gnaeus Pompey's legions at Oculbo. To say such a thing is easy enough, but consider this. Caesar travelled nearly twelve hundred miles by land in a month's time, negotiating the Apennines, the Cisalpine Alps, the Pyrenees and the Sierra mountain ranges. And after such a journey he arrived with a fighting force of six thousand men. Such a thing ought to be beyond mortal capacity. It had certainly never been accomplished in the history of warfare, but that was Caesar's way. From Narbonne Legio V marched six hundred miles in two weeks averaging forty miles a day. Cavalry, with the exception of the most senior officers and some couriers, packed their horses with grain and supplies and trotted on foot like everyone else.

We did not bother with anything but the weapons and

armour we carried; we had no wagons to haul tents. We brought no siege instruments. Nor had we any of a legion's complement of essential non-combatants. We bought and butchered livestock where we could. Sometimes we baked our bread on campfires. At other times we ate only the rations of hardtack every man carried on his belt. Two weeks passed without scouting parties or walled camps. At the end, we did not even light fires. Caesar's only defence in a land committed to open rebellion was to move so quickly no force could possibly anticipate his arrival.

Hispania Ulterior: December, 46 BC

Once beyond the Pyrenees, Caesar sent messages by courier to his most trusted friends in the north. These were local nobility who had served him in his last campaign and were able to provide cavalry and whatever intelligence they could gather on the disposition of Pompey's siege at Oculbo.

By the time Caesar arrived in Andalusia, Legio X's cavalry had joined up with the Larks. Counting our allied cavalry, recruited quite literally on the run, we numbered some nine hundred horsemen against Gnaeus Pompey's six hundred. As to the infantry, we had added only a few scouts to our solitary legion. That meant we were outnumbered two-to-one in infantry, which is the only fight that matters.

Two days before our arrival at Oculbo, Caesar sent the cavalry of Legio V and certain of our allied cavalry west through the mountains. In all we were five hundred horsemen. We had orders to stage our attack at sunrise two days after our departure. Not a moment before. The journey was off road, and we depended entirely on local guides to take us across winding goat trails that ran above vertiginously steep ravines. Matters were bad enough at night. In daylight we had to cover the heads of the horses before they would consent to walk along those treacherously narrow paths. In all we travelled forty hours without sleep. Arriving well before dawn, we settled down in a sparsely wooded gorge overlooking the plain west of Oculbo.

Oculbo, Spain: December, 46 BC

It is fifty years since that morning, and yet I can still recall the emotions I felt as I anticipated my first battle. I should have been exhausted from a fortnight of hard travel followed by our two-day march through the Sierras. Instead, like the perfect fool I was, I felt only euphoria.

Our cohort's prefect gave orders for us to feed our mounts and then make ourselves a breakfast of hardtack and spring water. We were told to finish with our toilets as quickly as possible and then to wait beside our horses, mounting up only when he gave the order. All of this we did in complete darkness, not even daring to light a few solitary torches. At just the moment when night turns grey and the first songbirds begin their cry, we heard elements of Pompey's six-hundred-strong cavalry riding across the plain in our direction. I imagined they had discovered us, but our decurions whispered to their squads to remain as they were. Only when the enemy had passed did I finally understand. Pompey, his staff, and all of his cavalry had abandoned the fight. They were riding at full gallop in the direction of Cordoba.

Nearly an hour before, Caesar had sent Legio V against Gnaeus Pompey's two legionary camps. These were set close together and fortified with an outer ditch and an encircling palisade. Outnumbered two-to-one, Caesar had to count on darkness and uncertainty. Sentries raised the alarm the moment Caesar's men broke from cover, but it was still too dark to know the full extent of the attack; this meant Pompey's legionaries spread across the camp to defend it, as military protocol dictates. Caesar, however, had concentrated his force at the east gate. When that gate fell less than a quarter of an hour after the initial attack, Pompey's legions might still have prevailed. They had the numbers to overwhelm our men, but again darkness and uncertainty proved the deciding factor. And the western plain was temptingly open.

Pompey and his officers took off first. Then the cavalry departed. After that, the legionaries began stealing away. Soon a general panic flooded the plain with infantry. Through all this Caesar waited. He wanted the enemy combatants to believe they had found safe passage. When they were confident the way was clear, they began running without regard for their units or any kind of military formation. Only then did Caesar give the order to chase them down.

Caesar's cavalry came out of the east, riding through the mist of a winter dawn. We came out of the west, five hundred cavalry bearing down on the vanguard of ten thousand infantry caught in the clutches of panic. When they saw us, Pompey's men had no place to turn, nor any chance of fighting as infantry do. Making matters worse, there were only a few officers left. A centurion here and there formed men into a knot of resistance, but these were like tiny islets in a raging stream.

—⟨⟩—

The first men we encountered threw down their weapons and raised their arms. As per our orders we killed them where they stood. Then we went after the rest. It was wanton slaughter with the aim of demoralising Pompey's less determined allies, but in my innocence it seemed only a great sport. I rode with the same men who had tumbled me from my horse so often I had thought they hated me, but that day we covered each other exactly as we were taught to do in a rout.

Two horsemen would flank a man on the run, one to hold him from breaking away, the second to pierce him with a spear. This need not be a mortal blow, only enough to take him down and keep him there. This is best done, as we had been taught, in the lower back at about the kidneys. Once a man was no longer running, our infantry could follow up at its leisure and finish him off.

Sometimes the enemy did not even see us coming; sometimes, at the last moment, they turned to fight. A few legionaries carried spears, which made them more formidable; most possessed only a sword. When the enemy went low in the hope of cutting the legs of our horses we simply spread out a few paces. This forced a man to commit to one rider or the other. That meant he had to turn his back on one of us.

The only real danger came from slowing down and making a fight of it. That presented others with a chance at our backs, and these men were understandably desperate enough to leap upon our mounts from behind. I saw it happen to a young cadet. I knew his name in those days, but the years have taken it from me. An enemy combatant mounted his horse from behind and slit his throat before he even understood his mistake. I thought to chase the fellow who did it, but my companion roared at me to stay with him. We turned at once and found another.

If someone gave us even a moment of resistance we raced on and found easier prey. That left the man to deal with our infantry or perhaps even escape. No matter. We had orders to kill as many as possible, and there were plenty to find. When it was over, six thousand enemy casualties littered the plain. Even then Caesar was not finished. He sent the Larks to kill every enemy still breathing and then to identify Pompey's fallen officers, any corpse at or above the rank of a centurion. The heads of these men he ordered impaled on stakes that soon enough decorated the ramparts of Oculbo's city wall.

—————

There was no rest that day, despite our victory. The infantry secured and fortified the camps they had attacked that morning; the cavalry began reconnoitring the region, more to discover other forces than to hunt down those who had escaped. That night, after our sentries were picked from Pedius's forces, Legio V, the cavalry of Legio X, and our Spanish allies occupied Pompey's camps. Caesar and his staff claimed one of the great houses inside the city.

In a celebratory mood we ate well, drank plentifully, and slept the night through in tents. It was our first full night of sleep in a fortnight. Next morning Caesar ordered his forces to feast and relax the whole day through. The necessary scouting and patrol duties fell to Pedius's forces. Locals, commandeered for hard duty, cleared the plain of the dead.

Once it was obvious Gnaeus Pompey had no intention of returning in force, Caesar set about rewarding his Larks. By that I mean he brought in women. These were not commandeered like the burial details. Bad business that, especially when a general is trying to recruit allies. No, he scoured the ports and cities and hired any female, slave or free, willing to join us in our camps. No obligations other than to come and drink and eat; they earned a sack of coins for their troubles. Naturally there was more to be earned for those willing to sell themselves. There were no virgins or wives and quite a few were up for rough trade as long as it paid, but others were young widows who came for the chance to find a husband. The money for this, as Caesar made sure we knew, came from Pompey's camp payroll, which we had just seized. It was Gnaeus Pompey's party, in other words.

Such was the generalship of Julius Caesar. He demanded the impossible from his men and got it; afterwards he rewarded them with the extravagance of an oriental potentate. I believe on the fourth or fifth day of our luxury, the women departed, though more than a few of them settled in the city, now the wives of Gauls.

Even after we had returned to our soldierly duties we continued to eat well on Pompey's stores and livestock, and we drank like men on leave, so that our mornings started slowly. But we had earned it, and Caesar knew to give his men their ease after the march they had endured for his sake.

———

A fortnight after our battle, the first cohorts of Legio X arrived, along with the full baggage train of Legio V. Within a month the remainder of Legio X, the *Equestris* as they called themselves, arrived in the company of Legio III and VI, the *Gallica* and *Ferrata*. Those cohorts of the *Equestris* which had stayed at Marseille until they took the city joined the fleet as it sailed south along the Iberian coast. Among the officers travelling with these legions was the commander of Caesar's cavalry, Publius Cornelius Dolabella, my patron.

On orders from Caesar, cohorts of the legions began working inland. Caesar meant to take the fight to Pompey and kept the pressure on through the winter months. He employed his most senior officers, however, in the recruitment and training of another four legions of auxiliary infantry. From Africa, just across the straits, he summoned those same allies who had helped him finish off the last of the senate's forces the year before. Caesar's friends in Numidia shipped horsemen across by the thousands.

Hispania Ulterior: January to March, 45 BC

My training now concluded, I joined Dolabella's staff at the rank of a junior tribune of the auxiliaries. Whereas cohorts of the legions were attacking and securing positions in the countryside surrounding Oculbo, Dolabella's cavalry penetrated enemy territory far to the west. For over two months I was second-in-command to some three hundred cavalry recruits as we took the fight to Pompeian sympathizers in the countryside around Seville.

It was at this time I met Marcus Ulpius Traianus –

Trajan. He was a wealthy eques living outside Seville and purportedly indifferent to Roman politics. In fact, Trajan was a Caesarean who happily provided us with a great deal of useful intelligence. With it we were able to intercept enemy couriers, rob payroll shipments, and set fire to enemy towns, farms, mines, and granaries.

We lived as highwaymen do, hidden away in mountain camps, never in one place for more than a few days. We ran couriers to Oculbo once a week, but got nothing in return by way of orders. Our job was to find targets of value and either seize or destroy them. By the time Dolabella called me back to Oculbo in late February, I considered myself an accomplished officer. In fact, I was more outlaw than soldier. Enough of one at any rate that I resented my return to military discipline.

My resentment lasted right up to the point Dolabella appointed me senior tribune to a cohort of his cavalry. These were all fresh recruits from the Pyrenees, murderously efficient men who had lately come to Caesar's side. I was astonished by my sudden promotion, for I had not yet turned twenty and was only one step below a prefecture. But this was the way it went in Caesar's army. Officers in love with war did not languish in the lower ranks.

I don't think Dolabella anticipated any radical changes in strategy when Caesar ordered his staff to report to him one fine winter morning in early March. This occurred only days after I had assumed my new responsibilities as a senior tribune. There was too much to be done in the countryside for new orders to make any sense. We were still actively recruiting men-at-arms. Gnaeus Pompey waited with thirteen legions forty miles southwest of Oculbo, but he was showing no interest in advancing against us, and unless he did so everyone expected we would face him in late summer, when our forces might begin to approach parity.

Most of the senior officers assumed that Caesar wanted to discuss the possibility of sending more cohorts to Cordoba. In that city the younger of the two Pompey brothers, twenty-year-old Sextus Pompey, was putting up more fight than anyone expected. So long as Cordoba remained in enemy hands, Caesar was incapable of moving against Gnaeus Pompey's thirteen legions. At least that was the thinking of men who knew anything about military campaigns.

Dolabella did not generally bring all of his tribunes to staff meetings, but it was customary for a senior officer to have an escort of a tribune or two, and that morning it fell to me to join him. I heard Caesar's voice within his office as we waited with several other officers in the atrium of his house. He was ordering ships sent out to make a search. For what or whom I could not fathom. This I knew: there was urgency in the matter. A moment later I saw one of his staff leaving his office. A voice that was not Caesar's called to the steward, who then escorted our party into Caesar's office.

I had seen Caesar frequently on our six-hundred-mile march from Narbonne to Oculbo. He often sat on his horse at the side of the road as we jogged by. Whenever he saw a man he knew, centurion, optio, decurion, or legionary, he would call to the fellow by name, taking the tone of an old friend. He generally liked to play with the fellow's pride and asked if Caesar led an army of men or pansies. On other occasions, when he could see we were all close to exhaustion, Caesar promised gold and women when our march had finished. He swore on Jupiter's Stone he could smell both coming on the breeze out of the south. Other times he would be frank with the fellow he addressed. 'A few more days of it, friend,' he would say, 'and we'll repay those bastards for all our suffering!' Curiously, I had never seen Caesar except astride his horse. My first impression of the great man dismounted was more than a little disconcerting. In his headquarters he looked to me like an old man dressed up in a general's uniform. I believe he was fifty-five that winter.

Caesar was completely bald. I had not noticed this previously because of the helmet he wore. His dark leathery skin was wrinkled, close to ruin from an active life lived outdoors. His eyelids were so hooded one could hardly see his eyes. In his youth Caesar had been handsome; I had seen his image so often I thought he must still be that fellow, but no, he was mortal after all.

Caesar stood up from his desk at our entry. There were

some twenty officers in our party; fewer than a half-dozen of these men were actually important. The rest of us were there to observe the protocols of command and learn how Rome fought her wars. Caesar had already started toward us with a greeting when he stopped suddenly. 'Octavian?'

He spoke hesitantly, with a shadow of anger in his tone. To my astonishment he was looking past the legates, focusing on the back row. In fact, I was quite certain he was looking at me. My expression told him all he needed to know. I had no idea what he was talking about. Caesar seemed to shake himself out of his trance. 'By the gods, lad, I thought you were my nephew Octavian.' The officers parted as Caesar signalled me to come forward. He wanted a better look, if only to be sure.

'Quintus Dellius, Caesar,' Dolabella said. 'One of our tribunes.'

'Well, Quintus Dellius,' Caesar answered, 'I can see the differences in a better light, but as you stood in the shadows you seemed the very image of Octavian. I thought that rascal had come sneaking in to surprise me.'

'No word of his fate?' one of the legates asked.

Caesar looked at the man with the courage of a relative who fears the worse. 'It is still possible he is detained somewhere needing to repair his ship. I am sending the fleet to look for him.' Caesar shook his head, suddenly furious. 'He insisted on manning his own ship with young men loyal to him. Even the ship's captain was no better than a boy.'

'Marcus Agrippa, wasn't it?' Dolabella asked.

'A bright lad,' Caesar answered with a distracted nod of his head. 'A raging bull in a fight. Still, he's only a lad. I wish I had forbidden it. They were taking off a week behind the rest of the army because they were waiting for Maecenas to cross from Greece. I'll wager whatever you like Octavian thought to arrive before the fleet by sailing due west for Corsica. From there straight to the Balearic Islands. At that age I would have done the same. Arrive a fortnight before everyone else and greet our ships as they sailed into the harbour!'

'From Corsica to the Balearic Islands is three hundred miles of open sea.' This was muttered by another of the legates. Caesar nodded miserably, this time not daring to meet the fellow's gaze. Better than most men Caesar knew the dangers of open water.

———

Caesar had called his legates together for the purpose of arranging an immediate advance on Gnaeus Pompey's position in the south. The idea caught even his closest advisers unprepared. The countryside was not yet pacified. Our forces were not up to strength. Worse still, the siege at Cordoba had bogged down. By waiting until summer Caesar might perhaps find himself in a better position to advance.

Caesar gave his officers the chance to protest because he could see they were distraught. All the same, he was unmoved by their arguments. He told them frankly, 'I do not have the luxury of waiting for summer. If I am still in Andalusia in three months my enemies in Rome will take advantage of my absence.'

'Surely Mark Antony can control the situation.'

'Antony has trouble enough controlling himself. Only Caesar can quiet those wolves, and even Caesar cannot be in two places at once.'

The seriousness of the situation seemed to settle over the room. Finally, one of the legates answered. 'Surely you are not anxious to engage Pompey in open battle?'

'I am, actually.' Caesar smiled as he said this, though it was not a pretty smile. 'More to the point,' he added, 'with thirteen legions at his command, I expect Pompey will be eager to take the field. Otherwise he might be tempted to force us to tear down walls to get at him.'

'And what about Cordoba?' another of the legates asked. 'Caesar surely does not intend to leave a powerful army at his back.'

'We have Sextus Pompey contained. Let's destroy Gnaeus Pompey's legions and then see how much fight is left in the younger brother. My question for you, friends, is how soon can we get our legions to Ronda?'

With cohorts of every legion scattered over hundreds of miles the question was not easily answered, but soon enough a consensus formed. Eight weeks, sometime in early May. Caesar shook his head. That was not good enough. Revised estimates followed: a fortnight, ten days, a week at the absolute minimum.

'A week it is,' Caesar declared.

And so it came to be that Caesar prepared to advance against an enemy nearly twice the size of his own army, leaving open sedition in his wake and an enemy force encamped some forty miles behind him. I had never doubted Caesar in my life. He was the paragon of a fighting man, a genius at war; but seeing the faces of his legates that morning I felt a chill of uncertainty. Had the old fellow lost his wits? Even I could see that Caesar was courting every kind of disaster with his impatience.

But Caesar did that to men. They would follow him happily to the gates of hell. They were charmed by his manner, mad for him even, but there was always a moment when he defied reason and wilfully broke every principle of war. Then even those who loved him balked. No matter. He pushed his men through gates they had thought were impossible to pass. More than his skill in directing a battle, this taking men to their very limits was Caesar's ultimate talent; this occasion was only one more in a long list. So we began packing for the march as our cohorts came streaming into our camp over the next few days.

As for Caesar's missing nephew, Octavian, I gave that poor fellow hardly a second thought. I had no time to worry about him. Truth is I soon forgot his name. Why not? I counted him lost at sea. There were so many casualties of war in those days one grew used to hearing about death. Even Caesar's kin were not immune. But of course our precious Octavian was far from finished with the worries of this world.

III
RONDA

Ronda: 15th March, 45 BC

Ronda, which Romans generally refer to as Munda, was a fortress town fifty years ago. It lay midway between Oculbo and Cordoba forty miles to the south. The way there was mountainous and hard going. Before the town lay a great undulating plain leading up to a nest of high rocks, where the city stood. With steep ravines at his back and covering his flanks, young Gnaeus Pompey had picked his site with care. Caesar might come at him in force from only one direction. Pompey had meat, grain and fresh water in abundance. More importantly he had time. Caesar was the one desperate for battle. Caesar had spent the winter fighting skirmishes, taking towns, and negotiating with potential allies. None of the fighting had value except as it persuaded certain wavering allies to commit fully to him. What really mattered was defeating Pompey's army at Ronda. All the rest was propaganda.

We arrived on the broad plain below the fortress in the early afternoon of the Ides of March and proceeded to build eight interconnected legionary camps. These Caesar fortified with a staked ditch and high palisade. I was not privy to Caesar's battle plan; I only knew that Dolabella's cavalry was supposed to wait in reserve with our forces spread out evenly before the ditch. When called forward, we might come in smaller units and be expected to support a folding line. If the battle was going well we might arrive in force, hoping to break through the enemy line at its weakest point. At the start, however, our only job was to wait. This allowed me the chance to watch Caesar's army take the field.

Caesar anchored his line with Legio X at the far right wing, where he would fight as well. This legion Caesar trusted beyond all others, and they loved Caesar as men love their fathers. Why not? He had turned them all into heroes with his book, *Caesar's Conquest of Gaul*. What man, once named and lauded for his courage in a famous book, can ever back down from a fight? No, he will die before he will run. The same as Caesar would do. Leaving aside Dolabella's reserve cavalry, Caesar amassed five thousand horsemen evenly at either end of the line. When the army had settled into formation, each legion was clearly marked out on the field. Eight legions, each with its own reserve cohorts behind it.

After his army had formed for battle Caesar rode across the frontline. We could see Caesar's scarlet cloak even from our camp. Caesar's inspection was a leisurely one. He called out to men in every legion, officers and infantry alike. As I learned later, he made light of the high ground Pompey commanded. He said when a man has filled his army with slaves and untried boys they've only enough courage to run downhill. He also made the point that their great numbers meant Pompey had plenty of gold in his camp to pay them. 'That's our gold, friends!'

When he had finished his survey, Caesar took his position with the cavalry on the right flank, just behind Legio X. An hour passed, and Pompey still remained in his camps. After that Legio X started with the catcalls. Soon enough some of the more animated fellows began running out before their frontline. Turning their backs to the rebel camp, they lifted their tunics to expose their arses.

When it was clear that Pompey's son had no intention of coming out that day, Caesar ordered the flagmen to signal the legions to return to camp. They formed their lines again, grew quiet, and left the field with the good cheer of men who haven't played the cowards. As for the talk that evening, it was uniformly in praise of Gnaeus Pompey. The lad had finally looked at Caesar's legions and resisted the impulse to run away.

Next morning, Caesar's army spilled out across the plain again exactly as before. As on the previous morning, Gnaeus Pompey remained behind his palisade while we

41

formed for battle. I thought he might refuse to fight again, but once Caesar's army was in place, Pompey ordered his army to the field.

With thirteen legions, Pompey's fighting men numbered well over sixty thousand infantry. In addition to these men, he enjoyed another six thousand cavalrymen. This against Caesar's thirty-five thousand infantry and eight thousand horse. Using his numbers to advantage, Pompey's legions spread across the plain with reserve lines twice as deep as those of Caesar's legions.

The open ground between the two armies offered a slight incline for us most of the way. Only at the end did we face a steep climb. Caesar therefore made no order to advance. He wanted Pompey to leave his plateau and come across the plain before he answered. Pompey of course understood his advantage and refused. He had waited all winter. If Caesar would not attempt an uphill charge Pompey would wait another day. He would wait all spring and summer if he had to.

Once it was clear Pompey did not intend to move, Caesar sent a courier to one of his cavalry prefects. The prefect sent three hundred light cavalry between the two armies. These men were armed with two javelins each and carried a shield sufficient for stopping darts and small stones. They drifted quite close to Pompey's line as they crossed the field because Caesar hoped to lure the enemy cavalry forward. From there the fight might spread and leave Pompey no choice but to come off his high ground. Pompey refused to take the bait. Instead, he answered with two cohorts of archers. They came before their line in a cluster and began raining arrows down on our horsemen.

Caesar's cavalry turned toward them at once, forming a slender column. When the first men were in range, they threw one of their javelins, then turned away at a ninety degree angle. The rapid breaking away from the column after a cavalryman threw his spear allowed the next man in line to throw his javelin, decimating the archers with a continuous barrage.

A second cohort of heavy cavalry left Caesar's line in anticipation of Pompey sending horsemen forward to save his archers, but Pompey refused to engage. He let his archers run back to cover without assistance. With Pompey's line standing at attention and offering nothing by way of a fight, our lancers came forward and chased them down with impunity, then retreated to the open plain, where both of Caesar's cavalry units proceeded to gather the wounded and those men who had lost their horses. From there they returned to Caesar's line.

Having no choice if he wanted a fight, Caesar sent his army forward in a cadenced march. In the old days, Roman armies came with rhythmic shouts as they beat their shields. This was to excite fear in the enemy. No longer. Caesar's men came silently, thirty-five thousand strong with only the centurions calling out orders. Every centurion's optio watched the flags in case the orders were suddenly changed, but the centurion watched the men in his century. On command, they could stop midstride or advance at a run. This is how they drilled: every man ready to obey his centurion.

As the distance between the armies closed, Caesar sent his archers forward, a cohort at either end of the line with cavalry standing by to defend them. Pompey's archers answered, this time with cavalry in support. For the moment neither side wasted ammunition. Caesar called a halt when the two armies were a furlong apart, roughly an eighth of a mile. When Pompey still did not move, Caesar cut behind his legions and rode as far as the centre of his line. There, passing off his cavalry shield to one of his staff, he took up a legionary's long shield and walked briskly through the files of his men. Passing his frontline, Caesar kept walking.

Thirty steps before the line he finally came to a halt and drew his sword. Holding it high, he shouted across the field: 'If you're looking for Caesar, children, HERE I AM!'

Not a sound came from either army, but Pompey's archers before the lines let loose. The arrows came from both flanks. They climbed like hundreds of migratory birds, closing together as they soared. They were black specks against a blue sky, moving as if directed by a singular intelligence, rising, cresting and then curving down en masse toward a single point.

They snapped into Caesar's shield with such force those closest to Caesar later said it sounded like hail cracking against tin. Caesar's shield stopped nearly a hundred darts. At Caesar's feet were more than a thousand arrows. In the next instant, without any order given, Pompey's line broke and ran at us.

Our legions stepped forward, not yet running, but eager to cover Caesar. Once his army had overtaken him, Caesar called out to his men as they marched by. He showed them his ruined shield, if only to give them courage. As for his person he had received not so much as a scratch.

Much as he might have wanted, Pompey could not call his men back. They ran downhill in a ragged, insane charge; they roared as if every man expected a chance at Caesar himself. Caesar's line stayed in better form. At twenty paces, both frontlines let fly their spears. These hit with a hollow thump of steel against wood, an odd cacophony that served as preamble to the thunderous crash of two lines colliding.

There was no subtlety here, nothing of our general's genius at play, only a mile-long line with thousands of mortal duels transpiring at once. If one man proved stronger he would slip his gladius beneath the other's guard or maybe over the top. A quick wound to the belly or the eyes, a twist of the point as the blade exited: that was all that was needed to take a man down. The next enemy came for more of the same, shields cracking again, blades slithering forward. If that failed to bring blood, both men pulled back. Then a second collision, one man suddenly taking ground, the other giving it away grudgingly, playing out their duels in tight confines, backs always to their own men. The blades slipping high or low or around the side of the shields, like serpents lunging.

Two or three duels saw a legionary finally brought down with a wound or too tired to fight another. Back he went along the files to the congratulatory shouts of his mates. The next man stepped up, happy for the chance to spill blood. Taking a charge, falling back, then pushing forward, the shield, swinging like a scythe, as much a weapon as the gladius. Up and down the line it went like this, anonymous men fighting in dust so thick they could hardly breathe. Young men eager for glory. Old fighters taking the measure of their foes before getting too serious.

For the first quarter of an hour I could see both armies; after that, the dust covered all but the back ranks of our legions. I could only listen to the fighting, the song of steel, the screams of the wounded.

<hr />

Sometime during the third hour of the battle Dolabella began riding along our line of reserve cavalry. He called to his prefects as he went. I looked at the battlefield, but

I could not see that anything had changed. On the right, Legio X had edged forward slightly, but this seemed to me only another of the permutations of the battle line.

In fact Caesar had suddenly pushed his men to take ground, and that is what prompted Dolabella to act. To my surprise our attack turned toward the army's left flank, opposite Caesar's position.

The enemy commander on our left, Titus Labienus, had served as Caesar's second-in-command in Gaul for many years. He must always have resented Caesar, for when the time came to pick a side, Labienus had joined Pompey Magnus. And now, having no choice but to live with a very bad decision, he rode with Pompey's son.

He saw us coming at the start of our attack and being hated by Caesar imagined we came for him. That was the point of Dolabella's charge, but as we closed behind our left wing a few hundred of our number hit Labienus's cavalry. As for the rest of us, we turned toward Caesar. Now completely screened from the enemy's view by the dust in the field we rode at a controlled canter. I was coughing and blinded, like every man and horse out there.

Circling behind Legio X, I could see the fight being pressed with terrifying fury. Caesar's cavalry had come against the infantry's flank. Pompey's cavalry answered with every man available. I heard horses and men screaming; I saw hundreds of combatants from both sides down with wounds or already dead.

At the centre of it the two cavalry forces had mixed completely together. A man could be fighting one enemy even as another closed on him from behind. The heavy lances were gone; this was sword against shield, and sometimes only the naked blades.

And all so that we might pass by like a stream of ghosts through clouds of dust.

⸺⸺

We took arrows and stones from squads of archers and slingers at the rear. A few hundred reserve horsemen started to intercept us. Realizing our number exceeded three thousand, they turned back at once and retreated.

We met three cohorts of men on horseback close to the camp palisade. We hit them with our lances lowered and broke through without any trouble. I brought down one rider in this charge; those behind him had already turned back toward the open gates of their camp. I stabbed another's back as he rode away. I was ready to chase down a third victim when one of my decurions shouted something.

He was pointing at the battlefield behind us and I pulled up for a better look. Gazing through the dust it was impossible to guess the number, but a mass of enemy cavalry had started across the plain in our direction. As I considered them, I felt my horse's hindquarters dip; then the animal skittered excitedly.

It could have been an arrow struck its haunches, or my horse might have stumbled on a corpse, but I knew the truth. I had committed the great error. I had let one of the enemy on the ground leap up behind me. As his grip closed around me, I lifted both arms. I sought to block easy access to my neck. Stopped in one assault, my assailant drove a dagger through my cuirass and into my ribs. The pain of the steel coming into me was like touching fire. Cold, then white hot. Having no chance of resisting the man as long as he hung on my back, I could only think to throw myself to the ground. My assailant came off my horse as well.

We hit the ground together, his weight leaving me stunned. He rolled away. I blinked and tried in vain to breathe. I watched him pick up a heavy lance and tried to reach for my sword. A sharp pain in my shoulder stopped me; I had broken my collarbone without realising it. I hadn't even strength enough to grip the weapon.

I sat up facing him, thinking I might dodge the killing thrust. As for fear, I was strangely without it. Utterly calm, if you can believe it. I hoped to anticipate him, somehow to dodge the blade. This was pure folly, but in my innocence I was not prepared to admit this was my death.

Dolabella rode over the man at a gallop; I had not even seen him coming. My would-be-killer flew several paces before landing in a heap. Once he hit the ground Dolabella's Guard finished him, and that was it. Two of Dolabella's men dismounted and lifted me up and carried me toward the enemy camp, which was already in our possession.

I saw a slave coming for me with clean rags. I looked down at the dagger in my side and realised, finally, that I was close to death. I felt myself fading. I let my head settle into the dust as the slave bent down to inspect the wound. I heard the clap of horse's hooves, the shouts of men. Then the dagger came ripping out of my ribs.

After that, I heard nothing at all.

———

The enemy cavalry charge I had observed might have overpowered Dolabella's force if Pompey's legions had not panicked at the sight of Labienus's entire cavalry leaving the battlefield. Who can blame them? They had seen it before. They could only imagine their right wing had collapsed and Labienus was fleeing the field.

Convinced a rout had started, Pompey's army turned at once and ran. Those who got away first found their camp gates closed, already occupied by the enemy, but the city was not far away. And so they ran on without a backward glance and made it to safety.

Those who followed them had mixed success. Some made it; some did not. For the rest it was death. Caesar's left wing, led by his nephew, Quintus Pedius, began the rout. Once it had started, Caesar's right wing was able to join them. Closing behind the cavalry were Caesar's legions, all of them now coming at a run. It was Oculbo all over again, only with greater numbers. We came at the enemy's back and into its vanguard; we swept up around their flanks. The killing continued all the way to the city walls. Once more, we took no prisoners. When it had finished, thirty thousand enemy lay dead or dying on the field. Of Caesar's men only a thousand had perished, though a great many of us had been seriously wounded.

―――

I had lost quite a bit of blood after the surgeon pulled the blade free, and with my collarbone broken as well I was in serious peril. According to my doctor, a Greek slave formerly in Gnaeus Pompey's army, the collarbone was easily set. As for the wound that had pierced my lungs, I nearly drowned in my own blood. For several days my doctor drained my wound and worried about infection. I hung between life and death, tied to my bed to keep me from moving.

I ingested a mix of narcotics including opium, but the medicine was hardly sufficient for the job. I was in constant misery. Awakening I tasted a bit of broth, then I would sleep and dream. I asked about the battle at some point but could not follow anything beyond the simple fact that Caesar was victorious. Of course I ought to have concluded that much from the fact that I was still alive. A week afterwards my doctor was more hopeful, but he still worried about infection. For the sake of my broken collarbone and ribs, he kept me in traction several days longer.

I learned at some point that Gnaeus Pompey had escaped once more. Titus Labienus had not been so lucky. His head presently decorated the entrance to Caesar's command tent. This was presumably so that the two old friends might look one another in the eye.

———

I was still bound to my bed when Caesar came to visit his wounded officers. I thought he only meant to see a few of the senior men and then move on. We were in fact a great number, including Dolabella, who had been struck by an arrow during the rout. Caesar had already started a siege against the town of Ronda, and he had sent a force back to reinforce the ongoing siege at Cordoba. So there was much for him to do and some worry still that he might not yet be as victorious as he seemed. Despite everything, Caesar took his time with his officers, 'friends' as he called us. Officer, legionary, or ally: his friends needed a personal thank you, and Caesar never failed to give it. When he came to me, his attending slave read from a scroll and whispered my name and rank, but Caesar spoke at once, as if needing no prompt, 'Quintus Dellius!'

He covered my hand with his own. I feel it still these fifty years afterwards, the warmth of the man, the charm, the mastery over others he possessed like no other I have ever known. 'I owe you a debt of gratitude, my friend.'

Can any words ever be sweeter? But even then he was not finished. He told me he intended to make war on the Parthians the following year. He looked in my eyes with all the sincerity of a father and said that he was going to need me with him. If I would only promise to make a full recovery, he meant to promote me to the rank of prefect at once.

If I had not loved Caesar before, I would have loved him then. It was his way to draw one into his circle, to offer confidences and ask help, though he was Caesar and had all the world ready to serve him. Would I go to Parthia? I would have followed him to the ends of the earth. I will tell you something else about Caesar, a thing I only learned some years later. He made much the same speech to every young officer in that hospital.

<hr />

Caesar's forces found and killed Gnaeus Pompey a fortnight after the city of Ronda surrendered. Cordoba fell soon afterwards. There was some concern when it was reported that Sextus Pompey had escaped capture, but Caesar did not let it spoil his victory. Sextus Pompey was twenty, just a boy. By Caesar's reckoning, hardly worth the trouble of chasing down. Or so went the argument. His victory now secure, Caesar travelled back to Rome. This time he managed a leisurely pace. His victory in Spain had quieted the seditious parties in Rome.

Not long after Caesar's journey began, Octavian joined the procession. Octavian's ship was in excellent condition. The problem was that Octavian himself had become ill during the voyage. Fearing for their friend's life, Octavian's companions spent the winter on one of the Balearic Islands. Caesar was so relieved to see him alive that he invited the lad into his carriage. This is of course the highest honour an imperator can bestow on one of his subordinates.

When Antony joined Caesar at Marseille, Octavian got shuttled out of the carriage and onto a horse, but he still basked in the great man's glory as he rode beside Caesar's carriage in the second highest position of honour.

I missed these happy reunions and changing of seats. I spent the spring and summer not far from Seville on the grand estate of Ulpius Trajan. His granddaughter, Ulpia, a girl of seven or eight years, was often in my room to care for me. I recall her reading various histories to me and even a novel about a kidnapped princess. She was a sweet child and always worried that the slaves neglected me.

I recall when I left, most of the family was there to see me off, but once my carriage was on the road only Ulpia kept watching as I rolled away. I never expected to see the girl again, but I must say it was hard to forget her sweet temperament and beautiful brown eyes. In the years that followed, I often wondered if she had become the perfect beauty her childhood had promised.

Rome: October, 45 BC

From Seville I caught a ship to Ostia; from there I hired a carriage and rode to the Camp of Mars like a gentleman. The senate had awarded three Triumphs for the war in Spain, two for legates under Caesar's authority, the last for Caesar himself. The year before Caesar had enjoyed three Triumphs as well. Those had commemorated Caesar's conquest of Gaul, his campaigns in Egypt and Pontus, and his victory over Pompey Magnus in Greece and Cato in Africa. Perhaps the three Spanish Triumphs failed to live up to the spectacle of the year before. Perhaps it was the sheer number of Triumphs in such a short amount of time that spoiled the mob. Whatever the case, the first two Triumphs passed quietly, notable only for the mob's lack of enthusiasm. When Caesar's turn came and he paraded his full army through Rome, the mob jeered and hissed. For the glory I had won in Spain I was treated to a barrage of rotten fruit, dung, and rocks. By the end of my journey along the Via Sacra, such was the fury of the spectators, I counted myself lucky to get by with only that much abuse. In the history of Rome there had been nothing like it. The outrage left all of us who rode with Caesar bruised and disenchanted.

In the days that followed Caesar's ill-fated Triumph I heard a great many theories about why the plebs had turned against their man. Part of it must be credited to Caesar's enemies. No sooner had the senators been defeated in battle than they stirred up a whisper campaign. All the old rumours about Caesar got fresh paint. It is also likely that a certain portion of the mob's rage was bought. But some measure of blame rested with Caesar himself.

He knew better than to celebrate the victory of Romans over other Romans; he had carefully refashioned his Triumph against Pompey as a fight against Macedonia; the battles with Cato in Africa were said to be against King Juba. Caesar, however, made no attempt to disguise the victory in Spain. That was Roman against Roman.

I think after Spain Caesar was tired of placating his political rivals. The job was one of ceaseless flattery and compromise. He had enough of that with his friends. For those who opposed him, Caesar's famous charm finally wore out. Lest his opponents fail to notice, he dressed his floats with the heads of their former colleagues. The effect was much the same as a warlord's threat. Even the plebs did not care for it.

IV
THE IDES OF MARCH

Tuscany: January, 44 BC

I had originally intended to spend the winter in Rome. A decorated and newly promoted prefect, I hoped to make the acquaintance of several of the more powerful individuals in the city. After the mob pelted me with refuse, I lost my taste for the city. A lot of us did. I took my pay and a bounty of slaves for a bonus. The slaves I sold at market for an abysmal price, always the case after war. I paid down some of my debt to my mother's relatives, about a third of what I owed, then asked for and received Dolabella's permission to spend the winter at my father's estate in Tuscany.

Dolabella required me in Rome again before the third day after the Ides of March. This was the date upon which Caesar planned to depart Rome, bound for his Parthian campaign. Until then I was a free man.

My father was surprised to see me. I had sent him news from Seville of my promotion and said in that same letter I would spend the winter in Rome and did not expect to see him until I returned from Parthia. I think he saw my discouragement at once, though I tried to hide it from him. This was not because I had been wounded. This was a failing of the soul. I had worshipped Caesar too long not to feel something was very wrong if those whom Caesar defended could turn against him so quickly.

I was not able to discuss this with my father; I did not even admit that we had been abused by the mob. I am not sure why I couldn't tell him. We had always enjoyed an open and honest relationship. I suppose a part of me wanted to protect him from disillusionment.

He had always admired Caesar, both as a soldier and a political reformer. There was also in me a deep feeling of shame. I could not understand the sensation, but it was quite real, and so it was impossible for me to admit that I had been pelted and abused like a prisoner tagged for execution at the Triumph's culmination.

One evening, as if divining my mood, my father remarked almost casually, 'Life is not only to be measured by public accomplishments, Quintus. There is contentment to be reckoned with as well.'

Such a comment was entirely foreign to me. Life was about winning glory. What else could it be? My father, to his credit, was not suggesting I resign my officer's commission and come back to Tuscany; no, he was only planting a seed, as farmers do. In time, I might realise new desires. In a long life one can find solace in the fruits of every season.

I heard the echo of such sentiment many times that

winter, but that was all. I think he knew it would take a few years before I could possibly come to the wisdom he possessed: that a public life is a busy one but not always fulfilling. A long life has taught me what my father thoroughly understood: some men are eager for accolades and when they have won them know only to reach for more; others seek the quieter pleasures of this world and in winning them know at last perfect contentment.

One afternoon in early February I came back from a hunt with fellows I had known from childhood. We were weary from a fruitless search, ready for a bath and refreshments, but my father insisted on leading us out to one of the paddocks behind our stables. We followed curiously and discovered a three-year-old colt named Hannibal, which he had purchased just that morning from a horse trader on his way through Tuscany. Hannibal was taller by two hands than any horse I had ever seen; he possessed a powerful neck and already had the prominent jaws which usually only older stallions develop. His chest was wide and deep, his haunches massive. Here was an animal bred for war, spirited and bold, and yet possessing the refinements of an aristocrat: a delicate step, a fiery eye, an elegantly lifted tail. In colour Hannibal was a blood red sorrel. He had a slender blaze of white on his face and one high white sock rising over his back right hoof.

The former owner, a Roman eques named Seius, had intended to make a fortune breeding Hannibal to the best mares in Italy. The recent troubles of our civil war, however, had brought him to a point of desperation; so he took what money he could get from a quick sale and left it to the next man to earn the real money. My father always kept gold on hand for such an opportunity.

I naturally congratulated him on the purchase and remarked that he would be the envy of every man who saw him riding such an animal. 'I bought Hannibal as a gift for you, Quintus. Your new rank accords you the privilege of bringing your own horse on campaign, after all.'

My exhaustion only moments before vanished, and I soon persuaded my companions to help me break the animal to the saddle. This I will say: Hannibal sent me to ground only once. Of course he tried a dozen times more, but that is the way of an animal with high spirits. Finally I walked him around our riding arena without a quarrel.

Within a week we knew one another like old friends. Before I rode to Rome I had Hannibal accustomed to me. He was not yet ready for combat; that takes a great deal of training, but he was ready for what came next. And so was I.

I had begun the winter profoundly discouraged; by March, I was nearly as enthusiastic to ride with Caesar as I had been the year before. For many years I credited Hannibal with my complete restoration, but that was only because I was still quite young. The truth is I possessed a wise father.

Veii, Italy: 15th March, 44 BC

I was at Veii, ten miles from the heart of Rome, when I learned that the world had changed forever. I recall the place and my precise thoughts because even then I knew what the news meant. I was thinking about the Claudii, whose vast estate the road passed through. The members of that famous clan took no pleasure in the work of a farmer. They had others herding their flocks and churning their cheese. Instead of a handful of clients in their debt, the family's patriarch owned whole cities of men committed to his service. His fortune was so vast no one could make a proper estimate of it.

Just as I was reflecting on these matters, I noticed a man on horseback galloping toward me. He was obviously in a hurry, but at the sight of a youth who wore the thin purple stripe of an eques, he pulled up. 'Have you heard the news, sir?'

Of course I hadn't. I came from the north. In fact it occurred to me he might intend to rob me. I carried all I owned on the back of the mule I led. As for Hannibal he was worth fifty times the going rate for the average riding horse on a bad day at auction. This fellow wouldn't be the first brigand to walk up to his victim with glad tidings; I had employed the tactic myself for a few of my robberies in Spain. I looked around for possible confederates, but it was a sorry place for an ambush. 'What news?' I asked, cautiously.

'Rome's tyrant is dead.'

I recall the strength leaving me. I knew what tyrant he spoke of, though I could not really believe it. If it were really so I didn't think the sun could still be shining. 'What tyrant?' I asked.

'Julius Caesar, sir. The senators cut him down in chambers this morning. The only shame is they didn't think to do it years ago.'

I pulled my sword and went for the fellow. A moment of sanity pulled me back from murder, but Hannibal's chest collided with the shoulder of the nag he rode. I kept my blade high, pointed at his heart. His horse skittered back at the impact. He swore roundly, but he made no attempt to grab for his weapon. I had dropped the lead line of my mule and was free to circle him, which I now did. He had no chance of outrunning me and knew it. Nor was he a man capable of outfighting a youth in peak physical condition. 'Draw your sword and fight me, you filthy rogue!' I shouted.

'Go on to Rome if you want blood!' he growled. 'There are plenty of men there who'll be glad for the chance at you.'

I was still holding my sword as he rode off. I did not catch all he said by way of farewell but this I gathered: '... should kill the whole lot of you.'

Only then did it sink in. Julius Caesar was gone. With his passing the lives of all who supported him were in danger. A few decades before, one of Dolabella's ancestors,

Cornelius Sulla, had taught Rome how to break political factions: first murder every enemy in sight, then search the city for anyone not cheering the carnage and murder them as well. By nightfall, if Sulla had taught Rome anything, the streets of Rome would be filled with corpses. Mine included, if I were foolish enough to be there.

I left the Via Flaminia as soon as possible and rode north over farm lanes and through hill country. Worried that the man I had threatened might find confederates and come looking for the Caesarean with the fine horse, I made camp inside a grove of olive trees and was careful to light no campfire.

In the morning I rode as far as Capena. There I settled down to await more news. Men asked me if I had heard about Caesar's death. Then came the question of where I stood on the matter. How does one stand anywhere once the ground has been pulled out from under him? I heard myself saying I was a landowner in Tuscany. I cared nothing for politics.

Rome: Spring, 44 BC

The oddest thing was that Rome remained quiet in the wake of Caesar's murder. I might have ridden into the city without concern for my safety. I heard the first reports of this stillness and could not believe it. But it was indeed true. In the first hour after the crime the assassins, some sixty senators led by Junius Brutus and Cassius Longinus, fled the Temple of Tellus, where the senate had convened that morning. They took up a defensive position at the Temple of Jupiter, high atop the Capitoline. With their freedmen and clients in support, the assassins numbered nearly half a legion in strength. Because that temple also serves as an armoury, they were prepared for any contingency. Despite their immediate concern for security, I am told they hoped the city would eventually celebrate their crime. This is of course the kind of delusional nonsense that occurs when philosophers play in the deep end of the pool.

While the assassins waited to know the disposition of the city, Mark Antony, Caesar's fellow consul, stirred himself to act. Leaving the outer porticos of Pompey's theatre, which houses the Temple of Tellus, he made his way to the fortifications guarding two temporary legionary camps. These had been established on the Camp of Mars, not far from Pompey's grand theatre. The camps were commanded by Proconsul Aemilius Lepidus. Lepidus was under orders to depart for Narbonne in southern Gaul three mornings hence. This would have been on the same morning Caesar was to have left the city to join his army in western Macedonia.

Such was Antony's charisma with the rank and file that he might have walked into the camp and taken command of it. Perhaps he even considered doing so, but the truth is Antony needed Lepidus more than he needed two legions of fighting men.

Antony said nothing to Lepidus about the fortune inside Caesar's house. No, what Antony offered Lepidus was the office of Pontifex Maximus – High Priest of Rome and perpetual guardian of the Vestal Virgins. In those days, the holder of that office resided in the Regia; that meant that the Regia had been Caesar's residence for many years and the place where Caesar kept his money.

Whether or not Lepidus remarked on the fact that Antony hadn't the authority to appoint anyone to an elected office, I cannot say. What I do know is that it took very little persuasion for Lepidus to agree to Antony's proposal. Almost as an afterthought the two men arranged for the eventual marriage of two of their pre-adolescent children.

———

The city was stirring with rumours of Caesar's murder when Antony and Lepidus arrived at the Regia. They were escorted by enough friends and clients to secure Caesar's house. With that accomplished, Antony and Lepidus walked up the Palatine Hill and approached the house of Cornelius Dolabella.

Antony and my patron had never been friends. I believe everyone in the city knew this. In fact, Antony was convinced his former wife had slept with Dolabella, though she denied it. Dolabella had publicly announced that it was possible, but he simply could not remember.

This was of course worse than denial, and Caesar had generally tried to keep the two men in separate provinces, if not on different continents.

One may wonder why, of all people, Antony went to Dolabella, but the answer is simple. With Caesar's death, Dolabella had suddenly become the commander of Caesar's sixteen legions. This army was presently camped in Western Macedonia, but that was not so very far away. With such a force at his back, Dolabella had become the sort of friend Antony needed.

Antony was not prepared to bring Dolabella into his family, but he could offer Dolabella a consulship. The office was available, after all. Of course Antony had no more right to offer a consulship than a vacant seat at the head of the college of priests, but Dolabella was certainly not the man to object. He grabbed the title as if it were his due.

Only then did Antony introduce the question of protecting Caesar's gold. As consul, consul-elect, and Pontifex Maximus-elect, Antony, Dolabella and Lepidus returned to the Regia. There they promptly divided Caesar's money and portable goods, each taking a piece of that great prize to a secure location. As for Caesar's widow, they gave her until dawn the following day to vacate the premises.

Antony then sent an invitation to the leadership of the assassins to meet with him that evening. Some hours later, word came back that Junius Brutus and Cassius Longinus would come for a meeting on condition that both sides exchange family members to serve as hostages. This was arranged and that evening Cassius and Brutus settled down to a meal at Dolabella's mansion. Neither Brutus nor Cassius dared taste the food or drink the wine. No matter. Antony feasted as per his custom, and Dolabella tipped his cup as carelessly as an honest man.

The first order of business, according to Antony, was to establish a truce among all parties. No need for more bloodshed. Brutus protested at once; the first order of business, he said, was the restoration of the Republic. There would be no more tyrants or dictators or talk of kings in Rome.

Clearly he thought Antony aspired to replace Caesar. Antony answered him enthusiastically, 'You are right of course. Unless by restoration you mean my consulship is illegitimate.'

'That is exactly the case,' Cassius answered.

'Then I suppose I haven't the authority to call the senate to session for the purpose of voting immunity to those involved in Caesar's death?'

After a long, thoughtful pause Brutus asked, 'You would do that?'

'If I were still a consul I would. Of course, if you want

to declare me illegitimate and arrange elections at once, I cannot help you. You want a Republic and that, I'm afraid, comes with courts and the right of Caesar's family to bring the charge of murder against all of you.'

'Caesar was a tyrant!' Cassius answered.

'Perhaps he was, but he was also a citizen. Under the laws of our Republic his family can make you answer for his death in court. You know how it goes: lost fortunes, exile...' He gave a shiver. 'Juries can get very testy about the murder of a man they once loved. But as you like. I'll not worry about it. It's your court date, not mine.'

<hr />

The agreement that followed was the sort of sham only Mark Antony could have conjured, as worthless as a roll of wet papyrus in the long run but sufficient to keep the peace for the next few days.

Antony, in his role as consul, called the senate to session next morning before dawn and got a unanimous vote on a single measure, the details of which had been negotiated the night before. Antony's and Dolabella's consulships were confirmed. Lepidus received his pontificate. Caesar would have a funeral at public expense, and the assassins were all immune from civil and criminal prosecution. Should anyone care to protest the senate's decision Lepidus stood ready to advance his legions into the city.

The city was still quiet when I arrived on the Camp of Mars. I left Hannibal and my pack mule at a stable and walked into the city with a hired slave pushing a rickety cart filled with my gear. This was the evening before Caesar's funeral. Rather than seek out a public house or my family's Tuscan friends, I went directly to the great house of the Cornelii, for I had promised Dolabella I would report to him before the third day after the Ides of March.

As soon as I had identified myself, Dolabella's steward informed me that I would walk with Dolabella's party next morning. This actually meant I would serve as part of Dolabella's security force, though we didn't use terms of that kind. A client walked with his patron as a show of respect. He might carry a gladius and dagger concealed beneath his toga and even a stout walking staff with a steel point on it, but it was not appropriate to appear in the city in military armour. Good friends in great numbers? Well, who is not envied his popularity?

I joined some fifty friends in a makeshift barracks inside Dolabella's house. Not all the fellows were busy when I entered, but a great number of them were honing the blades of their weapons.

———

As a consul, now officially appointed by the senate to his office, Dolabella had an escort of lictors to accompany him in public; these men surrounded a standing consul as a mark of honour. They were sworn to protect the consul with their lives, but their numbers might not be sufficient against determined assassins. With another fifty friends close by, Dolabella would be far safer. My patron's anxiety for his personal safety seemed out of all proportion to any danger I could imagine until I saw the mass of people gathered in the Forum next morning.

In the wake of Caesar's assassination, the mob had stayed quiet, but that is not to say they were content. On the morning of Caesar's funeral they filled the Forum, spreading across the steps of all the temples and crowding along the basilicas Julia and Aemilia to the north and south of the great plaza. Even the rooftops and alleyways surrounding the Forum were filled. Man or woman, it made no difference: wherever I looked, I saw a murderous scowl.

Caesar's corpse had been set atop the speaker's platform with only a solitary squad of lictors posted around his funeral litter. Directly behind him was the dreary old Temple of Saturn, black with the smoke of centuries. Behind it was the Capitoline, with Jupiter's gleaming white temple pre-eminent at the top of the hill.

Caesar was propped up on one elbow in the traditional manner of the dead; the effect suggests a fellow reclining on his couch at a feast. He was wearing a senator's toga with the broad purple stripe and holding a drinking cup. This is the Roman way of bidding our world farewell and certainly not the worst of our customs. Brave and careless, yet honouring the amenities of life, we leave the light of day.

Caesar's co-consul, Mark Antony, delivered the funeral oration. He began his address with the usual tropes. He spoke of Caesar's kindnesses to his friends and family. Eventually he turned to the matter of Caesar's long and honoured service to Rome. I did not listen closely, for although Antony was a skilled speaker I soon found myself thinking about Caesar at my bedside: the touch of his hand on mine, his assurance that I was much needed.

A rumble in the crowd brought me out of my reflections. Once more I awakened to the terror of the mob. I could see nothing at first. Antony was quoting the oath that men had taken to serve Caesar: '...a sacred oath given freely before gods and men!' Then he named the men who had taken that oath: Gaius Trebonius, Cassius Longinus, Junius Brutus...

He continued naming the assassins, and as he did he walked over to Caesar's corpse. He pulled the toga away, exposing the stab wounds, more than twenty in all. 'Look and see how these men kept their sacred promises.' And touching the wounds, he cried again, 'Look and weep, Romans!'

It was a call to battle, and the plebs answered with a roar.

—◦—

Our captain called to us to get around Dolabella and take him up to the Capitoline, which was the closest fortification. He might as well have asked us to fly. We could not move. I could hear the plebs tearing into shops and looting goods. The Curia was soon put to fire. The old senate house was not the site of Caesar's murder, but that fact bothered no one. The senate house was handy and had long symbolised everything the plebs hated about their overlords. Once it was ablaze, the pressure of the mob shifted.

With swords drawn we were able to evacuate along the Via Sacra up the Capitoline's slopes and safely beyond the crush of the mob. As the road lifted us above the Forum I caught a glimpse of the melee from high ground. I could see both basilicas along the Forum's perimeter had already been trashed and set on fire; here and there the bodies of senators and equites were already down. Those men who had been hemmed in by the crowd or were too witless to escape when they had the chance were presently pursued by gangs of plebs. It did not matter if a man belonged to the assassin's league or Caesar's; a purple stripe that morning was enough to mark a man as an enemy of Rome.

Looking down at the Forum from the porch of the Temple of Jupiter we watched the mob destroy everything within reach. Despite the chaos, neither Antony nor Dolabella appeared anxious to summon Lepidus. To be honest, I think the consuls rather enjoyed the fulsome slaughter.

When they had seen enough and finally sent for him, Lepidus stormed into the city with every man he had. By late afternoon, the fight was over. Next morning hundreds of corpses of men, women, and children littered the Forum and streets beyond; pleb thugs had fallen over murdered aristocracy. The corpses of children were stiff in the arms of their rigid mothers. The shops were charred from fire. And ten thousand legionaries stood at attention throughout the city, even as squads of cavalry patrolled the streets.

It was at this point that a great many of the senators decided it might be a good idea to spend a few weeks at their country villas. Those actually guilty of murdering Caesar applied to the consuls for permission to leave Italy altogether.

Rome: April, 44 BC

For the moment Mark Antony's coalition ruled Rome, which is to say Antony ruled the world. Caesar's enemies were on the run, and the plebs were certain Antony embraced their cause. Nor did he play the tyrant. He took all and sundry matters before either the senate or the people's assembly. Nothing became law without a vote.

Nor was there any more murder of the aristocracy. Both Antony and Dolabella were happy to write passports for any of the assassins who asked the favour of them. At that late date, there were no senior positions to be had, but a minor office in some foreign city gave them the legal excuse to leave Italy.

As for the legions available to Antony and Dolabella, the two consuls made no personal use of them. Lepidus marched off to Gaul in a matter of days after Caesar's funeral. The great army in western Macedonia remained in camp for the duration of the summer.

For the better part of my life I have wondered how fortune turned so quickly against Antony. Within a matter of weeks everything he had accomplished began to unravel. Did he not understand the dangers he faced? Was he overconfident of his popularity with the mob? Too certain of the loyalty of the legions?

Only in my old age has it come to me. Antony acted quite properly. He was not interested in becoming another Caesar. He only wanted to serve his term as consul and then retire to a prosperous provincial government, where he might amass a fortune that even he could not exhaust. It can never be said that Antony was politically inept or stupid. Quite the opposite: he proved himself a political genius in the aftermath of Caesar's murder.

That he lost his power so quickly makes it seem as if he misjudged matters terribly or somehow let his success blind him to danger. There is some truth in both views, but a better assessment of the situation is that Julius Caesar came back from the dead. After that, no mortal could anticipate what might happen next.

V
A SULPHUROUS FOG

Rome, Macedonia, and Brindisi: April, 44 BC

Some days after the riots in Rome we awakened to find the city under a heavy fog. This was not the usual kind of moist air that forms around a river on a cold morning. Ashes drifted in the air and a vile sulphurous stench permeated everything. We thought it would pass with the first wind, but it stayed in Rome through the whole summer. It limited vision and burned the eyes. It wore on men's nerves as it lingered and made everyone wonder if it would ever depart.

The plebs were quick to assume the gods had sent this fog as a punishment on Rome. This was of course pure nonsense. With the coming of Octavian, Rome was going to have all the punishment she could endure. The more thoughtful of the superstitious eventually decided that the fog served as a harbinger of his coming. Another view, and certainly a less romantic one, is that Mount Etna blew its top.

Caesar's grandnephew had been in western Macedonia with the army when he learned of Caesar's assassination. At the news, Octavian's two closest friends, Marcus

Agrippa and Cilnius Maecenas, advised him to return to Italy at once. His mother and stepfather sent a letter by courier to counsel delay; the city, they wrote, was unsafe. Octavian hesitated only until he learned of the riots at Caesar's funeral. At that point he took courage and crossed the Adriatic and came to Brindisi, at the boot heel of Italy.

In Brindisi, still three hundred miles by road to Rome, there was more news. Caesar's will had been read. Legacies and gifts aside, Caesar had named Octavian his sole heir. Caesar had also adopted Octavian as his son. Having no other heirs with whom to share Caesar's fortune, Octavian quite suddenly became the richest boy in the world. Of course the law in those days was anything but clear on testamentary adoptions, but Caesar's will provided Octavian enough justification to call himself by his adoptive father's name, Gaius Julius Caesar.

Feted in Caesarean-friendly Brindisi as Caesar's avenger, our new Caesar rode north along the Appian Way with veterans of the legions joining him as he went. Perhaps because of his popularity with the plebs, very few of the great families offered the lad hospitality. It is said that Marcus Tullius Cicero received him at his villa in the south, albeit without offering him either a bed or a meal. Octavian pretended not to notice the slight and laid out his plans to Cicero in clear and simple terms.

Cicero pretended to approve of Octavian's ambitions and sent him on to Rome with much encouragement. Of course Cicero expected Antony to dismember the young fool in short order, and Cicero was almost never wrong in his assessment of things political. But, like everyone else, he was wrong about our boy Octavian, badly wrong.

In Cicero's defence, no thinking person could imagine Octavian was up to the challenges of political and military leadership. Only passion could stir men to support such an unlikely hero, but it was not a time for clear thinking. The plebs wanted revenge for Caesar's murder and backed the only man who promised it.

Rome: 5th May, 44 BC

Octavian's veteran legionaries settled on the Camp of Mars one morning in early May. They made no show of force against the city; they did not have armour, just swords and knives for personal protection. Armoured or not, their presence won Octavian a meeting with Rome's consuls, Mark Antony and Cornelius Dolabella. Octavian had declared in advance of the meeting he desired two things: the assassins of his father brought to justice and the inheritance Caesar's will had promised. Having nothing to give the lad, Antony and Dolabella might have hesitated granting a meeting, but Antony insisted on bravado. 'Best to put the lad in his place,' he declared. 'If he returns to his army empty-handed, the men will lose their enthusiasm for him. No soldier adores a man who proves too tender for the fight.' It was sound advice then and seems so even now. Certainly delay in granting a meeting or a pointed refusal to talk with him could only stir up trouble with the veterans.

There was no plan to assassinate him. For one thing, he wasn't worth the trouble. The subject did come up for discussion but only as one discusses killing a pestering fly. Whether Octavian feared the event or only thought to be prudent I cannot say, but he demanded hostages from Antony and Dolabella and offered his sister and mother and several of his family in exchange. All parties agreed to an honour guard of friends to stand in attendance; these men were to keep their daggers politely concealed. For his escort Octavian brought Marcus Agrippa and a handful of young thugs loyal to Agrippa. Cilnius Maecenas also stood with Octavian, though I seriously doubt he bothered to conceal any kind of weapon. Maecenas had a fine talent for political intrigue even in those early days, but no one ever accused him of military accomplishment. In a fight, Maecenas was always the fellow hiding behind the largest column, right next to Octavian.

I stood with a dozen other men at Dolabella's back. Antony surrounded himself with family and a few of his favourite pleb drinking companions, all good men in a brawl. In addition to the principal parties and their escorts, several senators were present to witness the event. We met at Caesar's former house, the Regia. The atrium was barely large enough to accommodate our number; in all there were some fifty men standing about. But a public building would not do; it was essential to avoid any appearance of conducting a formal meeting. This was a matter to be settled among family and friends. Hinting otherwise only served Octavian's cause, but of course everyone knew Octavian had forced the meeting and the entire city awaited the outcome. What they expected the lad to accomplish I could not imagine.

As I had neither met nor seen Octavian prior to this occasion, I was anxious to have a look at the young man. I can tell you I was disappointed. I could not help thinking that Octavian looked nothing at all like me. From my own youthful perspective that was the critical issue of this gathering. Nor could I understand Caesar having confused me with this boy. Let me be honest here. I spent years wondering what Caesar had seen in my features that allowed him to mistake me for Octavian. I was a head taller. I was thicker and more athletic as well. I looked to all the world like a young man. He, with longer hair, some makeup and a stola, could have passed for a pretty young matron trembling at the prospect of her wedding night.

I expect now the cut of our silhouettes was not that much different, and of course in a room full of older men a very young officer probably caught Caesar's eye, because he desperately wanted to see Octavian when he looked in my direction. There was also a fact I could not know in those days. Caesar had not been well acquainted with Octavian at that point. He spent a great deal of time with Octavian in the summer after the Spanish campaign; prior to it he had been engaged in a thousand-and-one intrigues. In such a life one has precious little time for a sister's grandson.

None of this, of course, was of the slightest importance to what followed, but fifty years on I still recall my acute agitation over Caesar confusing the two of us. So we all live, I suspect: obsessed with the silliest issues, missing entirely the surge and flow of that great river we call Time.

———

Antony and Dolabella received Octavian as one receives a child. No handshake was offered, nor did Octavian seem to expect it. Antony was a tall, powerfully built man but he was already going to fat. He often used his physical size and imposing baritone voice to intimidate men and thought to make the most of his mass with the waif-like Octavian. Dolabella, the more calculating of the two men, hung back throughout much of the exchange. He offered support when Antony appeared to falter. He answered in sensible tones whenever Octavian began gaining ground with his arguments.

To Octavian's credit, which I give grudgingly, he appeared hardly to notice Antony's bluster; he certainly showed no respect for it. There was a child-like peevishness in his tone at the start of the meeting, which no one could admire. In fact, at his worst moments during the meeting, Octavian seemed like a screeching, spoiled brat. Nor did it help that his toga made him look utterly ridiculous, especially as neither Antony nor Dolabella bothered with anything more than belted tunics. The day was quite hot, the very worst occasion for a man to bother with a toga.

Octavian's first order of business was to demand to know why Caesar's murderers had walked freely about in the city after their crime. Dolabella took this question. He explained that the assassins had surrounded themselves with their clients. 'You had the entire city under your authority,' Octavian responded. 'They had murdered a consul of Rome. You did nothing. Were the two of you in on it?'

'I'll not have talk like that!' Antony bellowed. He seemed to cool down once his two brothers made a show of taking his arms. 'You were not here, lad,' he added in a quieter tone. 'You cannot possibly understand the desperate nature of the situation. True, they had murdered one consul, but most thought they intended to kill the other as well.'

'And after him,' Dolabella added, 'any of the senate who had ever voted with Caesar's faction.'

'And what are your plans for them now that you have let these murderers escape?'

'If you want to know the truth,' Antony answered, 'I encouraged the senate to provide them with immunity from prosecution.'

This excited more youthful outrage, though I was fairly certain from watching Cilnius Maecenas it was not fresh news. It occurred to me, actually, that Octavian was following some kind of script, as an actor does. I shrugged off the notion, for it seemed utterly ridiculous, but in fact much of his later life followed a script written by another; in those early days Maecenas and much later his wife. He only acted his role. My assessment from this remove? Maecenas did indeed write this bit of theatre and Octavian recited his lines. The strategy, apparently, was to push Antony to folly. As a hothead, Antony needed only a bit of encouragement.

This theory credits a great deal to children, I know. But as those same children never seemed to take the advice of more experienced men in the years that followed, I think it is exactly what happened. Octavian pretended emotional outrage. Antony and Dolabella, eager to acquit themselves in the court of public opinion, sought to justify their behaviour.

The chief advantage of granting immunity to Caesar's assassins, according to Dolabella, was the agreement which had allowed Caesar a state funeral. His corpse would otherwise have been tossed into the Tiber, befitting a traitor's death. As Dolabella explained the matter, he sounded quite reasonable. The next point he made was equally praiseworthy: Antony's truce with the assassins had saved all the reforms that Caesar's government had accomplished, especially the acts granting land to retiring legionaries. It was at this moment that Maecenas struck.

'Your deal with the assassins protected Antony's status. It also got you promoted to consul without the bother of an election.'

'The government needed to continue with as little change as possible,' Dolabella answered. His face remained impassive, but there was tension in my patron's voice. I could see Maecenas's shot had struck its mark.

Octavian rose to Dolabella's comment like an actor responding to his cue. 'In other words, you were only interested in profiting from my father's murder.'

'If you want justice, go find the assassins yourself!' Antony roared. 'As for us, we have dealt with the matter as men do. We have averted war. We have saved the Republic!' Antony's fury could hardly obscure the fact that Octavian was right. When one came right down to it, neither Antony nor Dolabella cared a whit about honouring the corpse of Caesar; they certainly cared nothing about land reform for the plebs. For that matter neither man had acted as if he wanted to avert a war or save Rome. The deal with Caesar's assassins was all about Antony and Dolabella protecting their own interests.

'Rest assured, Antony,' Octavian answered, 'I intend to hunt down the assassins. Every last one of them. If that means war, so be it. But that brings me to my second concern. In order to pursue these criminals I am going to need my inheritance. From what I am told, the two of you arranged with Lepidus to take possession of my father's treasury. I assume you are holding it for me?'

'We have taken possession of nothing,' Dolabella answered. He kept his tone civil, for he was in fact a very skilled liar.

Antony spoiled the effect by trying to explain what they had actually done. It came about as close to a confession as I ever heard. 'After Caesar's murder,' he said, 'Dolabella, Lepidus, and I came here to Caesar's house. We intended to secure Caesar's fortune from looters, but as it happened all we found were Caesar's papers. What Caesar had not spent in the form of payroll for his legions he wasted on spectacles for the mob. There was no gold. No money at all.'

'What he possessed in abundance was debt,' Dolabella added.

The voice of Antony's brother, Lucius, broke from the crowd of Antony's clients. 'If I may be so bold as to offer you a bit of advice, Octavian... '

'My name is Caesar!' the boy screeched.

Antony's crowd rumbled derisively at Octavian's peevishness on this point. Within the year we would all embrace the name of Caesar and think nothing of it. A man is what he calls himself after all, but at that moment Caesar was more title than name. No one in Rome was quite ready to call this little sissy Julius Caesar. He might stamp his feet and screech as long as he liked: there was only one man deserving that name.

'My advice, lad,' Lucius Antony continued, once the jeering had died down, 'is the same that your mother and stepfather gave you some weeks ago. Repudiate Caesar's will. If you accept it, you will bankrupt yourself trying to pay off his debts.'

Octavian turned to the senators present, his witnesses, speaking quite calmly now. 'If Antony and Dolabella and Lepidus insist on stealing my father's money...'

'How dare you call me a thief, you little twit!' Antony's voice boomed with rage. He stepped forward with his great fists doubled. And he meant it.

'A thief and now a liar too.'

Antony's brothers pulled him back at this point, and there was no acting this time. Had they failed to do so there would have been violence. To give Octavian his due, he neither pretended to want to fight nor displayed the first tremor of fear. Struggling fiercely against his own men, Antony pointed a menacing finger at Octavian. 'Don't imagine you and I are finished, pretty. I'll see you cut to pieces and fed to the plebs for a banquet!'

Octavian turned his attention again to the witnesses. 'Let it be known I intend to pay out all of Caesar's legacies with my own money, including the three hundred sesterces Caesar's will promised every citizen of Rome.'

Antony cursed the boy as a fool. 'You make a promise that will ruin you, lad. Don't think we are not witnesses to your folly. I shall tell the whole city what you have promised!' I could discern nothing in Octavian's expression as Antony launched his threat, but Maecenas seemed actually pleased, as if Antony had taken some kind of bait.

'Shall I tell you what my father said to me in Marseille,

Antony?' Octavian had his feet under him now; his voice betrayed a strange confidence.

'Your father or your lover, sweetheart?'

'He said he thought it was better to bring you inside his carriage for the journey to Rome; otherwise one morning you were bound to be too drunk to ride and you'd end up falling off your horse and breaking your ugly neck.'

Antony went for the boy once more, but Octavian's bodyguards stepped forward. I recall my first impression of Marcus Agrippa at this moment. He had roguish good looks, calm eyes, and quite obviously the heart of a man who isn't afraid to use his fists. Even against a consul of Rome.

Antony and Dolabella consoled themselves with drink and talk after the meeting. Of the two, Antony was decidedly more animated. He called Octavian's promise of paying out Caesar's legacies 'a fatal miscalculation'. Antony said he wanted everyone to know the promise the boy had made. He signalled to one of his men, who withdrew and set about publishing this news to the plebs. 'Three hundred sesterces for every citizen,' Antony muttered, as if trying to calculate the sum. 'That is something like…'

'Fifty million sesterces,' I answered.

Antony glared at me, for I was not expected to speak, certainly not to him. He repeated the figure, however, as if checking my arithmetic, then quite suddenly howled with delight. 'Don't think the plebs are going to hear a promise like that and forget about it. When they don't see their money they'll hang our Little Caesar by his prick!'

'He can borrow on the value of Caesar's estates,' Dolabella answered.

'He may think so, but we have only to threaten encumbrances on the properties. Some question about the validity of the will is enough; no one will dare advance money to the boy until the will is settled, and that won't happen until Rome has new consuls. If he can't sell or use his property as security for a loan, all he can do is try to explain to the plebs why he hasn't got their money. Personally, I'd rather steal cubs from a lioness. At least a cat would be quick about it!'

━━⟞⟡⟜━━

Octavian, as it happened, had not made a frivolous promise. He was in the Forum next day with a league of his clients in attendance, all of them about the business of paying every citizen of Rome the three hundred sesterces promised in Caesar's will. Dolabella was as furious as Antony when he learned about it. It was impossible for Octavian to possess that much cash and yet he had it in hand and paid it out like a magistrate going about his public obligations. As for the propaganda that ought to have come with it, he said nothing at all. Antony had already made sure that everyone knew Caesar's bequest was to be paid from Octavian's own private funds.

In terms of political genius it surpassed all expectations. It certainly left Octavian's enemies gasping in confusion. Where had the money come from? That mystery was solved some days later when Dolabella's informants reported that Octavian had appropriated the treasure Caesar had sent to Brindisi to finance his Parthian campaign. I can still recall Antony's look of confusion when Dolabella told him about it. Of course both Antony and Dolabella had known about that money, but with a fortune in Rome to be purloined they had not bothered securing it as well. Besides, it was money set aside to pay for the services of sixteen legions. Sacrosanct – or so they had thought.

'Seven hundred million sesterces,' Dolabella announced, although both he and Antony knew the precise figure. At the time I was quite sure they regretted their failure to confiscate the money themselves, but I think now their real concern was Octavian. The lad had not only flanked their position in his first political outing, he had routed them in the aftermath.

After the funeral riots Antony had believed the mob was his to manipulate; suddenly both he and Dolabella had been exposed to the citizenry as thieves of Caesar's fortune, a fortune Caesar had intended to share with the plebs. Worse still, Octavian's subsequent propaganda branded them both as conspirators in Caesar's murder.

VI
ANTONY

Rome: Summer, 44 BC

Judah informs me that I have said very little about Mark Antony's personal appearance and the qualities of his character. Large and going to fat hardly covers it for a man of Antony's fame. Judah is of course correct. Not everyone knows about Antony these days. Once upon a time his effigies abounded, but his death is now thirty-five years past. In Rome one cannot even find his image. The young know how he came to his end but not all that happened before that. In the year of Julius Caesar's death Antony was forty. He was fit enough for a hard march and still a perfect terror in battle, but anyone could see that fondness for debauchery of every sort had begun to take its toll. In his youth Antony lifted weights to build his strength. After a day or two of feasting and recovery, he would plunge into his manic exercises again, lifting for hours on end.

The effect was said to be quite extraordinary. No one in Rome could lay claim to such a physique as his, and in fact it was a commonplace for people to call him Hercules. I am told he did actually resemble the figurines of the legendary strongman that one sees so often in houses. As a young man Antony liked the comparison so much he took to wearing an unfashionable beard to enhance the effect. He would even arrive at parties wearing a lion skin and carrying a club.

Atop this muscular figure was an aristocrat's face: long, serene and noble in character. The neck actually was a bit longer than normal, but I know of no one other than Octavian who ever called it ugly. Antony's family had risen in the world a generation or so earlier, but by bloodline he came from pleb stock, the same as Octavian's father's family did. Neither man liked to admit his plebeian origins, though it was hardly a secret, and in my opinion their discomfort with their common blood drove them both to the heights of patrician affectation. As to his character Antony was a creature of impulse, which perhaps explains both his genius and folly. He was a generous patron. Better than most, I would say. He had enjoyed the best education money could buy. He was especially skilled in speechmaking. Perhaps it was the discovery of brains inside that beautiful physique, but whenever he spoke at some length he thoroughly affected both men and women. He had a deep golden voice, but that was only part of it. He possessed an actor's skill and was not ashamed to lay it on thick. He could weep on command or cut loose with a series of jests, jokes, and puns. More than once I saw him turn a sombre gathering into a riot of laughter.

The stories that were told about Antony were always outrageous. Everyone who knew him could tell some awful tale, always of the same genre, though never quite the same incident. These began differently but ended with Antony vomiting into his toga, over an altar, into a matron's lap, on the Forum's speaker platform, or across the senate house floor. He was the last dignitary anyone wanted to see presiding at an official celebration and yet his prestige often required his attendance. He despised Roman pomp, claiming it always smacked of sham, and so he got himself roasted for the great festivals. After that, he either threw up or fell down.

Antony's chief virtue as a commander was his principal deficiency as well: he faced his fears head-on. He was unafraid of low ground in a fight and so had no instinct for avoiding military disaster. His considerable political skills were quite as easily compromised for the same reason. He did not care that all of Rome whispered stories of his sexual predilections, which were essentially boundless. It never occurred to him to enjoy his vices more quietly and thereby avoid political attack. Nor could he anticipate that others might be quite as clever as he was. His failure in this respect had less to do with his natural talents than with his lack of preparation, as for instance on the occasion of his interview with Octavian.

Grab his hand in salutation and you knew the legendary strength of his youth had not departed. Trap him in a corner and you would discover a man cut from Homer's cloth. Let him bask in glory and taste good wine, as he did in the days after Caesar's murder, and you would soon discover a fool having a run at the nearest cliff.

Enough? Judah is silent.

Not long after Octavian had paid out Caesar's legacy to the citizens of Rome, Cicero, the grand old man of the senate, delivered a speech before his colleagues. In it he charged Mark Antony with political corruption, theft and, for good measure, sexual immorality 'of a nature too vile for a decent man to describe'. Antony would have done well to ignore the matter. Cicero had no power beyond his own moral authority; certainly no party claimed him as its champion. He was simply a great man. Much admired, very little loved. But Antony, being Antony, thought he could put Cicero in his place. Launching into a diatribe against Cicero that reached back to scandals over two decades before, Antony struck with a fulsome broadside of half-truths and innuendoes. The worst of it came when he attended to Cicero's personal life, namely two divorces of recent date. The first was to a wife of many years so that he might marry an adolescent. The second divorce came soon after Cicero's new bride 'begged release from her vows'. When Antony had finished with Cicero's domestic tribulations, Cicero looked like an old fool besotted with youth. This was of course a road down which many old men had gone before. Hardly high crimes and treason. Antony had less success with his insinuations that the noble Cicero had helped himself to money from the public treasury, but Antony only wanted to stir Cicero's passions.

The strategy Antony employed can work quite brilliantly even against a talented orator. It is especially potent when one can charge an opponent with being an old man or accuse him of crimes he has most assuredly not committed. In either case the accused will become indignant and thereby look guilty. Cicero, however, failed to take the bait. Instead, he proceeded as the pedagogue does, with a detailed critique of Antony's rhetorical shortfalls. After a painstaking illustration of Antony's discordant logic Cicero proceeded to excuse the consul his excesses. Antony had not, after all, engaged his intellect in forming an argument since his schoolboy days. Any speech delivered without the aid of a few sacks of wine, he added, must be a terrible ordeal for one whose brain had rotted away from constant inebriation.

And so forth. It might have played out as comic theatre in less tumultuous times. As it happened the game was deadly serious. Cicero intended to pave a road by which Brutus and Cassius, the chief assassins of Caesar, might return triumphantly to Rome. Instead, his assault on Anthony gave young Octavian an opening.

Octavian, imagining Antony was down and out, proceeded into the city with his newly purchased legions, every man paid at five times the going rate. His judgment was sound in one respect; there was no one capable of opposing him, but Octavian made the mistake of establishing his military camp in the Forum. At once he lost much of the goodwill his money had bought him with the plebs, for they had no more love of tyranny than the aristocrats.

Not content to run his ship aground with the plebs, Octavian summoned the senate to convene before him. He let it be known he intended to ask for a vote that would name Antony and Dolabella enemies of Rome. To Octavian's chagrin, the senators stayed home. Within a day of the rebuff Octavian's officers mutinied and withdrew their forces from the city. Octavian had no choice but to follow his army out of the city, looking to all and sundry like a young whelp with his tail tucked between his legs.

Antony now rallied for a counter-assault, returning to the city with a great show of confidence. Nor did he proceed as a rank amateur by leading armed soldiers into the city. He covered himself only with a few friends and of course a consul's escort of lictors. And when he summoned the senate, the old men gathered like cattle to a feeding trough.

As a standing consul Antony was legally entitled to call the senate together, and after the recent occupation of the Forum, the senators were undoubtedly in the mood to declare Octavian an enemy of Rome. On the appointed morning, however, the senate sat without Antony. He had made a late night of it celebrating his revived fortunes. He only fell into bed an hour or so before the senate gathered. When his slaves awakened him in a panic, he threatened them with their lives. Knowing their master to be a man of his word the slaves let Antony return to his slumbers. And so Octavian was never officially declared a public enemy.

Was the fate of Rome really subject to an awful hangover? I am not wise enough to know the answer to that. What I can say with confidence is this: a vote to designate Octavian an enemy of Rome would not have influenced the legions supporting his cause. Perhaps Antony knew this and never planned on attending the meeting. Perhaps, deep in his cups, he finally understood the absurdity of voting. Only a battle was going to settle the issue. Perhaps his debauch was an eloquent answer to Cicero. Yes, he was an outrageous drunk, but he was also a general of considerable talent who was about to become Rome's new tyrant. Complain as men might, vote as they would, there was nothing anyone could do to stop him.

With Antony, all intentions were possible at once or none at all. He followed impulse and despised discourse and counsel. He hated discussing how others might react to any given action. It was not that he was stupid; rather he was impatient with lesser mortals. Whatever he chose to do was generally best. Who cared what his enemies planned?

At any rate, once Antony had recovered from his hangover, he travelled to Macedonia and took command of the legions there, though their number was now greatly reduced because of Octavian's poaching. Antony then crossed back to Italy with his army and marched north into the province of Cisalpine Gaul. This was the same province from which Caesar had launched his attack on Rome. He was a few months early for his proconsul appointment and in the wrong province as well, but no matter. He ousted the sitting governor, an assassin named Junius Decimus, and proceeded to recruit Gauls by the thousands for the coming fight against the boy who called himself Caesar.

VII
THE WILD BOAR

In theory, Dolabella had sixteen legions waiting for him in Macedonia. In fact, Octavian, having absconded with the Macedonian army's payroll, soon brought more than half of these legions under his own standards. Except for two legions, Antony took the rest. That left Dolabella scrambling for auxiliaries.

I played no real role in any of Dolabella's exchanges with the men of the senate that summer, but he brought me to several of his meetings. Observing Dolabella's negotiations turned out to be something of an education in how serpents dance. It was usually never a question of a willingness to provide Dolabella assistance; the issue always came down to price, but of course no one ever spoke of *quid pro quo*. An aristocrat would simply begin talking about a piece of property Dolabella's family owned or a house in a fine neighbourhood by the sea he had always wanted to purchase.

Fighting men were at a premium and no one cared to give away what could be sold. Some men wanted political office;

some few wanted a priesthood. Others sought a position of command for a son or nephew or younger brother. But the strangest *quid pro quo* came at the house of the Claudii.

Campania, Italy: Autumn, 44 BC

In his youth, elected a military tribune of the legions, Tiberius Claudius Nero rode under the standards of Pompey Magnus. Following this, Nero served as a legate in Gaul under Caesar. Caesar later appointed him admiral of his fleet in Egypt. A sparkling military career, in other words. Nero's influence in the senate was a different matter. For the sake of his fortune and noble bloodlines Nero's peers endured him patiently. They even praised him on occasion, but no one ever turned to him for advice. According to Dolabella, who quoted his good friend Gaius Trebonius on the matter, 'Claudius Nero was the dullest blade in an armoury of rusty swords.'

One had only to examine his performance as a military commander in detail to understand just how dull Nero really was. In Gaul, his only accomplishment was to be trapped and then rescued by Caesar. As Admiral of the Fleet in Egypt, he lost all of Caesar's ships without ever leaving Alexandria's harbour. Along with the fleet some portion of the great Alexandrian library burned as well. No blame ever accrued to the noble Claudius Nero, of course. Such mishaps are the fortunes of war. In the aftermath of the Egyptian debacle, once Nero had paid lavishly for the honour, Caesar let him stand as high priest of some temple or another. Dolabella forgot which it was and I never had the curiosity to look it up in the state archives.

Although Dolabella was too clever to quarrel with Nero the two men had no fondness for each other. Nero in fact had spoken out openly against Dolabella's sexual immorality, which is to say he disapproved of Dolabella's mixing with the lower classes. It is, after all, one thing for a Roman senator to tup his boy slaves, if that is his inclination. It is quite another matter to let actors and gladiators climb on.

Through much of the summer Dolabella had avoided Nero chiefly because he expected his visit would be a waste of time, but by autumn, resting at his estate in Campania for a few weeks, Dolabella found himself still in short supply of competent cavalry. If Nero wanted to cooperate, he could provide Dolabella with five hundred Spartan horsemen of the finest reputation. It was not an essential visit, but once he learned that Nero was in Campania as well, Dolabella decided it would not hurt to spend a few days courting the great man for the sake of the finest cavalrymen in Greece. In the worst case, he could expect to eat and drink quite well; Nero was rather famous for the spreads he put on. In the best circumstances, Nero might actually deliver the needed cavalry for the promise of a praetorship.

I expected Dolabella to pull his claws in and present only his best manners. That was the kind of behaviour I had witnessed all summer, but my patron had a real genius for divining moral depravity. With Nero he came charging in with the sort of wickedness he generally reserved for his transvestite and gladiator friends.

———

Nero was a good two decades older than Dolabella, in his late-forties or perhaps early fifties. That seems a vigorous age to me these days. At the time, he appeared to be a veritable ancient, all the more so once I discovered his new bride was an adolescent cousin from some branch of the far-flung Claudii gens. Nero was a tall man with thick, flabby limbs and a great gut. He had a long wobbly neck topped by a solemn square face that might have been carved of stone for all the animation it demonstrated. He generally wore a grim, pasty expression that never quite seemed sociable. He was slow moving and slow thinking, a man of extreme gravitas without so much as a spark of wit to make it bearable. Dolabella announced he had come to his 'old friend' hoping they might 'crack cups, get drunk, and throw up together.'

Nero reacted to this banter exactly as a man does who's been slapped and doesn't know what to do about it. Nor did Dolabella give the poor dolt a chance to respond. He dropped names the moment he arrived, choosing from among the nobility he had courted that summer. He disparaged and sniggered at their pompous airs and middling fortunes, a bleating flock of hypocrites, the whole bunch of them. It was blasphemy and slander to Nero's ears; it was also delicious gossip. Soon enough Nero was drinking it down in gulps. To give Dolabella his due: not a word of his chatter was untrue.

'A fine villa,' Dolabella said of one senator's country estate, 'even if it is mortgaged to the hilt with three different lenders. Better hope they don't find out about each other. Oh, I mean it's a perfect fraud: up to his ears in it with other people's money.'

Of another: 'Besotted with one of his own slaves. A pretty boy, no doubt of that, but I mean, really. When the master plays wife to his own slave it's not going to end well.'

Of one senator's wife Dolabella said, 'I tell you, friend, I've seen prettier horses.' This comment was part of Dolabella's rant against men who married ugly women. Nero's bride was not only sweet and unspoiled, she was gorgeous. I say this without exaggeration and with no argument from any man living in those days. All who met Claudia Livia Drusilla found her small stature and round, sweet face the very essence of sensuality. One can find a well-formed body and a pretty face at every bend in the road. It's the distinguishing feature of youth. They are babbling brooks of delights, soon enough enjoyed and forgotten. But there are some young girls with a sensuality that smoulders for decades in a man's memory.

Such was Livia's power. Rather than pretend he did not

appreciate her delicious beauty, Dolabella declared he could only respect a man who married a beautiful woman. By that standard he put Claudius Nero above all other men in the senate. Nor did Dolabella offer the usual formulaic praise for a good wife, nonsense muttered about docility and homemaking skills with a passing reference to her stature and self-possession. No, he was mad for the girl's pert round arse, and he made sure to let Nero watch him drool for it.

'So many men marry old crones for the sake of their fortunes these days. Even our hero of the Republic, Mark Antony. Fulvia!' Dolabella shuddered as if chilled by a sudden winter frost. 'Castrate me if I am ever so hard-up for money. Not my friend Nero. No second leavings for his marriage bed. But tell me, friend, do you intend to trade her off for another cousin once she's twenty and gone to the dogs or will you keep her on a bit longer out of sentiment?'

Nero had no idea how to answer such talk. I don't think anyone had ever confided in him about anything, least of all women. Certainly not in those terms. No matter. Dolabella could talk enough for both of them. He loved young girls. Not exclusively of course but well enough that if Livia had a sister looking for a husband he was freshly divorced and in the market.

In private, quite certain Nero's spies were listening, Dolabella declared he envied Nero as much for the little filly he mounted and rode each night as for the fortune his family possessed. 'What I wouldn't give for one night with that delicious cunny, Dellius. One time. By the gods, one time! I'll wager when a man plunges into her, she sizzles!'

'Tell me, Nero,' Dolabella whispered at dinner one evening, 'did Livia weep on her wedding night? You lucky bastard! I bet she did. Is she still the bashful girl in bed or mad for the old thyrsus now she knows what it's all about?'

Another time he said, 'If you're not happy with her, I'll take her off your hands. I'll be glad to pay you for the trouble of finding another wife.'

'How much would you give for her?' Nero asked.

It was a strange, cold question. I think he was joking, but who could tell with that dour soul? Dolabella laughed, all in good fun. 'I'd make you king of Rome if you gave me an hour with Livia.'

'I'll have my coronation before I agree to it.'

'What surprises me,' Dolabella remarked one evening when the two men were deep in their cups, 'is that you haven't thought to take hold of your colleagues and shake them like the spoiled brats they are.' Nero could imagine a crown on his head or at least joke about it; he could not fathom how he might bully his colleagues. They intimidated him, much as Dolabella did.

'I don't mean you ought to bother about them; they're frankly not worth the trouble, but what a good many of them need is a sword in the guts, and for the rest the threat of it. By the gods, we need to cull out the bankrupts and banish every man who's married to an ugly woman!'

'My husband is too kind for that sort of thing,' Livia answered. She was supervising the slaves as they served us, quietly listening to Dolabella's rant. She spoke up, I believe, because her husband was too shocked to say anything.

'That's a pity,' Dolabella answered cheerfully. 'Here we have Rome's last hope, and he's too decent to do what is necessary.'

'I don't think it's quite decency that stops me,' Nero muttered.

A slave came to the villa one afternoon, this on the third or fourth day of our visit. He informed Nero that one of the estate's herdsmen had spotted a wild boar in the mountains. Dolabella, overhearing the news, called at once for a hunt. Blinking and nodding in response, Nero answered, 'Yes, that would be the thing to do.'

Dolabella suggested that Nero send invitations to the aristocracy and gentry of the neighbouring estates. By dawn next day we had gathered more than a dozen young men of quality. Most of the hunters were the sons of Roman nobility on holiday at their Campania estates. A few were indigenous gentry who knew the mountain trails well enough to lead the hunt.

To the considerable surprise of all, Nero's bride expected to be included. I recall Livia arriving at the stables just as we were all preparing to mount our horses. Nero asked her what she thought she was doing. 'I've decided to join the hunt,' she answered.

'That's impossible,' he said.

'You've taken me hunting before.'

'A wild boar is considerably more dangerous than the game we've hunted. It isn't safe for you.'

'With all these armed men about? You have to be joking.' To her slave, she said, 'Fetch Artemis and be quick about it!'

'Stay where you are!' Nero told the fellow.

'Go!' the girl answered petulantly. The slave was naturally torn between commands: the refusal of either would get him a beating.

Fortunately for the poor fellow, Dolabella inserted himself into Nero's domestic affairs. Dolabella of course cared nothing about the fate of a slave; he simply loved scandal of every hue and thought to nurture this one in its infancy. 'Let her ride with us, Nero,' he said. 'Dellius will keep her safe.' He turned to me. 'Won't you, Dellius?'

I knew better than to complain of losing my chance at riding in the vanguard and answered my patron crisply. 'On my life!'

'You see? On his life. She will be perfectly safe.'

I expect Nero knew he had been turned into a laughing stock. All the same, he relented, for he dearly loved that girl. Let the neighbours make their jokes; nothing is as sweet in life as a happy wife. Of course, at the time, I was astonished that a senator of Rome would submit to a mere child. I had no respect for the old fellow. In my bachelor's ignorance I believed a man must never submit to the whims of a woman, especially if she happened also to be his wife. Time has softened my opinion considerably. When I was Nero's age, somewhere in my fifties, and about the business of my second marriage, I did not let my new bride hunt wild boar with the young gentry of our neighbourhood, but like Nero I spoiled her at every turn. Those who make us happy we learn to indulge. It is partly our sentiment for their sweet compliance and partly a desire to give them a life that is kinder than the one we have endured.

At any rate, Livia was athlete enough to ride with the men, a better athlete than most, if truth were told. Nero knew this and was not worried about her tiring or falling from her horse. He did, however, take the precaution of keeping his wife from danger by sending all but Dolabella and me ahead. With luck we could hope to join up in time for the kill, but there would be no adventuring at the front of the chase.

For her part, Livia appeared to agree to Nero's conditions until her mare was brought out and saddled. By then the rest of the hunters were a mile or so up the mountain. When Artemis bowed down to allow Livia to mount, she took her seat and brought the mare up quickly, kicking her flanks as she did. Nero called her back, for all the good it did. Livia departed at a full gallop, and nothing was going to turn her back. Still on the ground and having no chance of catching her anyway, Nero looked at me angrily. 'Your life, Dellius, if anything happens to her!'

—◦◦◦—

The land around Nero's estate was wooded, hilly and wild. Livia knew every ridge and ravine from her morning rides and soon left the trail by which the hunters had ascended the mountain. Her path was more direct and thereby more treacherous. There were jumps over logs and ditches. Then there were the breakneck descents, which I took at a gallop for the sake of keeping up with her. The fog that shrouded Rome that summer had covered all Campania as well; if anything the air was thicker and more foul.

Before long I found myself utterly alone. I knew Livia had gone off trail to lose me. Realising that there can be no pleasure in such a game if one is unavailable to be laughed at, I turned back and headed down the mountain. Soon enough Livia came ambling out of her hiding place. She began at once to tease me about my equestrian talents: 'I'm not sure you are the fellow I care to have guarding me. You can barely keep up.'

'Have you ever encountered a wild boar, Lady?' I asked.

'They are no longer common in Campania.'

'They are still plentiful in Tuscany, where I grew up. I've hunted enough of them to tell you when you find one you had better not be alone.'

'You have your spear and sword. Where is the danger?'

'They charge whatever frightens them. Even a mortal wound will not take them to ground at once, and with tusks as long as your arms they can impale you before they even know they are hurt.'

'How are they killed then?'

'It's best done with three or four men in a circle about the animal, all of them on foot and wielding spears. With danger on all sides a boar will try to threaten everyone. To do so it will turn from man to man, allowing the others a chance to strike its flanks.'

'I should like to witness that.'

'For that we need to join the others.'

With Nero's great mass it had been impossible for him to race his horse straight up the mountain. Accordingly, he had followed us by a more tortuous trail with Dolabella keeping him company. As we rode back to find them Livia took the opportunity to interview me. She was particularly concerned about my father's estate in Tuscany and the extent of my military experience. When I answered her in general terms, not caring to brag about my father's wealth or my extensive combat experience in Spain, she pressed me for details.

Her interest flattered me, of course, and I eventually gave her all she wanted, like the innocent dolt I was. I am not sure how long we talked in this fashion, for there is no topic as delightful as one's own life. Whether we are young or old, time passes quickly when we pursue the topic in earnest, especially with a perfect beauty quizzing us. This I can say, when we finally came upon Nero and Dolabella, it seemed only a short while and I resented losing the girl's attention. But such is the bachelor's fate.

Nero was in a terrible mood when we arrived. I imagined some portion of his anger must be directed at me, if only for the intimate conversation I had shared with his wife, but I was nothing to him. The moment we came together he began scolding Livia for the danger she courted. Livia called him an old grumpy-face, or some such nonsensical term. Rather than complain of her impertinence, as any other man would have done, Nero's wrath simply melted. He began by explaining himself and was soon apologising for losing his temper. 'It's just that I was worried, my love.'

—◦—

We had heard the baying of hunting dogs intermittently through the morning, but at midday the pack gave an excited cry. They had found their prey. Wild boars are wily creatures, but they rarely outrun a pack of dogs. Once sighted, they are soon surrounded. When that occurs, a boar has no choice but to stop and fight.

Nero, like the rest of us, was suddenly anxious to join in for the kill. Livia's safety no longer an issue, his only real concern was that we might be too late. With a perfect knowledge of the mountain's trails, Livia pointed out the most direct route. This happened to be along a cliff's edge, not really a trail at all, but she promised her husband we could save a quarter of an hour by taking it. That was sufficient argument for Nero, who led us now. Out of deference to our host and his wife, Dolabella and I brought up the rear.

On a clear day the horses might have refused us, but the summer fog covered the drop-off so that the animals galloped fearlessly along the very edge of the world. Once we had returned to safer ground the forest opened into a large natural clearing, and Nero pulled his horse up to have a look at two different trails.

The dogs were still baying, but to my ear they seemed to have lost sight of their prey. They were back to chasing its scent. Livia came up beside her husband and started to point out the better way just as the boar broke from cover. The beast charged right at them. Their horses shied in separate directions, and by chance the boar turned toward Nero's horse, goring its belly with long tusks. The violence of the attack took the horse down with a sickening equine scream and sent Nero tumbling.

I kicked Hannibal into a gallop. As I did I brought my spear to my right hand and leaned out as one does when he is preparing to strike the back of a fleeing infantryman. I could not hope for a mortal wound. I simply wanted to turn the boar away from Nero. I had trained Hannibal for such charges all spring and summer, but he had never encountered anything like this. As I rode forward at a gallop, Hannibal's terrified instincts overpowered his training, and he balked unexpectedly. Having already shifted my weight forward for the attack I was suddenly flying. I struck Hannibal's neck with one shoulder. My legs arced overhead. It happened so quickly I hadn't time to freeze up with fear, and so, while my legs passed gently over my head in a somersault, I twisted my entire body so that I might watch the ground on my descent. I landed on both feet, perfectly balanced. Only I was facing the wrong direction. I could see Dolabella's horse rearing up, still a good twenty paces behind me. He was, for the moment, a useless ally. I saw Livia staring at me in perfect disbelief. Dropping the reins, which I had carried over the top of Hannibal's head, I pivoted. The boar was tearing at the ground. Its focus was on me. Some fifteen paces separated us. Equine blood had smeared across the boar's tusks and jowls. I lifted my right arm, and only then discovered my hand was empty. I had lost my spear.

The wild boar came at me fast. I answered the attack with a bellowing shout and raced headlong toward it, pulling my sword as I ran. Closing together we built speed with every stride. A step before we collided, I hurdled over the animal's head, one leg leading, the other trailing. The animal lunged upward with its tusks as I passed over. I parried this attack by driving my sword down through its neck. I had aimed for the mortal juncture of spine and skull, and I thought I had caught it. In fact, the blade slipped past bone and plunged into the thick fat guarding its neck.

In the next instant the sword ripped from my hand and I went tumbling across the animal's back. I tasted the beast's wiry black hair right before slamming painfully into a network of bare tree roots. I felt rather than saw the boar turning back for me. Then I saw Livia charging at us. Artemis refused to come close, but the feint distracted the boar. Even as it pondered attacking Artemis, Dolabella came running in on foot. He drove his spear into the beast's flank. The boar turned on him, and Nero came now, striking the beast with his spear. I was kneeling behind the boar, knife in hand, and quite pleased the animal had forgotten me. Livia pushed Artemis forward again, and the boar turned, brushed past me with its flanks, and raced for cover.

I found my spear not far from Livia. After I had picked it up, I looked at the girl. Artemis had lost her wits with the repeated feints. She was dancing and rearing up in perfect terror, but Livia stayed with her expertly. A flush of excitement coloured her cheeks, and her eyes were fixed on me in a way that left me hopelessly affected. I glanced across the clearing to see if Nero noticed. He and Dolabella were walking toward Nero's horse. The animal had given up the struggle to stand, which in a horse amounts to the end.

I was attempting to retrieve Hannibal when I heard the dogs closing on our position. Distracted by Hannibal's refusal to allow me to approach, I did not at first realise they were chasing their prey again. In fact, they were coming quite close to our position. Then it struck me: they were chasing the boar in our direction. I turned from Hannibal and gave a cry of warning as I ran toward Dolabella and Nero. With my spear poised to throw, both Dolabella and Nero looked at me in confusion. Only when the boar broke into the clearing, did they finally understand.

I could see my sword still buried in its neck. This limited its speed and might ultimately have proved fatal, but at that moment the blade served only to madden the animal. At the sight of Dolabella and Nero, it turned toward them in fury.

From twenty paces I had no choice but to throw my spear. The point pierced the flesh just behind the shoulder and took the animal down; even then the hind legs kept driving forward. Nero danced behind his horse, looking like a whirling bacchant instead of an aging and overweight senator of Rome.

Dolabella, who had been leaning upon his spear, came to life with admirable speed, twirling his weapon toward the downed beast and driving the spear point into one of the kidneys. Nero now stepped forward, drawing his sword as he did. With a ferocious downward slash he opened the boar's neck.

VIII
QUID PRO QUO

There was some talk about who should give up his horse for Nero's sake. By this time several of his clients had arrived and were all volunteering their animals so that Nero might ride back to his estate. Before her husband could decide which offer to accept, Livia dismounted Artemis and handed the reins to him. 'I'll ride behind Dellius,' she said, and turned toward me. She reached up, and I caught her forearm as she took mine in turn. I lifted her as she jumped up behind me, exactly as cavalry are taught to do under battle conditions.

Nero stared at his wife and me, mouth open but speechless. I think he knew better than to protest. He was the butt of enough jokes already. Why throw oil on the flames?

For the next two hours, as we rode down the mountain, Livia pressed her pert breasts into my back and held me so tightly in her arms I could almost imagine she feared losing her balance.

At the estate the hunters retired to Nero's luxurious bath. As we soaked away the aches of a long ride Dolabella regaled those who had missed the kill with a comic rendition of my 'arse-to-sky Tuscan dismount'. As for my attempt to hurdle over the boar, Dolabella insisted I had only jumped the beast in the hope of tupping it.

Meanwhile the beast roasted slowly through the late afternoon and evening, carefully tended by Nero's slaves. When we had finally settled down to feast on our kill late next afternoon, it was a banquet that did not soon end.

———

After our feast, as per my habit, I came awake before dawn. I thought I might run for an hour before the rest of the household had stirred, but as I washed myself a slave girl knocked at my door. 'The domina would like to speak with you,' she told me.

We made our way under the extensive porticos connecting the various buildings on the estate and soon came to Livia's residence. I heard the chirping of some twenty or thirty songbirds within. These were imprisoned in a gilded cage that stood in the atrium, directly behind a shallow pool. Farther on through the house I could see a splendid garden from which Livia approached. She wore a floor-length sleeping gown. It was tied primly around her neck, showing nothing of her delightful figure. Her long black hair hung down loosely about her shoulders and across her back, not yet combed and curled for the day.

'Leave us,' she told the girl. The slave backed away and vanished beyond the gate. 'Come closer, Dellius,' she told me. I knew better, but I walked around the pool and stood before the young matron. 'I want you to tell me what Dolabella desires from my husband.' This without even a good morning.

'You must ask Dolabella that.'

'I'm asking you.'

'I don't know. He doesn't confide in me.'

Livia pulled upon the slender cord at the neckline of her gown. As she did, the garment fell in a rush about her feet. I stared at Livia's naked flesh with a mix of terror and desire. Her husband might suddenly come upon us; for all I knew he might be asleep somewhere inside the house. At the very least there would be slaves who might see us together and tell Nero what they had observed.

But for all that, I could not bring myself to flee. How could I? I knew only the party favours who had congregated at Dolabella's orgies and the slaves one can buy in brothels. Too thin, too fat, foul of breath, bruised by beatings, low, crass, loud, all of them eager to have a man quickly so as to be done with the business. I had seen nothing to equal Livia's sweet nubile athleticism. Her beauty robbed me of breath and left my heart aching. 'If you lie to me again,' she whispered, 'I will scream until my slaves discover us. What do you suppose my husband will do to you if he thinks you are here to rape me?'

I could see in her eyes she had no fear of her husband's

displeasure. What torture he might inflict on me was another matter.

'Dolabella believes your husband can provide him with a cohort of auxiliary cavalry.'

She thought for a moment. 'The Spartans?'

I nodded absently, looking around the atrium fearfully. Were we alone? Did she mean to ruin me? Or was this how the girl seduced her lovers? 'Might you at least cover yourself? In case your husband should find us.'

'Am I so horrid to look at?'

I looked because she invited it. I looked because I could not stop myself from it. 'Think of the danger, Lady.'

'I am. I rather like it, if you want to know the truth. Now tell me. What can Dolabella offer my husband to make it worth his trouble?'

'I heard Dolabella mention a praetorship.'

'Dolabella and Antony have made a great many promises this summer. I am wondering if they have promised more than they can deliver.'

'What my patron promises your husband he will deliver, but please cover yourself. I do not want to be discovered with you like this.'

She stepped closer, touching my tunic with her fingers. She explored and then teased my awaking sex. As she did this, quite expertly I must admit, she said, 'You are assuming Antony will return to Italy next summer.'

'What?'

She wrapped the tunic about my shaft. Slowly, for the pure pleasure of watching my fear wash into desire, she brought me to full tumescence. 'Mark Antony cannot promise my husband a praetorship if he cannot return to Rome in time to control the outcome of the elections, Dellius.'

'All that stands in his way is an army commanded by a boy.'

'That would be the same boy who chased him out of Italy this summer.'

'Antony has already…'

To be honest, I forgot what Antony had already done. I did not trust the girl, nor think us safe from discovery, but neither could I resist her. She was bargaining for something I could not understand. Robbing me of my wits in the process.

'My husband puts faith in neither Antony nor Dolabella. You, on the other hand, he believes he can trust. Is he right?'

'When I make a promise, Lady…'

I did not finish the thought, was not sure myself what my promises meant.

She caressed me still, even as she bargained. 'I'll see to it Dolabella has the Spartan cavalry he covets,' she told me. 'In exchange, you must promise that Dolabella and Antony will see to it that my husband is elected praetor next year. Your promise, Dellius, not Dolabella's.'

'You will see to it?' I stammered.

She let go of me and took my hand, leading me across the atrium in the direction of an open doorway. 'My husband will proceed exactly as I recommend.'

'I must speak with my patron before I can say what he will do.'

She brought me into her bedroom. 'I can also provide you with four legions of veteran Italian infantry.'

I stopped our advance for her bed. I stared at her in disbelief. 'Four legions?'

'For that gift I have other conditions,' she announced primly.

Was she mad? Lost in fantasy? 'Just where are you going to find twenty thousand veteran infantrymen who will answer your directives?'

'Aulus Allienus has command of them in Alexandria. Allienus owes his appointment to my husband's patronage. He will do whatever my husband asks. All you will need is a letter written under my husband's seal and signed in my husband's hand.'

'And you can arrange this?'

'I can if you promise to meet my conditions.'

I stared at her naked body, and yet I knew it was something else. Something I would hate. 'What conditions do you require?'

'When you deliver the letter to Allienus, you will need to show him the head of Gaius Trebonius.'

'The head?'

'Without it – or with some counterfeit – Allienus will not only refuse your request, he will have you executed.'

My tumescence was gone, and suddenly I was more afraid of this girl than of being discovered by her husband. 'You want Dolabella to assassinate the governor of Asia?'

'I did not say that. I want you to assassinate the governor of Asia. You may present Dolabella with your legions once you have them, if that is what you desire, but they will be yours to command. I have already spoken to my husband. He agrees with me. They should answer only to you. They will serve whatever cause you deem best.'

'I hope you understand that, as the governor of Asia, Trebonius surrounds himself with an army.'

'You should have no trouble getting him to let down his guard. Trebonius and Dolabella are old friends.'

'What makes you think Dolabella will agree to let me assassinate a man he calls his friend?'

'For the sake of four legions I don't think Dolabella will quibble over a lost friend or two.'

'And you say I must be the one who kills Trebonius. No one else?'

'On your word of honour, Quintus Dellius. You and no one else. And before you strike the killing blow, I want you to tell him I am the one who sent you. He must know that.'

As she said this, Livia stepped forward and put her arms over my shoulders. There was no resisting her spell. I kissed Livia's mouth and felt her body press tightly against me. I inhaled the sweet scent of her flesh. The moment she felt her effect on me, she lifted herself up and wrapped her legs about my hips. Only my tunic and loincloth separated us, and these she soon pulled out of our way. For a long moment we touched without penetration, a playful mime of lovemaking. Finally, she snaked her hand between us. There was a moment of hesitation, the feel of hair and then of her wetness. And finally the impalement of lovers.

I shivered helplessly as I sank into her. Her mouth covered mine, her tongue teasing, tasting, probing. I could not bear separating from her even to walk to her bed, so I staggered with her still clinging to me, faces, torsos and groins touching. Her grip on me as insistent as hunger.

Campania, Italy: Autumn, 44 BC

Dolabella's door was still closed when I returned at midday, though the rest of the house was up and about. He had taken one of Nero's slaves for his night's entertainment. I can't recall the gender, but with him it made very little difference. I gave him time to awaken and then asked to have a word in private. Dolabella had no patience for interviews with his junior officers and signalled me into his room as if suffering a terrible inconvenience. Of course he was miserably hung over and still stinking from sex and drink. I told him I could not speak inside the house.

He was curious at this but agreed we should take a ride together, in a little while.

I waited for him at the stable nearly an hour before he joined me. When we were alone and could not be heard, I told him Nero would provide him with the Spartan cavalry he coveted in exchange for the promise of a praetorship. 'Happy to do it,' he answered, and I knew him well enough to know he was lying. He had no more praetorships to give away.

'You will want to give Nero what he asks for,' I told him.

'I'll do anything I please, Dellius, and mind that you take care before you give me instructions again.'

'In addition to the Spartans, Nero offers me command of the four legions stationed in Egypt.'

Dolabella brought his horse to a halt. 'Offers you?'

'That is the condition of the gift, that I command them. But as I serve you, I will naturally remain under your authority.'

'Nero asks you to command four legions? And he actually has them to give away, just like that?'

'His wife makes the offer actually. With one condition.'

Now he laughed. 'Livia is offering it! Yes, well, she does have her way with the old boy. Pray, tell me, Dellius, what is her condition? A good tupping?'

'She insists I take the severed head of Gaius Trebonius to Egypt. Once I present it to the Roman commander in

Alexandria the legions will be mine to command.'

Before that moment I had never seen Dolabella speechless. He was pre-eminently the man with a clever riposte. Not on this occasion. Perhaps he imagined I was joking and did not want to appear the fool; perhaps he was adjusting his understanding of the world. Whatever his thoughts, they were his own; then, quite suddenly, he burst out laughing. 'That delicious little tart! I wonder what Trebonius did to her?'

'I didn't ask.'

'Nor should you have done. No, we'll ask Trebonius, while he still has tongue to answer. I'm sure he'll be glad to confess.'

'You agree to the conditions?'

'For four legions, Dellius, I would give the girl every head in the senate, save my own.'

Returning from our ride, we found Nero waiting for us. I feared the man as I had not previously done, but he did not bother looking in my direction. He handed Dolabella a letter. 'Have Dellius take this letter under seal to Egypt along with his package. I'll send your Spartan auxiliaries directly to the Hellespont to await your arrival. And I should like to be elected the urban praetor, if you don't mind, next in power to the consuls. There won't be a problem with that, will there?'

IX
LEGATUS

Smyrna, Asia Minor: February, 43 BC

Gaius Trebonius, Governor of Asia, assassin of Caesar, old friend to Cornelius Dolabella: I see him still in the torch-lit hall of his palace at Smyrna.

There was such laughter that evening it was difficult to remember we had come to murder these men. Such was my strange mood I could almost believe they had somehow divined our intentions. The hilarity seemed unreal. Perhaps, I thought, they dissembled just as we did.

I reminded myself that Trebonius had not bothered with security, but it was no good. I was sure they suspected us. There were only two men guarding the entrance to the Triclinium. They were there to keep out unwanted intrusions. Trebonius brought all his senior officers to the feast. Like our own officers, they were young gentry and nobility, every one of them in his fighting prime. None of us was armed for the banquet, of course, but knives naturally lay on the tables.

In the weeks leading up to that night, Dolabella had

crossed the Hellespont and marched south through Troy. From there he continued as far as Attalia, which is guarded from open water by the enormous island of Lesbos. There he made camp. This was fifty miles north of Smyrna. He then sent one of his two legions along with his Spartan cavalry to lay siege to Sardis. Sardis lies on the Hermus River, fifty miles east of Smyrna. Having Smyrna now threatened from the north and east, Dolabella gathered his officers together and boarded two warships that he might sail into Smyrna's city harbour.

Those legionaries escorting Dolabella surrendered their weapons as they left the ships. Dolabella and his officers came forward dressed in togas, which is to say completely unarmed. Presenting a passport that declared him Proconsul of Syria by authority of the Roman senate, Dolabella requested an audience with the Governor of Asia. Nor did he make any demands for hostages. In other words he put himself at the governor's mercy. We walked under an armed escort into the city. There were no chains on us, but we were prisoners all the same.

Once Dolabella stood before Trebonius he announced that he had come to Smyrna to surrender his army to his old friend. He offered his own life in return for the safety of the two legions under his command. He said his officers had served him faithfully, that he alone deserved to be punished for betraying 'the principles of the Republic'. By this, of course, he meant that Caesar was a tyrant and had deserved to die.

I recalled the face of Trebonius. I had seen him at one of Dolabella's parties, though we had never been introduced. He was a young man, in many respects very much like Dolabella, especially with his fondness for good wine, cruel wit, and pretty boys. Trebonius played the grim-faced magistrate as he listened to Dolabella's plea for the lives of his officers and men. He watched imperviously as Dolabella fell to his knees in supplication on our behalf. Finally, with a theatrical flair worthy of Dolabella himself, Trebonius rose from his curule and walked toward his old friend. Only as he pulled Dolabella to his feet and threw his arms around him did Trebonius finally smile. He called Dolabella brother. Dolabella's eyes filled with tears, his cheeks suddenly streaked, as if his friend's magnanimity was entirely unexpected. At this, Trebonius scolded him for imagining he might not be welcome. Were they not old friends? Not good friends still?

We all took an oath to serve Trebonius and his allies, Cassius Longinus in Syria and Junius Brutus in Greece. The blood of a pig was spilt, followed by vows taken in the name of Artemis, the supreme and most ancient cult deity on the Ionian coastline.

Afterwards, Trebonius and his staff played host to Dolabella and his officers. Our sailors, marines, and rowers bivouacked on the ships; our legionary escort was quartered elsewhere in the palace, but as they had also taken an oath they were not kept under lock and key.

At midnight, while the officers still celebrated their newly formed alliance, certain of Dolabella's legionaries slipped away and eliminated the guards at the city gate. After that it was a simple matter of letting our Spartan cavalry into the city. The Spartans had left the siege at Sardis early in the morning that same day and arrived in Smyrna at midnight. Once inside the city, they eliminated every soldier they encountered then surrounded the barracks of Trebonius's Guard.

At the first cry of alarm inside the city, Trebonius seemed vexed. Before either he or his officers could work through the matter, Dolabella's men took up carving knives and struck at those closest to them. Smiling one moment, cutting a throat the next. One or two of our party failed his task, and the fight was on. All the same, it was bad odds for Trebonius's men, and the room soon belonged to us.

Trebonius seized a knife when I came at him. His men were either down or backed into corners and outnumbered. I came at him boldly, eager for the fight. I grabbed the handle of a long-necked amphora and smashed the vase against his wrist as he threatened me. Bone broke. The knife clattered across the marble floor. I stepped up and pummelled Trebonius's ribs with a flurry of punches. Trebonius had served as an officer in the legions of Caesar and was a veteran of a great many fights, but he had not spent the past year training for his next encounter, as I had done. He was at my mercy after only a few blows, but I kept at it. I meant to soften his resolve. In his pain Trebonius cried out to Dolabella. What was going on? What about the oaths we had sworn?

Dolabella gave a careless shrug. 'No truer, I'm afraid, than your oath to Caesar.'

Before Trebonius could speak of Caesar's tyranny, as he seemed about to do, I slammed my fist into his nose. I required him to focus on me; I had no interest in hearing his justifications for murdering Caesar. I wanted him to answer my questions. I wanted to hear what terrible thing he had done to Livia. I ached to know the details so his death might be all the sweeter when it came. After he was broken and bloodied and straining to stay conscious I picked up the knife he had tried to use against me. I began cutting him. These were light quick slashes that soon awakened his attention. Finally I spoke. I told him I wanted the truth. He said he would give it, but when I asked him about Claudia Livia Drusilla he claimed not to know the girl. I cut him for his ignorance; I slammed my fist into his ribs hard enough to break more bones. 'She is the bride of Claudius Nero. Do you know him?' This confused him, or perhaps he was simply too stunned to think quickly.

Dolabella had watched my performance up to this point without interfering. He was half in the bag with drink, letting me 'earn my legions' at the cost of his friend's life. Now he told Trebonius it did not pay to be slow about answering. 'Not with earnest young Dellius here. Tell the lad you deflowered the girl, and we can all have a good laugh about it.'

'I tell you I don't even know her!' Trebonius cried. His eyes were wet with tears. He was in pain, but I think the shock of Dolabella's betrayal had broken his courage. He seemed sincere in his protest, but every man under torture begins with sincerity.

'Of course you know her,' Dolabella answered. 'When she married that old bore Claudius Nero last summer you had plenty to say about it. Don't play coy!'

'I made jokes about it! But I don't know the girl. I only said I pitied her.'

'By Dis!' Dolabella cried. 'He's telling the truth.' I stared at my patron uncertainly. 'He just told you! He pitied the poor girl having to lie under a tub of guts like Nero! That's what you said, wasn't it?' Trebonius nodded without enthusiasm. 'So kill him and be done with it,' Dolabella muttered.

By this time our men had fetched weapons from the armoury. One of the other prefects, as I recall, handed me a long sword. Trebonius, seeing it, suddenly begged for his life, but I paid no attention. 'This is from Livia,' I told him. I expect I hurried my stroke. I was a bit drunk as well. At any rate, my aim was faulty, and I cracked open his skull. He gasped and groaned, still alive. I pried the sword from bone and heard a cry of mortal pain. He lay on the marble, blood pouring from his scalp. At least the begging had stopped.

I used both hands this time as I brought the sword down and through his neck. The sword itself shattered. The head rolled across the floor like some kind of ball. I sloshed through the pooling blood after it. I gave it a vicious kick. I followed the thing as it tumbled along a macabre serpentine path, blood and brains spilling in its wake. I slipped and nearly fell before I kicked it again. Even then I was not finished but started after it once more.

'Easy, Dellius,' Dolabella called. He was laughing at the great mess of it all. 'Allienus needs to recognise the face. Mash it up too much and you won't get your legions.'

I stared uncertainly at the head, then back at its bleeding corpse. Finally I focused on my patron. I was like a man who awakens from a nightmare, no longer capable of distinguishing reality from dream. I grabbed the head by its ear and carried it over to one of the palace slaves who had been serving us when the carnage began. He was twelve or thirteen, quite small for his age. I dropped the bloodied pulp in his lap. 'Put it in a jar of wine and seal the lid shut with wax,' I told him. The boy looked at the face of his last master in perfect terror, his breathing fast and shallow. The poor lad seemed incapable of speaking, but at least he did as he was told.

After all these years I am still not sure if Livia sent me to kill Trebonius for the sake of revenge or to see if she could accomplish a murder simply by asking for it. I expect she hardly knew herself; she was only a child acting the part of an adult. For me, however, the real curiosity has always been the inexplicable rage I felt after taking the man's life. Was it for the sake of the murdered Caesar or for Livia's hurt pride that I kicked that head? I cannot answer with certainty. I am even inclined to wonder if something else excited my emotions, a feeling of having betrayed my own principles, perhaps.

I realise that, as a rational creature, I ought to be able to explain myself, but there it is. I am lost for a reason or had too many to understand my true motive. This much I can say, for I remember that evening in every detail. After handing the severed head to the boy I walked out of the governor's banquet hall and ordered a weeping slave girl to draw a bath for me. I settled into a smooth stone tub of hot water and called for more hot water at once. When that cooled I demanded more. After I had soaked away whatever emotions stirred my rage, I pulled the girl into the water and tore away her tunic.

Later, I sent her to fetch fresh clothes for me from the governor's wardrobe, his and no one else's. I dressed myself in a handsome long-sleeved scarlet tunic cut in the Greek style. I had never before worn such a gorgeous costume; such airs in Tuscany and Rome would win a man scorn. In the orient such finery was customary, assuming one could afford it. After dressing, I fitted the governor's ceremonial long sword and scabbard at my belt. Finally, I appropriated the finely woven wool mantle Trebonius had worn when he greeted us. Only then did I study my figure in a brass panel. By a trick of light the man staring back seemed a perfect stranger.

Dolabella's Spartans had taken possession of the city. The only opposition remaining had withdrawn to the citadel. This meant it would be safe for my party to go at once to the harbour. Dolabella wrote out my passport in his own hand and impressed his signet ring into hot wax at the bottom of the letter. The parchment declared my name, my rank as a legate, and the authority under which I travelled, Cornelius Dolabella, proconsul of Syria. When he had passed the document to me he said, 'Caesar once told me a legate does well to act exactly as his most experienced centurion advises, but if he is absolutely convinced he has a better idea, then he must "grit his teeth, pull his sword, and kill every son of a bitch who stands in his way!" I've found it the best advice I ever received. I suggest you follow it as well.'

⟶⟨⟩⟵

I left the governor's palace in the company of those officers who had helped me murder Trebonius and his staff. Also in our party was the slave boy to whom I had entrusted the head of Trebonius. I claimed the slave as my property by right of conquest. To my delight, once young Nicolas began speaking again, he demonstrated a rare talent for language, being fluent in Latin, Greek, and Aramaic, the popular language of the East. Like most Roman officers newly arrived in the East, I had studied the Greek of Homer and Plato, which is to say the ancient and classical dialects. I was still some years from being comfortable with modern Greek, called koine. Having an interpreter at my side would make my life easier.

At an island just west of Chios next evening our ship joined up with five transport ships in the service of Dolabella's fleet. These carried a cohort of veteran legionaries, the horses of our officers, payroll for the men under my command and an armoury of weapons. I did not take inventory at once. I was eager to get on to Egypt. I simply assumed Hannibal was on one of the ships. I learned he was missing in Kos, when we were forced to take shelter from a storm and unloaded our livestock in the dead of night.

With so few horses making the journey it did not make sense that Hannibal had been forgotten. I knew a legate's horse is never misplaced or overlooked; a general's horses are accorded nearly the respect of the general himself. I could only conclude that Hannibal remained in Asia on Dolabella's orders. Dolabella of course had no intention of keeping Hannibal as his own; of that I am quite sure, but he knew how I loved that horse and could not resist playing the prankster. And of course, since the horse was in Asia while I was in Africa, he took care to give the animal some exercise. Funny though it may have seemed from his perspective, I can tell you this: I found no humour in it.

Our fleet carried water and supplies capable of sustaining us a fortnight at sea. It was enough, with good weather, for us to sail directly to Egypt. Between Smyrna and Alexandria, Cassius Longinus and his allies in Judaea owned the islands and the entire coastline. Any stop was dangerous, but a storm we encountered close to Kos obliged us to find harbour and cost us a fight with the Roman garrison there. In fact, we used up almost a week of our supplies. With our scant forces we could not take the fortifications on the island, but before we left we damaged their ships so they could not give chase or warn Cassius's allies on the mainland.

Three days more got us to Cyprus. There we stopped for fresh water and supplies with only a minor skirmish as we left the harbour. Afterwards, it was five days and nights against the wind to Egypt.

Alexandria, Egypt: May, 43 BC

We saw what looked to be a second Venus in the night sky. It hung low on the horizon, shimmering like a star that none of us had seen before, but our pilot knew it for what it was. By first light we could see the faint outlines of Alexandria's famous lighthouse under the great flame. It had been a long haul without coming to port, and the men began cheering. Egypt and land at last.

The lighthouse of Alexandria is situated on the island of Pharos, which is about a mile distant from the city. Pharos is a long, thin rectangular strip of ground that serves as the harbour's primary breakwater. It also functions as the city's outer fortress. A mile-long causeway had been constructed between the island and mainland, this perhaps a century after the city's creation. Militarily, the effect was perfect. The island could be fortified with men and supplies; should it fall to the enemy the causeway was easily closed off from the city. As a result of the causeway, Alexandria enjoyed two large harbours, one for ships on imperial business, the other for commercial traffic. To either side of these harbours the land had been extended into the sea and fortified with artillery. The effective encirclement of each harbour, much as one finds at Brindisi, makes the city quite safe from attack by sea.

The royal palace sits on a spur of land along the eastern perimeter of the harbour. A temping jewel on view, seemingly for anyone to take, it is surrounded by water on three sides. Because the outer walls plunge down into the sea, access to the palace comes only from within the harbour. The first of these access points is a long and easily defended stairway that snakes its way up a steep incline from the harbour to the palace gates. This makes an attack on the palace quite costly, if not thoroughly impractical. A second point of access is the boulevard that connects the palace complex to the city of Alexandria. Like the stairway leading up from the harbour, this boulevard only appears open and inviting. For all its luxury and spaciousness, it is, in reality, a narrow defile designed for trapping and killing an invading force.

Thorough as these defences of the royal palace are, the city itself is also protected by a high wall and numerous towers. Alexandria's chief fortification, however, is nature itself. There are no harbours close to the city. To the south and east one encounters the Nile Delta, swampy ground filled with fast running streams over which only a few roads and bridges afford access. To the west the pastel green fields soon fade into an inhospitable desert landscape. All of which has given Alexandria a relatively uneventful history during its three centuries of existence. In fact the only significant disturbances have arisen from internal unrest, the most recent being the civil war between Queen Cleopatra and her younger brother. This was the conflict that Julius Caesar famously settled, though he lost a fleet of ships in the process.

—⊸∞ᘰᘊᕊ∞⊷—

As we were Roman soldiers, our ships entered the imperial harbour without first being boarded by agents of the harbourmaster, but we were not permitted to disembark until I had presented my passport to a Roman freedman.

This fellow was nominally in the service of our legions, but, as I quickly discovered, there were no legions in Alexandria. They had withdrawn to Memphis at Queen Cleopatra's request.

Once this freedman had examined my passport, he asked my business. I informed him that I had a letter from Claudius Nero, who had asked me to deliver it in person to Aulus Allienus. This excited some curiosity, but I would not explain my business to anyone but Allienus. The freedman promised my request would be passed on to Allienus. He then suggested we stay on our ships until he could arrange accommodations for us within the palace compound. I answered him bluntly that we were coming off our ships with or without invitation. This was not well received but, having no rank, he would not quarrel with me.

Caesar had put Roman soldiers in the country. Any attempt to control or impede the Roman army was the same as open revolt, punishable by crucifixion. Accordingly, I ordered our men and supplies off the ships. We met no resistance from either the citizens or the Queen's Guard.

I took up a defensive position in one of the basilicas close to the harbour. For the sake of our equipment and the great number of rowers and sailors in our company, we ended up commandeering three additional buildings, all of them adjacent to one another. This is the sort of activity that turns locals against standing armies, but I had no choice in the matter. I did not care to build a camp outside the city, lest we be locked out. While we were yet unloading our gear I sent men to collect food and supplies from the local merchants, writing promissory notes rather than parting with the meagre cash Dolabella had given me for payroll.

X
CLEOPATRA

One of Queen Cleopatra's eunuchs came to us at sunset, begging forgiveness for not coming sooner. He offered me and my staff a suite of rooms within the palace. The invitation came with a certain degree of flattery to our high station and a report of the queen's enthusiasm for our cause. In those days I had no understanding of the Macedonian's innate talent for duplicity. What stopped me from accepting the offer was the impracticality of it. I had arrived in the full expectation of finding some part of my army in Alexandria. Had that been the case, I might well have enjoyed the comforts of palace life while my army made ready for its march. As matters stood, I needed to stay close to my men. We had too much work to accomplish for me to waste even a part of each day in luxury. Had I accepted Cleopatra's invitation and made my residence in the palace I am sure I would have been poisoned.

My first order of business was to turn my rowers, sailors, and marines into infantrymen. I also recruited nearly a hundred men from the city's teeming Jewish population. I then commandeered the city's stadium, which offered a magnificent field for a force of about a thousand men.

We drilled and marched and trained from dawn until sunset. Two weeks is hardly enough time for recruits to become soldiers, but it is a start. I spent most of my days supervising this process. I was especially interested in finding men of talent among our recruits. These I soon promoted to the ranks of junior officers who would answer to a centurion. By this means I hoped to retain the potency of my one cohort of legionaries. Otherwise, I would be removing a great many of the best legionaries for command in the auxiliary units.

During all this time I did not neglect my own training. I was planning on leading hard marches through a merciless land; so I ran and rode hard in the hours before dawn or late into the evening, after the others retired. I also spent a part of each day training with the gladius and shield, like a common legionary, for in a desperate battle a commander needs to lead at the front. I worked opposite my staff for my own combat training until I discovered that none of them could stand against me in a fight. After that I began calling out centurions and legionaries to train with me. This got me a few good fights, and so I continued the practice until one morning I asked my *primus pilus*, Cassius Scaeva, to stand down from training for an hour or so, that he might give me a contest.

Scaeva had everyone's respect. He had been a rank-and-file centurion in Caesar's legions through most of his career, but Caesar had promoted him to first centurion after a desperate battle against Pompey Magnus at Dyrrachium. In that battle, some weeks before the decisive engagement at Pharsalus, Caesar's army nearly broke and ran, which would have been the end for Caesar and his army. As it happened a lone century led by Scaeva had stopped the Pompeian thrust. Scaeva had lost an eye early in that fight and yet continued on, rallying his men against the enemy and holding a line that ought to have crumbled before an entire legion but refused to do so.

Every man in our cohort knew the story and gave the old centurion nearly the respect of a divinity, one of Caesar's best men. Scaeva was somewhat surprised by my request, no one ever sought to train opposite him, but he took the request in good humour. I must say up front I was not looking for the man to teach me any new fighting skills. I quite frankly thought I was extremely talented with a sword. I was more curious to learn how much fight the old Cyclops still had in him. To that point I had not seen him lift either shield or sword. I wore armour and carried a heavy wicker training shield and a wooden gladius. For his part Scaeva tossed aside his *vitis* and grabbed a couple of training swords, saying as he did, 'Come on then.'

I stepped in to strike, using my shield to block his right arm and got stabbed for my troubles with the gladius in his left. I stepped back to try it again. This time I trained my attention on the sword in Scaeva's left hand and got hit by the right. We ran a few more contests in this manner, and when it was clear to me that I could delay my demise but not overtake the old centurion, I tossed my shield aside and took up a second training sword myself.

Scaeva was a born fighter and proved nearly impossible to beat. Once I had managed it a couple of times, this after several days of attempting it, he suggested we might do well to take on some number of legionaries together, if I cared for a proper challenge. At that point we began inviting three and then four men to come strike a 'mortal' blow against us. After that it was five or six, and so forth until we were overwhelmed; usually seven would do it.

I will not call what we had a friendship, not at that time, but after we began training together, we talked more freely with each other. That led to a few cups of wine late one night and finally to the wily veteran's wise counsel.

This came after a fortnight had passed and we still had no word from Allienus. When I consulted my senior staff on the matter, their advice had been that we must be patient. 'It's the Egyptians, General,' the cohort's prefect told me. 'They're just slow to get down to business.' The Egyptians, of course, had nothing to do with it. The delay came from Queen Cleopatra, a Macedonian Greek.

After thinking about the matter a few days more, I said to Scaeva, 'I need your opinion on a matter of some importance.'

'I'll give it if I have one,' Scaeva answered.

Rather than ask at once, I invited him to dine with me that evening. We were well into our meal and had enjoyed several cups of wine before I finally broached the subject. 'Why do you think I haven't heard from Allienus?'

'That's easy enough. The queen has either detained him, or she hasn't told him you're here.'

'For what reason?' I asked.

'Whatever your business, it can't be good for her. She won't oppose you openly, but if she lets the summer drift by and nothing happens, that's all to her advantage.'

'I was under the impression she despises the men who murdered Caesar.'

'I suppose she does, but whatever happens between Mark Antony, Dolabella, and the rest of them, the queen wants to have her head on her shoulders when it's all finished. If she chooses sides too early and by chance chooses incorrectly, she won't survive. She's got a sister locked away in the Temple of Artemis in Ephesus. They can put her on the throne in Cleopatra's place if they care to. After that, they can pack Cleopatra off to her mausoleum; so long as a Ptolemy is running the show the local aristocrats aren't going to complain.'

'She risks the wrath of Rome.'

'The woman is a Macedonian, General. If she is not playing some deep game it means she is already dead.'

'You're telling me I'm not going to see Allienus?'

'Not until things are settled up north between Cassius and Dolabella.'

I gave this some thought before I asked him if he thought we had the manpower to burn the city to the ground. 'You can burn it easily enough,' he answered simply. 'If you mean can you threaten to burn it if she doesn't send Allienus to you, that's a different matter. The longer our men stand around making a threat like that, the more likely it is the city will rise up against us. Once you make the threat, you might burn some of the city, but you won't get out alive. The same is true if you threaten to destroy the Temple of Serapis or Alexander's mausoleum. You won't just have the Queen's Guard to worry about. The people won't stand for it.'

'I need to force the queen to send Allienus to me.'

'What you might do is threaten to burn her museum with all her bright fellows locked inside it. Folks in the city aren't going to care about a few million books gone to ash – they can't read anyway, and I never heard of anyone mourning a dead philosopher.'

I spent several hours in conversation with Scaeva that night. What he suggested had a beautiful logic, but of course, as we discussed the matter, I found there were a great many problems. Once we had worked these out, I called my staff from their beds and gave them their orders.

By dawn our legionaries had taken control of the harbour's artillery installations. We also held the gate from the palace to the harbour as well as the gate from the palace to the city. The remainder of my force waited until the museum was filled with scholars, at which point I closed the gates and began building 'altars to Prometheus'. These makeshift stations provided fire and pitch, which we could take inside once I gave the order to burn the museum. Having arranged these matters, I sent Nicolas to deliver a note to the queen. Half-an-hour later one of the queen's eunuchs, the same I had dealt with previously, came scurrying out in his long skirts. 'The queen,' he declared, 'desires to speak with you at once.'

'Perhaps I should start a decent blaze so she will know I mean what I say.'

'Please, General. Hear what Her Majesty has to say before you do anything that cannot be undone.' I gave the order to destroy the museum if I was not back within the hour. Then I walked to the palace grounds with only Nicolas to escort me.

—◦—

I expected to be taken into the hall where the queen met with foreign dignitaries. Instead, I was led into the royal residence. The rooms in this wing of the palace were extensive, all gorgeously decorated, full of curiosities and books. Some of the books were bound tomes of parchment; the greater number were scrolls, which is the more ancient form of bookmaking.

After a long walk I came to a room in which a great number of the Queen's Guard stood at attention along the walls, effectively encircling the room. Additionally, there were perhaps a dozen domestic servants also at attention. At the centre of the room was a battered cauldron, the sort used for burning refuse out-of-doors. It was half-filled with scrolls. A lone female slave was busy pulling scrolls from the shelves and carrying these to the cauldron. As I entered the room this same slave began speaking to me in Latin, even as she continued her work. 'If Dominus feels compelled to burn the treasures of Egypt, he ought to begin in this room. Look!' She waved a scroll at me impertinently, as no Roman slave would dare to do. 'Here is a copy of Hesiod's work that Caesar himself sent to the queen from Pontus. It was in the library of Mithridates for many years. It is imagined by some to be the earliest copy in existence.' She tossed this scroll into the cauldron as carelessly as one might discard a broken toy. 'Certainly that will do for your sacrifice. Oh, and here is some of Homer's nonsense brought from Sparta, where it was preserved as the oldest copy in existence.' Again, into the cauldron. 'And here is the poetry of Sappho. Ptolemy Soter acquired it even before he had begun building the museum. Some believe this manuscript is written in the lady's own hand. Let it taste the flames, Dominus, before you burn humanity's lesser achievements.'

A second inspection of the people in the room suggested to me that this was no slave but Cleopatra herself, though to be honest I was not really sure. The woman was in her mid-twenties, which tallied with the facts. She was, however, a bit too slender for nobility. In fact, she looked like one who lives in constant want of enough to eat. She was also a grey-eyed blonde, like one of the race of Celts who over-populate our slave holdings, not the famous black-haired Egyptian queen I had heard about in Rome. She certainly had none of the regal bearing one encounters in nobility. In fact she possessed such a nervous energy she seemed quite incapable of commanding respect. I learned in later years this agitation came and went, according to the drugs she used or avoided. With the proper amount of medication the woman could look like stone itself. Her show this morning, dressed in slave garb and without her customary wig, was for the sake of a Roman legate of no great importance; she meant to embarrass me. She had no other weapon at hand. Even a barely literate Roman ought to know better than to destroy the sacred writings of Homer and Hesiod. 'I ask only to meet with Aulus Allienus, Majesty. Give me Allienus and we will burn nothing.'

'Majesty? No, no, no, Dominus! I am the slave of General Quintus Dellius. Please, do not employ such grand titles for your slaves.'

'Where is Allienus?'

'He is in Memphis, Dominus. As I understand it, he is quite ill. If you want to see him, perhaps you should travel to him.'

'I will see Allienus in Alexandria tomorrow by sunset, or I will burn every book in your museum. As for these scrolls, do with them as you please; my business is with the museum and nothing else.'

Fairly sure I had made myself the mortal enemy of the queen, I withdrew from the palace and took up arms with my men, half-expecting a breakout from the palace. The queen had an armed force sufficient for the fight. What she lacked was a foothold from which to launch her attack. And if she tried to gain it, she risked her museum and the million books within it.

I received word next morning that Allienus would be in Alexandria by evening. Concluding this note was a plea for patience in case he arrived an hour or so after sunset. I had, at last, the queen's complete attention. Lest she was readying an attack at sunset, I put our men on alert that evening. As for the scholars, they were still hostages within the compound. Once I received word that Allienus was on his way, I sent Scaeva and three centuries of our auxiliaries on the road to Memphis. Scaeva had orders to build a camp midway between the two cities and have it ready for the rest of us.

At sunset I received word that Allienus had arrived, if I cared to visit him. I proceeded at once. I took my slave,

Nicolas, and the head of Gaius Trebonius: otherwise I was alone. As before, when I left our camp, I gave orders to our legionary cohort's prefect to burn the museum if I did not return within the hour.

Allienus was a considerably older man than I had anticipated, in his late sixties as it seemed to my young eyes, though I never learned his exact age. He was ill, but the illness had overcome him after my arrival in Egypt, the result of a mild case of food poisoning. Cleopatra's work, or so I have always believed.

The hundred-mile journey from Memphis had left Allienus physically exhausted, and I worried that he might not be able to make the return trip with us. Still, I had no choice but to use him as best I could, even if it killed him. As per my instructions I handed Allienus the letter from Claudius Nero. When his slave had read it aloud to him he asked to see the head. I signalled to Nicolas, who broke the seal on the amphora. The head came out dripping red wine, blood and bile. Allienus studied the head with the aid of a torch. He seemed curious about the features, for they were quite deformed from the kicking, but once satisfied he nodded.

'Very well,' he told me. 'I relinquish my command. You must understand something, however. Caesar left three legions in Egypt. Another joined us after he departed. They were to be paid from the queen's treasury. This she did faithfully until last year. Since Caesar's death the pay has stopped. Over the past year, I'd say we've lost more than half the men.'

'I want you to send a courier to Memphis tonight letting your men know you have handed authority over to me; make sure they understand that I intend to pay them their back wages and add, as well, five times every man's annual salary in advance of service for the coming year. To any man returning to the legions during the next two months, I will pay a year's salary and add as well the promise of no disciplinary action. Any men refusing my offer can stay in Egypt and pray Dolabella does not come looking for them.'

The old man blinked. He cleared his throat. 'I'll give you some advice about the ways of the world, lad. When you talk about paying a man, you had better have the money at hand when he shows up to receive it.'

I did not care for the advice and disliked even more being called a lad. I have more sympathy for Allienus these days. He had surely seen his share of fresh-faced beauties like myself grow old and get slow and learn wisdom by degrees. I am sure he only meant to help. I advised him to mind his own business and to take care how he addressed me in the future; I was no one's lad. I left him at that point and went to find someone who might arrange an audience with the queen. With Cleopatra's museum under threat of destruction I got my meeting at once. She came to me in the garb of a slave again. I let her pretend she was not the queen of Egypt; I hardly cared what games she played, but I made sure she knew to deliver forty talents of gold by next evening. She protested her nation's poverty and spoke of a famine in the land. She was lying or exaggerating; I could not tell which. Nor did I care.

'Deliver the gold I ask for and you will see me depart for Memphis,' I answered. 'Give me anything less, and I will destroy every book in the city. The choice is entirely yours.'

XI
BEYOND ALEXANDRIA

The Road to Memphis: May, 43 BC

I sold our ships next morning to a wealthy merchant. I used the proceeds to pay off my promissory notes in the city and to acquire, among other necessities, lumber, wagons, and sheets of the leather used for tents. Finally, I purchased several mules. When Cleopatra's gold arrived that evening I had it repacked and loaded on the mules.

At midnight I gave the order to leave the city, just as Caesar would have done. I arranged a carriage for Allienus, who was still unfit for riding. The few horses I possessed I used to scout the road ahead and to keep watch on the road behind our formation. My officers and I marched with the veteran legionaries, who were divided at the front and rear of our column. I had no cavalry to cover the column's flanks, but there was not as much danger in this as one might expect. Through most of the journey that first night the marshlands and waterways shielded us from surprise attacks.

We finished our march through the delta at just after

dawn. This was a thirty-mile journey in about eight hours. Exhausted as we all were, we took an hour for a breakfast of hardtack and spring water. It was at that point I realised we had lost my slave Nicolas. I made enquiry at once but no one had seen him since the beginning of the journey. I had no time to worry about the matter, though a slave of his value was a considerable loss of fortune. To put his value in perspective, think of it in this way. I could have sold him at market for an amount equal to the yearly salary of a *primus pilus* centurion.

There was a chance he would be coming along, a chance as well he had fallen into the river at some bridge; but in my heart I knew Cleopatra had tempted him to leave me. I had sent him to her often enough for her to have recognised his value and persuaded him to stay under her protection with promises of freedom and a life of luxury, all so she might cut me deeply.

<hr />

I gave the order to push on at double-time and got grumbling even from the veterans. I was tired too, but I did not care to die from laziness, so I rallied the men with promises of wine and women at journey's end. We continued on the road south, the river guarding our eastern flank, our mounted scouts now keeping watch at the rear and on our western flank. By late afternoon we encountered Scaeva's scouts, who promised us an open road and a camp already in place. Scaeva's auxiliaries had travelled with less equipment and with considerably more speed than our own party. According to orders, which I had developed in concert with the wily old Cyclops, Scaeva had built a camp fortified by dirt ramparts and ditches, there being no available timber in the region. My wagons carried the lumber for the gates, as well as the leather used for tents. We had several barrels of pitch as well. As soon as we arrived, Scaeva's men went to work erecting four gates with a makeshift tower guarding each. I appointed two additional centuries of our auxiliaries to erect tents inside the camp.

When all was ready, I toured it with Scaeva. I commented on the stink of pitch. His squads had painted the stuff everywhere. Scaeva thought the night breeze ought to take the worst of it off. Otherwise, it was perfect, and I commended him for his work. I left a squad of Scaeva's bravest auxiliaries to defend the towers and tend the campfires, every man to win a purse of gold for the risk he ran. As for the rest of us, we withdrew to the trenches Scaeva's men had dug for us. These were located in flanking positions about a mile away from the camp. The trenches proved sufficiently deep for us to hide both our men and animals.

The men newly-arrived ate hardtack again. Fires were not permitted. They rested through the afternoon and evening, sleeping if they could. Those of Scaeva's auxiliaries not inside the camp pulled sentry duty for the men in hiding. I sent no scouts out to watch the countryside, however. I did not care to let the enemy know I anticipated an attack. About two hours before dawn we heard a mass of riders coming at a gallop. Our men, who had slept in their armour with their weapons at hand, had sufficient time to come awake and ready themselves for an attack. As they did this, the enemy cavalry, which ran to some five thousand men, swarmed around our camp's four gates.

Scaeva's auxiliaries within the camp raised a shout of alarm, as if we all waited inside. They quickly manned the towers for a fight, simulating a determined resistance with archers and slingers, and adding fellows to the fight as it progressed. There were others below whose job was to shout orders, though there was no one around to obey them. The fight went on for only a short time before our men abandoned the defence of the gates and fell back into the camp, calling out to ready against incursion.

Once the enemy had broken down the main gate and started through in force, Scaeva's men set fire to the pitch. The enemy no doubt saw thin lines of fire racing along tracks of pitch, but it was difficult in the dark to understand what it meant. They rode heedlessly into the centre of camp, looking for men to kill and bringing fire to burn us out of our tents. Meanwhile, all four gates erupted in flames, closing off any hope of escape. We had caught perhaps a thousand men, less than one in five, but for those inside there was no hope. At least none they could discover. In fact, the camp contained several carefully concealed tunnels by which our squads escaped the smoke and flames that quickly engulfed the entire camp.

The explosion of light at the gates served as our command to attack. We ran across the field on foot quickly and quietly, hitting the enemy cavalry at each gate simultaneously. While the bulk of the enemy had gathered at the main gate on the camp's northern perimeter, large groups of horsemen also waited at each of the other exits. These men hoped to slaughter us as we fled the camp. We overpowered the smaller groups, killing them in many cases before they understood we were at their backs. Where it was possible we took the horses of the fallen men but did not mount them, lest our own men be mistaken as enemy combatants.

The darkness and suddenness of the attack gave only a few of the enemy the chance to escape. Those gathered at the main gate were in a better position to fight and soon rallied against our forces there; here we took the majority of our casualties. Even so it was more skirmish than battle, with the enemy soon retreating. This is easily accomplished in a fight between cavalry and infantry. Nor did we give chase. Instead we formed a line to receive them should they turn and attempt a second charge on our position, but these were not regular cavalry in the Queen's Guard. They knew nothing about turning flight to their advantage with a sudden reversal. Beaten in a skirmish, they ran without looking back.

At dawn, using legionaries on the captured horses to scout the area, I determined that the enemy had truly gone and gave the order for the men to build fires and bake fresh bread. Some of my Jewish auxiliaries assisted me in the interrogation of those we had captured, many of whom spoke only some local dialect of the indigenous Egyptian population. Our prisoners claimed no one had sent them; they had heard about the gold in Alexandria. Their captains thought to steal it from us and had recruited them with the promise of easy money.

They were probably telling the truth, they suffered enough for the sake of their stories, but I had no doubt that Cleopatra's agents had arranged matters, letting the forty talents of gold we carried serve as bait. At noon, I ordered our dead loaded into wagons. Any man with wounds also had the use of a wagon if he wanted. The rest of the cohorts formed into a column, infantry and officers alike. Using the river to guard our eastern flank and a screen of some three hundred cavalry to the west of the road, we marched south. We met no more resistance and continued through the night, arriving at the legionary camp outside Memphis late afternoon next day.

From Memphis to Ashkelon: June, 43 BC

Once we had secured ourselves at Memphis I ordered funeral rites performed for our dead. Afterwards, I issued the pay I had promised. Then we feasted and drank, exactly as Caesar had treated his men in Spain after our long march. For my part, I slept more than I had done previously. When I was awake, I spent all my time preparing for our advance into Judaea.

As for the deserters, they came in slowly over the next few weeks, sometimes singly, sometimes in squads that had no doubt survived by means of banditry. When the first of them received their salary promptly and without punishment the rest began pouring in. With the arrival of the summer solstice I had gathered my forces and ordered an advance on Ashkelon. This is the first fortified Judaean port beyond the Egyptian border. We hadn't the four full legions that Livia had promised me, but I could call them four legions. With auxiliaries and the non-combatants in our baggage train we numbered something like ten thousand souls; four half-legions, if you will.

In preparation for our march into Judaea I interviewed a number of our Jewish auxiliaries. I also read whatever I could find about the recent history of that region. As even the most casual observer of Judaea soon learns, the population is divided almost equally between Jews and Greeks. Those who are called Greek are in fact people of diverse nations. They may have adopted Greek religious and social customs but the majority are otherwise Asian or Greek-Asian in character and race. Most speak and write at least some Greek but carry on in Aramaic at the market place and in their domestic lives. They are the remnants of many nations: Macedonian, Persian, Babylonian, Armenian, Arab, Syrian, Egyptian, some of them even outcast Jews of mixed parentage. Having neither a racial history nor any political aspirations what they want is autonomy within their cities, and for a price they have it.

The Jews, on the other hand, amount to a nation. In many of the larger cities they coexist with the Greeks and yet still manage to follow separate customs and laws. For almost a century the Jews held authority over all the people of this region. This was thanks to the powerful Hasmonean family, a Jewish dynasty accorded royal status for having won Judaea's freedom from the decaying Seleucid empire.

The Hasmoneans had fractured a quarter of a century earlier when two brothers quarrelled over who should sit upon the throne of Judaea. The ensuing civil war ultimately persuaded each man to seek the aid of Pompey Magnus, who was then in the east at the head of a massive army. Pompey appointed the elder brother, Hyrcanus, Ethnarch of the Jews. As the term implies, Hyrcanus ruled only ethnic Jews and had no authority over the rest of the population. Hyrcanus used this appointment to assume as well the office of High Priest of the Temple. That station at least offered some royal dignities. His brother spent the remainder of his life fashioning one revolt after another, and when he had finished with the light of day, his son, Antigonus, continued the tradition. As for the hard task of keeping the peace between Jews and Greeks, that fell to a Roman procurator.

The Pompeian solution enriched Pompey, rather the point of all of his politics, but it did nothing for the stability of Judaea. Without a Roman army residing permanently in the region one uprising after another followed until Julius Caesar discovered the talents of Antipater of Idumaea. One of Hyrcanus's generals, Antipater was the son of a man who had converted to the Jewish faith. He also enjoyed a close link by marriage to one of the great families in Petra, which is the capital of Arabian Nabataea. Antipater possessed an extraordinary talent for administration. After awarding Antipater Roman citizenship at the rank of an eques, Caesar appointed him Procurator of Judaea in perpetuity. Hyrcanus continued as Ethnarch of the Jews, but the truth was obvious to all. Hyrcanus answered to his former general. As for the opposition, they grew quiet, though by no means content.

When Cassius Longinus seized Syria earlier that summer, Antipater provided him with an enormous amount of gold and also sent a large portion of his army to the Syrian border. This kind of support gave Cassius the ability to confront Dolabella as he marched against Syria, but it also left southern Judaea exposed. I was not sure how much resistance Antipater intended to offer my forces. For all I knew, he might welcome me as a liberator. In the more likely event that he opposed my legions, I intended to stir up his enemies and reignite the Judaean civil war.

To that end I contacted one of Antipater's governors, a man named Malichus. According to my informants, Malichus had refused Antipater's order to provide a tribute of gold for Cassius. Curiously, when Malichus failed to present Cassius with his portion of the total tribute, Antipater made up the amount from his own treasury.

This told me two things. First, Antipater feared disappointing Cassius. Second, Antipater had not the resources at hand to break Malichus for insubordination. In my letter to Malichus, written while I was still in Egypt, I congratulated him on his principled refusal to serve one of the assassins of Julius Caesar. Rome, I said, would not soon forget his friendship.

With that promise to Malichus smuggled into Judaea by one of my Jewish auxiliaries, I ordered my army to decamp from Memphis.

Ashkelon: Summer, 43 BC

We marched past two unfortified towns at the Judaean border. When these offered no resistance, we continued to Ashkelon. There we made camp before the gates of the city. With Egyptian and Judaean enemies now at our backs and a walled city before us, I had brought my army into some jeopardy. The risk was calculated, however. I did not care to come into Judaea ravaging and burning whatever I found. Instead, I sent word to the elders of Ashkelon that

I required hostages before I moved north along the coastal road. Nor was I much disturbed when they answered that the city elders must consult Antipater in Jerusalem before they responded to my request. That was fine with me. As they awaited instructions, I dug in for a siege.

That evening, only hours after I had issued my request, a party of a hundred women and children appeared at our gates. These were the hostages I had requested. The man presenting them asked that I come into the city and speak with Herod and Phasael, the elder sons of Antipater. I was somewhat surprised to find the sons of Antipater waiting for us, but I knew Antipater was well informed about all matters dealing with Egypt.

I took Scaeva and a small legionary escort with me and entered the city. Inside the citadel I left my escort and appeared alone before the two brothers. Both men stood at my entrance and came to me as fellow citizens of Rome. Other than the handshake they both offered, neither man appeared to be Roman, though in fact both men enjoyed Roman citizenship and possessed the gold ring of an eques. They wore beards and long hair and decidedly oriental tunics. Phasael, the older of the two brothers, was nearly as tall as I. He was considerably thinner and also quite bald. Phasael was then only a few years past thirty, though I imagined him a man in his fifties. There was nothing cheerful in his manner; nor did he show any willingness to offer more than the barebones of Roman courtesy. I knew

Phasael had served at his father's side in combat, but it was clear to me that he was not the man to inspire the rank and file. He was a born magistrate, this one, cool and detached, made for meetings like this – not the chaos of battlefields.

His brother, at least on the surface, seemed the very opposite, as brothers often do. Handsome, full of passion, mercurial in all things, Herod was a fighting man's general. A single glance at his powerful physique promised a commander who rode in the vanguard of the charge. Men would follow Herod into war, I thought, because he asked it of them. Herod was then about thirty years of age. With long thick black hair and a neatly trimmed beard, he was a handsome man; I should say even charismatic. When we shook hands he actually seemed pleased to meet me. In fact, as I later learned, he was pleased. He already knew what I had done to Cleopatra and dearly wished he could have acted against her as I had done. Of course I did not understand this at the time. I imagined he was simply putting on a bit of a show for the latest Roman visitor.

We began our meeting in Greek, but to my relief Herod switched to Latin after only a few exchanges. Phasael followed his example but would sometimes interject the occasional Greek expression, for he was not as talented in Latin as Herod. Our introductions finished, Herod told me he was afraid he had some bad news. I was surprised by this. I had expected our discussion to be about my sudden appearance in Judaea. 'What news?' I asked in perplexity.

'Cornelius Dolabella is dead, General.'

'Dead! How? When?'

'Less than a month ago. We are told he took his own life rather than surrender to Cassius.' I pressed for details but got very little more. Dolabella had been trapped in Laodicea, on the Syrian coast. When it was clear Cassius had taken the city, Dolabella ordered his legions to surrender. Before Cassius arrived at the citadel, Dolabella took his own life. What was left of Dolabella's army now belonged to Cassius. While I still struggled with this news, Herod added, 'There is more, I'm afraid.' I stared at the man dumbly. Trapped in a hostile land with enemies before and behind me, my only ally dead, I could not imagine more bad news. 'The legions of the new consuls of Rome, Pansa and Hirtius, have defeated Mark Antony in northern Italy.'

'I don't believe it,' I answered.

'Neither did I, when I learned the news,' Herod remarked. 'Nonetheless, I'm afraid it is true. It seems Antony effected a brilliant manoeuvre in his first encounter with Pansa by coming at the consular forces from a swamp and striking a deadly blow at their flank. Then, as Antony's army returned victoriously to its camp, Hirtius hit Antony's column. Antony lost half his men before darkness ended the fight. A second battle some days later gave the consular armies complete victory.'

'So Antony is dead as well?'

'Actually,' Phasael answered, 'Hirtius and Pansa are dead. Antony has escaped into the Alps.'

'Caesar now commands the consular armies,' Herod added.

'Caesar?' I could not help myself. The named elicited an image of my Caesar. A moment later I knew he meant Caesar's heir, the little twit.

'We are told,' Phasael added, 'Caesar remains in the north with his army. He demands to be made consul when he returns to Rome.'

'A consul? At nineteen? Perhaps I should seek a consul's chair next year.' My sarcasm failed to affect either man.

'Cicero is urging the senate to accept the proposal,' Phasael explained.

'Cicero? Siding with Caesar?'

'His support is on condition that Junius Decimus assumes the second chair.' Decimus was the ousted governor of Cisalpine Gaul and one of the assassins of Julius Caesar.

'At the moment,' Phasael explained, 'Caesar refuses any form of compromise. He claims he will not share power with one of the men who murdered his father. More than that no one knows.'

I cannot describe the despair I experienced at learning these things. It was closest, I suppose, to the emotion one must experience as one falls from a great height; midway between heaven and earth the moment hangs without resolution. While it does, a man must certainly imagine there is something he can do, even as he knows he is doomed. Should Octavian – Caesar, as we were now calling him – consent to Cicero's proposal, it would mean peace. Pleasant as that idea might be in the abstract, peace meant that Cassius and Brutus would become legitimate; by extension I could expect to be named an enemy of Rome.

'May I be so bold as to offer my opinion, General?' This from Herod.

'By all means,' I answered. 'To tell you the truth, I am not sure what to make of any of this.'

'Cassius believes Caesar will refuse any form of compromise with the assassins. Caesar has taken an oath to avenge his father's murder. His army marches with him for the sake of that oath. If he now forms a political alliance with his sworn enemies, he risks losing the support of the very men who have elevated him.

'Cassius may be wrong, of course,' Herod continued, 'but at the moment he prepares for war. He welcomes every nation to his army, but what he values most are Roman officers who know how to command his auxiliary forces.'

'Matters with Cassius are more complicated than they appear,' I answered.

'You are worried that Cassius will want revenge for the murder of Gaius Trebonius?' Phasael asked me.

I looked at him in surprise, but I did not bother dissembling. He obviously knew the truth, or at least some part of it. 'Even if Cassius pretends to accept my oath of loyalty,' I answered, 'I fear he will avenge Trebonius once I am in his power.'

'If you imagine you can escape by ship to Caesar,' Herod told me, 'you should know Cleopatra has her navy patrolling our coast. They have orders to board all ships not in the service of Cassius or Brutus. They are looking for any officers involved in the assassination of Trebonius.'

'As it seems Cleopatra affords me no opportunity of escape, perhaps I should turn around and march back into Egypt.'

'Make an alliance with our father first,' Phasael answered. 'Once you do that, you can remain here on the Egyptian border, ready to attack.'

'And where is my advantage in that?' I asked.

'Cassius desires tribute from Cleopatra,' Herod answered. 'So far, she has refused to send him anything. If allies of Antipater hold an army at her border, the queen may well discover some gold in her treasury after all. If she still refuses, Cassius will want to send a punitive expedition against her. All the better if the core of that invading army is already waiting here and ready to move quickly. Especially one commanded by a general she utterly despises.'

'Can Antipater protect me from Cassius?'

'Cassius treats Antipater's allies as his own. He requires

none of them to swear an oath of loyalty to him but is content if they are sworn to Antipater.'

'But sooner or later,' I answered, 'Cassius will want revenge.'

'Deliver Egyptian gold to him in enough quantity,' Herod answered, 'and I promise you Cassius will soon forget the name Gaius Trebonius.'

Jerusalem: Summer, 43 BC

Before I committed myself to their proposal, I returned to my camp. I called together those officers who had participated in the murder of Trebonius and explained the situation. There was considerable consternation, and I let them talk through it. Eventually, they came to my conclusion. We ought to turn around and attack Egypt but only with the support of Antipater. With reinforcements, even a few mercenaries recruited from the Greek cities in Judaea, I thought we could sack Alexandria; even the possibility of it would inspire Cleopatra to hand over enough gold to buy the favour of Cassius. I gave any officer who wanted it the chance to escape by sea, but no one doubted Cleopatra's determination to capture and punish us.

Once they had finally embraced the idea, I proposed that every officer guilty of breaking his oath at Smyrna ride with me to Jerusalem. There we would swear our allegiance to the Roman procurator of Judaea and by doing so enjoy protection from Cassius. When all had finally approved the plan, I sent word to Phasael and Herod that we would be ready to ride to Jerusalem at dawn.

I left Allienus in command of the camp, taking with me only a squad of mounted legionaries under the centurion Scaeva's command. Herod and Phasael rode with a large escort of Celtic mercenaries from the region of the Black Sea. We made our way east forty miles, coming to the city of Hebron in late afternoon. At that point we were still some twenty miles from Jerusalem, but the horses were tired. We settled for the evening at Antipater's palace; he of course had a fine house in every major city in Judaea. To our delight, Phasael offered us the use of a Roman bath. This was followed by an evening feast that would have satified even the discerning tastes of poor Dolabella.

XII
JUDAEA

Jerusalem: Summer, 43 BC

Only a few of us rose early next morning; most of the men were slow to leave their beds and the comfort of the slaves who slept with them. All the same, we were on the road to Jerusalem by midday. That put us inside the gates of Jerusalem before darkness fell. We entered the city from the south, well below the two mountains that form that ancient city, Zion to the west and Moriah to the north. At the Pool of Siloam, inside the City of David, we turned into the citadel of King David; this was the Jewish monarch who had captured the city a thousand years ago.

We were treated to yet another Roman bath and, with the assistance of Antipater's palace slaves, dressed ourselves in togas for a feast that commenced an hour before sunset. Our bodyguard of legionaries, also given residence inside the citadel, enjoyed their own banquet in the company of certain of Antipater's Guard. Scaeva, as an eques entitled to wear the purple, joined Antipater's feast.

Before we lay down to our supper, Herod introduced

me to Hyrcanus, Ethnarch and High Priest of the Jews. Hyrcanus was a greybeard of indeterminate antiquity, though not nearly as old as I guessed him to be. He played on his dignities and would not shake my hand, though he welcomed me with a courteous bow. When I met Antipater I discovered he was much more like Herod than Phasael. He gave me a cheerful salutation in Latin and shook my hand gamely. After this, Antipater took me around the room and introduced me to his civil magistrates and various generals, all of them old and dear friends, or so he declared.

At this stage of the proceedings I met Malichus, Governor of Peraea and the only man to refuse to offer tribute to Cassius Longinus. As with many of the others that evening, Malichus did not offer his hand to me; instead, there was a quiet nod of his grey head and a murmured greeting spoken in Greek. I looked in vain for a light of recognition in his eyes as Antipater introduced us. Had he received my message? Given his cool manner I could not know. Perhaps, I thought, he was only a very good actor.

As it happened, Phasael had intercepted my letter. But of course I only discovered this after it was too late.

⦿

When it came time to dine, most of Antipater's Jewish friends departed for business in the city. Hyrcanus and Malichus remained, as did Phasael and Herod. I joined Phasael and his father at the table of honour. I believe Herod insisted that Scaeva dine with him, for he was anxious to hear the untold stories of Caesar's most famous battles. Those of Antipater's party who remained for dinner were the senior officers in his army, all of them non-Jewish mercenaries of longstanding.

I was curious that no other Jews had remained for the meal. I knew from interviewing my own Jewish auxiliaries that many of the more zealous Jews prefer a certain distance from those who do not share their faith, but as neither Phasael nor Herod had acted uneasily on this count I assumed the prejudice against foreigners was only practiced among the lower classes. Eventually, I learned that Antipater and his sons had long ago set aside the custom of avoiding foreigners. This made them politically potent outside Judaea. Within Judaea a great many of the Judaean Jews despised them for it.

⚭

Antipater was a man of Julius Caesar's generation. Unlike Caesar, who had still been vigorous in his final years, Antipater suffered a great many maladies, tender and swollen joints mostly, but weak eyes as well. In fact he was nearly blind. Nevertheless, he appeared indifferent to his failings – at least on the night I met him. 'The process of getting old can be cruel,' he remarked casually. 'Even so there are also a great many delights to console a man.'

Like any youth, I had trouble imagining what delights these might be. To my thinking, old age meant the loss of strength, a wandering mind, a lack of vitality. For such things there could be no compensation. I know better now. An old man may know serenity, where the young cannot. The old may enjoy the quieter passions; the young must always be about the business of earning. The old may enjoy the children of their children; the young must raise them up. Most prominently the old have earned the right to tell their stories.

Antipater was no different from many others in advanced years; he loved to gab. Very few foreigners could claim the acquaintance of so many Roman commanders, and he was proud of this, especially in the presence of a young Roman legate. The whole evening through Antipater regaled me with recollections of his encounters with Pompey, Caesar, Mark Antony, Sulla, Crassus, and of course Cassius Longinus, to name only the more prominent Romans he had entertained. He spoke frankly of the virtues and moral failings of those men already claimed by history; he was more circumspect in his remarks about the living. He seemed especially fond of Antony, whom he had met in Antony's youth. Antony had served as a senior tribune during a military campaign in Egypt, in the service of Ptolemy, Cleopatra's father. Antipater, Phasael, and Herod had joined the legion to which Antony was attached and all three of them had come to appreciate Antony's magnetism.

From that experience Antipater claimed he could not believe Pansa and Hirtius might outwit Antony with a fatal ambush. 'I expect it was more likely an accident, one army stumbling into the other.' Then with a shrug, 'Of course Antony fights at his best when the odds are against him. Much like Julius Caesar in that respect. Antony's problem, as it has always seemed to me, is that when things go well he grows lax. After an easy victory against one army, I can imagine him drunk with success.'

Phasael took a delicate sip of wine, interjecting quietly, 'Or simply drunk.' Antipater smiled but said nothing more on the subject.

Late in the evening, Antipater suddenly began a story he had already related. As this is a common malady with old men, I thought nothing of it, but then he forgot a famous name. Phasael supplied it for him. Pompey, as it turned out. After that he began slurring his words. I thought this curious; Antipater appeared to be a careful drinker. Then sweat broke across his brow. At that point Phasael called to his father's secretary, who was close by. Together they lifted the old man to his feet. I stood as well. I recall Antipater resisted being pulled away at once. 'I am suddenly not feeling well,' he said to me. 'I don't understand it. Tomorrow, Dellius, tomorrow we shall...'

There was no more. Antipater collapsed.

———

'We need to get to the legionary barracks, General.' I looked at Scaeva without comprehending his concern; then he added, 'Romans are always the first to be slaughtered in a general uprising.'

Taking his point, I gathered my officers with a signal. We made our way from the banquet hall to the outer perimeter of the citadel. Once we had joined the rest of the men, we got about the business of arming ourselves and fortifying a somewhat tenuous position inside the citadel. Then, like everyone that night, we waited. At dawn a servant came to inform us Antipater had died. He offered nothing about the cause of death.

An hour afterwards, I was composing a note of condolence for Phasael when one of his servants came to tell me his master desired to see me. Phasael wasted no time listening to my condolences. He only wanted to know what I had witnessed after his father's collapse. This meant he thought his father's death was murder, and I took a moment to recall exactly what I had seen. My only distinct memory was that Hyrcanus and Malichus had been the first to depart the hall. 'Others followed them, though not at once. Most of the men,' I said, 'were anxious to know what had happened to your father.'

'Malichus did not seem curious?'

I hesitated. 'I do not mean to accuse anyone.'

'Of course not. A simple question.'

'My sense was that Malichus and Hyrcanus were eager to inform others of the event.'

'Would you say they left together or at the same time?'

'I am not sure.' As I said this, it dawned on me that they had left together. This detail I kept to myself.

Phasael now pressed with a series of questions. Had they seemed worried? Was there urgency in their departure? Stealth? Did it seem they were involved in a conspiracy?

'They spoke to some men,' I said, but when he pressed for details I shook my head. 'I heard them without comprehending the language they spoke.'

'With whom did they speak?'

I could not tell him, which was curious because of all the men I met that evening I recalled only Hyrcanus, the ethnarch of the Jews, and one governor, who happened also to be the very man I had contacted by letter before entering Judaea. The others were a blur, and though I could not be sure, I feared Phasael noticed this detail.

'I apologise for asking about such matters,' Phasael remarked at last. 'It was not your responsibility after all to keep watch over my dinner guests. I ought never to have let my father's health distract me.'

'Perfectly understandable in the circumstances,' I

answered. I was not really sure I believed his apology. Phasael did not strike me as a man who might lose his wits in a crisis. I even feared he questioned me about these peripheral matters because he actually suspected my involvement.

'Herod believes Malichus bribed the wine steward to poison our father.'

'Malichus?' I asked. I knew as I spoke that I ought not to have an opinion about who might or might not want to harm Antipater, but I could not help myself. The idea that Malichus had murdered Antipater frightened me; if it were so, I was sure to be dragged into it eventually. From the look in Phasael's eyes I thought he must know about the letter.

'The governor of Peraea,' he said.

'Yes, I know the man,' I answered guiltily. 'Your father introduced us. I am only surprised to hear that he is suspected of murder. I was under the impression he and your father were cousins by marriage. Has Herod found any proof against him?'

'The steward has confessed to the murder. Of course a man will admit anything when he is being tortured. That is what bothers me. The steward claims to have received a bribe for delivering the poison, but he cannot produce the money. He tells Herod he used poison but he cannot identify its type or even the vial that contained it.'

'He confesses so the pain will stop?'

'One supposes so, but the fact remains that he was the only person with access to our table.'

'Does he implicate Malichus with his confession?'

'He does, but once again what he tells us does not conform with what we know. He changes his story every time he is pressed for details. First, a man came to him. Next, the man was Malichus. Nothing at all about what he tells us is credible.'

'But the steward is the only suspect?'

'Well, I suppose you or I could have done it.' Phasael offered this as if it were the most unlikely of possibilities, but after he spoke his dark eyes bore into mine. I was a suspect; I was sure of it.

'Are the physicians certain it was poison?' I asked.

'They are.'

'So it was the steward.'

'I am sure of it, but he must have had help, someone who arranged for the evidence to vanish. Herod is questioning the others in our kitchen as we speak. If we are lucky someone will be able to connect this to Malichus.'

'Has Malichus a motive?'

'He does not gain directly by my father's death, but he supports Hyrcanus. With my father now gone there is a chance Cassius will appoint Hyrcanus either King of Judaea or its new procurator, though it is by no means a certainty. Should that occur, Malichus would then take command of the armies Herod and I now lead.'

'Surely Cassius will investigate the circumstances. Especially if Malichus is responsible for your father's assassination.'

'Cassius hardly has time for such matters, and even if he does investigate, it will cost us the rest of the summer before he makes a determination. That is time enough for Malichus to act against us.'

'Do you think he intends to incite a civil war?'

'He is a more subtle man than that, General. Malichus will more likely incite protest and rioting in various cities. He will encourage the governors there to make no move to stop it. If Herod or I move to quell the rioting, he will complain to Cassius that we have usurped our father's office, without having the authority to do so. And if we do not act but let the rioting go unchecked, Malichus will complain that we are useless without our father.'

'But surely you must act to keep the peace?'

'That is the point. Herod and I have no authority outside our own provinces. The provinces we command will be quiet. The rest will see fire, protest, and open revolt.'

'Cassius surely prefers peace to the prospect of another civil war in Judaea.'

'There will be no peace unless Roman troops enforce it. Any other solution will see Malichus quietly steering power to Hyrcanus. Cassius may appreciate all that our father has done for him, but he will not jeopardize the tranquillity of the region for the sake of our friendship.'

'You could ask his help, I suppose.'

'If we ask for assistance he will hardly see the advantage of keeping us in power. What we need is your assistance. If you act, then all the provinces will remain quiet and Malichus will have no complaint to lodge.'

'I have no mandate to act.'

'You have simply to write to all the governors who served my father. I will send a letter to Cassius on your behalf. I will explain that on his deathbed Antipater asked you to keep the region safe by using your army to ensure the peace until such time Cassius appoints a new procurator.'

'I was not at the procurator's deathbed, Excellency.'

'I was. My father asked me to speak with you about this matter. He knew he had been murdered, that he was dying. Even so, he was lucid enough to anticipate how Malichus and others would attempt to turn this to Hyrcanus's advantage.'

'Antipater spoke my name?' I asked.

'He did. He thought you should make it clear to all the governors that you will act only at the request of individual governors. That will put every governor to the test. They can let the violence in their provinces continue but only by appearing incompetent. I should think you might order three or four cohorts of your legions to join your staff at first opportunity. Bring others up if necessary, but I doubt you will even need to act. A letter to the governors ought to be enough.

'The fortress city of Samaria,' he continued, 'will serve you best, I think. I can send word to let them know you are coming. From there you will be well placed to move rapidly into the most contentious provinces.'

'Cassius will no doubt suspect me of seizing Judaea.'

'You act in his service, General. He may not like what you have done to Trebonius, but when Judaea remains perfectly quiet at no cost to him, I will be sure he understands to whom he is indebted.'

Seville, Spain: Autumn, 3 AD

A lifetime before the assassination of King Herod there was the assassination of his father, Antipater, procurator of Judaea. Of course in those days I was still young and foolish. Contemplating that death for the first time in many years, I find myself wondering how matters would have turned out for Judaea if Phasael had become king instead of Herod. The sons of Antipater hadn't the bloodlines to hope for such promotion. Of course, the world changes quickly and often capriciously. All the more so when we least expect it. Monarchy was two years away for Herod, but the crown he wore ought to have been Phasael's, if Phasael had only lived.

Knowing Herod's character, I am sure he would have stayed loyal to his brother. No family infighting for those two. That would have been essential to Phasael's success.

With that caveat, I believe Phasael would have been the more successful monarch. I do not belittle all that Herod accomplished, but where he failed, he failed spectacularly. I think the worst of it came at the end, when he charged two of his sons with treason and tried them before Caesar. Phasael would have rid the royal family of ingrates and traitors by using poison. Exactly as he did with Antipater, whom he murdered for the sake of the old man's mounting incompetence.

Yes, I awakened one night several weeks after my interview with Phasael. I was in a prison cell, and suddenly I knew, with perfect clarity, that Phasael had poisoned his father; I could even remember the moment he delivered the liquid into the old man's cup. Herod knew nothing of the assassination. He had not the fortitude for such villainy. In the aftermath of Antipater's death, Phasael directed Herod's attention to the steward, even as Phasael was convincing him that their mother's cousin, Malichus the malcontent, had bribed the poor man. Hot irons against the hapless steward got the necessary confession. Then Phasael persuaded his brother to hold off taking revenge. In the meantime, I went off to Samaria and a prison cell and by doing so kept the peace in Judaea.

As king, Herod ruled Judaea like some overwrought actor in a Greek tragedy, boasting and lamenting by turns to a chorus of dancing sycophants. He tried one of his wives for adultery, saw two sons, a wife and a younger brother executed as traitors and imprisoned a third son as he lay on his deathbed. He could never pull his heart away from the desperate quarrels that characterise court life. He had no talent for political intrigue. No, Herod was more comfortable crashing into opposition at the head of his cavalry.

Anyone will tell you Herod's gifts to the people of Judaea exceeded in sum the gifts of all the Jewish kings to their subjects in the whole long history of that nation. He fed his people through famines, he built cities by the dozens, and finally he turned a decrepit old temple into one of the wonders of the world. Phasael would have done nothing of the sort. He would have let famines teach the stiff-necked complainers a hard lesson; he might have created a few cities, as needed, but nothing so grand that the treasury suffered. As for the temple, a votive offering to decorate one of the old porches would have sufficed. And when he had come to pass from the light of day Phasael would have left a son like his father, cool, calculating and fully capable of political murder.

Samaria: Summer, 43 BC

My staff and I rode north to the town of Samaria with Scaeva and our squad of mounted legionaries for escort. Phasael, in the meantime, had already sent carrier pigeons to inform Cassius of our plans. I knew nothing of those fabulous birds at the time. I could not imagine that Romans in Syria would learn where I was going ten hours before I departed. I imagined Antipater and his sons got their news by rumours from the sea like the rest of the world.

At Samaria our party was met by a freedman who directed his slaves to show our legionary Guard to their barracks. He then led the officers to the great hall, where we were supposed to meet the city's chief magistrate. Within the hour I was trussed in chains and sitting alone inside my new home, a prison cell of stone far below the palace cellars. For most of the next year I saw no one, not even the man who lowered bread and water to me twice a day. What happened, besides the rising and setting of the sun, I could only guess.

—◦◦◦◦—

At some point during my sojourn in Samaria, the prefect who had arrested me led a century of infantry to Ashkelon. He announced to Allienus that Cassius Longinus intended to bring eight legions against him if he did not surrender at once. The prefect had not even bothered marching these legions down the coast; he made only the threat of it and that was good enough for old Allienus, who opened his camp gate at once and surrendered his army.

Of course Cassius had nothing like eight legions. From the start he was scrambling for fighting men, buying mercenaries at inflated prices like all the rest of the warlords.

Once he had swindled Allienus out of four legions he could boast a full eight legions but not until then. Allienus stayed on as the commander at the Ashkelon camp and his legions remained with him until the following year. At that point the entire force marched north to join Cassius and Brutus in Macedonia; there they served under Marcus Livius Drusus Claudianus, Livia's father. Allienus, I am told, died in his bed at the camp in Ashkelon at about the time the winter rains began. I have no way of knowing for sure, though I expect it was an honest death.

That same autumn Malichus rode with Hyrcanus to Lebanon to meet Cassius. Cassius had sent a man to tell Hyrcanus he wished to discuss the possibility of naming Hyrcanus Procurator of Judaea. Hyrcanus asked his long-time friend, Malichus, to provide an escort. Malichus undoubtedly imagined himself now at the right hand of Judaea's most powerful man. A squad of Roman tribunes at the head of a century of men came along the highway to greet Hyrcanus's party. These men murdered Malichus as he saluted them. Hyrcanus and his bodyguards stood by and watched, no doubt wondering if they were next. Quite amazingly, the assassins bowed to the Pontifex Maximus of the Jews, thanked him for his service to the Temple, and then withdrew without another word.

I am told this was the last occasion on which Hyrcanus showed any ambition. He returned to Jerusalem a chastened man and contented himself with the Temple's many colourful ceremonies. Some weeks after the murder of Malichus, Herod and Phasael rode to Lebanon to meet Cassius. Cassius appointed Phasael procurator of Judaea, Samaria, and Idumaea. Herod became procurator of southern Syria and Galilee.

XIII
THE PROSCRIPTIONS

Italy and Gaul: Autumn, 43 BC and Winter, 42 BC

Caesar took his seat as a child-consul. For his companion he sat with his cousin, Quintus Pedius. This was the same Pedius we had rescued in Spain. Young Caesar's refusal to compromise his stance with respect to the assassins was bad news for Cassius. So bad, I expect, that Cassius gave no further thought to avenging the murder of Gaius Trebonius.

Good news came to Cassius late in the summer, however, when he learned that Aemilius Lepidus had surrounded Mark Antony's army. In fact, Cassius was told that Lepidus was presently starving Antony into submission. This was good generalship, if not the bravest, but Antony, ever at his best when things went badly, answered by calling the legions of Lepidus into his camp and making converts of them. Soon Antony had more of Lepidus's soldiers than Lepidus. Antony did not rub it in, of course. Lepidus was family – or would be when their children finally grew up and married one another. Once Lepidus had surrendered his remaining cohorts to Antony, they marched together into Italy.

Cassius of course had hoped to see the end of Antony, but he was not especially disturbed by this odd turn of events. Cassius imagined that Antony and young Caesar would bash into one another for a second round of fighting, with Antony probably winning this time. In either case, enough corpses would litter their battlefield that the assassins might hope to return to Italy and collect the spoils.

Bologna, Italy: Autumn, 43 BC and Winter, 42 BC

But then young Caesar executed another of his remarkable pirouettes. As a newly elected consul, Caesar left Rome and joined his legions in the north. Rather than fight Antony and Lepidus, as everyone expected him to do, he asked for a meeting.

They convened on a small island in the River Lavinius in northern Italy. This was not far from where they had fought only a few months before. Elements of their respective armies lined either side of the river. Hostages were exchanged as per custom. Lepidus, in his role as Pontifex Maximus, played the negotiator. The three of them very quickly divided the empire, that is the empire that still remained in their power: Sicily, Gaul, western Africa, and Spain. They all agreed to share and share alike in the plunder of Italy. Their map would prove to be of no consequence a year later, for after their victory over Cassius and Brutus, the Triumvirs, as they called themselves, drew up a new map. Still, the first map is telling in one detail: they grabbed all the provinces of the empire as their own and left nothing for others.

Their map drawing finished, Caesar and Antony turned to the more troubling issue of how to pay for the legions they commanded. The wages for a fighting man had reached unimaginably high levels, five or six times the amounts paid only two years before; even the divine Julius Caesar's purloined fortune was insufficient to carry them forward. In later years Caesar blamed Antony for the idea of the proscriptions. This is our august leader at his best, for he has always held that any lie told often enough becomes the prevailing reality, if not exactly the truth. The truth is quite simple. Caesar proposed murdering the aristocracy and seizing their fortunes. Estates were to be sold at auction even as the bodies of the murdered aristocrats cooled. For the better part of the next two years, murder created a steady stream of cash for army payrolls. All of it Caesar's idea, though he never owned up to it.

Antony told me some years later he could not speak when young Caesar made the proposition. It was not the idea of mass murder that astonished him; Sulla had employed proscriptions when Antony was still a boy. 'It was the serene manner with which the little twit proposed it, as one speaks of raising taxes or selling slaves.' Antony was quite good at mimicking 'the little twit' and often performed a pitch-perfect recitation of Caesar's proffer. I think his astonishment was genuine; Antony was capable of any abomination, but for that he needed wine to fuel some bit of mania that he kept buried in his soul. Caesar committed his abominations in the clutches of a chilling sobriety.

Of course, Antony always finished his version of the story at the proffer. He claimed that, after Cicero, he had no grudges. The truth is once he got his voice back, if one can believe anything would ever rob Antony of his speech, he realised he actually had quite a few old grudges to settle. Rumour has it, from slaves and attendants at that infamous congress, the Triumvirs divided the world within an hour but spent the next two days negotiating The List. Lepidus stayed out of it mostly, or claimed as much in later years; I expect, however, he too managed to name a few of the men who had scorned the manner by which he had won the office of Pontifex Maximus. It is only human nature to want revenge, and on such a long list, what mattered a few names more?

With a sack of wine for his inspiration Antony eventually rattled off a few hundred family patriarchs who had irritated him at one time or another; he even threw in a few freedmen of great fortune who had loaned him millions and still held his mortgages. He admitted this to me once but claimed he offered their names by way of negotiation. He quarrelled for none of them. Only one man was essential for Antony. He wanted Cicero. More specifically, he wanted Cicero's right hand and tongue nailed to a stake beneath his accursed head and set upon the speaker's platform for everyone to see until Cicero's flesh rotted to oblivion. The other names were only bargaining chits to that end. For his part, young Caesar made sure he named every patrician who had snubbed him on his first journey from Brindisi to Rome. By chance this did not include Cicero. So a head, hand and tongue for Antony, the fortunes of the wealthiest patriarchs of Rome for young Caesar. I am told both men eventually gave up friends and family for the sake of keeping their most cherished rivals on the lists.

Having posted their list and then, subsequently, several versions of an expanded list in the Forum of Rome, Caesar, Antony and Lepidus were finished with the worst of that business. They had simply to make sure the estate auctions followed in a timely fashion. The actual murders were conducted by gangs of bounty hunters. These fellows were required by law to deliver the head of a proscribed man in order to earn their fee. Yes, it was all sanctioned by the divine name of the law. The slaughter was quite indiscriminate. If any man assisted someone on the list he was fair game as well, and naturally, as a traitor to Rome, there was a bounty for his head once his property went to auction. Blood eventually stained every family of any reputation before the killing ended. And not only patriarchs. Mothers and children perished in great numbers during the proscriptions, for the gangs cared nothing about the details of their task. Having killed the father legitimately they raped the rest for the pleasure of it. After that the usual policy was to leave no witnesses.

There are tales about a few loyal wives and sons – and even slaves – who dared to hide men named on that fatal list. Even strangers would sometimes spare a desperate nobleman on the run. Humanity is not always as morally bankrupt as the worst of our kind would have us believe. On the other side of it, lest we get too sentimental, quite a few sons brought the heads of their fathers into Rome for the sake of the bounty. With no patrimony, they thought at least to gain a few coins for the old boy's head. Then there were the neighbours who denounced gentry not originally on the lists. Denunciations of treason were never examined with much care. Once the charge was made, it was treason. And so men expanded their fine estates by buying the land of their neighbours at auction.

Our Caesar, so beloved these days that we build temples to him throughout the empire, earned his divine status in the worst way imaginable: trading the lives of friends and even family for the fortune he stole. What astonishes me still is that he so cleverly managed to shift the full blame of it to Antony. But of course that is the enduring genius of our princeps. He has always been able to dress others in his own most egregious crimes and take wholesale the virtues of better men.

Tyre, Lebanon: Summer, 42 BC

Roman officers brought me out of my cell and ordered slaves to wash me, trim my nails, and cut my hair and beard. Finally, pale and shivering in my nakedness, the officers instructed these same slaves to slip a plain tunic over my head, the customary purple stripe of an eques quite forgotten for the likes of me.

I spent some days at the coastal town of Tyre before being pushed into a carriage and taken to the marbled suburb of Daphne on the outskirts of Antioch. Daphne is where the Roman proconsul to Syria makes his home.

While I was still in Tyre one of my guards befriended me. He informed me of a good many details about developments in the world since my imprisonment; this came like casual gossip from a bored attendant. I would learn later that the part this fellow played was for my rehabilitation. First I learned Allienus had surrendered my legions. Then I heard about the proscriptions. I did not even think about my father. How could he be affected? My guard was less certain about this matter but promised to find out if his name appeared on the list.

Both Cassius and Brutus had gone to great lengths to

learn the fates of men who had not escaped Italy's new tyrants, and this fellow had only to approach one of his superiors for a glimpse of the latest proscription list. Eventually, my friendly guard returned to tell me my father's name was on the list. He promised to ask his prefect if anything else was known.

I had some days of worrying about my father's fate before learning that his head did indeed decorate the speaker's platform in Rome's Forum.

So I came first to worry and then fell at last to mourning. Of course my guard knew everything even from the beginning. I was only being manipulated so that I might rage all the more against the Triumvirate of Antony and Caesar and Lepidus. When I had finally got the full news I did not even weep. Instead, I recalled Octavian baiting Antony into a rage at their first meeting, the sly Maecenas standing beside him like a playwright watching his work being acted out. They were children with their schemes, incapable of empathy.

And so I moved from disgust for our young Caesar's impertinence to loathing him for the sake of his indifference to the lives of the innocent; almost fifty-years later I still want Caesar's blood for the crime he committed against my father. I want it, but I do nothing. In all our decades together since that time, I have thought about killing Caesar every time I stood before him. For all that, I bow and call him by his title, just as everyone else does.

Well, isn't it the same with the gods? They sit by and watch nations burn and men of character murdered. They are quiet while the innocent are raped, and yet still we come before them whispering our adoring salutations and secretly loathing their indifference.

Daphne-by-Antioch, Syria: Summer, 42 BC

To my inexperienced eyes Cassius Longinus seemed a great man: silver-haired and handsome with a dignified voice and the cool assurance of one long familiar with power. He was then some forty-five years of age, a veteran of a great many campaigns. At first glance he appeared to be a far more impressive figure than Julius Caesar had been when I saw him in Spain.

I would know Cassius better a few months later, when indecision and obstinacy characterised his every decision. In a palace, with no enemy to threaten him, he was the epitome of the old Roman imperator.

At my appearance in his praetorium Cassius announced, almost conversationally, 'I am told you nearly burned Alexandria to the ground, Dellius.' This remark came without so much as a handshake.

'Only its museum, Imperator.'

Cassius liked this. At least he laughed. 'Caesar set fire to it as well.' He spoke as if he had been fond of the man he had murdered.

'Let me make this easy for you, Imperator,' I answered. 'I was the one who murdered Gaius Trebonius. I made it a fair fight, my fists against his knife, but it was murder all the same.'

'I know you did. I also know about the vows you swore to Artemis. She will not forget that you used her name for your crime, Dellius. But that is between you and the goddess. What I want to know is how you persuaded Allienus to give you command of his army?'

'Allienus had no army. They had deserted him and gone into the hinterlands to become bandits. I brought them back to service with gold Queen Cleopatra gave me.'

'I have been trying to get gold from Cleopatra for almost a year. I tell you this: that woman is freer with her virtue than her money.'

'Give me my legions back, Imperator, and I will bring you all the gold in Egypt!'

A wistful smile. 'Would you swear an oath to that effect?'

'Happily.'

'I cannot trust your oaths, Dellius. If you lie to the gods, you will lie to me.'

'That is not true. I do not believe in the gods, Imperator. You, on the other hand, are quite real.'

'An Atheist? I despise such men. At least your fellow officers felt some remorse at swearing an oath they had no intention of keeping.'

'What have the gods to do with us?'

'They care about the Law.'

'Then why did you kill Caesar? If the gods cared that he had broken faith with Rome they ought to have struck him down; instead they let him prosper.'

'The gods expect us to care, Dellius. When their laws are broken we must act or suffer the consequences.'

'The gods are a fantasy, else there would be justice in the world.'

'You do not know why the gods do what they do.'

'Turn me loose on my father's murderers or kill me for my crimes. Do not tell me about imaginary creatures who love justice and punish the wicked.'

'The gods will teach you the truth in time, Dellius. Until then, we shall leave Cleopatra's gold for another day. I need to get ready for the army of the Triumvirs. I have released your fellow officers and I intend to do the same with you. I will make you a senior tribune of the cavalry. I mean to assign you to a cohort of the Thracian auxiliaries who will form part of my Guard. They are a difficult race to manage but by all accounts excellent fighters. Cassius Scaeva will serve as your first centurion of the cavalry. He assures me, by the way, he would rather ride with you than with any officer in the legions, save only Brutus and me. High praise from a man of his reputation.'

'I will try to be worthy of it, Imperator.'

'Give me young Caesar's pretty head, lad. If not his, then Mark Antony's will serve as well. For such a trophy I will not only restore your father's estate to you, I will give you all of Tuscany as your own.'

Beyond the Hellespont: Summer, 42 BC

Scaeva and the others had already departed for Thrace by the time I interviewed Cassius. That left me to travel with several centurions, tribunes and prefects on their way to Hellespont. Our cavalry escort included a mix of Parthians, Medes, and Arabs, a thousand horsemen in all. We averaged forty miles a day and reached the Hellespont within a month of our departure. From there, I was only a few miles from my new camp, but it took a week before I caught one of the ferries across.

I reported to the prefect of the Thracian cavalry, the son of one of the assassins, as it happened. He informed me that, for the time being, the entire Thracian cavalry would answer to Junius Brutus. Once Cassius arrived, our cohort would join Cassius's Guard. I did not expect a temporary assignment in the army of Brutus to make any difference to me, but as it turned out Brutus enjoyed frequent and large gatherings of his officers, including all his senior tribunes. To his thinking it was important for everyone to understand what we were doing.

Brutus processed military decisions exactly as men shape law in the chambers of the senate. He was anxious to play the role of Rome's liberator. To his thinking liberators do not give orders in the same manner as tyrants do. Rather, they build consensus. He was an idealist, of course. That created a certain degree of the unintended silliness in his command, but I must say whenever he spoke of liberty he affected all of us. I cannot recall any decision he made which did not include some philosophical touchstone. He was a hard man to despise, for all that I had loved the man he had murdered. But then, to be fair, I did not become well acquainted with the true character of Brutus at that point.

Once Cassius crossed the Hellespont, I joined his army. Unlike Brutus, Cassius had no interest in the opinions of tribunes and prefects; I attended none of his staff meetings. Still, I could see differences in the commands of the two men. Our food and fodder came punctually into our camp without the usual sorts of reminders being sent up the line. Our equipment was always in perfect order and when there were problems we had replacements or repairs often on the very day we made the requisition. A real general, in other words – not a philosopher on a horse. Or so Cassius seemed in the beginning.

If I had started to love my new patron, it all came to a halt on the morning Cassius finally rode out to inspect his legions. To my astonishment he sat atop Hannibal. It was easy enough to understand how Cassius had come to own my stallion: he had defeated Dolabella. In the aftermath of their battle he claimed Dolabella's property as the spoils of war. Except that Hannibal was not Dolabella's horse.

I sent word through our chain of command that Hannibal was my horse, bought from the eques Seius through the services of a Tuscan horse-trader whose name I provided, if verification was required. I concluded my letter by explaining that Dolabella had taken Hannibal without my permission. As such, the animal was still my property, and I should very much like him returned to me.

Cassius, who possessed the wealth of the orient, ignored my letter.

XIV
PHILIPPI

Hellespont: Summer, 42 BC

Our Thracian mercenaries were exceptionally skilled at the kind of fighting that patrols encounter, but this particular cohort was new to Roman discipline and needed extensive training. Scaeva performed this task admirably. That left me with the responsibility of bringing my staff of junior tribunes up to standard. These fellows were mostly from the great families of Rome, all of them splendidly educated in Greek literature. They could ride and most had some concept of which end of a sword to grab, but they were soft and spoiled. Schoolboys really. The worst of it was their fondness for jeering at the weakest fellow in our corps, a chubby tribune named Quintus Horatius Flaccus – Horace. Horace had originally been in the army of Brutus, severing as a legionary tribune. Brutus had loved Horace's wit and poetry and assumed he would do well in a command position. When there were a number of complaints, Brutus sent his friend to serve as an officer in the auxiliaries. Whether by chance or design, Horace ended up in the army Cassius commanded.

Horace's father had bought his son a fine education, but neither he nor his son had any interest in a political career. That meant Horace had never intended to become an officer in the army and was ill prepared for the challenges of such a life. He knew enough to ride a horse, but he was not good at it. When it came to handling a weapon he was perfectly awful. Nearly everything he attempted brought gales of laughter from the others. Seeing nothing funny about incompetence I made sure the abuse stopped. Rather than speak to the issue of hazing directly, I called out the loudest of the bullies to pair with me when we practiced sword fighting. I always gave the fellow a practice shield and a proper helmet so we might make a fight of it, then I grabbed up two practice swords for myself. I never bothered with anything more than the cuirass, which I wore habitually. If two fellows had abused Horace or if one had laughed harder than the rest at someone's joke, I called them both forward for a session. A swipe at their helmeted heads, a hard poke in the chest, a crack on the fist, or a slap across the back of his thighs: I delivered the blows with the easy indifference of a master swordsman. Bright fellows that they were, they caught on to what I was doing and the hazing soon stopped.

Horace was actually a remarkably clever fellow; he had simply no talent for war. In fact, no one in our army possessed a finer command of the Greek language, with the possible exception of Junius Brutus and the Athenian nobility. For the chance to miss extra training sessions, Horace was happy to write my reports and was soon issuing orders in my name to our Thracians. These fellows knew no Latin and refused to comprehend what Greek I spoke to them.

At our evening meals, with a sack of wine passed around to loosen our cares, Horace would often recite the most wonderful poems. All were original, though some were satires of quite familiar verses. His most popular recitations were wickedly scatological, but sometimes he was simply clever; others answered him with their own creations, for we were erudite in the extreme, but these were never to Horace's standard, and Horace was soon recognised as our corps' unofficial poet laureate.

In the beginning, Scaeva was not really charmed by Horace. To his thinking Horace performed the same clerical work for me that a slave would do, if I had owned one. As for his wit and poetry, that counted very little in Scaeva's worldview. A lifetime in the legions had taught him to appreciate martial valour and little else, but one evening Horace turned the old Cyclops into a hero with a poem in the heroic meter, the dactylic hexameter that Homer employed. It celebrated the day Cassius Scaeva lost his eye as he commanded a century of men in a battle that had famously stopped one of Pompey's legions.

When Horace had finished his recitation old Scaeva

was so touched he had to leave our campfire. A few days afterwards Scaeva confided to me that he thought Horace might be useful holding our horses, should we ever need to go somewhere on foot. Scant as it was, it was more praise than he offered the other officers under my command.

Philippi, Macedonia: September, 42 BC

In late summer, we received our orders to move in advance of the army on its march to Philippi. Our patrols, finding no enemy resistance, soon discovered a splendid site for the army, two miles west of the city. Our position actually straddled the Via Egnatia, with a camp to either side of the highway. A rugged line of cliffs along our northern flank and a vast marsh to the south guarded our flanks. The marsh actually spanned a distance of eight miles from north to south and ran from the very edge of our southern camp all the way to the sea. From east to west the marsh extended nearly three miles. The ground was inhospitable to a man on foot, utterly impossible for horses, so it served as a barrier against any flanking manoeuvres by enemy cavalry.

Our army occupied two large hills rising up to either side of the highway. Cassius claimed the southern hill, Brutus the northern one. The river, which fed the marsh, lay to the east of our camp. This provided us with the luxury of fresh water, while requiring the enemy to use well water.

The highway that our two camps straddled kept supplies coming from Asia Minor, so long as our fleet guarded the Hellespont. In total, our generals commanded seventeen legions, divided evenly between the two commanders. There were another fifty thousand auxiliaries in the combined armies; almost half of them were cavalry. Most of our legions were close to full capacity, roughly five thousand men per legion. I would guess our total number of combatants amounted to one hundred thirty thousand men, with another ten thousand slaves and servants. Add to that number sixty thousand horses and mules. Antony and Caesar fielded roughly the same count of infantry, though easily ten thousand fewer cavalry. As with our own army, their legions were filled with veterans. That meant neither army was likely to panic; it also promised heavy casualties on both sides once the fighting began.

To keep the loyalty of their soldiers, each of the four generals paid his men from his own purse. They also promised their men splendid bonuses in the wake of a decisive victory. Having lost everything to the proscriptions that winter, those of us in the service of Cassius and Brutus were especially hungry. To put it plainly, paydays and the prospect of bonuses meant everything.

⋙⋘

Once Antony's legions began their march across Macedonia

I spent nearly two weeks in western Macedonia on patrols with my Thracian cohort. Twice we encountered Antony's scouts and made a fight of it, but these were quickly finished, as cavalry fights so often are. From the men we captured in these skirmishes I learned that Antony was coming at our position with eight legions. Caesar had crossed the Adriatic after Antony but, for reasons that were not entirely clear, he and his legions remained on the coast. All the men we interrogated said the rumour in Antony's camp was that young Caesar was ill. Some said dying. This was critical news, which I sent back to Cassius at once, though Cassius did nothing with it.

*

Antony arrived with his eight legions at Philippi in mid-September. Quite unbelievably, he established his camp only a mile from our fortifications. Our splendid position was suddenly compromised by Antony's choice of a campsite. It meant that after the armies had formed for battle they would be quite close to one another. Nor would there be any room at either side of our battle lines for the cavalry to manoeuvre. I expected Cassius if not Brutus to understand the problem at a glance. All we had to do was attack before Antony could set up his defences. We needed to drive him back three or four furlongs. Instead, our generals allowed Antony to place his camp where he pleased.

Antony established a ditch on the evening of his arrival. While this was being dug we had orders to remain behind a long palisade that fronted our two camps. Afterwards, we watched the enemy bring down timber from the forest. With these logs they erected a palisade behind their ditch, exactly like our own.

It made no sense to me that we let Antony construct such elaborate defensive works. We outnumbered his force two-to-one. Whether we swept down against his army with our own or simply harassed those parties collecting timber, we might have damaged him. Instead, we watched quietly until, a week later, Caesar joined Antony's army.

From that point forward our armies began turning out each morning for battle. Because the legions of Cassius and Brutus enjoyed the high ground, much as Gnaeus Pompey had done in his battle against Julius Caesar at Ronda, Brutus and Cassius were content to form a battle line then wait for an attack.

My cohort was supposed to defend the army's left wing, reinforcing the legion closest to the marsh. Should our infantry break through the enemy's right wing, I would naturally lead my Thracian cohort forward, taking as many of the enemy as possible as they ran for their camp. In normal circumstances there would be ground to our left and considerable space between the back of our legions and the camp palisades. At Philippi there was no room for movement. Cassius and Brutus had let Antony compress the distance between the two armies. This meant our cavalry, far superior in number to Antony's and Caesar's, would have little or no effect on the outcome of the battle. Only in a rout would the majority of us be let loose to fight. And of course since we intended to establish a defensive posture a rout was unlikely.

Of all our cavalry, my cohort had the very worst of it, for we were set against the marsh with a legion immediately before us and our camp's ditch and palisade close behind. I might send messengers behind the lines so long as we stood at formation, but there was no space available to take all my men at once.

That is not to say all of our cavalry units were useless. Once the armies faced one another, there was any number of skirmishes between the cavalries on both sides. We employed four thousand Parthian archers who spent their day riding between the two armies firing their arrows into the enemy. Antony's and Caesar's lancers came out to clear these fellows away and to form a cover for their own archers. We answered with attacks by heavy and light cavalry. So there were always horses and archers on the narrow strip of ground between the armies, but the infantry, with which battles are won and lost, stood by quietly like spectators at the races.

Our high command gave repeated assurances that time was on our side. We had no shortage of supplies, and once the fall rains began Antony's and Caesar's camp, necessarily established on low ground, would turn into a swamp. With the coming of winter and supplies becoming more difficult for them to acquire, Antony and Caesar must either retreat or make an uphill charge. In either event we would possess every advantage. Before that day came, however, we spent our time standing in a hot dusty field learning patience.

Philippi, Macedonia: 3rd October, 42 BC

A week into our standoff, Cassius learned from a captured cavalryman that Antony's engineers were building a road deep inside the marsh. The road itself was two miles distant from our camp and ran parallel to our position. We could not see or hear the work and only learned of the road by a chance confession. I joined a squad of legionaries and tribunes who waded into the marsh to confirm the information. It took most of the day to travel the two miles out and back, but we found the road. It was primitive in form, being only a dirt road, but it was wide enough for two chariots to pass, which is to say it was up to military standard. The ground was supported by timbers then covered over with mud. The mud soon baked into a hardpan surface, sufficient for both infantry and cavalry, at least until the autumn rains came. Unchecked, it would have proceeded past our camp and come out on dry land somewhere behind our position. Once completed the very existence of such a road might compromise our supply line. In the worst case, it would allow enemy legions to come in behind us.

The answer ought to have been to build fortifications once the road was nearly completed. The road was narrow and therefore easily blocked. A few cohorts might defend it. With a large cavalry ready to pursue the enemy as they retreated the danger would suddenly belong to Antony's men. It might also have been a wise precaution to secure our camps with palisades along our flanks and at the rear. Cassius, however, thought to cut the road off in the very middle of the marsh.

To do this he built a wall running due south from our camp. This eventually blocked all further progress on Antony's part. Of course, behind our wall, we had been forced to build our own road, which was quite as good as Antony's. What Cassius seemed not to notice was the fact that our road completed Antony's work for him.

———

We interrogated men we had captured as a matter of routine. The road through the marsh was only a distraction, until of course it became a disaster. What interested every man in our army was the rumour that Caesar had died. Not one of the men whom we captured had seen him since he had left the litter that bore him into camp. Antony was alive and well, of course. He rode before his legions every morning, his massive frame and scarlet commander's cloak easily discernible. Caesar's legions, in contrast, were leaderless. They would not pledge themselves to Antony, nor to any man but Caesar, who still paid them, and though Caesar's legates turned out for battle each morning there was no supreme commander to review the rank and file and coordinate the various legions during an attack.

One morning, soon after we had blocked the construction of Antony's highway through the marsh, the armies formed for battle as usual. As per my custom I rode forward to have a look at the enemy. Nothing appeared to have changed at first glance, and yet as I studied Antony's legions, they appeared to be very slightly diminished. It was not immediately apparent, but here and there a centurion was not in his usual place, nor did I see that century's standards, all of which, in my boredom, I had begun to recognise.

A few centuries missing is odd, nothing more. There might be any number of reasons for using them on some other task, but as I continued down the line, I noticed that every legion under Antony's command appeared somewhat reduced. Caesar's army, however, stood at full capacity. Riding back along the line I finally realised Mark Antony himself was missing too. That seemed one too many.

'Horace!' I cried, when I had returned to my cohort. My friend pulled his horse next to mine. 'Send a man to Cassius. Tell him Antony may be leading as many as half-a-legion of men through the marsh. If it is true, they're coming for our camp.' Horace stared at me without comprehending how I could know such a thing. I shouted at him to do as I ordered, and he turned and repeated my message in Greek to one of our Thracian captains. This fellow rode away in the direction of Cassius, but at that very moment I heard the shrill cry of a whistle deep within enemy lines.

Other whistles answered and then the flags at either wing signalled the enemy to advance. Suddenly all nineteen enemy legions began a cadenced march in our direction. Our light cavalry darted before them in columns, the lead men tossing javelins, then turning away so the next horseman might have his turn. They were answered by lancers who rode into their flanks. Our own lancers and the Parthian mounted archers came to the rescue, but the ground between the armies was vanishing quickly. Antony's and Caesar's legions were on the attack.

For a time the march was a slow one, then the flags moved again. Cries from the enemy centurions sent every century into a slow trot, and the cavalry of both armies retreated behind their legions. I rode forward to watch the advance, and still saw no evidence of Antony. I rode back along the lanes and checked our camp gates for activity. My warning to Cassius had apparently gone unheeded. He was not sending reinforcements into our camp.

I rode toward the command position, thinking Cassius had not received my warning or had misunderstood what I was telling him. Seeing me, one the prefects came out to block my way. 'What do you want, Tribune?'

'To tell Cassius we are under attack in the marsh!' I cried.

The fellow looked at the quiet marshlands then pointed his finger at the enemy on the battlefield. 'Turn around and have a look, lad. That's what an attack looks like.'

'Antony is missing.'

'Sleeping one off likely.'

'On the day his army attacks?'

'Get back to your position.'

'Mark Antony is in the marsh with three thousand picked legionaries.'

'We've got men out there to stop him. If Antony was really attacking them, we would know about it. Now get back to your men while you've still got skin on your back!'

Cassius had placed two cohorts to defend our wall in the marsh. A dozen centuries, well armed and guarding a single point of land, ought to have been sufficient, but under cover of a new moon Antony had sent a hundred squads into the soft ground to the north and south of his road. Some of the men came with axes, picks and shovels; still others carried ladders.

They moved slowly under cover of perfect darkness and came so close they could see our sentries as they stood on the ramparts of our palisade. At sunrise Antony appeared on the road at the head of two thousand men. They came running along the road, taking volleys of stones and arrows. To cover themselves from the withering assault, Antony's men formed a testudo, shields up and interconnected. Against the testudo only heavy artillery stops an advance. In this instance, Cassius's men had catapults loaded and ready.

Antony's men suffered heavy casualties as they closed on our palisades and were soon driven back. But the testudo had done its work; Cassius's forces came away from their redoubts, running to the aid of those holding the road. Once that happened Antony's squads came out of the heavy grass, striking at the palisade up and down the line. With few men available to resist them, they crossed the palisade and took possession of Cassius's road with very little trouble. Once that had happened, the men Cassius had sent to defend the marsh could no longer send him messages. From the camp, none of this was visible. Cassius presumably learned about the possibility of the attack from my message but getting no distress signal from the cohorts defending the marsh concluded there was nothing to worry about.

Once Antony's squads had crossed the palisade, they cut down the enemy where they stood. With that fight won, Antony signalled for a cohort of his cavalry to come forward. These followed behind Antony's infantry attack until they had broken into our camp. At that point several squads of Antony's cavalry raced forward to hold the gates between the battlefield and the camp. As a result, Cassius could no longer enter his own camp. The remainder of Antony's cavalry and infantry turned to the business of looting and burning our southern camp. Antony himself robbed the praetorium, where the army payroll was kept. Once all the tents were ablaze, Antony sounded the retreat. Our men, finally able to enter the camp, began pouring through the gates, but it was too late. All had been lost.

—◦◦◦—

On the battlefield, Antony's and Caesar's armies attacked our legions at about the time Antony took possession of our camp. Some have speculated that Cassius hesitated because of the attack on his camp, but in my opinion, he refused to advance his forces because that had been his strategy from the beginning. This cost lives at the front, but it was a strategy that reduced the chances of a rout, which could amount to the loss of his entire army in an afternoon. So the fight on the battlefield proceeded much as Cassius anticipated it would do, with neither army taking ground.

Brutus gave his army the same orders, but as Caesar's legions closed for the fight their formation grew so ragged that one of Brutus's legates could not resist giving the order to charge against them. It was folly not to. Once one legion began the attack, the rest followed. With Brutus's army far in advance of Cassius's legions, the fight that erupted on the northern half of our battlefield occurred in the middle of the field, rather than close to our palisades.

An hour into it, Caesar's legions finally broke and ran. This gave Brutus's cavalry the opening they needed. Again without Brutus giving the order, his cavalry raced forward for the kill. Had Brutus led the cavalry assault instead of trying to stop it, he might have turned it against Antony's exposed flank. Owning the entire northern half of the battlefield he had only to roll up the rank and file behind Antony's front line, just as Julius Caesar had done against Pompey Magnus at Pharsalus. Instead, as I learned later, Brutus lamented his army's lack of discipline as they raced headlong toward Caesar's camp.

—◦◦◦—

I saw none of these things from my position. The field was soon covered in a thick screen of dust, and I was tucked away behind the lines, pressed against the marsh and our camp palisades. From my perspective, all of our legions were being pushed back even as our camp burned. At the rear of our battle lines men were turning from their appointed places and crowding the camp gates in the vain hope of saving the camp from annihilation. The result was chaos at the gates and a blockage of the ground behind our army.

Realising there was no chance of receiving orders from Cassius, I gave the order to abandon our horses and enter the marsh. Soon the entire cohort, three hundred Thracians and a handful of Roman officers, crashed into the murky water and began wading through the mire. I went last, making sure the men formed a column and moved as quickly as possible away from the battlefield. When a volley of arrows came swarming into us, our centurions ordered shields up and directed the men to continue their slow retreat from the battlefield. Once beyond the reach of Antony's archers I ordered the wounded to be taken to dry ground, where their wounds might be treated. As this occurred I brought my staff together and explained my intentions. The moment their complaints began I shut them off. 'Any man disobeying orders will lose his head.'

Our long summer of training paid off. Not another man dared protest, and when we returned to the Thracians my officers were quick to keep their centurions and the rank and file from protesting, repeating my promise of severed heads. So it is with armies; the officers assume the manner of their commander. Up and down the line, men behave exactly as their superiors do. Hesitation breeds cowardice;

confidence makes for courage. I was taking our men into the fight, not away from danger as they had at first hoped, and though every man in our cohort dreaded my decision he pressed forward without daring to protest. So the armies of Caesar had fought. The real Caesar, I mean.

As we made our way we encountered legionaries who had fled death on the battlefield by plunging into the marsh and escaping into the wetlands. These I pressed into our column, and I was soon commanding four hundred men. Sometimes we were in water, sometimes deep in the mud, but there were also soft fields of dead grass atop mud flats, which was as close to hard ground as we could hope for.

———

We were closing in on Antony's road when two of the legionaries I had pressed into service broke from our column and ran. I tossed my lance and shield to Horace and took off after them. I knew that if I let these deserters get away, I could expect to lose a great many others as well. They were fit and fast, but they had foolishly kept their shields, and I was soon closing on them. Of course a legionary is loath to abandon his shield, for he fights as much with it as with his gladius. We raced along the soft dead grass, sometimes sinking into water, sometimes running on ground firm enough to let us run flat out. I was barefoot of course. Like everyone else I had lost my sandals soon after entering the mud. Two furlongs on, a quarter of a mile at most, I began to close the distance. The legionaries stopped and turned to face me. Each man drew his gladius.

I expect they hoped I would be afraid to face them. We were certainly too far from the others for me to get any assistance. When I kept coming for them they spread out to either side to receive me. Several paces away from them, I stopped to catch my breath. 'Don't be a fool, lad!' the older of the two men called to me. 'Turn back and save your own skin.'

I pulled both of my swords out. 'I'll turn back when I've got your heads.'

'They might be harder to take than you think!'

Saying this, they came at me. These men were not like my officers, who had grown wary of my talents and fearful of being hurt. They had spent their lives on the line and had survived against every sort of enemy; so they had no fear of me. They were veteran brawlers and supremely confident of their abilities. Best of all, from their perspective, I was without a shield.

The first to lunge at me was on my right. He swung his shield at my sword, holding his gladius close to his hip at the ready. Only a step behind his companion, the second man came against my left side, pushing close and ready to end it at once. He too used his shield in an effort to pre-empt my attack. Like his partner, he kept his gladius close to his hip. Rather than getting caught between their shields, I threw all my weight across the shield of the second man. With my left hand I blocked the gladius that came for me. With my right hand I reached around and cut a deep gash across the tenderest part of the fellow's arm. Rolling off his shield, I heard his scream as the blood spurted wildly from his wound. I turned to find the second man coming in for the kill. I had not the balance to meet his attack. Instead, I went under his shield. I blocked his sword thrust with one gladius, then cut his tendon with the second.

Coming to my feet again, I faced the man whose arm I had cut. He had dropped his shield and sword because he was desperate to bind his wound. I stepped toward him hoping to plunge a sword into him. Rather than trying to recover his weapons, he ran for his life.

I finished the man on the ground; then I took off after the other. We had not gone another half a furlong when I suddenly went face down in the mud. I kept a grip on both swords but with the wind knocked out of me I was slow coming to my feet.

By then, the fleeing legionary had vanished. I knew he was in the high grass; I knew he had to be close, not more than fifty paces away, somewhere in front of me. I watched the grass in case he tried to circle behind me. He was without shield or sword, but he had a dagger and there were fieldstones lying about.

I went forward slowly, listening, turning, watching for an attack. When I came to a large pool, I realised he could be somewhere in the high grass at the centre of it or already over the small knoll on the opposite bank. The water was moving but where exactly he had gone I could not tell. As I weighed my options, I heard the cry of what sounded like a girl just beyond the pond. I waded into the pool and crossed to the opposite bank. Crawling out of the water and over a low grassy bank, I pushed forward to have a look, only to discover Maecenas and Caesar alone in the marsh.

It was Caesar's cry I mistook for a girl's. I knew this because he was at it again. Maecenas, the larger of the two but a very soft man, was pulling his friend by the hand. Caesar begged him to stop. It was over, he panted. They were dead men! Maecenas whispered to him that there was still hope, but Caesar was having none of it. 'We've lost!' he cried. 'I only wish I had the courage to kill myself!'

Maecenas started to answer, but at that moment they saw me. I had come to my feet without even thinking. I fixed my gaze on Caesar. My heart was brimming with a terrible passion for revenge. The slick little thief, sending thugs to murder honest men that he might claim their fortunes! I cannot explain how thoroughly my emotions seized me. He was alone for the taking, or practically so, at any rate. Maecenas was certainly no protection.

Caesar begged me or some imagined god for mercy, but for a long beat he did not move. I must certainly have presented a terrifying sight. I was covered in mud, an officer of the cavalry, with a gladius in each hand. When I stepped toward them, both of them shrieked in terror and turned to run.

They were thirty paces from me, neither really capable of running full out at this point, nor armed with anything more than a dagger. I smiled at my prospects. With the head of young Caesar I hoped to own all of Tuscany.

At just that moment the man I had been pursuing came up out of the tall grass. He was a step behind me when I saw his shadow. He carried a large boulder, which he threw at me as I turned toward him. I ducked under his assault but the rock hit my back and shoulder, and I went down under the force of it.

I heard the drawing of his dagger from its sheath. Then, only half-conscious of what was happening, I rolled toward him. I brought the gladius in my right hand under his leather skirt. The blade plunged into soft flesh. The legionary howled. I gave a twist of the blade as I pushed up and then pulled the sword free. Blood washed across his thighs as he swayed over me. Then he collapsed beside me, his dagger useless in his hand. For all that, he was still alive when I took his head.

Maecenas and Caesar had vanished in the high grass by the time I had got to my feet again. I sheathed one of my swords and took the head of the man I had killed in my free hand. Scaeva waited for me where the first man lay. I took the second fellow's head and carried them like a couple of gourds with my fingers locked into their open mouths. I meant to show my men I was as good as my promise. When I did, the Thracians stared at me as if I were some kind of monster. Which I suppose I was.

Five decades on I still curse the fool who came out of the grass for me. Had he only stayed hiding, he could have kept his head, and I would have taken Caesar's instead!

XV
JUDGEMENT

Philippi, Macedonia: 3rd October, 42 BC

Antony had secured his road through the marsh with several redoubts. Each was guarded by a century of infantry and several squads of artillerymen. Rather than battle through each fortification, I took our men toward the last of the redoubts, the one closest to Antony's camp.

Before we were out of the marsh the enemy hit us with a volley of spears, arrows, and slung stones. Up went our shields and then our legionaries were soon coming out of the water, meeting the enemy head-on, exactly as the legions are trained to fight. Our Thracian auxiliaries swarmed around the enemy flanks, as cavalry are taught to do. Antony's men had the superior position, but we outnumbered them and were soon pressing them back. Once I had secured the redoubt against those centuries farther down the road, I turned the remainder of our cohort against the camp ditch.

I went in the vanguard with our legionaries, racing toward perhaps a hundred defenders. We caught a volley of spears, but kept our formation as we raced up the bank of the ditch. I threw myself against a man directly before me and heard the men to either side of me cracking shields at the same time. My opponent reached around my shield with a deadly thrust. Anticipating him, I slashed at his arm with my shield. As he fell back with a broken arm, I cut at the tendons of the man to my right then struck the back of the leg of the defender to my left.

Soon we had pushed the last of Antony's men back into their camp. Rather than drive into the camp with my entire force, I sent three centuries forward to loot and burn what they could. I led the remainder along the perimeter bank. We caught another fight but soon drove the enemy back into the ditch. After that we got to the corral and caught up fifty horses. We did not bother with saddles, and many times used only a halter and a lead line instead of bridle and reins. Most of us grabbed up javelins and lances but I made sure some of the squads also got hold of lit torches. We rode through one legionary camp, setting fire to the tents as we went, but a quarter of an hour after we had taken the horses, Antony's rearguard began pouring into the camp. Taking what small victory we had, I ordered our cohort's immediate retreat.

We used those on horseback to guard our rear. The rest advanced in tight formation down Antony's road. The redoubts were built to protect the camp from external attack. With an enemy at their backs, the defenders of the redoubts simply fled into the marsh. Two miles on, we found the broken palisade where Antony had crossed that morning; after that we were safe.

Philippi, Macedonia: 4th to 22nd October, 42 BC

I rode forward with a handful of my officers, calling out the day's password to one of the sentries. This let us enter the fortified area, where we discovered two legions belonging to Cassius now defending our camp's southern perimeter. They were of course twelve hours late for the party, but no matter. At least we were ready to turn back a second attack.

Once I knew our army still possessed the camp, I sent for my men and asked the prefect of the Night Watch to take me to Cassius.

'Cassius is dead. He killed himself an hour ago,' came the answer.

'Killed himself? I don't understand.'

'Nobody does. They're saying he thought we lost the battle.'

I looked at the smouldering ruins that had been our camp. 'Didn't we?'

'While we were getting battered about, Brutus's legions broke through Caesar's line. They destroyed the better portion of four of his legions. After that they looted Caesar's camp, including his payroll.'

'How bad was it for Cassius's legions?'

'The camp is completely destroyed, and Antony made off with our payroll. As for the legions, we took heavy casualties across the line, but we can still turn out nine legions tomorrow morning – assuming Brutus is willing to pay us.'

———

Food for our evening meal came from the hardtack tied to every man's belt, the food of last resort. After that we went looking for the ruins of our tents, but with no landmarks to guide us and the roadways blocked by rubbish, we were as disoriented as the rest of the army. Finally, Scaeva put our men to work clearing an area. We were all barefoot and suffering with bruised and cut feet; I don't think a single man had made it through the marsh with his sandals still on his feet, but no matter. We were alive.

By midnight we collapsed close to one another around small campfires. There were no bathhouses remaining and in the chilly night no one cared to bathe in the river; so we slept as we were, covered in blood and mud; the worst of it was that we stayed in our armour. We feared the enemy might attempt to take our palisade under the cover of another moonless night. Some of the men wrapped themselves in half-burned blankets. I recall I slept covered by a charred leather tarp.

At dawn, neither army bothered to turn out for battle

formations. Instead, following a breakfast of hardtack, the legionaries set to work clearing the camp of debris in earnest. The auxiliaries retrieved the dead from the battlefield. From these, my men and I found footwear.

———◦———

Brutus's camp had survived without any damage, and although my men had pierced the membrane of Antony's camp and burned perhaps a hundred tents, that damage was more symbolic than actual. Antony still possessed his payroll, plus the one he took from Cassius. Brutus owned his own great fortune and Caesar's too. The critical issue on both sides of the battlefield was money. Antony, once he learned Caesar still lived, offered to pay Caesar's legions from his own purse.

Bankrupt though he was, Caesar would not allow it. Instead, he borrowed money from Antony, and you can be sure Antony arranged the interest rates to his advantage. Not coin exactly but power, which amounts to the same thing in the end. They did not make a formal arrangement – not without Lepidus, who was in Rome – but the agreement was settled nonetheless. Antony would take possession of upper Gaul, Greece, Macedonia, Asia and the biggest prize, Cleopatra's Egypt. Lepidus would have western Africa, Spain and Sicily, as before. That left Caesar with Narbonne, the southernmost province of Gaul

– asliver of the empire, in other words. As before, the spoils of Italy still belonged to all three men. Their bargain left Antony preeminent, assuming they were victorious, but Caesar had no choice. Without a payroll for his men he knew they would abandon him and join Antony.

Brutus, having no partner remaining, was the real winner of the first battle at Philippi, and though he talked about restoring the Republic, even an idealist knows when he suddenly owns the world, which would be the case if he defeated Antony and Caesar. All Brutus had to do was embrace the legions and auxiliaries that had formerly pledged themselves to Cassius. No one competed with him for the command of these forces because no one but Brutus had the money at hand to pay them. To seal his new contract with the legions of Cassius, Brutus issued a thousand denarii bonus to every fighting man in our camp, regardless of his rank or nationality. That his own forces might not grow discontented, Brutus awarded the same bonus to them. We received our bonuses promptly next day, but of course the men who had formerly been under the command of Cassius could not help but think that they had lost everything when their tents were looted and burned, while the men who served Brutus still possessed the money they had already earned. In fact, the legionaries and auxiliaries in Brutus's camp suddenly had more money than most of them had seen in their entire lives.

By such small matters are armies ruined. For his part

Brutus proved incapable of understanding the problem. To his mind he had been even-handed in his generosity. His army had seized a fortune, and he paid out a bonus to everyone; Cassius had lost his camp, and Brutus would assume responsibility for feeding and paying these men going forward. What more could anyone expect of him? It was not his fault we had lost our money.

Had Brutus been less even-handed about the distribution of money, had he given his officers something like half-a-year's salary for a bonus and provided less to the legionaries and less still to the auxiliaries, his officers would certainly have quelled the mutinous rumblings. As it was, resentment came chiefly from the officers, who complained about the foreign auxiliaries getting the same bonus they received. As with all armies the attitudes of the officers soon trickled down through the ranks. Before any of us saw his next payday, every man in the legions Cassius had once commanded cursed the name of Junius Brutus. More to the point, they did it openly and without fear of disciplinary action.

Cassius's legions lost ten thousand men. Caesar lost almost twice that number, fully a third of his army. Antony and Brutus, in contrast, kept their legions intact, counting fewer than a thousand dead on either side. A week after the battle, we learned that on the same day we had fought at Philippi, Caesar lost an armada of transport ships in a storm off the Peloponnese. Two legions, bound for the Hellespont, gone. Had they succeeded they would have cut off our supply lines and left us poorly placed. As it was, Brutus now possessed every advantage.

With news of the disaster, Brutus took heart and spoke to his officers of our coming victory over the tyrants. 'Even the gods hate tyranny!' he told us. A confirmed atheist, I could name a great many tyrants whom the gods permitted to thrive, but I was happy nonetheless. I thought Brutus would take courage from the news and press forward. But no, he refused to change from his defensive strategy. In fact, he now insisted his legions stay behind the camp palisade. 'No need to risk another battle,' he said. 'We will wait for Antony and Caesar to make a second attack on our camp, and when they fail to breach our defences, we will turn our cavalry loose on their retreat!'

Brave words and fine policy – if only the enemy had behaved as halfwits. Instead, Antony had his men construct a siege camp between our southern camp's palisade and his own fortifications. He set it close to the marsh for defensive purposes and then arranged for a low wall to connect the new camp to his old one. By this means, he meant to keep his advance position well stocked with artillery. This new wall included several redoubts. These were all bristling with artillery, though the effort was wasted. Brutus made no attempt to stop the construction of Antony's new camp or the wall connecting it to the old camp. Once it was established, Antony's artillery began sending stones into our southern camp. Brutus's answer was to order us to move our bedrolls back half-a-furlong; in that way the stones landed harmlessly on vacant ground.

Our real worry was the road Antony and Cassius had built through the marsh, for it connected us with Antony's camp and could not be easily destroyed. Even after it had become impassable for cavalry because the hard-packed mud washed away in the rain, it still functioned for infantry. The only answer was to build a palisade along the southern perimeter of our camp.

———※———

Antony's and Caesar's camps did indeed turn into mud pits, and supplies grew progressively more difficult for them to acquire. None of this mattered. With Brutus cowering behind his camp palisade, our men were the ones who lost heart. The desertions began with our sentries fleeing to Antony's new camp. When Antony happily received these men, entire cohorts of auxiliaries began going over. Then even the legions lost courage. With reviving fortunes, Caesar came from his sickbed and began to appear each morning on the battlefield. And still Brutus preferred to keep his army behind the camp palisades. As for himself, he rarely left his commander's tent except to attend his staff meetings.

Within a fortnight Brutus had lost five thousand men to desertions, though no one would admit such a number. Some of these men rode as a complete cohort into Antony's camp with their officers in the lead. They took whatever grain and supplies they could carry as a bribe. Others, like the Thracians I commanded, slipped away into the east, going back home with their thousand denarii bonuses wrapped in their packs and whatever goods they could steal. A patrol might be sent out and never come back. Sentry posts were routinely abandoned overnight. Those officers foolish enough to make a search for deserters would often lose the search party as well. The stones Antony sent into our camp now carried notes promising amnesty to every deserting officer and money paid to him at once if he brought his men along. Those who refused such generosity were told not to hope for mercy later. And of course every day it rained. Without a tent, and no one in the southern camp had one, high ground is only slightly better than low. I can still recall shivering in the dark as I listened to rocks falling out of the sky, each with a promise of amnesty or death.

<hr />

Brutus's staff of legates pressed for a fight while they could still put an army in the field. Brutus's speeches, which became more convoluted as time went on, assured us we had only to wait for our victory. I will not say the man rambled or that he seemed to be growing mad as time passed. He had come to his conclusion half-a-year before. Unable to admit the dynamics had changed, he argued the old opinion in the face of new evidence. To his thinking, nothing in the plan was faulty. Why adjust a perfectly logical strategy? We were winning this war! Body counts had given us all some assurance in the beginning, but after the desertions no one cared to hear about our splendid advantages. In the end, Brutus still argued that our moral superiority would answer, but I must tell you the word freedom, so lovely in the abstract when Brutus had said it in the early days, very soon came to sound like 'death-by-sword'.

Brutus compared himself to Pompey Magnus at Pharsalus, pressed by his staff to fight when waiting would have meant victory. His history was accurate, but the situation he faced was quite different. At Pharsalus. Caesar was trapped and vastly outnumbered. Hubris and a lust for Caesar's blood caused Pompey's staff to insist on finishing matters at once. Here we enjoyed the advantage of high ground in a potential fight, but our numbers were dwindling and our legions were in a mutinous mood. There was no certainty of winning anything without a fight. When Brutus finally relented and turned his army out for a battle, he still insisted we would be better off waiting for winter. He said he acted against his better judgment. It was a sorry way for an army to take the field.

Philippi, Macedonia: 23rd October, 42 BC

The day was cold and cloudy, but there was no rain. Rain might have given us an advantage had we come to fight in earnest. We had been told we were going to fight if the enemy answered, and of course Antony and Caesar came out to dance.

My Thracians now gone, I commanded a cohort of our Spartan lancers, these in the service of the very legions I had recruited in Egypt. We were grouped with several thousand other auxiliary cavalry at the northern reaches of the battlefield. We had a forest and hills to our right. It was not good land for a flanking attack but I thought we might see skirmishes if Caesar sent archers to harass our wing. I was well placed to have a look at the enemy, and without the dust of summer to hinder my vision, I could see Caesar's legions as they formed for battle, with Caesar riding a fine white horse. He was a proud boy with that great army at his back; no tears for Maecenas to wipe from his cheeks on this fine morning.

I did not waste my breath whispering to the gods, but at the sight of young Caesar I did pray to whatever daemons inhabited the forest and marsh that I might have one more chance at the coward. But of course the perverse spirits of that great marsh at Philippi had teased me with the only opportunity I was ever going to have.

The fight lasted less than an hour, time enough for Brutus and the rest of the nobility to escape. They took with them our camp guards and the two legions holding the marsh. And of course the money. Once we knew what he had done, those of us left behind threw down our weapons.

—◆—

The remainder of the day was spent sorting out the officers from the rank and file. Our camp was plundered. Nothing we owned stayed with us, even the hardtack tied to our belts. Half of us, those belonging to the southern camp, had been living without tents for the better part of a month; so another few nights in the open was no more onerous than usual. Those officers at or above the rank of a centurion were held in the new camp Antony had built. The rank and file were taken into the armies of Caesar or Antony after swearing an oath of loyalty. Men were happy to serve Antony. Those obliged to join Caesar made a brave face of it. All the same not a soul had any regrets leaving the armies of Cassius or Brutus, the one a fool, the other a coward. As for the auxiliaries, most were relieved of their property and set free.

We stayed on that field until news came that Brutus

had committed suicide. He did this not in shame for his cowardice but to escape capture. After his death his staff turned themselves over without a fight. The day after these men arrived, the officers were all taken to the battlefield. First in line were the great men. After that, no one bothered sorting us out by ranks; they only insisted we stand in an orderly fashion. Scaeva stood before me, Horace behind. The three of us had been together as prisoners since our surrender. This was a consolation for me, for I counted them as my friends.

Caesar and Antony waited at the front of the line. They were seated and wrapped in robes, for the day was quite cold. They were attended, naturally, by friends and counsellors who might help them make their choices. Antony had fortified himself for the occasion; Caesar was cold-bloodedly sober. The captives stepped forward to receive judgment. Many of these men were known. If Antony or Caesar did not recognise them, one of their friends usually did. Men who were known on sight were generally proscribed. Their property was already gone. It only remained to take their heads. Others were sons of proscribed men. These men Caesar thought might be quite dangerous in the future, and so he took their lives while he had the opportunity. That is to say, he nodded his golden locks like Homer's Zeus atop Mount Olympus, and a bloodied centurion stepped up to execute the man. The stroke was with a gladius. Properly aimed, the sword slipped under the ribs and into the heart. The heads of the proscribed nobility were removed at a distance from our party and placed in wine jars for the long journey home. Once in Rome the heads would be set up on the speaker's platform in the Forum. Nobility had the right to speak before their execution, but any fellow giving a political speech was taken down at once. Most men asked a favour for their families; these appeals were always directed at Antony's party, where one of Antony's slaves took notes.

Those not recognised were asked to identify themselves. This involved giving a name and home, a declaration of citizenship, and of course past military experience. Caesar took the lead in these interrogations, chiefly because Antony soon grew bored with the whole spectacle. He remained only that he might cull out old friends or a bright young officer of reputation; otherwise, if he did not bother to speak up for a man, Caesar usually killed the fellow.

As we got close to the front of the line I expected I would die and only cared to do it with dignity. It was difficult in the circumstances. I could hear Caesar's petulant voice as we came slowly forward. In Rome, young Caesar had been playing the role of an outraged prince denied his inheritance. At Philippi, he was a mighty imperator dispensing justice. In both instances he sounded like a boy out of his depth.

To those not related to a proscribed man, Caesar held out hope as he interrogated them; he even pretended kindness. In fact, he let a few of the young officers of no importance walk away with impunity so that the others might hope. With many he played games of chance. Some of the wagers involved dice, but the ones I witnessed were far stranger. A young officer with no political coin had the chance to guess the direction a certain bird would fly when it left its perch. 'Quick now. Tell me where it goes!' The fellow pointed, and all present, even Antony, waited curiously until the bird finally departed. Down went the man, for the bird had not flown in the direction he had indicated. This game hadn't gone quite fast enough, so the next victim had to guess the number of fingers Caesar held behind his back. 'You can trust me. I'll play fair.'

'Three!' the poor youth cried, trembling at the prospect of one-in-five odds.

'On your life, you wager it is three and not *four* or five?'

'It is four!'

Caesar pulled his hand from behind his back, 'Too bad for you. Three was the right answer.' The flash of the gladius. The sound of another body hitting the muddy field.

'What is your name?' This to Scaeva.

Scaeva gave his name.

'Cassius Scaeva? Are you a relative of the assassin Cassius Longinus?'

'I have relatives who were freed by his ancestors.'

Caesar nodded, and the executioner stepped forward. The blade of the gladius swept into Scaeva's side. As the blade withdrew Scaeva fell to his knees with a heavy grunt and rolled forward, nearly touching Caesar's feet.

'What is your name?' Caesar was speaking to me, but I had no voice. I could hardly breathe, for I had thought Scaeva, of all men, would earn Caesar's mercy. 'Do you have a name?' The voice seemed to come from a great distance. I heard him without quite understanding that Caesar was talking to me. I was watching the body of a man I counted my friend dragged away.

'His name is Quintus Dellius.'

Caesar glared at Horace, who had spoken up for me. Of course Horace had not been asked to speak; for his impertinence he was now in mortal danger.

'Mine is Horatius Flaccus – Horace,' he added, though Caesar had not asked his name.

Mark Antony opened his eyes and blinked, for he had dozed off as we approached. His face became drunkenly animated as he cried out, 'By the gods, Horace! What are you doing here?'

'I really don't know, Antony! Brutus got me so drunk I was an officer before I knew it. I have never been so drunk in my life.'

'That is saying a good deal. Tell me, did our friend Brutus by chance promise you undying glory?'

'He promised me the glory of Achilles.'

'Achilles died young, Horace.'

'It seemed only a small detail at the time.'

'I expect so. I'll take this one, Caesar. Horace promises me he will never again lift a sword in anger. Don't you, lad?'

'I swear it, Antony! But will you bring Dellius with you as well?' Antony looked in my direction without seeming at first to recognise me. 'He is really the most amazing man with a sword! The bravest man I have ever known – after you, that is. And Caesar, of course. You won't regret it. I swear to you he is a fine and honourable man as well.'

'What is the name?' Antony asked, for I apparently now looked vaguely familiar.

'Quintus Dellius, Imperator,' I answered.

'Dolabella's creature? The mathematician?'

'I served Dolabella, Imperator.'

Antony looked at Caesar. 'I'll take Dellius as well.'

Caesar shrugged indifferently, then turned his gaze to the man behind me. 'What is your name?'

XVI
HORACE'S WAGER

Philippi to Athens: Autumn, 42 BC

Caesar returned with his legions to Italy, where a great many were disbanded. Antony took his army as far as the Hellespont. Horace and I were both temporarily assigned to Antony's Guard, but this did not mean very much. In fact, neither of us had any responsibilities. We simply moved in Antony's entourage. One morning, however, Antony showed up quite drunk and called Horace into his carriage. This of course is a singular honour for any man, especially so for a junior tribune of the auxiliaries. A man of my rank watched Horace enter the carriage and muttered something about Antony needing a morning blowjob.

I took the fellow down from his horse and set upon him with a flurry of punches. I knew Horace was fine entertainment on a dreary trip; if there was something more to it than conversation I wasn't ready to admit it of my friend and certainly would not allow anyone else to comment on the matter. Antony of course had a famously voracious sexual appetite, but unlike Dolabella I never knew him to use a citizen of Rome as a female. Not when he was sober enough to notice, I mean.

At the Hellespont several of our legions crossed into Asia, where they made their winter camps. The remainder sailed to Athens. Horace was assigned a secretarial post at the palace where Antony resided. I joined the junior tribunes at one of the armouries in Athens. We hadn't any duties and a great many of the young officers spent most of their time pursuing the pleasures of the city. As I had no money, none at all until the first payday, I remained at the armoury and used the entire day for training.

I would see Horace when he had time off from his duties. On these occasions Horace assured me he was a tireless promoter of my talents. I would not languish forever in the lower ranks, not if he had anything to say about the matter. I answered these promises as nobly as I could. I was content, I said, to make my way by my own merits. This of course speaks plainly to my youthful folly. Fortunately, Horace did not listen to such nonsense.

Athens: Winter, 42 – 41 BC

Antony was enjoying himself that winter. He really had no reason to be on the lookout for talented officers. After Philippi, he expected the next year to be relatively quiet. So Horace's relentless promotion of Quintus Dellius no doubt left him irritated. Nor could Antony imagine that Horace knew enough about war to recommend someone. So at first he ignored Horace; then he said he would have a look at the boy, meaning me.

He was insincere in this; he only wanted Horace to shut up. When Horace pressed again, Antony decided to teach the poet a lesson about real fighting men. If Quintus Dellius was so remarkable would Horace be willing to place a wager on him in a fair fight – one-on-one?

Horace said he would wager a fortune on Quintus Dellius, if he only had one. Antony arranged for loans to be extended to him; then he set the entire amount before Horace. Would he really wager it all? Against any fellow Antony might choose? Horace answered him that he would do it gladly, so long as Mark Antony himself was not the opponent.

I knew nothing of these matters; I simply spent my days running, riding, and fighting. Once or twice I noticed a stranger watching us train at the arena, but I thought nothing of it. As for Antony himself he never trained with us, nor did he bother visiting our armoury. I only saw him when he mounted a litter or walked in the streets surrounded by his clients and flanked by his Guard, of which I occupied the outer perimeter.

One morning, however, Antony arrived at the armoury with his entourage, including freedmen, secretaries, legates, old friends, and a few of the Athenian nobility. Horace was in this crowd too, though it was a while before I noticed him. Our training centurion spoke briefly with Antony's freedman then called us from the sand. He arranged a duel between two of the better tribunes and after these two he arranged another. The men used heavy wicker training shields and wooden practice swords. Like the shield, the training gladius is quite a bit heavier than a real sword. After these two duels the centurion called the two winners back to fight me.

I picked up my wicker shield, placed one training sword in my belt and took another in hand. The arena was covered in hard-packed sand and ringed about with heavy marble markers. The space was sufficient for as many as a dozen fights at once. Horace shouted heartily at my appearance, standing and clapping his hands. He was the only one in Antony's entourage who appeared to support my cause.

I slammed into one of my opponents, careful to slide away from the second man as he charged at me for any easy hit. When the second fighter had gone a step too far, I bounced away from the first opponent with a hard push. I wasted no time in play but with a sweeping motion of my shield knocked the shield of the second man away from his body and reached over for a thrust into his head. The blow was hard enough for the call of a kill but not quite enough to put him down with an injury.

Our centurion judged it a mortal wound, and the young man so struck retired from the fight, even as I turned against his partner. This one came charging at me in the hope of catching me while I still attended to the other man. I gave ground because he had the momentum, and for a moment we made a decent fight of it for Antony's sake. Still, I did not care to play the incompetent and at first opportunity struck my opponent's ribs with a gentle thrust.

'Well done, Dellius!' Antony called. 'Are you up for another?'

'I'm ready for as many as you care to watch, Imperator.'

Antony whispered something to one of his attendants, who turned and left the training area. All waited curiously until he returned in the company of a veritable giant. The fellow was a blond-haired Celt, who, I later learned, came from lands to the north of the Black Sea. In his mid-thirties, he was a head taller than I and perhaps half-again as heavy. He wore the skullcap of a freedman, and I guessed him to be a retired gladiator.

'Let's make it interesting for you, Dellius,' Antony said. 'Beat this man in combat, and I will give you five thousand denarii.' The prize on offer was equal to a first centurion's annual salary, a very enticing sum to someone who had recently been stripped of all he owned. But of course the amount of the prize intimidated me nearly as much as the giant himself. I could not imagine Antony expected to pay out a sum of that magnitude. For such a grand offer he had certainly acquired a champion. Still, I could not help but think what the money could buy.

We were each given a legionary's pilum and military-grade shields. The pilum, with a thin, barbed point, is a mortally dangerous weapon. Its more practical purpose, however, is to pierce and then hang upon an opponent's shield, thereby ruining its efficacy. Of course it is always possible to keep fighting with a spear dangling from one's shield, but the pilum is heavy by design and makes any movement with a shield awkward. The main fight would be with practice swords. These were decidedly non-mortal weapons. As per my custom, I carried a second gladius in my belt. My opponent could see no advantage in a second sword and refused the offer.

The legionary's shield is considerably lighter than the wicker shields used for practice; it is also a weapon in its own right, having the potential to cut a man if the edge comes into play. I appreciated the relative lightness of the shield; I had been carrying weighted wicker shields for a few weeks, but I did not care to fight with real weapons against a giant. I frankly expected to be beaten and really only wanted to come away with my skin intact.

We began at opposite ends of the arena and ran towards one another on the training centurion's signal. We both heaved our spears at about the same moment. By a deft turning of his shield the Celt caused the pilum I threw to slide away and scoot across the sand to the far reaches of the arena; his spear however pierced my shield. We kept racing forward, each of us drawing his sword. The collision jolted me as if I had run into a galloping horse. I stayed on my feet but reeled away, scrambling for balance.

I had hoped the collision would clear my shield, but the pilum remained dangling from it. The tip was now hopelessly bent, something more like a fishhook than the barbed point of a spear. Having no time to pry it free, I tossed the shield to the side of the arena and pulled my second training sword. I am quite sure the Celt had several reports on my fighting skills and may even have watched me without my noticing, for he stayed close but would not charge me.

When I came at him with a wild swatting of both swords against his shield, he stood his ground in a defensive posture. Had he not set himself in this manner, I meant to parry his first thrust and then go under his shield with a blow to the back of his leg. When he refused to do anything more than fend off my assault, I settled with beating his shield with my weapons, three strokes with each sword, then backing away. I retreated to my right, away from his sword hand.

He scooted towards me as I charged again, left foot forward, right bracing. He still held his gladius close to his hip, covered by his shield. I cracked his shield in the same rhythm as before, but on my last stroke, with my right hand, I reached around it as I fell away. Had he been pushing into an attack, as men will do when an opponent is about to back away, I hoped to catch flesh; instead, he swatted my gladius away with his shield.

I advanced again with the same dance, repeated the same series of hard blows and then retreated as before; but this time I did not reach in. I only feinted it. His shield swept before me as before. Reversing course, I stepped in suddenly, swatting his gladius aside. I lunged forward with a killing thrust, but the giant leapt nimbly away before I could touch him.

—◁◁◁▯◁◁▷—

So long as his right leg was planted, the Celt's reach was insufficient for a killing stroke. The moment he stepped forward with his right leg it would be to strike at me, whether low or high I could only guess. A man may try to disguise his intentions but the feet will expose him every time. That is the trick I had learned from Scaeva. Moreover, with two swords in play I did not need to brace and lunge. I might strike with either foot forward, whenever the opportunity presented itself. The Celt, on the other hand, must step forward with his right leg when he attacked. So he came shuffling forward, feet braced to receive an attack, always waiting for his chance in the same posture.

Neither of us was willing to give the other an opportunity to retrieve the loose spear at the end of the arena, so we stayed within a few steps of one another, turning in a wide circle. I used my gladii in brief, furious attacks, striking at various angles, searching for a chance to slip one of the blades past, then backing away a few steps. I would take a moment to watch him then charge in a second time. On the second retreat I always went a few steps farther back. This forced him to follow me, lest I get away from him and run for the pilum at the end of the arena. But that was all I could do. I could not tempt him to lunge at me with his sword.

So I danced, harassing him, backing off, coming in a second time. The rhythm never changed. Finally, as I returned for a second assault, I saw his right foot move forward. I sprang away suddenly, swinging my gladius at full extension. This time I struck his bare arm. I fended off his attack by retreating and circling, then looked toward the training centurion for a call. A cut must be deep enough to stop a real fight; tapping the flesh is not sufficient. The centurion shook his head. At least he had seen the blow. It was a fair call, I will give him that, but for five thousand denarii I could have hoped for a more generous one. I circled back in the direction of my spear and the Celt moved to intercept. I attacked again, tempting him with my sudden assault. He feinted a lunge, and I fell away as before, reaching behind his shield as I did. He was waiting for me this time and swung his shield at my hand. This left a deep groove in my sword and might well have ruined my hand had we been only slightly closer.

I changed nothing in my step, though I slowed the tempo, as if tiring of the game. He let me repeat my dance a few times then, suddenly, as I came at him, I saw his right foot leave the sand. I went down, rolling under his shield and snapped my gladius across the back of his sandal at the Achilles tendon. I rolled away and then jumped up, my arms extended overhead. This was always judged a maiming stroke, which is the same as a kill. With a sharpened blade my opponent would have gone to the sand with his tendon cut.

I looked at the training centurion and saw him raise his hand calling it a victory. No matter. The Celt, in his fury, charged me. The match was over, or at least it ought to have been. Of course I had no interest in getting battered by a shield and a wooden sword. I took a defensive posture, giving ground as he pushed his shield at me like a battering ram. I stepped aside but did not bother with another stroke across his arm. The training centurion was in the arena now, still signalling a victory, but Antony called from the benches: 'They fight until one of them asks to stop.'

I saw the Celt breathing hard, and I knew his best days on the sand were behind him. Too many drinking bouts, too many long mornings in bed with adoring fans. I stepped into range again, confident now I could wear him down. He rushed at me again. If a wound counted nothing, he meant to use his size against me. He swung his shield at me as I backed away and very nearly cut me. Then he gave a savage lunge of his gladius that was all fury and no art. I parried it and reached around his shield with my right hand, driving the dulled point of my sword into his jaw with all the force I could muster. It was a solid hit and ought to have taken him down, but it seemed to have no effect, except to enrage him. Again he came at me artlessly, this time trying to club me with his gladius. As I retreated from his mad charge, he turned back suddenly, moving to the side of the arena where my ruined shield and the bent pilum lay. He dropped his sword, stepped on the shield, and pried the pilum free with a ripping screech of wood and steel. The tip may have been curled, but it was steel against two sticks.

I moved back and to my left, always left now. This forced the Celt to keep turning the spear out from his body if he wanted to keep aiming it at me. He could throw it, but that only gave me the weapon if he did not take me down with it. Better simply to keep it in hand and force me to keep backing and spinning away. I swung my swords at the point of his pilum but that was only to frustrate him; it gave me no advantage. Nor could I move in close. So I circled him, swatting at his weapon. There was no way under him, no way through. Always to my left, always forcing him to turn. I was breathing hard now. After another of his lunges I backed away several steps and stopped as if desperate to catch my breath. Thinking I was too beat to resist him, the Celt charged me.

That was when I took off at a sprint, heading for the spear at the end of the arena. He was on my left, three paces behind. I let him come within half-a-stride; he could not yet reach me with his pilum, but when I bent down to pick up the spear he would be on me, driving his weapon hard into my back. Still a few steps away from the undamaged spear, I broke stride, closing the gap between us. At the same time, I swerved into him, batting the pilum away with the sword in my left hand and rolling into his legs.

I hit the side of his knee with the weight of my entire body. I heard the crack of bone, a scream of pain. When he was down I rolled away and came back to my feet. Tossing both swords away I grabbed the good pilum and held the weapon over him, threatening him with it until he cried for mercy.

I turned from the Celt, still holding the spear, and looked at Antony, who sat within range of my weapon. I was seething in rage for having been played the fool, and I thought about challenging Antony himself, which would have been bad business. Then I thought about the money. Walking away from the giant I dropped my weapon, my arms extended overhead, as if a mob cheered me. In fact my training mates were crying out enthusiastically, for they had all been beaten by me and were happy to see there was a good reason for it. From the benches where Antony sat I heard only my friend Horace howling and clapping his hands. I didn't know it, but he had just become a very rich man. The others in Antony's entourage, all with heavy wagers against me, stared down at me with sullen faces. So, too, Antony.

Without a word of congratulations or a glance at the fallen Celt, Antony finally stood up and departed. His entourage followed until only Horace remained at the benches. He was still clapping his hands and shouting the salute one might offer a victorious gladiator. Finally, he left too, scurrying after the nobles like one of their servants. As for the fallen Celt no one came for the poor fellow. We had to summon a few legionary slaves to carry him off to a doctor – for all the good it would do; he would walk with a crutch for the rest of his life.

I went for a bath afterwards, long before the usual hour. I wanted no company; I was angry at Antony and at the Celt, whom I had been forced to cripple. It was better than getting run through by a spear, I can tell you, but I did not like hurting a man in the practice arena. Nor did I care to be treated like some low-rent gladiator.

I cooled down that evening when my fortune arrived. I expected a note of congratulations from Antony, but no, only the coins, a great mass of them of every description. Most of the money though came in the form of a letter of credit over Mark Antony's signature.

A week or so later, Antony called me to his palace in the city. We met where Antony routinely received his clients each morning; I was first through the door. 'Come in, Dellius.' Antony left his chair and walked toward me. As he was my commander I stood to attention. He was then a very heavy man but still tremendously powerful and wonderfully handsome. He walked around me I think to compare his physique with mine, or perhaps he meant to compare my build with that which he had possessed at my age. I was no Hercules but I was strong enough to hold my own against one.

'I thought we should have a talk about how you managed to lose four of Dolabella's legions in Judaea.'

'They were not Dolabella's legions but mine, Imperator. They were a gift from Claudius Nero, on condition that Dolabella and you would arrange for Nero to be elected the urban praetor.'

'Nero enjoyed his praetorship, but Cassius Longinus received the legions. Without a fight as I understand it. I want to know why that happened.'

'I failed to act as Caesar would have done, Imperator. The real Caesar I mean.'

'Don't let our new Caesar hear talk about the real Caesar, Dellius. He's rather touchy about his shortcomings.'

'I only meant…'

'I know what you meant. What happened? Did you lose your nerve? I've asked several people, but no one tells the same story.'

I began my tale with my arrival in Egypt. I hardly cared to confess to murdering Gaius Trebonius for the sake of taking his head to Allienus. From Egypt to Judaea and there my meeting with the sons of Antipater.

'I had the Queen of Egypt waiting for me if I turned back and Cassius Longinus ready to oppose me in Syria. Once I had learned that Dolabella was dead and that your army had been destroyed, I sought to negotiate with Cassius through the auspices of Antipater. Antipater seemed ready to help me, but of course he was poisoned on the very night we met.'

'And what do you imagine Caesar would have done in your place?'

'With four legions ready to fight? He would have marched through Judaea, slowing down only long enough to persuade another two or three legions of auxiliaries from the Greek cities to join him. In fact, Cassius had nothing like the eight legions he advertised. What few legions he did have were spread across the whole of Syria and Asia Minor. Caesar would have understood that. He would have doubled the speed of his march and arrived at Antioch before Cassius could defend it.'

'So why didn't Quintus Dellius do that?'

'I let the sons of Antipater deceive me with promises.'

I told him the full story of Phasael's betrayal, how he let me imagine I might serve in Judaea and keep command of my legions. 'Two weeks after leaving Egypt, Imperator,

257

I could have been lord of Antioch had I only stopped for a moment to consider what Caesar would have done.'

'You may be right. Then again Cassius might have defeated you as he did Dolabella.'

'Better to go down fighting than lose four legions without lifting a sword.'

'On that we agree, and I have to tell you my chief concern with respect to you is that you lost those legions without a fight. You see, I'd like to offer you a commission as a senior tribune in my guard. More to the point I want you to take command of those men closest to my person all recruited and trained by you. We will be travelling through Asia Minor and Syria next spring,' he added. 'There will be crowds and meetings with dignitaries, sometimes quite a tumult of bodies. I do not expect any trouble, but it is the perfect venue for an assassin to strike, and I cannot think of any man I should like to have closer to me than you.'

I nearly jumped at the chance, but my instincts told me I could have more. 'I will require a prefecture, Imperator. If I am responsible for your safety, I want to have your entire guard under my authority.'

'I already have a prefect of the Guard, lad.'

'Promote him.'

Antony blinked at my impertinence, then surprised me. 'Done,' he said.

'I should like a bonus, as well.'

'Count your five thousand denarii as quite enough bonus,

Dellius. Don't ruin good fortune with too much greed.'

'I won that money at considerable risk to my skin, Imperator. I want the bonus as a courtesy.'

'How much courtesy do you require?'

'I should like to have the horse Cassius Longinus rode at Philippi, the tall red stallion with the narrow blaze and one white sock; you brought the animal to Athens and keep him presently in your stable.'

'That horse and no other?'

'That and no other.'

'But I like that horse.'

'No doubt you do, but the horse was mine before Dolabella stole him from me.'

'Dolabella a horse thief? You can't be serious.'

'It was more of a prank, actually, but of course once Dolabella was dead, Cassius took the horse as his own. When I wrote to Cassius to say that the horse was my property and provided information on how he might confirm the sale of the animal to my father, Cassius ignored my letter. Now you have won the animal by right of conquest, but I want him as a gift from my new patron – that I may know you value me as you ought to do.'

Antony turned to one of his staff. 'Draw up papers for the prefect's command and get him that damn horse – the tall red one I call Cassius.'

At some point in the following days Horace found me in my new apartment inside Antony's palace. He was anxious to give me my share of the winnings. This came in the form of a slave he had purchased on my behalf. As a prefect I would need someone to attend me, he said, and he feared I might be cheated at market, if I went looking on my own for an educated Greek. This one Horace had tested in Greek and Latin. I might trust his grammar as being nearly perfect, only a small issue with the Latin ablative, but he was working on that. I could also count on him to train me in Greek pronunciation, which, Horace told me as kindly as he could, I needed to improve. I was astonished by the generosity of my friend until I learned the amount he had won in his wager, two hundred thousand sesterces from Antony alone, and smaller though quite handsome sums from the others on Antony's staff. Not a bad hour's wage for sitting on a bench. Of course he had risked bankruptcy if I had lost; so I could not complain that he had assumed no risk at all.

Horace reported to me that he would be leaving Antony's service at the first breath of spring, when the sea was open again to traffic. Antony had agreed to award him an honourable discharge owing to a non-existent injury. With this document my friend hoped to get secretarial work with the government in Rome and afterwards begin running in circles where his poetry might help him make a name for himself. He had money now and, possessing good relations with Antony, hoped for patronage either from one of Antony's friends in Rome or, as it actually turned out, someone in Caesar's circle.

I arranged to send money with Horace to give to the patriarch of the Tuscan family with whom I had lived when I first went to Rome. This gentleman, as I mentioned earlier in my history, had assumed responsibility for a debt I had foolishly incurred, and I was happy finally to discharge my obligations to him and even supply a bit of interest in my gratitude. As it turned out, the man had perished in the proscriptions, but the money I sent with Horace went to his heirs, who were understandably rather desperate for it.

XVII
BACCHUS

Asia Minor: Spring, 41 BC

A few weeks after Horace sailed for Italy, Antony's court departed for the orient. Antony's entourage moved through the very provinces that had opposed him only six months earlier, though it was impossible to imagine it by the way people turned out to receive him. One would have thought Bacchus himself had come back to life. Kings and nobles vied for his affection and bandied about the term 'divine' so often that Antony began to believe it. Standing close to him after these great shows of affection, I heard his drinking companions laughing at the oriental's fondness for sycophancy. Antony laughed too, but a month into it one of these rude fellows made a mockery of the elaborate adorations Antony had lately received with a vague reference to one of their debauches in Rome. It was one of those occasions when Antony had ended up vomiting over something or someone of high repute. Antony laughed cheerfully at the memory, but when the fellow had departed he instructed his freedman that he wished never again to see the man.

Antony had come to Asia for money, but of course Cassius had robbed the land of its wealth. No matter: kings found something to give, even if they had to steal it from their neighbours. They wanted Antony happy, for no man, not even Pompey Magnus, excited more terror in the orient than Mark Antony in the wake of Philippi. There were chests full of money instead of the wagonloads of former times. When Antony took his gifts he did not fail to grumble at the miserly offerings. To compensate for their lack of fortune the potentates of Asia recruited fresh dolls from the mountains to play the bride of Bacchus for a single evening. For a season I believe Antony slept only with virgins, sometimes two or three at a go and sometimes only the solitary princess of a local monarch. Wives were offered when there were no suitable virgins available, even sons in a pinch. Theatre, banquets, lectures on the arts, and then a long night of drinking and debauchery. Dionysus himself could not have played the role with more gusto.

My duties were to arrange my men to best advantage and to worry even when there was obviously no danger. Antony let me go about my business as I pleased, but he was watching and judging my abilities. Of course he did not worry over my good opinion of him: he had not concerned himself with the opinion of his fellow senators; why bother with his lowly prefect of the Guard? I am sure, however, he assumed I was impressed by his magnificence. To be honest I found the man too pleased with himself to feel much admiration. I could not help recalling the manner of the divine Julius Caesar, who was sober and abstemious, lest he must begin a march at midnight. A lover of women, yes, but not as the satyr loves them. I could imagine Caesar had been interested in their conversation and quite charming in his seductions. With Antony it was the scream of a torn hymen, then the girl abruptly shoved from his bed.

No, it took me quite a long time to discover the virtues of Mark Antony.

Syria: Summer, 41 BC

Antony received a number of ambassadors from Jerusalem. These men were quick to note the crimes of Phasael and Herod in their roles as procurators of Judaea and Galilee, respectively. They knew the amount of money given to Cassius and complained about the brutal efficiency of Herod, whose mercenary army had fought in defence of Cassius and Brutus. When he had collected all the information he could, Antony told these visitors he fully intended for Phasael and Herod to answer for their actions; he also assured them he would rid both provinces of Roman procurators. This pleased the ambassadors greatly and they returned to Jerusalem in the certain belief that they would have no more dealings with the hated sons of Antipater.

Phasael and Herod, like all the rest of the potentates of the East, had spent all they possessed in support of

Cassius; nevertheless, they dug about their palaces for a few talents of gold. They also dished out the usual platitudes concerning Antony's magnificence, only falling short of calling him a god, as all the rest were so happy to do. Antony apparently did not mind. He knew Jews are loath to call any man a god.

Curiously, neither Phasael nor Herod noticed me. I was one of those faceless creatures in an officer's uniform who attends important men. Then too I stood purposely in the shadows that day because Antony had promised me I would have my chance to confront them. I intended to step forward as an accuser, and I looked forward to watching those two begin with their pathetic excuses.

Antony took their presents as if not much pleased by the paltry offerings, though in comparison to what others had given they were wonderful: finely wrought silver for the banquet hall, a beautiful shield, and silk from the land beyond India. It was more than enough to make a common man wealthy, though insufficient to delight a man of Antony's fortune. Antony set these gifts aside indifferently and said to the brothers, 'My concern is that I counted you both as friends, yet you served Cassius as if he were the one who rode with you into Egypt so many years ago as a comrade-in-arms.'

Herod was the first to speak. 'We helped secure Rome's eastern frontier, Imperator. Not one of our soldiers stood against you at Philippi.'

'By that faithful service you allowed Cassius to bring his entire army against me at Philippi.'

'If I may say so,' Phasael remarked, 'we were obliged to serve Cassius six days a week. On the Sabbath, however, it was Mark Antony for whom we prayed.'

'Well, your prayers were answered. But what I want to know is what happened with Dolabella's man, Quintus Dellius? Do you know the fellow I'm talking about?' Phasael shook his head, though I believed he recognised the name. 'Oh, surely you remember Dellius. He came into Judaea from Egypt with four of Caesar's legions.'

'Oh, yes, Dellius! Of course,' Phasael answered. 'What of him?'

'I am told you imprisoned him.'

'It is a lie. We did no such thing.'

'Dellius, are you a liar?'

I stepped happily out of the shadows intending to level my accusations at these two deceivers. 'I am not, Imperator.'

'Were you imprisoned by Phasael?'

'I was indeed. In Samaria. I lay in chains in a dungeon for nearly a year of my life.'

'If you will allow me to question your man?' This from Phasael, who for all his confidence seemed a bit pale at that moment. Antony nodded his permission, and Phasael said to me, 'Did I escort you to Samaria, Excellency?'

'Not personally.'

'Did my men escort you?'

'You sent me.'

'I sent you? Did you travel under my passport or is it more accurate to say that I merely suggested you travel to Samaria?'

'You had no authority to send me, but you...'

'No authority. Yes, I told you I had no authority to act. I suggested you might be able to keep the peace in the region. I said that could be accomplished if you went to Samaria?'

'Well, yes, but...'

'And while it proved inconvenient for you to remain in chains for so long, it did keep the peace, did it not?'

Antony laughed, but I saw no humour in the joke and pressed my prosecution. 'You told Cassius I was going to Samaria. You betrayed me!'

'I betrayed no confidence. I informed you I would contact Cassius and explain your intentions to serve him.'

'You deceived me with your offer of friendship.'

'I told you what I planned to do, Excellency. You deceived yourself, if you imagined Cassius would not order your immediate arrest. Tell me, in Samaria, were my soldiers there to receive you and keep you imprisoned?'

'Your slaves were there to lead me into a trap.'

'They were not my slaves. The men at the palace in Samaria were acting on orders from a local magistrate. He had surrendered to the Roman prefect who arrested you. The fellow acted to save himself, not to satisfy me. I had no involvement with anything that happened to you in Samaria. I believe I informed you of this matter before you left, so that you might know I could not protect you. Is it so or do I only imagine it?'

He waited for me to answer, but I could not respond. First to be tied up in chains, now to be tied up in a game of sophistry!

'Please, Excellency. Tell me your complaint, if I have wronged you in any manner.'

When I still could not answer him, Antony laughed again, as if he had witnessed a great comedy, which I suppose he had. 'My friends, I have promised a delegation from Jerusalem that I mean to rid Judaea and Galilee of her Roman procurators. I must tell you their pleasure at the news disturbs me. I think they are already up to mischief and want only an incompetent to rule their land so they may start a revolt. But not to worry – my secretary has all their names and will give them to you after our meeting. I believe they hate you because you will not betray Rome; that is high praise for you by my calculations. Dellius here is a perfect example of your treatment of Romans. You might have resisted him with arms or arrested him and placed him in your own prison, but you took care to have no part in harming any Roman. What Romans do to Romans is their business. Rome must not lose such friends. So I am dissolving your positions in Galilee and Judaea as procurators. You will no longer monitor the civilian government but will now act as the absolute rulers of those two provinces, having the power of life and death over anyone, excepting only a Roman citizen. I should like the two of you to recommend two more men to rule in the same fashion over the provinces of Idumaea and Samaria. Four provinces, four rulers. Tetrarchs, if you will. We shall also dissolve the title of Ethnarch of the Jews. Hyrcanus may continue to serve as the High Priest of the Temple but only at the pleasure of the Tetrarch of Judaea. From this time forward that office will have no civil authority over the Jewish people.'

—▬◖▬—

So the sons of Antipater prospered, and I was left looking the fool. I expected consolation from Antony in the aftermath of that meeting, but he had no interest in my feelings. A few weeks after their interview with Antony, however, Phasael and Herod sent me two beautifully crafted gladii of the Spanish style. I carry them still. The pommel of each was formed of ivory and trimmed with steel, the guards were of ivory as well, though likewise trimmed with steel, for these were fighting weapons and not merely for show. The handles were made of a composite of hardwood and inlaid ivory with silver and gold braiding securing the grips. The sheaths were identical, each of Corinthian bronze – a glittering alloy of copper, gold, silver and tin – decorated with precious stones; the scabbards could be clipped tightly together, allowing me to hang both swords together under my right arm.

I could not guess the value of such a gift, nor even consider selling such a prize had I needed the money, but this I can say: after that day I knew why Antipater and his sons were the eternal favourites of Rome.

Tarsus: Summer, 41 BC

Antony settled finally in the harbour town of Tarsus. Tarsus used to be a haven for pirates. It had been lately dressed up a bit. It was not the grandest city Antony might have chosen, but its location was advantageous. Situated between Syria and Asia Minor, it was secured by the sea before it and an impressive mountain range at its back. Antony had begun quarrelling with the Parthians over some principalities east of Syria. He had legions already positioned in Syria with an experienced commander taking the fight into the kingdom of Armenia. He did not expect the Parthians to answer with an invasion into Roman territory, but, in the worst case, if that did occur, Tarsus was well guarded by its mountain range and unlikely to be swiftly overrun.

Antony's interest in Parthia was the same interest all Roman commanders possessed. This was a land of fabled wealth not yet plundered by the Roman sword. The last westerner – which is to say the only westerner – to drive successfully through that great expanse was Alexander of Macedonia, three centuries ago when a Persian monarch ruled the land. To match the accomplishments of Alexander excited the ambition of every great general, Antony no less than Julius Caesar before him. There was also a political excuse. Two decades earlier Rome had lost several legionary standards to the Parthian king, this on an ill-fated campaign into Parthia. The legionaries carrying these standards were long ago dead or utterly lost to lives of abject slavery, but Roman pride would not let their sacred eagles remain hostages forever. The eagles would be returned to Rome or there would never be peace between the two empires. Antony's personal animosity with the Parthians came from the fact that the Parthians had supplied Cassius Longinus with a great many auxiliary troops, including Parthia's famed mounted archers. The Parthians had been under no compulsion to provide men to Cassius. Since they had done so willingly, Antony thought retribution was due.

In retrospect it seems foolish that Antony looked to the east for a fight when all that stood between him and total authority of Rome's vast empire was a sickly coward in Rome. From Antony's perspective, however, Caesar was not really a problem. He expected the young man to simmer slowly in Rome's great cauldron of political and military troubles. No sensible individual gave the lad more than a year or two to live after Philippi. First, his health was precarious, though I had already detected a pattern: Caesar really only grew sick when he was travelling in the direction of a great battle. Second, there was no money in Italy. His legions were filled with aging veterans who were anxious for retirement. The trouble was there was no land to give them unless Caesar first confiscated it from others. Finally, and most critically, young Sextus Pompey, the last living son of Pompey Magnus, owned a fleet of ships and several legions loyal to him. He had lately come out of Spain and seized Sicily, Sardinia, and Corsica as his own. His army might cross to the Italian mainland at any moment, but for the time being Pompey contented himself with a blockade of the western coast of Italy.

I realise that in my discussion of the political state of the empire I have entirely neglected the existence of Lepidus, but that is for good reason. The third member of the Triumvirate and our Pontifex Maximus had lost Sicily and Sardinia without a fight. Rather than building an army and making some attempt at winning back what he had so ignobly lost, Lepidus contented himself with plundering western Africa of its wealth and playing no greater role in Rome's destiny than a provincial governor would have done in other times.

Antony hoped, in the best of circumstances, that his provocations against Parthia might bring about a moral victory at very little cost. The return of the legionary standards to Rome without a long and gruelling campaign would crown Antony with new praise for his wise

272

diplomacy and surely turn public opinion against young Caesar, who hadn't accomplished very much, for all the glory his name evoked.

Failing a negotiated truce, Antony assumed he would have to fight, but for an extended campaign he needed a great deal more money than he possessed. To get it he turned his attention to Egypt. Egypt alone had not lost its wealth to Cassius, and though Cleopatra habitually pled great poverty Antony knew, from his visit to that country in his youth, that he might carry gold out of Egypt by the ton.

Cleopatra liked to claim she had personally led a fleet of ships to Rome in the hope of supporting Caesar and Antony in the run-up to Philippi. This fleet, according to her ambassadors, had been nearly destroyed by storms. Eventually, even though she had wanted to press on, Cleopatra, the leader of that great armada, had been forced to return to Egypt.

The trouble with Cleopatra's tale was that she could offer no proof for any of it. And in fact nobody had even heard the story until after Philippi. Despite Cleopatra's claim of support for the Triumvirs, she had not bothered sending any gifts to Antony, either before or after Philippi. Divine Antony, Bacchus incarnate, thought he deserved better from a girl who owed her very existence to Roman swords.

Antony therefore decided to summon Cleopatra to Tarsus. He meant for her to answer for her insolence and bring gold by the talent, if not the ton. If she refused him or delayed her journey Antony knew he would have no recourse but to send his legions against her. That would do nothing to enhance his reputation and might, in the worst case, risk sending the queen into the arms of the Parthian king. It would be better, he thought, to sweeten his invitation with temptation, Cleopatra's half-sister, Arsinoë. This sister was living in exile at the famed Temple of Artemis in the city of Ephesus. So long as Arsinoë remained alive, Cleopatra's enemies might use the exiled princess to incite another Egyptian civil war. Rather than keep the girl as a threat to the queen, Antony decided he might gain greater advantage by giving Cleopatra what she wanted: the girl's death. But only if Cleopatra came to Tarsus as a supplicant to Bacchus.

I expected Antony to send a legate or senior magistrate to Egypt for the summoning of Cleopatra; instead he thought I would make the perfect ambassador. I can see his thinking at this remove; I had nearly burned the queen's museum. What better message than a summons from the Tuscan barbarian Quintus Dellius? At the time I could only imagine Cleopatra would make me her prisoner if she did not murder me outright. When I protested to Antony that the queen hated me, he scoffed as if dealing with a child.

'You flatter yourself, Dellius. Cleopatra gains nothing but my enmity by harming you.'

'There is always a quiet death by poison.'

'You are my man, Dellius. If the queen forgets it, she is a fool.'

Alexandria, Egypt: Summer, 41 BC

I sailed in the company of a single century of my men, though I had requested two cohorts. I had in addition to these several officers from my Guard. We went in military dress, though no one expected trouble – at least none from the queen. At the port of Alexandria I presented a passport bearing Antony's signature. I expected delays, perhaps even the news that Cleopatra was travelling and unavailable. To my surprise, she invited me to visit her court on the very day I arrived. Perhaps she feared for her books and thought better than to play games with the likes of Quintus Dellius! More likely she was anxious to know how Antony intended to deal with her.

Whatever her reason, I made my way into the palace with a full escort. The queen received me without remarking our previous encounter. She wore a black wig and dark makeup, Egyptian to the bone, but she could not disguise those pale blue Macedonian eyes. This was the skinny blonde actress I had met: the impertinent slave tossing scrolls into a cauldron and calling me Dominus. Cleopatra's son, Caesarion, the purported offspring of her liaison with Julius Caesar, sat on a second throne. As the Egyptians require a husband and wife to rule them,

Caesarion was also his mother's husband. Such customs satisfy the Egyptians' exotic taste, but of course marriages of parent and child leave Romans in a state of physical revulsion. Caesarion was still some years from puberty, so the marriage was, presumably, symbolic. But with that woman who can say? As for his authority, the boy took his orders from his mother, like everyone else.

A great many counsellors and attendants surrounded the two thrones, but I found Nicolas, my former slave, close to Caesarion's throne. As it happened, soon after Cleopatra had persuaded Nicolas to leave me, she had appointed him Caesarion's tutor. Nicolas was only a few years older than the boy, but with his command of several languages he proved the perfect teacher. I had no hope of reclaiming my property at that moment, and I did not wish to give Cleopatra the satisfaction of listening to my complaints; so I said nothing about my ownership of the boy.

I announced in the bluntest manner possible that the Imperator Mark Antony required Cleopatra's presence in Tarsus at once. No flattering titles for the queen, not even Antony's salutation and warm regards. I spoke to the queen as one addresses men who have dropped their swords.

Her answer was in Greek. Practiced in that language by that point I hoped to understand her, but it was so nuanced with ambiguity I needed my secretary to repeat it to me in Latin. The gist of Cleopatra's remark was that she would come in late autumn but if not then, surely sometime the following spring or summer. This was about what I expected, and I answered her promptly. 'Princess Arsinoë will be delighted to learn of your delay.'

This piqued the queen's curiosity, and she said to me in Latin, 'And why should my sister rejoice that I cannot immediately travel to Tarsus?'

'Once you arrive at Tarsus, Antony intends to ask you to decide her fate. As long as you remain in Alexandria the princess may still hope for life and perhaps even a throne.'

Cleopatra's blue eyes cut to one of her eunuch counsellors. He stepped forward at once, announcing in a high-pitched Latin so mellifluous it was nearly impossible to comprehend, 'Her majesty may be able to arrange a journey somewhat sooner than the autumn, though of course there is much to do before she can depart.'

Having accomplished my obligations, I turned without farewell and made for the harbour without seeming to be hasty. There I gave orders to set off at once. We were gone by late afternoon and rowed through two nights without stopping until we came to the Judaean harbour of Ashkelon.

Rome: Summer, 4 BC

A decade after I discovered Nicolas at the court of Cleopatra he joined King Herod's court as counsellor to the king and tutor of his children. By the time I learned that

Nicolas was living in Jerusalem a great many more years had passed. Herod was pleased with the man's service, and my claims of ownership, though still justified, were by then quite ancient. I also lacked sufficient proof that he was my property. Not a soul still living knew Nicolas had ever been my slave, and of course I had no written evidence of it. I could have appealed to Herod's belief in my integrity and so have won my property back, but I had enjoyed a great many gifts from Herod and judged that if I insisted he return my slave I risked the loss of his friendship, for Nicolas was one of his favourites. I was not financially harmed, I had paid nothing for him, and I had endured several years in Egypt in the presence of the fellow without ever complaining to Antony that he was my property. So I let it go. At the time, I congratulated myself on my self-restraint, but two decades afterwards I paid dearly for failing to return the scoundrel to slavery.

Nicolas and I were in Rome arguing before Caesar about the fate of Herod's kingdom – this in the wake of Herod's death. Nicolas supported Archelaus, Herod's eldest surviving son, as a successor to the king. I proposed the elevation of Herod's grandson, Herod Agrippa, the legitimate heir to the throne, though he was then just five years old. There were a great many technical issues to cover in my arguments, including Nicolas's sabotage of Herod's government and the likelihood, in my humble opinion, that Herod's death was in fact an assassination perpetrated by none other than Nicolas and Prince Archelaus. While I was still building the logic of my case and not yet ready to point my finger directly at him, Nicolas apparently guessed my intentions. To neutralise my charges against him, he struck first, declaring he was astonished that a man of my unsavoury character stood in the same room as Caesar.

This unspecified slander against me excited Caesar's interest, for beneath all his dignity Caesar was a hopeless gossip. Pretending to defend one of his 'most noble equites' Caesar asked Nicolas to explain himself or face serious consequences. Nicolas had already written a gushing biography of our revered princeps. To put it plainly, he had no worries about stirring Caesar's wrath. Still, he proceeded diffidently, as if concerned that he may have overstepped. 'I only meant to say that it was Quintus Dellius and no other who instructed Cleopatra on how to seduce Mark Antony before the two villains met at Tarsus. I say this as one who witnessed Dellius's visit to the queen in Alexandria, when he advised her to come in all her splendour to meet Antony, explaining to her in great detail about Antony's tastes in lovemaking.'

This was an obvious attempt to put the blame of all that followed from that disastrous love affair squarely on my shoulders. By that time, strange as it may sound, no one remembered the true nature of Cleopatra; by some accounts she was an unpleasant mix of a sphinx and that murderous creature of the orient, Medea; by other accounts, Cleopatra was only a quarrelsome girl who got swept up in Antony's intrigues. It has never been the Roman way to give women too much responsibility, either in accomplishment or disaster. And of course Nicolas and I were the only ones in Caesar's court that day who knew the truth; so Nicolas's remarks had the authority of an eyewitness. In his version of the event, I became Cleopatra's favourite for my cunning advice and remained in that high station until she discovered that I often arranged a suitable bed mate for Antony whenever he did not sleep with the queen. Further, on those occasions when my selection did not entirely please Antony, I happily fulfilled the role of his lover myself.

I made several protests as these lies were being put into the public record, but Caesar would not allow me to stop the fellow. Nicolas was not passing along idle rumour but stating what he had seen. When Nicolas had finished I stood to defend myself against these scurrilous charges, only to be told by a very pleased Caesar that we were quite off topic and had better attend to the fate of Judaea. I complained that I had been ruined by this harangue and was entitled to answer the charges. At this, Nicolas quipped, 'Perhaps Dellius has some innocent explanation for being so often with Antony in his bed.'

Caesar and his court laughed at this; not one of them doubted that Antony had used me as his girl. I was sixty years of age at that time but still a good hand with a sword. Had I been armed with my gladii, Nicolas would surely have lost his head at a stroke. As it was, I punched him several hard blows before Caesar's praetorian guard wrestled me to submission. Even as they pulled me away Caesar scolded me: 'Come, come, Dellius. We were all young once. There's no reason to be angry because someone has a long memory.'

To his inner circle that evening Caesar quipped, 'I suppose it is time I admit our friend Quintus Dellius was not the Horse Changer I have always imagined, riding one horse and then another according to the political winds, but the horse so many rode!' Great fun on the Palatine.

Instructing Cleopatra how to seduce Mark Antony! Yes, and in my spare time I teach crows to caw and cobras how to curl up inside baskets.

Tarsus and Alexandria: Summer, 41 BC

When Cleopatra arrived in Tarsus in her royal barge Antony was on business in the city, adjudicating the claims of a couple of landowners, as I recall. All very dull stuff, but of course the city had turned out to watch the imperator. When word came that Cleopatra's magnificent vessel had docked, the entire city fled the agora and raced to the harbour. Plaintiff and defendant remained before Antony as well as Antony's Guard; otherwise the Forum was empty. Antony instructed the men to continue their arguments. He was not about to compromise his dignity by running down with the rest of the mob to have a look at the queen's great ship. The two litigants, however, begged permission to be allowed to settle. They were too eager to see Cleopatra to worry about boundary lines.

So Antony alone snubbed the queen, though I doubt she noticed it. He had me deliver an invitation to her for dinner that night. This gave me the chance for a look at her ship: it was festooned with flowers, trimmed in gold, and propelled by silver-tipped oars. Its size required six hundred oarsmen. At dock the vessel was magnificent; at sea, I expect it sailed as gracefully as a rudderless raft. When I delivered Antony's invitation, Cleopatra claimed she could not leave her ship. She was utterly exhausted by her long journey. She did, however, suggest that Antony might come to her that evening, if he cared to indulge in her ship's meagre offerings.

I suppose Antony was actually curious to see the barge, which now everyone in the city but Antony had seen; so he accepted the invitation despite his better judgment. I believe he had become inured to eastern sycophancy and found the queen's impertinence refreshing. At any rate, he boarded the ship and feasted his way through twenty courses of meagre offerings. Meats, sauces, fish of every variety, exotic fruit from Africa and the orient, and even, I am told, vegetables from Italian farmlands. All delivered by nubile black maidens clad only in diamonds and pearls. These girls were happy to tease the imperator at every service but left the queen to finish her guest off, with her hand and coconut milk, as I learned from the guards I had posted onboard. Antony staggered from the queen's barge at noon next day. The whole city, gathered at the docks for the occasion, roared with applause, just as fellows will do when a groom leaves his new bride on the morning after their wedding.

Next evening, Antony invited Cleopatra for dinner at his residence. This was supposed to be a banquet to equal the queen's sumptuous fare, but he had no servants to match her staff. Midway through what he had hoped would be the finest cuisine the queen had ever enjoyed, Antony turned to me with orders to execute the chef. I took this as a joke, but the chef learned of the remark and spent several days in hiding.

Having no hope of impressing the queen either with his dignity or his borrowed staff and palace, Antony surrendered. He ordered me to sail to Ephesus and arrange the execution of Arsinoë on the steps of the Temple of Artemis, for all to see. She was strangled with a piece of knotted silk, this a gift from Cleopatra. I oversaw the affair but let another take the poor girl's life. This murder broke any number of laws and religious sanctions and exposed me, once again, to the outrage of Artemis, had the goddess actually existed. In the meantime, Antony and Cleopatra sailed away blissfully to Alexandria in the queen's golden barge.

XVIII
THE PARTHIANS

Galilee: March, 40 BC

As my reward for attending to the execution of Arsinoë, Antony did not require me to follow him to Egypt. Instead, he provided me with a thousand Spartans from his Guard and sent me to Galilee. Officially, I was there to liaise between Antony's legions in Syria and Herod's army in Galilee. In practice, the job was chiefly administrative. I had to make sure couriers were set up for runs down the Judaean highway as far as Ashkelon. From there, ships took these reports to Alexandria.

As an intelligence officer I thought no one had more current information than I did, but one morning Herod came to me with news that there had been a revolt in northern Italy. Caesar's problem, I answered. 'Perhaps it is,' Herod said, 'but I suggest you inform Antony of the matter at once.'

I sent Antony what little I knew. Some days later Herod had more information. The revolt turned out to be something more than a local uprising; the leaders were none other than Fulvia, Antony's wife, and Antony's brother, Lucius. Joining these two was the freshly retired praetor, Claudius Nero.

I was not anxious to be the first to inform Antony of these matters and remarked that Antony must surely know about it. Herod's response startled me. 'Only if he ordered the revolt, Dellius. The news is five days old.'

Of course that was impossible, at least in so far as I understood the world. When I said so, Herod told me about his carrier pigeons. Antipater had long before established dovecotes in Italy, Macedonia, Asia Minor, and throughout the provinces of Judaea. The news he gave me had passed from bird to bird at the rate of sixty miles an hour! When I still would not believe him, he showed me one of his pigeons and then sent a message to Jerusalem. Within an hour another bird returned with an answer to his question. I suspected this was some kind of parlour trick, for I really could not comprehend such speed. Herod understood my scepticism, however, and explained how his family had come to learn about the secrets of this race of bird. He told me that centuries ago the Persians had discovered the male bird of certain types of pigeons have the power to find their nests even if they are hundreds of miles away. By creating dovecotes for these birds every two or three hundred miles, one might send messages across thousands of miles in a matter of a day or two, not weeks.

Only then did it dawn on me that the use of birds

in Judaea and Syria had made it possible for the Roman prefect who had arrested me in Samaria to know my intentions to travel before I had even departed. It also explained why Herod and Phasael knew within an hour of my crossing into Judaea that I was coming with an army of four legions. So they had arrived at Ashkelon on the very evening of the day I sent my ultimatum. I had very little time to reflect on these matters at that time, though I was later much fascinated with the flight of birds. I actually bred the birds in the hope of selling the concept to Caesar, but Caesar in old age was quite as dull as Caesar in his youth. He thought I had a brilliant idea if I could only get the same bird to fly in two directions.

Lebanon and Galilee: May, 40 BC

Though I was fairly sure Antony had incited the revolt in Italy or at least given his tacit permission, I sent the news to Alexandria. A week later Herod informed me that Caesar's man, Marcus Agrippa, had made short work of the revolt. Fulvia and Antony's brother had been captured.

I sent another courier to Antony with this fresh news and received his response a week later. I was to ride to the harbour town of Tyre and await his arrival. I took most of my staff with me, as well as three hundred Spartans for escort. Once there, we waited several weeks for Antony's fleet to arrive.

During that same period the Parthians suddenly broke across the border and defeated Antony's legions in Syria. Those cohorts managing to escape fled to Tyre in the hope of finding rescue. By the time Antony's fleet arrived, the situation had become critical. The Parthians had begun to lay siege to the city walls. Antony soon concluded that he hadn't enough ships to transport all of his men. Rather than abandon them, he sent to Tarsus for additional transport ships. We waited a desperate week, fighting at the city walls day and night until the ships from Tarsus arrived. When all was ready, Antony ordered his men to abandon the defence of the city and begin boarding the ships.

As Antony's prefect of the Guard I fully expected to join Antony's flagship. My only concern was securing passage for Hannibal, but when I attempted to arrange this, one of Antony's legates informed me that Antony wanted to speak with me. Antony had remained onboard his ship throughout the siege and was anchored close to the mouth of the harbour. During the week we had waited for the ships from Tarsus, I fought on the city walls. I had sent Antony several reports but had not met with him since his arrival. It took nearly an hour to get through the mass of ships in that harbour and board his flagship. Once onboard I waited another hour until I was escorted into his presence.

Antony had no time for greetings. As soon as I appeared before him, he ordered me to take my cohort of Spartan auxiliaries out of the city and return to Galilee. I was stunned, for it seemed to me that Antony had no idea what he was asking of me. First, getting out of the city with only three hundred men for escort might prove impossible. Beyond that, I could not imagine what he expected me to accomplish with such a meagre force. 'If the Imperator expects me to help to defend the Galilean border, might I request a legion?'

'I wish I could afford it. As matters stand, I require every fighting man I have to sail with me to Italy.'

'Herod does not have an army of sufficient size to stop the Parthians, Imperator.'

'I know that, Dellius. I want you there to make sure Herod and Phasael do not join the Parthian alliance.'

'If they decide to abandon Rome, I don't see how I can stop them.'

Antony went to a small sea chest that he had set up in the corner of his room. Unlocking it, he pulled two vials from a row of a half-dozen and handed them to me. 'If you cannot kill them by force of arms, murder them by stealth. My fear is that if the sons of Antipater join the Parthians, Egypt will fall within a matter of weeks. That simply must not happen.'

For many years I thought that Antony worried for Cleopatra's life. Old age has let me see the matter more clearly. Antony could hope to recover Syria and the Jewish provinces as long as Egypt remained an ally of Rome, but if Egypt was lost as well, it would mean the end of his Imperium.

Antony sailed for Athens on the same evening that we spoke. Using the cover of darkness, I broke out of the city with my staff and three hundred Spartan auxiliaries. We had some fighting with the Parthian camp guarding the road to the south of the city, but after we broke through their defences we had an open road, which we followed at full gallop.

Athens: Summer, 40 BC

In the wake of their defeat, Fulvia and Lucius Antony were given their lives, but Caesar exiled them both from Italy. Claudius Nero, their co-conspirator, had managed to escape the city before its fall and spent the summer as a fugitive. I learned much later that Nero's escape and subsequent survival in a hostile land was due in large part to the services of a loyal freedman and to his wife, Livia. At the time, I only knew that poor, dull Nero was the most wanted man in Italy.

As for Antony's wife and brother, they sailed to Athens to meet Antony, who had arrived there with his fleet and was attempting without success to communicate with Caesar in Rome. Antony was still awaiting a response when his mother arrived in Athens. Publically, she claimed she had fled Rome out of fear for her life, but in fact, the old girl was not quite the timid matron she pretended. On her way to Athens she had stopped in Sicily. Sextus Pompey asked her to tell Antony that he was not only willing but anxious to form an alliance and help him in his fight against Caesar.

Fulvia and Lucius fervently backed the idea of a new alliance but Antony could see no value in it. He would still be sharing power and, to his thinking, as he admitted to me some years later, it was better to share his authority with 'the little twit' than with Sextus Pompey, who actually knew how to fight.

He did not rebuff Pompey at once. Rather he left the offer open as he sailed to Italy at the head of a fleet of four hundred ships.

Brindisi: Summer, 40 BC

Antony was not permitted entry at the harbour of Brindisi. Rather than risking all on a naval battle, he sailed on and found anchorage at Taranto, due west across the isthmus. This permitted him to lay siege to Brindisi from the landward side of that city. Caesar's forces, commanded by Marcus Agrippa, soon arrived and forced Antony to lift his siege.

Over the course of several days cavalry skirmishes between Agrippa's and Antony's forces ensued. Then, once Caesar had arrived, the two armies faced one another. Curiously, the legions on both sides refused the order to advance into battle.

It was of course not as simple as that. Antony had

informed his centurions that should any of the men call across the lines and ask for a truce there would be no disciplinary action. So up and down the line Antony's legionaries called to Caesar's men. This was not Philippi. There was no reason for a fight. The legions loved both Antony and Caesar; the legions ought to insist on negotiations.

Caesar's men, tired of so many fights against Roman forces and fearing Antony's reputation for unpredictability, soon responded. Caesar and Agrippa had no choice but to enter into talks with Antony. Hostages were the first to cross the no man's land between the two armies; then finally the leaders met and a truce was sworn.

Once again Caesar and Antony made a pact without consulting Lepidus. This time Caesar gained the advantage, receiving all of northern Gaul to go with Gaul's coastal province and with it the eleven legions stationed there; for his part Antony got a new wife, Octavia, the elder sister of young Caesar. Fulvia, Antony's former wife, had remained at Athens. By a happy coincidence Fulvia became ill soon after Antony left her. Before Antony could ask for a divorce, he learned she was already dead.

Lucius Antony also died of stomach ailments that same summer. As part of the negotiations, he had been awarded a governorship in Andalusia but died while still on his journey to Spain. Most suspected Caesar, but for years after Antony always had a shifty look whenever he accused Caesar of the crime.

Judaea: Spring, 40 BC

The Parthians that had invaded Syria were led by a proscribed Roman commander named Quintus Labienus. This Labienus was the son of Titus Labienus, second-in-command to Gnaeus Pompey in Spain, proving – if proof is required – that it is a small world for the Roman aristocracy.

Labienus, with a clear understanding of the crisis in Italy, took advantage of Antony's predicament and, having seized Syria, turned next to Galilee. Herod sacrificed no lives in a losing struggle at the border. Instead, he retreated into Judaea where he took command of the armies of his fellow tetrarchs. As Antony had expected, Herod received friendly correspondence from Labienus. Herod might share in the riches of Asia and Egypt, if he would only join him.

Herod spurned the offer but not without informing me of it first. When he told me about it he added that his brother had been contacted too. I knew of both offers before Herod informed me, for I had men under my command bribing servants to keep watch. Whether Herod understood this or not, I cannot say, but I do know that he did not appear to be tempted by the offer.

Of course Labienus, once rebuffed by Herod and Phasael, had only to make his offer to the outcast royalty of Judaea. This faction was led by the nephew of Hyrcanus, a charismatic young prince named Antigonus. Antigonus embraced the alliance at once, and soon incited rioting in a number of Judaean cities. Herod's forces answered these challenges admirably, but once the Parthians broke into Judaea, Herod had no choice but to find shelter with Phasael behind the high walls of Jerusalem.

Jerusalem: Summer, 40 BC

Jerusalem was not then as well-fortified as it would be some thirty years later. The chief deficiency was the citadel, which had no access to large reservoirs of water. The city gates were quite strong, but they were not well defended against attack from inside the city. In later years Herod would erect the magnificent Antonia Fortress to the north of the Temple Mount. This massive citadel defended much of the northern perimeter of the city on both sides of the wall.

Herod did what he could with the resources he had. He ranged most of his army along the northern walls and sent the remainder of his troops out before the gates to keep the land clear of siege machines. For a time the fight might have gone either way. When rioting broke out inside the city, however, the city's defence grew more problematic. Late one afternoon, partisans of Prince Antigonus inside the city attacked the gates. After a brief skirmish, they were able to open them up to Antigonus's army. Those of Herod's men holding the ramparts along the northern perimeter of the city were cut off from retreat. Most threw down their weapons at once. Those who fought on were slaughtered where they stood.

I was tasked with keeping supply lines open to the south of the city and found myself routinely skirmishing with Parthian archers, who devoted themselves to harassing caravans bringing grain and other essential supplies along the road from Bethlehem. When I learned the Parthians had broken into the city in the north I brought my men through the southernmost gate as quickly as possible. While the fighting still raged in the northern quadrant, we readied a defence of the citadel.

Jerusalem's citadel is now situated along the western wall of the city and fortified by great towers designed by Herod's most trusted architect. In those days the citadel was set upon a ridge of hills at the eastern edge of the city, just south of the Temple Mount. High walls and towers guarded the palace from attack from forces inside the city. The outer walls were built over the Kidron Valley, making siege engines impractical. The citadel provided sufficient space to house a thousand or so combatants, and of course the palace was home to Antipater's four sons as well as his daughter and her husband. On this occasion, however, there were also more distant relatives taking refuge. With my cavalry of a thousand Spartan auxiliaries, our numbers pushed the total to some two thousand fighting men in all, with another three or four hundred non-combatants, including servants and slaves. We were safe for a week or so, but at that point, assuming we could still defend the walls, we would be facing diminishing supplies and a chronic lack of water.

Before matters became desperate, Herod and Phasael called the nobility together to discuss our options. I joined the meeting too. Everyone sitting in that room knew he would not survive capture; we were all men marked for death, and yet the overwhelming concern was how best to protect the families. Some believed if Prince Antigonus swore an oath before the people to spare the women and children we might hope for mercy for them, at least. Herod was not convinced. He said he had no faith in Prince Antigonus, recalling for our consideration the time before the Romans came, when Antigonus's grandfather crucified fellow Judaeans and then brought their wives and children before them as they hung on their crosses. That he might inflict even more cruelty upon those men already dying, he ordered the throats of their wives and children cut; thus, each family utterly perished as its patriarch watched helplessly from his cross. Such were the forbears of Prince Antigonus.

Phasael agreed with his brother. Antigonus could not be trusted to keep his oath. In fact, as an aspiring king, Antigonus would be sure to inflict terrible cruelties on the families of his enemies, signalling to his future subjects the danger of resisting his authority. The only hope, Phasael said, was flight. The fortress of Masada was thirty miles due south through the Judaean desert. With luck most of the civilians might make it there. That was assuming we escaped at night without the enemy realising it. It was possible, Phasael explained, to leave the citadel quietly using the sewers. Those who could not make the journey ought first to be killed, he said, that they might die quickly and not endure torture at the hands of Antigonus. Phasael included in this number his own mother and all of the smallest children.

Herod would have none of it. He thought it possible to use carts and wagons and carriages so that the weakest might be transported to Masada along with the rest. Another answered that if we took carts and wagons we must leave by the city gate. In that case we could not escape unnoticed. Others agreed with this opinion. 'Trying to save the lives of the weakest will get us all killed.'

'The only way for all of us to make it out is to send the cavalry away some days before the rest of us escape,' Herod answered. 'That will give them time to gather wagons and carts and bring them to us on the night the rest of us leave the city.'

'If we depart after sunset next Sabbath,' Phasael added, 'we will have a new moon.'

'Surely they will be looking for escape on just such a dark night,' one of Herod's generals answered.

'I will go to Antigonus at sundown,' Herod answered. 'I will tell him that we intend to surrender at sunset next day, once the Sabbath has concluded. My only condition will be that he swears to pardon our fighting men and spare the lives of our women and children. While I am negotiating with him, Phasael can lead the civilians to Masada. As for the soldiers, they can escape south to Nabataea.'

'You are needed to lead the retreat,' Phasael answered. 'I will negotiate the surrender.'

The brothers argued, for it was obvious to both of them that the man who remained behind would perish miserably at the hands of Prince Antigonus. Neither wanted to live so much that he would sacrifice his brother. In the end, Phasael announced it would not do for the tetrarch of Galilee to negotiate the surrender of Jerusalem. Phasael insisted the city was his to command and his to surrender. He would leave the citadel. He would negotiate with Antigonus.

At this point old Hyrcanus, to his glory, spoke up. He would accompany the tetrarch in his role as High Priest of the Temple. He would insist that Antigonus spare the women and children for the sake of their family's reputation. Antigonus was, after all, his brother's son and such a plea for the family name would be credible if he was there to make it. He added that if two dignitaries went out of the citadel Antigonus would also be less likely to suspect intrigue.

'And when he discovers you only meant to delay him?' Herod asked the old man.

Hyrcanus smiled bravely. 'By then I hope you will have taken our families safely away. My nephew is not a man who accepts disappointment lightly.'

There were a great many other matters to settle. Chief among these was to decide where and exactly when to meet a small force of cavalry from Masada. These were contacted by a carrier pigeon, with a confirmation returning a few hours later. Herod arranged for the meeting at the third hour of the Sabbath morning at a mountain twenty miles south of Jerusalem. Today there is a city there, which Herod built in memorial of his flight from Jerusalem. Then it was a desolate piece of ground that looked something like an enormous haystack.

He arranged for the infantry to pack what they would need for the journey: tools, weapons, medical supplies, food and water. There was of course some chance of discovery during the escape, in which case he appointed certain of the units to arrange for the wholesale execution of the families, that their deaths might at least come quickly.

<hr />

An hour before sundown, two nights before the Sabbath commenced, I led our cavalry out of the citadel. We fought a short way through the city before coming to the southern gate. There, we took a barrage of light missiles; these were arrows and javelins and stones slung down from the ramparts. I sent a century of men on foot against those on the ramparts; another century dismounted to take the gates. We were gone before reinforcements arrived.

But of course that was only the start of it. We had not cleared the plain when a cohort of mounted archers came after us. Rather than letting them pursue us at their leisure,

I turned back at once to face them. I had been fighting these fellows since my escape from Tyre. Experience had taught me their habits by heart. They are like pestering gnats, not especially dangerous but decidedly irritating. At first they have no effect on a large force of cavalry; only the occasional arrow connects with a rider or horse. Even then the wound is rarely life-threatening. That is their job: they hover around a numerically superior force striking from a distance of twenty or thirty paces, then race off at the first sign of a threat against them. Of course as they depart they always send one last arrow at those who give chase, the so-called 'Parthian Shot'. The moment the threat against them ceases, they return and commence launching arrows again.

Attack them in earnest and they will scatter. The answer to this tactic is to break apart with them, using ever-smaller phalanxes of lancers to chase them down. The Parthian archers wear no armour beyond some thick padding at their chests and backs; these are quite effective at dampening the force of an arrow but worth nothing against a heavy lance. Once within range of our lances they came down as easily as fleeing legionaries in a rout.

In the first attack against them we left nearly twenty of them on the field, killed or wounded. The moment I called our men back, the Parthians stopped fleeing and rallied for a second assault. We, in the meantime, crossed the plain and formed a line behind the first hills. This was perhaps a mile from the city walls. Those of our men who had lost their horses in the city or on the field now snatched up whatever free horses they could find after our first fight. Some of my Spartans had been wounded, but most were still able to ride.

We waited like a line of infantry, and soon enough the archers returned. We held our positions for as long as we could then broke from cover in several tight phalanxes, chasing them down as before. This fight lasted less than a quarter of an hour. By then the sun had set and the Parthians, fearing envelopment, rode back to the city. Once free of our pursuers we took up those men unable to ride. We gathered our dead as well and departed for the Judaean desert.

Herod had provided scouts who knew the way to the Engedi. This is a lush green valley cutting through the hard, dry desert hills. Here we might find enough cover to hide away some nine hundred and seventy men and horses. Not that it mattered. In the two days we waited we saw no scouting parties looking for us. As far as the enemy was concerned, we had fled Jerusalem with no intention of returning.

At the close of the second day we brought our horses out of that great canyon and headed back in the direction of Jerusalem. As we travelled I sent scouting parties out to appropriate whatever carts and wagons they could find. In addition, we commandeered several carriages and even some litters.

XIX
FLIGHT

Southern Judaea: 11ᵗʰ June, 40 BC

An hour before sunset and the commencement of the Jewish Sabbath, Phasael and Hyrcanus walked out of the citadel. They were immediately arrested and taken before Prince Antigonus. Phasael offered to open the gates of the citadel at sunset next day, which marked the Sabbath's end. In exchange he asked immunity for his mercenary soldiers and for the lives of the women and children in his party. He made no bargain for the lives of the others. Believing my cavalry had abandoned the citadel, Prince Antigonus had no reason to doubt Phasael's sincerity. Nor could he see any advantage in refusing the offer. So the sun set, and the Sabbath began with the promise of a twenty-four-hour truce.

———

Since the departure of my cavalry Herod had rearranged his sentries. They stood along the citadel ramparts close to towers and pillars. They did not move either at night or during the day. Once darkness fell over the city on the Sabbath eve, these sentries were replaced by uniforms stuffed with straw. They were held in place by ropes and timbers, exactly as the living sentries had stood. Herod then ordered everyone to gather in the sewers. He hoped the ruse of the sentries might last through the night.

At the third hour of the night, Herod began sending his infantry through the tunnels. These were followed by the families, the servants – including my secretary – and all the nobility. Herod and his Guard came last. The way was narrow and required the party to proceed in single file. The first ones out of the tunnel waited nearly an hour for the last. They could not be seen from the city walls, the night was pitch black, but neither could they see where they stepped.

I met Herod's party in the fourth hour of the night, just as the last of his party escaped the sewers. I brought with me the wagons, carts, litters, and carriages my scouting parties had been able to collect. The vehicles had seemed quite satisfactory on the roads, but on uneven ground they creaked and groaned incessantly. Nor were there enough for those who needed to ride. The ground was stony and uneven and great numbers went down as they tried to walk. After that they were unable to continue without assistance. Herod ordered the men in his Guard to help those who could no longer walk. But the cost was time. It took more than an hour to cross the plain.

Young mothers held the mouths of the youngest children. They whispered and prayed: 'Be good, child. Be still; on your life, be still!' Sensing the fear in everyone around them, some of the very youngest cried out in terror. These shrieks were soon muffled, but no one knew if they had been heard in the city. If riders came to investigate, all would be lost.

With only his infantry to command, Herod might have counted his escape complete once safely beyond the city walls. Fighting men could have run thirty miles before dawn. With so many elderly and children in his train, his work was only beginning.

A child shrieked and then fought the hand that muffled the cry. A wagon wheel hit a stone with an awful crack. Horse hooves clapped against the hardpan. And every time some awful sound erupted we all turned into cowards. I cannot count the times I looked at the city wall. I could see nothing beyond the dark silhouettes of its towers cutting into the night sky, but for all that I could not stop myself looking back.

Having no road, the carts and wagons actually slowed our progress. And the longer we went the more people needed them. At some point an axle broke on the biggest wagon, for it was terribly overloaded. In the face of such disaster any sensible commander would have abandoned his plan. Almost three hours after the escape we had yet to travel three miles. Herod's resolve, however, never wavered.

In this party he had his wife and son and mother and sister. With assorted nephews and nieces, old friends of his father, their wives and children and even their grandchildren, he could not bear to abandon the civilians, even if it cost him his own life.

Phasael was the wiser of the two brothers. He ought surely to have made the better king, for he was a creature of court life and knew to kill the weakest when necessary; but only Herod could have forced his will on us that night and by doing so saved everyone, from the most ancient to the very youngest.

—◦—

When we could no longer carry the injured or fit them all on the wagons, I ordered our cavalry to let those who needed to ride take their horses. This meant most of my men walked at the side of their animals for the sake of one whose strength had given out. I meant to stay mounted so that I might supervise the column with Herod, but I soon discovered a young woman limping and in obvious pain. As it happened this was Salome, Herod's sister, though I did not realise it until she was atop Hannibal and we had begun talking.

Salome was my age, a decade younger than Herod, and naturally already married, though yet without children. I expect Salome thought we had only a few hours more to live; I know I did. This escape was moving too slowly for us to have any hope of getting clear of Jerusalem. Knowing our lives had likely come to an end, we spoke of anything but that. I would have thought I had nothing in common with this girl from the orient, but Salome was quite well travelled and thoroughly acquainted with a number of the great cities I had seen. So we talked about architecture, of all things. Throughout our exchange Salome betrayed no fear of what might come next, though as a young woman of high station she had to know what happens to women before they are killed. 'I do not care for the gigantic proportions of it,' she said, 'but there is no temple in all the world as perfectly made as the one dedicated to Serapis in Alexandria.'

'Not even in Ephesus?' I asked. I did not like the simple lines and massive stones of the temple dedicated to Serapis, but I had been overawed by the Temple of Artemis at Ephesus.

'There is no art in Ephesus,' Salome answered. 'It is all a grand mishmash of columns and porches put together over centuries. There is no order to any of it. I prefer the tiny Temple of Vesta in Rome. I know it is not the popular opinion, but a thing perfectly proportioned is far grander than a heap of stones covering acres of ground.'

Talking so earnestly about the wonders of our world, I kept recalling with a jolt of dread that I was likely going to be dead in a few hours, but before I could dwell on such matters, the young woman drew me back from my despair.

It was one of those peculiar nights that makes for a lifelong friendship, for though I might not marry Salome without first submitting to circumcision, nothing at all prevented us in later years from an intimate friendship that served us both. All because of a bruised heel.

—◦—

At dawn we found a road, and Herod ordered us to march at double-time. The carts and wagons rumbled more quickly. The riders, often two per horse, bumped along uncomfortably as the animals were pushed into a trot; the cavalrymen jogged beside their mounts. I sent scouts to look for the cavalry coming from Masada. I ordered others back to watch for the enemy coming from Jerusalem. We passed Bethlehem, some eight miles from Jerusalem. We needed to cover another twelve miles before we could hope for the Masada cavalry to relieve us of our party of civilians.

Of course in Bethlehem there were partisans of the rebels who would send word to Prince Antigonus that we were fleeing Jerusalem. Eight miles by road to the city on foot would give us two hours. If someone went by horseback we might see the first Parthian archers within the hour.

Three miles more passed without incident, but at that point a great many of us had begun looking to our horizons: rescue from the south, attack from the north. Herod, on horseback, moved from the front of our line to the back, calling to everyone on foot to keep pace. He feared we might need to form our defences quite suddenly. And then finally one of my scouts came from the north. The Parthians, he reported, had not yet left Jerusalem.

Herod called a halt. We ate and drank our fill, resting a full hour. Those departing from the city had been moving for over twelve hours. My cavalry and I had been travelling for eighteen. I rested like the others, but I did so in the company of my officers, that we might arrange our forces for the coming fight.

—⟪⟫—

Back to our feet, sated and sore. Hard work even persuading the horses to move. Two, three, four miles slipping by.

Finally we came to the base of the hill Herod intended to use for his camp. Infantry and civilians alike began digging a trench along the edge of the plain. Behind the trench others brought stones down the mountain to build a low wall. To the back of the camp the mountain rose up steeply enough that very little was needed in the way of defensive works; our wagons and carts and carriages created enough of a barrier.

While the camp was still being fortified, my scouts returned from the road to the south. The Masada rescuers had not yet left the mountain. If they were coming they were still more than two hours away.

At that point I ordered seven hundred of my Spartan cavalry behind the crest of the mountain. The others remained at Herod's camp. I put scouts high on the mountaintop to watch for the enemy's approach. At their signal I came forward to see what we faced. Because it was a Sabbath, the Jewish regiments under the command of Antigonus had remained in Jerusalem. That meant we were fighting only the Parthians, a thousand cataphracts and some three or four hundred mounted archers, those same archers we had decimated at Jerusalem.

Our numbers and position gave us a slight advantage, but cataphracts are ultra-heavy cavalry, impervious to light missiles and even swords. They cover themselves and their horses with chainmail; they encase both their heads and the heads of their horses with iron masks. In our only fight against these faceless iron monsters some weeks earlier we had suffered heavy losses. Afterwards, I did everything I could to avoid engaging with them. But this time, like it or not, we had to fight them.

—◦⦿◦—

As per their custom, the archers came forward while the cataphracts waited a furlong behind them. My tribunes at Herod's camp ordered our cavalry to attack the archers, two hundred Spartan lancers against twice that number of archers. We were practiced at this game and knew to use tight formations so that one rider might cover another. In that manner we chased them down, breaking our phalanxes apart as they scattered and tried to regroup at our flanks.

As soon as we began winning this fight the cataphracts came forward. On pre-arranged orders, our riders refused to engage and fell back to either side of Herod's defensive works. With cataphracts now holding a position close to Herod's camp, the archers returned. For Herod's makeshift wall to provide any shelter, his infantry were obliged to stay down. As for the civilians, they found cover under the wagons and carts. For the moment no one cared about harming them. Some of the Parthian archers tried to flank our camp; most contented themselves with lofting their arrows high overhead, letting the missiles rain down on the camp. A few of Herod's men were wounded, but most kept themselves covered with their shields.

⸺◈⸺

The moment the Parthian attack commenced, I sent my forces to either side of the mountain. At the beginning we were unseen by the enemy. Once we broke from cover we formed into six long columns and pushed the horses into a gallop as we swept around the enemy and came toward the backs of the cataphracts.

Each column was comprised of one hundred twenty riders, four abreast and thirty deep. The idea, in the abstract, was to drive eight columns into the midst of the cataphracts, our six columns plus the cavalry at either wing of Herod's line. Hitting all sides simultaneously, we hoped to break through the outer perimeter and drive toward the centre.

This was not utterly suicidal. By the concentration of force a few dozen men can soon crash through any line. It is an especially effective technique against cavalry, where animals under the stress of assault quite naturally panic and give ground. Once in the midst of the enemy, I hoped our superior quickness would neutralise the advantage of the enemy's heavier armour. The trailing riders in each of the eight columns had orders to close down the perimeter, that we might keep the fight contained.

Before we hit the cataphracts, the archers came for us. Every man leaned close to his mount, covering himself with his shield. Because of our formation, the archers had some play at only one-in-four riders. Men and horses were hit but very few went down. An arrow scorched my thigh early in the charge. I had been intercepting another with my shield and simply did not see it coming. With a screaming curse I pulled the dart free. I saw blood seeping from the wound, but there was no spurt, which is the real danger. No matter. There was nothing to be done for it. I had either to fight or get trampled by my own men.

Foam gathered at Hannibal's bit; the pure white froth of a racing horse covered his neck. I hugged down close and tried to ignore the searing pain in my thigh. I was in the vanguard of my column, first to crash into the enemy. The man I came against pierced my shield with his lance. The force of the impact ripped the thing from my grip. My own spear slipped under his shield as I had intended but accidentally caught the pommel of his saddle. At impact, the shaft of my spear shattered.

We passed by one another, he to receive the fury of the men in my column, I to greet another iron mask charging me. I drew one of my swords and turned Hannibal into the flank of another rider, the way ships ram into one another. As we crashed into this animal, I swung my sword down across the rider's arm. I could not cut flesh through Parthian chainmail, but bone was still vulnerable and the rider dropped his spear.

I pulled my second sword and spun Hannibal, looking for another fight. The enemy was everywhere, but so too were those who had ridden in my column. I hooked an arm about the head of a man in a fight with one of my Spartan auxiliaries. As easily as that, I pulled him from his mount. At my own flank a rider came closing in and swung his sword at Hannibal's neck. I parried the stroke, then turned Hannibal into him, letting Hannibal's superior strength drive him back. As we fought, swords clashing, I heard Hannibal's scream. He reared above the smaller horse, striking with both hooves and biting the chainmail covering the enemy's mount.

One of my men closed behind the fellow and knocked him to the ground. I spun Hannibal about and charged another rider, ramming into the smaller horse. The other horse cried out and shied away, leaving its rider struggling to keep his seat. I had no chance to grab this rider's head, so I hacked at his wrist instead. His sword dropped, and I spun Hannibal on his haunches, looking for the next fight.

We lunged into another rider but were also hit by a man coming behind us. Hannibal gave another scream of rage and kicked at the animal with both back legs. The enemy's mount shied from this attack and I was saved from a sword swung at my head.

There was no line, no order to any of it; the fight was everywhere. A melee of swords and shields. Horses rammed into one another, reared up or gave vicious kicks, fighting like the men on their backs, and for a long time it seemed that neither side could gain an advantage.

Then suddenly we saw Herod's infantry wade into the fight. After that, melee turned to massacre.

The men on the ground came in pairs. One carried a shield and sword; the other a sword and dagger. These weapons slipped under the chainmail skirts of the Parthian mounts. Once a horse went down, the rider generally fell to the ground too. If by chance he landed on his feet, Herod's infantry tackled him. In any event, after he was on his back, killing him as he struggled to get up was as simple as giving his head a hard kick or a quick turn.

Our cavalry continued to engage the enemy, knocking them from their horses if possible, but Herod's infantry did most of the killing. I was turning, looking for another fight, when a wounded horse came backing away from a sword thrust and bowled broadside into Hannibal. Both animals went down with a scream of pain, but I was able to step free.

I was naturally worried for Hannibal but had no time to look for him. A Parthian rider came over me the moment I touched earth, swinging his long sword down toward my head. I parried the blow and then took his leg before he could swing at me a second time. Turning my back to his horse I pulled him from his saddle and down he crashed, nothing more than a heap of steel.

I kicked his head, breaking his neck, but when I turned from him, I saw another rider coming for me at a gallop. His sword was lifted, but he seemed determined to run me over. Caught between fights at either side, I had no chance to evade his attack. A stride before he struck me one of my own men collided with his mount. Both animals tumbled, but the Parthian himself came hurdling over the neck of his horse.

He struck me with his shield as he landed and sent me reeling back. I tripped over the legs of a corpse and went down. Sword lifted for a killing blow, the Parthian stepped over me. A horse came in behind him, the rider leaving his saddle and tackling my assailant. Only as the two men hit the ground did I recognise Herod.

Herod took the iron mask of the Parthian into the crook of his arm and gave it a hard twist. He then took my hand and pulled me to my feet. We turned now as an infantry team, playing out the remainder of the fight from the ground.

Plunge a blade into a horse's belly or break its leg with a slashing wound. Catch hold of an iron man's ankle. Pull and turn it. Get them on the ground and they were helpless: slow to rise, half blind, staggering like drunks.

The dust was so thick we were fighting shapes not colours. Everywhere came the shouts of men, the grunts and screams of horses colliding, the strident song of steel. And then suddenly our cavalry from Masada arrived. With fresh forces coming into the fray against them, the cataphracts abandoned the fight and sought only to break free of our circle. And breaking free, they raced back the way they had come, along with their archers. We let them go with only the Masada riders giving chase.

Looking about, I saw some five hundred horses had been brought down. Almost all of them still struggled. Of the cataphracts left behind, all were quiet, every man with a broken neck. I limped out of the centre of the fight, sore and worn out, but anxious to know how the battle had gone at the perimeter. My cavalry had taken the worst of it there. They had been the only targets the archers could shoot at. Most of the men in that position were wounded; some forty were dead or dying.

I found Hannibal standing off in the distance. I checked him for wounds, but he was fine, only very close to exhaustion, like every man and horse under that mountain. I led him back into Herod's camp and passed him to the care of my secretary, who had waited out the fight with the civilians. Only then did I seek medical treatment.

XX
A KING FOR THE JEWS

Nabataea: July, 40 BC

Salome cleansed my wound with vinegar and salt; then she closed it with plaster to keep it safe from infection. After that, she wrapped the plaster in bandages. Herod was sending the wounded and all the civilians to Masada; we were fifteen miles from the mountain fortress and though it was tempting to take the shorter journey I needed to stay with what was left of my cavalry. How else could I promise the men who went to Masada I would get them free before the next summer ended? Accordingly, I arranged for a litter and made sure my wounded officers had litters as well. For the rest of our wounded, some four hundred Spartans, there was no helping it; they went off to Masada, there to wait for the rescue I promised them.

Herod's mother's family still lived in Petra, which the Nabataeans claim as their capital city. Because of this familial relationship, Herod had every confidence we would be received at the borders of the Nabataean kingdom. Our journey required two nights and most of two days, but that was only because we had already exhausted ourselves. The Parthian archers returned late in the day following our night march. Instead of fighting them in earnest, we sent out squads of cavalry lancers to keep them at a distance. So we trudged across the land shadowed by the enemy. We lost very few men on our march but the number of wounded continued to mount.

Much of this business I missed because I was on my back, though I did find an arrow in my blanket when two slaves lifted me from my litter one evening. When we had finally arrived at the Nabataean border, I thought the worst of it was over. Instead, the border guards turned us away. King Malichus had lost a kinsman – also named Malichus – to Roman swords quite recently. Besides, he had no desire to risk a war with the Parthians.

Egypt: July, 40 BC

Having no choice in the matter, Herod turned west. We were two hundred miles from the Nile Delta, half of the journey over or around mountains, the rest across the scorching sands of the Negev desert. It took three weeks for us to cross, but at least our escort of Parthian archers abandoned us.

We ran low on food and water and feared for our lives until Herod engaged the services of a nomadic tribe. He spoke their language but, all the same, the terms he arranged were to their considerable advantage. They took his gold and most of our horses into the bargain. In return they provided us with camels and food and a guide who would lead us to water as we travelled.

By the time we had made the first of the tributaries of the Nile, I was walking again. With the last of our gold, Herod and I negotiated permission from a local magistrate to build a camp on Egyptian soil. Here, Herod's army and the remnants of my cavalry, three hundred Spartans, would wait together until we could summon them. From there Herod and I moved on with only a few of his officers and a squad from his guard for escort and a few servants, including my secretary. A month after our flight from Jerusalem had begun, we entered the Jewish district of Alexandria and stayed the night with friends of Herod's family. From there we sent word to the palace that Herod, Tetrarch of Galilee, came to the queen as a supplicant.

I stood with Herod and several other men while he spoke to the queen. After he had told his tale of escape from Jerusalem, Cleopatra offered him command of her armies. She did this on the sole condition that he led them south into Ethiopia, not east across the border into Nabataea and Judaea. In Ethiopia there were riches to be harvested, and she did not mind starting a war in the south if Herod led the campaign.

The offer was generous and apparently extended to the Roman eques standing beside him, but Herod refused her. He had no choice, he said, for he had not abandoned his family in Jerusalem and would not now leave them to perish at Masada. He begged only a passport and permission to leave the queen's harbour in a merchant ship. This she gave him, along with the loan of some gold, which Herod gratefully accepted. Nobody had seen a payday in over a month.

But that was all the queen gave him, no matter what she claimed some years later.

Egypt to Cyprus: August, 40 BC

Herod ordered his officers and Guard to return to our camp with the gold Cleopatra had provided; the men needed their pay. He and I then boarded ship with only our servants and horses. We set sail for Cyprus, where Herod had several friends with large fortunes. From these gentlemen he arranged letters of credit, which he used at once to purchase a large ship and crew.

While we waited, word came on the wings of a carrier pigeon that Phasael was dead; Hyrcanus yet lived, but his nephew, Antigonus, had cut off his nose and ears. These deformities disqualified him from service in the Temple; I assume that, for the sake of their blood relationship, Prince Antigonus let his uncle live. Herod suffered terribly at the news of Phasael's death; I believe his older brother was also his best friend.

Still quite young, I did not know how to console him and left him alone in his grief. One day, however, after we had set sail for Rome in Herod's new ship, he came to me as I watched the oars ply the waves. 'I count you as a true friend, Dellius.' He said this in the same tone a man uses to discuss the weather. I had no response for such affection, except to answer in kind, but I was obviously taken by surprise.

'The moment you left Jerusalem,' Herod explained, 'there were men under my command who laughed at me. They said you had left and weren't coming back. Phasael and I told them they didn't know you as we did. But I must confess, I wondered if I would see you when we came out of those sewers. I thought: if he has any sense, he will be a hundred miles away. But there you were. Because of you, my brother's sacrifice means something. Our family still lives.'

Rome: October, 40 BC

I have always marvelled that Herod insisted on arriving in Italy with his own ship, but I think he understood better than an Italian-born Roman that in Rome money is all. If a man has no money he had better pretend it isn't so; no one assists a penniless exile, no matter what title he used to own. He was a beggar, like Ulysses after one of his shipwrecks. And like Ulysses, he carried on as if his flight from Judaea were only a minor inconvenience.

We sent a messenger ahead to Antony as we neared the city and Antony, in turn, sent an escort of friends to find us while we were still on the road. It would have been a finer gesture had he come in person, but no matter – we were received. And that is the first necessity of dignity.

Antony's home had formerly been the residence of Pompey Magnus. It was the very largest house on the Palatine in those days and had been decorated with plunder from the orient, both Pompey's and Antony's. For all his show of wealth and power Antony seemed a changed man. He was, by then, already married to Caesar's sister, Octavia. That alone might explain some of his docility. Octavia was a delicate flower like her brother, as cold and heartless, too. Quite contrary to custom, Octavia waited at Antony's side to receive us. I could not help but recall the court of Cleopatra, where young Caesarion was honoured as Pharaoh alongside his mother but it was Cleopatra who made all the decisions. Antony was wretchedly sober and miserable on the morning we arrived. Every morning afterwards, for that matter. Gone were the louts he liked to keep at his side: dwarfs, actors, retired gladiators and certain ancient legionaries whose last skill was to drink until dawn without fading.

Missing too was Antony's morning hangover. He looked flush with good health but chastened and mournful for the sake of it. Of course he had recently lost a wife for whom he had great affection and the second of his two brothers as well. Or maybe his sorrow was all about losing northern

Gaul with its eleven legions. Or the companionship of Cleopatra. Then too it could not have been easy to leave behind the adoration he had so lately enjoyed in the orient; in Rome, after all, Antony was still the subject of several awful tales of debauchery. Defeat in Syria and the loss of the Jewish provinces weighed heavily too. But then Bacchus is nothing if not a creature of extremes: glorying in celebration one moment, wailing and broken the next.

He ordered wine and refreshments for us, but he would not taste more than a sip or two from his own cup. He permitted Herod to tell his tale, relishing the description of the battle against the Parthian cataphracts. And then Herod told him the bad news. Phasael had escaped crucifixion by killing himself; Hyrcanus lived but had been shamefully mutilated. And the worst of it: all of Herod's loved ones were presently trapped atop Masada and under siege.

Hearing these reports Antony showed sympathy, but that was all he had to offer. Until Rome reclaimed Syria he was unable to help Judaea.

'Surely there is something we can do,' Octavia interjected.

We were all embarrassed by this outburst. Finally, Antony answered his new bride. 'Our chief concern at the moment, dear, is holding the provinces of Asia Minor. If we succeed at that, we will turn our attention to regaining Syria. Only when that is accomplished, can we drive the Parthians out of Judaea.'

Octavia ignored this and looked at Herod with the bright optimism of an innocent, though she was anything but that. 'Perhaps my brother can help you.'

'If he has found legions who can fly,' Antony snapped, 'perhaps he can!'

'Will it hurt to ask his opinion?'

I thought Antony might explode in rage as he would have against a man. Instead, he gave his new wife exactly what she asked for. It could not hurt to ask, he murmured. With that, Octavia sent word to Caesar that there was urgent business to discuss with respect to Judaea. Whether she wrote something more I cannot say, but Caesar soon answered her letter with one of his own. He invited Herod and Antony and his sister to dine with him that evening.

We departed Antony's house and crossed the Tiber. There we found hospitality with Herod's wealthy friends in the Jewish district. I might have joined men I knew in Rome, but I wanted to stay close to Herod. I thought he would have news after his dinner with Caesar. Fortunately, I did not have to gather the information second-hand. Later that afternoon a slave arrived with my invitation to join the party.

I assumed I had been overlooked because I lacked any political resource. I am still not sure why I was finally included, but perhaps Caesar's wife, some distant relative of Sextus Pompey, became ill at the last moment and they had a vacancy. This I know: Caesar neither liked his wife nor trusted her; so her absence from an important dinner was not especially remarkable.

Naturally, I was unprepared for such an occasion. I scrambled about trying to arrange the loan of a toga that had the thin purple stripe of an eques. That was easier to acquire than a decent pair of slippers, but shortly before we departed for Caesar's house someone came to me with a pair that fit, or nearly so at least. Since my arrival in Rome five-and-a-half years before, nothing I had experienced compared to an invitation to dine with the two most powerful men in the world. In a city where every important man was anxious to speak with Caesar and Antony, business to which I was intimately linked took pre-eminence. Even having to wear borrowed clothing could not spoil the occasion.

⟞⟝

The fall of Syria and Judaea of course were not casual matters to be handled when the leadership got around to it. No, this was the fall of half an empire, presaging the political collapse of Rome's leadership. So our meeting concerned not only the fate of Judaea but the fates of Caesar and Antony as well. For all of that no one seemed especially concerned.

Caesar was pleased to meet Herod. He knew of Herod's friendship with his father, his adoptive father, Julius Caesar,

I mean. He mentioned as well that all of the Jews in Rome had gone into mourning on the day they learned of Caesar's murder. Herod answered this with the observation that his own father had counted no man a better friend than Julius Caesar. So the meeting was off to a good start.

There were only two tables set, with three diners at each. I lay beside Antony and his new bride, the only woman present at the meal. Caesar put Herod next to him; Caesar's friend, Maecenas, lay to the other side of Herod. It was all quite intimate, which is the way real power is exercised.

After the warm welcome, I expected the men to get down to business, but Caesar insisted on music through the first course of our meal. This was lettuce, arugula, and dormice, as I recall. There was no time for political discourse but there was much talk about the Jewish reluctance to eat Roman cuisine. Herod ate the rodent without complaint but as he did he entertained Caesar with a full description of Jewish dietary prohibitions. After the music, we had a recitation of some poetry in Latin that seemed, even to my untrained ear, desperately eager to be grand. During this phase of the banquet we helped ourselves to various stews that had been set about, all in spicy sauces. I detected game bird, chicken, pork, beef, and the brains of some creature. Wine sweetened with honey kept the heat of the sauces bearable.

Maecenas was responsible for selecting the poet and apologised when the fool had departed. It was difficult to find any but Greek poets, he told Caesar. Of those the really good ones all refused to translate their creations into Latin. Caesar complained, for his Greek was practically non-existent. Why couldn't Romans write poetry? 'We own the world and have nothing to show for it but armies and ships? No! We have a culture that far surpasses anything the Greeks have accomplished; it's time for us to take pride in that fact!'

Maecenas answered that any Roman youth wanting to pursue the study of poetry must live for a time in Athens, which spoiled his affection for his native tongue. Caesar stabbed his table with his dinner knife. I believe this was his first use of a weapon in anger, but I may be mistaken on that point. I know Antony blinked and looked at the young man for the first time that evening. 'There is nothing at all the matter with Latin, Maecenas. It is the custom of worshiping all things Greek that is the problem!'

I repeat so much of this silliness chiefly because I found it wildly improbable. The world was falling down around his ears and Caesar wanted poets to deliver their doggerel verse in Latin instead of Greek so he could understand it. More to the point, his chief advisor did not bother shifting the conversation back to matters of state but talked seriously about the problem of finding good poets. As the conversation continued I saw Antony watching the wine jar passing. He was on his best behaviour and had already refused a second cup, but that did not preclude desire.

I focused my attention on Octavia. She had arranged this dinner because, as it seemed to me, she had been touched by Herod's affection for his family. Hoping to inspire her to introduce the topic of Judaea's fall, I decided to entertain her with a story about Salome taking up a shovel and digging the fortifications for a battle line alongside the rest of her brother's soldiers.

Octavia enjoyed this or pretended to, at least. Soon she began speaking of Roman women who wore swords. She named two or three from extreme antiquity, then added almost innocently, 'And more recently Antony's late wife Fulvia. Then too one cannot forget our other allied women. Cleopatra, for instance. I am told the queen really is a warrior at heart.'

Antony swirled the dregs of his wine in his cup, adding as he did, 'This much I can tell you. She rides a horse as well as any man I've ever known.'

'Antony is quite impressed with the queen's athleticism; I imagine they played with swords when she was not riding him.'

'The queen enjoyed archery, not sword fighting, and when she rode me, she did it as if she enjoyed it.'

'So an actress as well. You know of course the queen is pregnant?' Octavia asked me.

'Unfounded rumour,' Antony answered.

'You saw her, Dellius. Rumour or fact?'

'I have no idea,' I answered.

'Brother, you must go to Egypt and have this creature yourself. You can't be the only man in Rome without her spawn.'

Caesar told his sister that he really did not care to visit a people who worshipped animals. As Antony snagged a passing servant and got his cup filled, Caesar talked at some length about the absurdity of praying to dogs and crocodiles.

Maecenas, who was considerably more sophisticated than his friend, agreed that there were strange aspects to Egyptian religion, but one could not deny their unsurpassed abilities when it came to astrology.

'Astrology and witchcraft,' Caesar answered. 'But for all their occult powers they have proven themselves incapable of winning battles without Rome's legions.'

Having brought the conversation back to national pride Caesar was soon discussing the need for a Roman culture in Rome, even a national epic to rival Homer's. 'Why always praise Greece and Egypt? They have nothing we do not possess in greater abundance. Except perhaps decadence.'

'Bugger the poets!' Antony exclaimed. 'Herod's wife, his mother, his son, and his sister are trapped on a mountaintop. He comes to us for aid and succour and all we can do is complain about the wretched state of poetry in our city. What can we do to help our friend?'

Octavia blushed at her husband's outburst. Maecenas looked frightened. As for Caesar, he seemed to me vaguely irritated by the interruption. He blinked, considering the matter, and then said, as if it were the simplest thing in the world, 'Perhaps we should make Herod King of Judaea.' Caesar thought about it for a moment more and then agreed with himself. 'Yes, I think that is best. King Herod of Judaea. It has a nice ring to it, don't you think?'

'But I have no claim to a crown, Imperator,' Herod protested. 'Perhaps you ought to consider Hyrcanus, who is, after all, heir to the throne of Judaea.'

'Hyrcanus is a mutilated old man. Besides, you will have the only claim you need once the senate has voted unanimously on the matter.'

'He still needs an army,' Antony answered drolly. 'Have we any spare ones around that I don't know about?'

'A king can always find fighting men. The difficulty is raising the money to pay for them; as for that, I'm afraid I can't help.'

Herod looked at Caesar as if he imagined the lad was making a joke at his expense. As for Antony, I believe he wondered quite seriously if Caesar had gone mad.

Of course Caesar was not mad at all. He simply had no notion of Judaean politics. If Rome made Herod a king, then he was a king. Like it or not, the king's subjects were not really a factor worth considering.

In fact, neither were the opinions of Antony and Herod. Young Caesar had determined the best course and returned to his latest passion. 'Latin poetry, Maecenas. Not always Greek, Greek, Greek!'

XXI
OLD FRIENDS

Rome: Late Autumn, 40 BC

Next morning, like old friends, Caesar and Antony walked at either side of Herod as they entered the Forum. An hour later Herod left the chambers of the senate a king, lacking only his kingdom. Antony proposed a celebration, but Herod had business in the city with several moneylenders, after which he meant to ride as quickly as possible to Brindisi. The seas would be closed to ships in a matter of days. He wanted to be in Cyprus before winter set in. Of course, he did not care to offend his patron and begged Antony's forgiveness, but he must think of his family.

A day or two more or less did not seem worth so much concern, but Antony gave his blessing. While he was in such an agreeable mood, I took the opportunity to ask Antony's permission to travel with Herod. In this matter, Antony was not nearly as obliging. 'I need you in Rome,' he told me simply. Like Herod, I had made promises to people. I told Antony the lives of the four hundred wounded Spartans I had sent to Masada depended on me. And there were also three hundred men in Egypt to whom I had promised to return; surely Antony could understand.

Antony did understand, far better than I, and cut off my complaints impatiently. 'This fortress of Masada cannot possibly survive the winter, Dellius. Antigonus knows Herod's family is there; he will soon enough learn that we have made Herod King of Judaea. Nothing will be more urgent for him than taking Masada. Herod must attempt the impossible because they are his family, but I will not waste your talents on lost causes. I am going to need you with me in Syria.'

'And what of the officers and men I left in Egypt?'

'They are at least safe. Let me worry about returning them to service, once Syria is ours again.'

So I remained in Rome while Herod went off to buy an army with borrowed funds. I was not officially engaged as Antony's prefect of the Guard, not inside the city, but I was always the man closest to his person, and men under my patronage were always at the edge of Antony's entourage, their gladii concealed under their cloaks.

Rome was uneasy, and that made a sudden attack on a Triumvir a very real possibility. The chief cause of complaint was Antony's and Caesar's inability to deal with Sextus Pompey's naval blockade along Italy's western coast. We were not starving, but neither had we sufficient grain for our population. Prices were rising at the very moment when fewer people had income. Antony was also worried that some radicals in Caesar's faction might launch an assassination against him. So in addition to his person, I arranged for men to keep watch over Antony's food and wine, lest he perish as Antipater had done.

With what little time I had to call my own I did manage to enquire about the new owner of my father's estate in Tuscany. I knew the man's name, he was a neighbour who had once possessed only a few hundred olive trees and some pastureland. His lack of fortune had let him avoid the proscriptions, but he did possess enough in his own right to provide surety for a loan, which allowed him to make the winning bid at auction for my father's estate. He had then, rather cleverly, sold off parcels of my father's pastureland at a profit. This allowed him to pay down his debt even as his income trebled from the produce of our orchards and vineyards.

When I wrote to ask him about the price he would take for all that remained of my family's estate, he did not play coy but gave me a fair price for it. Only then did I realise I could not earn the money I needed with an officer's salary. I proceeded to speak with a few men in the city, but all of them required me to own property before they would loan money to me. Of course, if they had loaned me the money I would have owned property, but when I made that argument they were not swayed by its logic. I knew better than to ask Antony for a loan, but one evening, when he was not in an especially sour mood, I asked him about my father's estate.

Might I not petition that it be returned to me on condition that I pay back the present owner's expenses?

It seemed a fair request, but Antony's face turned hard as stone. We had all lost a great deal, he answered. Of course, he meant others had lost a great deal. For Antony our civil war had brought an end to his perpetual indebtedness. He was then the wealthiest man in the world – after Caesar, of course, who had recently come to enjoy the wealth of Gaul.

⸺⁂⸺

Some days after Herod departed for Cyprus, I sent a brief note to Maecenas. Reminding him of our dinner at Caesar's house and Caesar's concern for Roman culture, I suggested he investigate the talents of my friend Horace, who was presently living in Rome. I was sure Maecenas received names quite routinely, all the clever young fellows wanted to write verse in those days, and so in my note I added how much Antony had enjoyed Horace's poetry. This was not exactly true, but of course nothing is sweeter than poaching a great talent from a jealous rival, and Maecenas soon invited Horace and me to his house.

Horace had by that time attained employment in the government through his friendship with one of Antony's clients, but no one at all in Antony's circle bothered to promote his poetry. Maecenas was impressed by Horace, there is no other word for it, and the two of them were soon lost in a discussion of prosody that I simply could not follow. No matter, Maecenas was a fine host with a bounty of foods arriving at his table, even if the rest of Rome was close to starvation, and he simply refused to serve a mediocre vintage.

Some weeks later Horace stood before the luminaries of Roman society reciting his poetry as if Pindar himself had risen from the dead and learned Latin. When he had finished, his audience, led by Caesar, stood to offer its applause. When their polite enthusiasm for Horace began to wane Caesar rallied them like a centurion in a desperate battle, and all stood and cheered as men do for the winner of a chariot race. Horace blushed, but he also knew he deserved their praise, and so as he blushed he smiled coyly as well. His hour had come at last.

Maecenas found me at the edge of the crowd afterwards. I was waiting my turn to congratulate Horace. Maecenas took my arms in his hands, leaning forward to whisper in my ear, 'Caesar is delighted, Dellius. Ask whatever you will of me. I am in your eternal debt.'

I thought to explain that I was helping Horace, but then I thought better of it. No one in all of Rome had more influence with Caesar than Maecenas. His gratitude was something to cherish, not throw away carelessly. So I took his fleshy arms in my grip, just as he had done to me, and I whispered softly: 'I have all I want seeing you pleased, my friend.'

From the look that followed gratitude was on offer anytime I cared for it, that very night if I were so inclined, but I invented business in the city and made my escape. Even if I had enjoyed that sort of dalliance it would have been utter folly to sleep with Caesar's lover.

I walked in public often with Antony and his friends that winter. I watched him operate with his political allies as well as his opponents. He was still a chastened man and always took care to mind his manners, but, as I soon learned, there was more to it than personal loss and frustration. As I have said, Rome was not pleased with its Triumvirate, but Caesar, up close, was especially disappointing.

Whether Antony feared being tossed out with Caesar or only wanted to appear the viable alternative, I cannot say. He might not have thoroughly understood his motivations himself. He was simply being careful, both of his person and reputation, perhaps for the first time in his life. This I know. When men brought up the topic of Caesar's various failings, Antony insisted on changing the subject. I watched him from close proximity that winter; he seemed sincere in this respect, but of course it was mostly that Caesar's chief spy, his sister, was now living in his house.

The worst of it for Caesar came on the Camp of Mars one day when he left the city and foolishly went to face a mob of angry veterans. A riot broke out before he could finish speaking; they were tired of being paid with promises. It started with shouts and shoves, moved to rock throwing and finished with swords drawn. Once more Caesar ran for his life. Experienced as he was in the art of flight, this time Caesar failed to make it to safety.

Antony, learning of the trouble even as events transpired, raced from the Forum, where he had been hearing civil cases in court. As he went, he called to his friends to follow him. We left the city running as fast as we could and came upon a mob of men shouting and striking out at Caesar and the rest of the men they had captured. Shoving our way into the melee we discovered many of Caesar's companions were already dead. Maecenas was held by a brute of a man who pressed a dagger into the soft flesh of his neck.

Antony's party was not nearly large enough to take the veterans, but Antony, always at his best at times like this, roared in that golden baritone of his, 'Harm Caesar and every one of you dies!'

Much to my relief the fellows shoved Caesar toward Antony with a laugh. Just expressing a difference of opinion. We gathered up what was left of Caesar's entourage, including a much shaken Maecenas, and made our way back to the city. Maecenas came to me on that walk. 'I thought I was dead,' he muttered, nervously touching his neck.

I smiled at him. 'I thought it as well, my friend. If not for Antony, I suppose you would have been.'

Maecenas glanced toward Antony's hulking figure. 'I wonder why he bothered?'

I had no answer for that, but some years later I asked Antony the very same thing. By then Caesar and he were finally and fully enemies. Why save the little twit? A bit of negligence might have made Antony lord of Rome. A thoughtless shrug and drunk's belch: 'I thought if they do it to him, they will imagine they can do it to me as well.'

I didn't believe him then, and I still don't. I think he went to rescue Caesar because he expected that Caesar would survive. That being the case, he wanted to appear to be a good partner in the alliance. Once he knew how desperate the situation was, he was in the middle of it and could not very well extricate himself. But I could be wrong. I am not sure Antony ever fully understood the danger that Caesar represented to him.

Sparta: March, 39 BC

With the first blush of spring I sailed with Antony and Octavia to Athens. Athens was Antony's first stop on his march into Syria. We spent some weeks recruiting auxiliaries in Greece and Macedonia while the fleet prepared to sail for Tarsus, which still remained under Antony's banners. Shortly before our departure, Antony sent me to Sparta for a fortnight. He hoped I might recruit some two or three thousand additional Spartan auxiliaries into his guard. I had by then a great many contacts in the region, including families of the men I had left in Judaea as well as the auxiliaries who had fought under my command in the last days of Philippi.

So it made sense for Antony to use me in this manner. I enjoyed a fine house in the city for my headquarters. Attending me were several of my most loyal and capable subordinates. As a show of respect Antony permitted me to negotiate terms with the lords of Sparta. Once I had arranged an agreement, I would send a courier to Antony in Athens for his official approval. Antony usually agreed to the conditions at once, but on occasion he would answer with a letter outlining his position with that particular noble. He was acquainted with them all or had information about them if he did not know them personally and therefore gave or withheld his blessing accordingly.

So sixty men from one lord, a dozen more from another, but with the next fellow I had to continue to haggle for a fair exchange of favours. It was all just as it had been in the summer Dolabella had sought auxiliaries: a son's promotion, a brother's appointment to command, a priesthood, land, or some other dignity sought and presently denied. Every lord having his price.

One morning I received a sealed parchment from a freedman I had not seen before. I had been courting the wife of an estate owner for some days. Her husband possessed more property than prestige and desired some local magistracy for the sake of twenty auxiliaries on offer. From my perspective the deal was not especially advantageous but the wife was a delicious golden-haired beauty, and she was anxious to see her husband's status increase.

Assuming my would-be lover had avoided sending the same servant twice, I opened the letter without worrying that the wax seal closing the scroll bore no identifying mark. Only when I noticed there was no signature at the bottom of the letter did I begin to wonder. This seemed strangely careful, even for a love affair. Especially so, as I suspected her husband of putting her up to the seduction.

When I read the note I realised the author was none other than Livia, wife of Claudius Nero. She spoke of the boar hunt we had enjoyed together, the friendship we had established afterwards. Should I care to see her, she was presently residing in the hills immediately west of Sparta. She preferred anonymity at the moment, and so had not signed the letter; the freedman who had delivered her note, however, could be trusted. He would lead me to her new residence at my convenience, but for the sake of her reputation I must come alone.

Having read the letter, I looked up at the messenger. 'I'll come within the hour.' The old fellow answered that he had hoped I would say as much. He would wait for me at the western gate of the city.

———

I had already learned that Nero had escaped with Livia and their infant son to Sicily. This came in the disastrous aftermath of the revolt Antony's wife and brother led in northern Italy. Nero's involvement in that matter had placed him at the very top of the proscription list. Of course, very few people on that list were still available to bounty hunters. Those who could manage it had escaped to Sicily and the protection of Sextus Pompey. The rest were dead. Discovering that Livia was now living quietly in Sparta I naturally assumed she had left her fool of a husband. The assumption was not especially naive. In Sicily, Nero was safe and might enjoy some dignity as a senator in exile. In Greece, he would be hiding in attics or under haystacks. Livia's care in remaining anonymous might have alerted me to the possibility that Nero was with her, but I was too happy to worry about it.

There are several great estates in the foothills just west of the city; these enjoy a fine trade in timber, grapes, and olive oil. I was sure one of the wealthy families kept Livia in perfect luxury while she negotiated her return to high society in Athens, presumably through my connections with Antony.

As I rode across the great plain surrounding Sparta, I thought about marriage. Why not? We had not seen one another for five years, but our morning in Livia's bed still burned in my memory. A divorce for her would present no problem, especially given my contacts with the high and mighty. I was then twenty-six and finally enjoying a handsome income, and though I could not afford to repurchase my patrimony I held a military rank of considerable distinction. Marriage to Livia could only enhance my position in society, for she belonged to one of the most ancient patrician families of Rome. That her fortune was lost mattered hardly at all.

Yes, I told myself, it was time to stop thinking about illicit love affairs and turn instead to the business of an advantageous marriage. All the better with Livia, who had excited passions I had never experienced with others.

The aging freedman Livia had sent to me was happy to talk about his life. He had spent, he said, twenty-five years in the house of Claudius Nero, more than half his life. In fact, he remembered my visit to Campania in the year Antony and Dolabella had served as consuls. He was still a slave at the time.

I didn't remember him. All the same, I told him I had recognised him without at first being able to recall just where we had met. This of course flattered him, and he proceeded with his story, to which I listened with genuine curiosity. Everything that had happened to him over the past five years reflected some detail about Livia's life. So when he tried to hurry his tale I pressed for details.

Put simply, he had won his emancipation on the very day Nero won the rigged-election for praetor. Since that time, he had enjoyed command of Nero's and Livia's household. After their escape in northern Italy, this fellow alone remained with them. I asked if he had not been afraid for his life; he told me he feared more for Nero's.

When they were hiding in Campania, this freedman had not only made himself useful by bringing food to the family but he had also made contact with the servants of Nero's former clients in the area. Most had refused to help. Not a few tried to sell them out for the sake of a reward, but on two occasions they had been given safe passage through the countryside. Finally, in the dead of night, he had rowed the skiff that carried Nero and Livia and their infant son safely across the straits of Messina to Sextus Pompey's rebel kingdom of Sicily.

Having listened attentively to all this, I finally asked the fellow the question I most desperately wanted answered. 'So what brings Livia to Sparta?'

'Domina will want to explain that to you herself, Excellency.'

'But you are newly arrived in Greece?'

'We are not three days here. I went into the city yesterday to arrange Domina's journey to Athens. She hoped to petition Mark Antony, but when I learned you were in Sparta, I returned at once to inform her of the news.'

'You recognised my name?' I asked in genuine surprise.

'Your name is well regarded in the house of the Claudii, Excellency.'

We came to a fine estate in the foothills, about three

miles from the city, but after we had passed it and then several more I asked the fellow, 'Where exactly are we going?'

'It will be another three or four miles into the mountains,' he answered. The road was quite ancient and so lacked Roman efficiency, which is to say there was hardly a time when we were not winding about ravines or climbing steep grades. We were in fact quite close to the sea, hardly half a day's ride to the west. For all that, it was mountain country in every direction. In her letter, Livia had asked me to come alone, but I was suddenly sorry I had not thought to bring along some men as an escort. With only Livia's freedman for company, I hadn't much protection if some gang of thugs decided to kidnap one of Antony's officers.

Finally, we left the main road and followed a lane that had been nearly swallowed up with briars and weeds. I could see nothing in the distance, certainly nothing cultivated, and I began to wonder just what I was riding into. Then, turning one last curve in the lane, I saw the burnt-out ruins of an ancient villa.

—◦◦◦—

I pulled Hannibal to a halt and looked down at the freedman, who had walked. 'Livia is here?' I asked. What remained of the main building was uninhabitable. Some walls stood; others had fallen. Elsewhere a column was all that remained of a portico that had once connected various buildings. Most of the property was swallowed up in high weeds if not already overgrown with mature saplings. There was a decrepit well close to the front gate. Otherwise the forest pushed against the main house.

'She was here when I left this morning,' the freedman answered.

'Run forward and have her come outside,' I told him. 'I will see her before I take another step.'

'As you like.'

He trotted easily toward the house. As I waited for the appearance of Livia, I studied the land about me. There was a deep ravine bordering the eastern edge of the property; it seemed to cut close to the main house and then circle behind it. To the west I saw nothing but trees and hills. The forest enjoyed a few old glories, but most of the trees were only a few decades old. There were no other estates about, and I realised this was some lord's stand of timber.

My chief concern was ambush. I knew of course with perfect certainty that the freedman who had brought me here had been Nero's servant, but times had changed. For all I knew the fellow might be in business for himself these days. I was still working through these matters when Livia came through the broken-down gate. She was dressed in dark, inexpensive clothes. She looked like a peasant. In fact, I was not sure at first it actually was Livia. Then, as she walked toward me, I recognised the rhythm of her stride and saw at last her dark glossy hair as she pulled away the veil she wore.

At that point, I slipped from Hannibal and led him forward. I could not stop myself from taking Livia in my arms and holding her with the desperate passion of a lover, my lips to her neck, pressing my body to her and recalling as I did every intimacy of our single morning together. It had been five years, but she answered my embrace with the same passion she had shown in her lovemaking.

'I hoped you would not disappoint me,' she whispered.

'How could I?'

She pulled away from me and looked back at the house. That was when Nero stepped beyond the gate.

He too dressed as a peasant, his tunic long, in the Greek style. It was filthy as well and without any mark of his patrician status. His hair was longer than a Roman usually wears it, and there was even a bit of a white beard. At the sight of Nero, I could not help myself. I pulled entirely away from Livia. I felt betrayed and of course quite foolish. 'What is he doing here?' I hissed.

'Dellius!' Nero called. His tone was cheerful, as if he had just encountered an old friend. It was, I believe, only the second time he had ever addressed me. The first had been when he threatened my life should anything happen to Livia.

I was obliged by law to take Nero's life the moment I saw him, that or make haste to report him to a local magistrate. Anything short of that amounted to giving aid and comfort to an enemy of Rome. 'You risk my life inviting me here!' I whispered to Livia. I was angry at her and at myself too.

'We have news for Antony,' she told me.

Despite my fury, I was curious. 'What news?'

Before she could answer, Nero walked toward us, calling out to me, 'You are looking well, my friend.'

Nero was not at all like the dull blade I had observed in Campania. Perhaps revolution suited him or he had learned a few social graces after a year of depending on the kindness of others.

'You as well, Excellency,' I answered, taking his hand as he extended it.

'We have news for Antony, Dellius.'

'So Livia tells me.'

'Come inside. I don't care to conduct my business in the open. Besides we are famished.' He turned and walked back to the house.

I brought Hannibal as far as the well, where I looped his reins over a post. 'What is this place?' I asked Livia, who had stayed with me as we walked.

'One of my father's properties,' she explained. 'Antony's estate now, I suppose. The house burned down the year I was born, almost twenty years ago. We still use the house to dry timber over the winter. Or did until my father's death.'

'But you can't be living here?'

'For the past two nights we've had no choice.'

We passed through the gate and came to a vestibule filled with debris from the collapse of its roof. Beyond that we entered a very large atrium which scavengers had stripped bare of its tile and marbles. The freedman had already set out olives and bread and a sack of wine. All of this he had brought with him from Sparta. Young Tiberius was already eating a piece of the bread. He was a large boy but hardly more than two or three years old. Curiously, he had the same dull expression his father wore: a look of bafflement, as if nothing in the world quite made sense to him.

The pool in the atrium was empty, but its size and the fragments of the mosaic that remained here and there hinted at the grandeur the place had once enjoyed. Further on, the house seemed already to have been overtaken by the forest. The roof had collapsed in every room for as far as I could see. The porticoed garden at the back of the house seemed already to be a part of the forest.

For all that, with the light breaking through the treetops and vines reclaiming the rooms, the effect was quite beautiful, though hardly a domicile anyone might willingly choose. No, this was a bandit's hideaway.

'Will you join us for a meal, Dellius?' Nero asked.

His remark that they were famished had seemed the usual hyperbole from one who has not eaten for a few hours, but I suddenly knew how utterly desperate their situation was: chased constantly by bounty hunters, they were probably half-starved most of the time. I was not even sure if the food their servant had brought with him was purchased or stolen.

I was hungry and all the more so once I tasted a piece of bread. I hesitated taking more of their food than that, but once I realised that the freedman had begun piling dried wood on the family's campfire in preparation of baking fresh bread, I helped myself to another piece. As I watched them eat, I could not help recalling our feasts in Campania. There we had meat of six or seven varieties and always fresh fish, though it had cost a fortune to stock the ponds where they were kept. I must say, for all the arrogance of the old boy in former times, I was not happy to see Nero ruined. Still, the sight of him so impoverished did give me some hope of persuading Livia to leave him and marry me.

Before we got down to Antony's business Nero asked about my life; he had some general idea of what had occurred but seemed genuinely anxious for details. This seemed quite strange to me; it had not previously been in his nature to care about others. I suspect now he was only anxious to flatter a man whose help he needed.

Soon enough I was telling them about the battle at Philippi. Livia's father had been one of the legionary commanders there and had in fact been executed in the aftermath. That they might know what sort of villain chased them I described the games of chance Caesar had played with some of the young tribunes. When I saw Livia's expression grow pale I hastened to add that the legates had been given a chance to speak before their executions. 'None were mocked or teased; the games of chance were only for the lower ranking officers.'

Livia was not sure I was telling the truth; to be honest, I had no idea if Caesar had mistreated the legates. They were at the front of the line, first to die; I had been standing a few furlongs behind them waiting my turn.

After my description of events at Philippi, Nero described the uprising in northern Italy. According to him, he was the one who had encouraged Antony's wife and brother to resist Caesar's tyranny. He assured me that while Antony knew nothing about their plans, all three of them had intended for Antony to be the sole beneficiary of their actions.

'When it was clear the city was about to fall, Livia and Tiberius and I made our way into the forest.' I noticed the freedman at the fire turn to look at his master, but he did not speak. It must have wounded him terribly to get no mention when Nero told the tale.

'You were at least safe in Sicily,' I told Nero when he had finished his story. 'Why come here and risk everything? Whatever news you had, you might have sent to Antony by courier.'

'Caesar is preparing to betray Antony, Dellius.'

'How?' I asked. Even though I did not suspect Nero of deep intrigues, I was not ready to believe Caesar was so foolish as to risk war with Antony.

'Caesar has been carrying on secret negotiations with Sextus Pompey. He intends to announce their alliance the moment Antony sails with his army to Syria.'

'You know this as a fact?'

'I was to be turned over to Caesar as part of a goodwill offering from Pompey. When Livia found out about it we escaped before Pompey could lay hands on me.'

'And what of Lepidus?' I asked. Lepidus, the third member of the Triumvirate, commanded western Africa with a great many legions under his authority. Should Lepidus throw in with Caesar, Antony would have no chance.

'For the moment, Lepidus has no involvement in Caesar's plans. From what I can see, he is not taken seriously by either Pompey or Caesar. Once Antony engages Labienus in Syria, they mean to come against him by sea with Pompey's navy and by land with Caesar's legions.'

'From what I have learned, they hope to persuade Labienus to join their new alliance,' Livia added.

I wanted to ask why Caesar would turn on Antony, but I knew the answer. This was all because of Pompey's naval blockade of Rome. With Antony away in Syria, Caesar feared more riots in Rome. Even if the population did not succeed in overthrowing him, Caesar must have known that a victory in Syria would make Antony preeminent. Should Antony suffer setbacks or even defeat, Caesar would be no better off. Antony's defeat would mean the end of the Triumvirate and Caesar's legions would lose faith in their man. On the other hand, if Caesar joined with Labienus and Pompey well before Antony attacked the Parthians in Syria, he would become preeminent with Pompey and Labienus assuming the role of junior partners in a new Triumvirate. Then all that remained would be to deal with Lepidus.

'Have you any proof of Caesar's intentions? Something I can take to Antony?' I asked.

'Only my husband's presence here, Dellius,' Livia answered. 'He would not have put himself in mortal danger if it were unnecessary.'

'I believe you, but I am not sure Antony will.'

'Antony is no fool!' Nero protested.

'His marriage to Caesar's sister seems to have changed him. All I can do is inform him of what you have told me; much as he might want to believe it, I am not sure he will let himself.'

'And what of us?' Livia asked.

I met Nero's gaze. 'I can take Livia and your son to Sparta. I assure you they will be safe. Anything else risks making me a criminal.'

'By standing in this room you are already a criminal,' Livia told me.

'What would you have me do about that? Kill your husband?'

'Arrest him! Take us both to Sparta and keep us under your authority until Antony decides what he will do.'

'Proscribed men are not arrested, Lady. They are killed on sight, along with anyone willingly in their company, wives included.'

'Take Livia and Tiberius,' Nero answered. 'I'll wait here until you return with Antony's decision.'

'No,' Livia protested. 'We must stay together.'

'Dominus!' the freedman called, his voice soft, urgent. 'There are riders outside.'

Nero and I hurried to the gate and looked out through one of the broken panels. A dozen horsemen had stopped at the edge of the meadow. It was not difficult to imagine what had happened, and had I known that Nero was with Livia I would have watched for trouble. Someone in the city had recognised Nero's freedman. By following the freedman they hoped to find Nero.

We had not watched them long before they started toward the house, spreading out as they came. The leader ordered four of his men to proceed toward the southern extremes of the property. Once these men rode into the forest, I could no longer see them, but I knew they meant to come at us from a flanking position.

'Have you weapons?' I asked Nero. At Nero's gesture, the freedman crossed the room and showed me two javelins tucked behind some rubble; I would have preferred lances for close fighting, but javelins would do. Nero walked across the atrium and picked up a gladius hidden in the rubble. He then wrapped his left arm in his cloak. The cloak would serve as his shield. I pointed at Nero. 'You will need to hide; make them come for you, but keep your sword ready.' Now pointing to Livia, 'Hold the child; do nothing else.' Now to the freedman, 'Set fire to the forest at the back and along the southern perimeter of the house. We need to keep those fellows who went into the forest from coming in behind us. And keep those spears out of sight until they find your master; then come behind them as they are fighting. Strike low in the back, as hard and deep as you can manage.'

I waited until the freedman had taken one of the brands from his cooking fire and began lighting the dry brush that edged into the house. Then I walked out the front gate. The riders studied me quietly as I approached them. 'Did you gentlemen miss the road?' I asked.

'Who is in the house?' called the man at the centre of the line.

He was a thickly built man in his forties, doubtlessly athletic in his youth but no longer. A Roman by his accent, probably ex-legionary by his dress and manner.

'Who wants to know?' I demanded.

'The man with the sword, sweetheart.' As he answered me he pulled his weapon and let me contemplate it.

I was wearing a long-sleeved belted scarlet tunic, which

I had purchased because it reminded me of the one I had taken from the closet of Gaius Trebonius. I wore as well the two gladii Herod and Phasael had given me under my right arm. With my costume and the precious stones decorating the twin scabbards, I suppose I did look like the perfect dandy; even so I did not care to be called sweetheart by any man. 'If you must know,' I answered, 'I am the one occupying this residence, at least for the afternoon. My lover and her child are within. And her servant.'

'What are their names?'

'She is another man's wife, so I will not tell you her name. As for the servant, I frankly never bothered to ask it.'

'And what is your name?'

'Quintus Dellius, Prefect of the Guard for the Triumvir Mark Antony.'

This startled the man, but he was not sure if I was lying or not. 'Prefect of the Guard is it? Well, Prefect, we have reason to believe a proscribed man is in that house with you.'

'What man?'

'Claudius Nero.'

'You're quite mistaken, I can assure you.'

'I may be, but I won't know until I search the place, will I?'

'I don't care to have the child frightened. I'll allow three of your men inside. No more.'

'I'll send as many in as I like.'

'If you send three men I'll stand here quietly. Send more than that,' I said, drawing both swords, 'and I'll have one of these in your guts before they cross the threshold.'

The ex-legionary did not care for this, but neither did he want to kill Antony's man without proof Nero was inside. He nodded to his second, who dismounted and took two others with him. I was now standing before five men on horseback, three of them occupied holding a companion's horse.

⊷∙∘∙⊶

I heard the gate creak open, then Livia's voice as she spoke to the men. 'What is this about? What is going on?' I turned briefly and saw the men push her roughly out of the way. She followed them, sounding like a common pleb who hadn't anything at hand but a sharp tongue and a shrewish disposition. Surprisingly, that sort of thing works with some men. Not these fellows. One of them laughed at her, calling her a whore. When she attacked him with her fists, he pushed her to the ground.

Only as she rose to follow did it occur to me that Livia had abandoned her son, expressly against my orders. Well, she had never obeyed Nero; why should I imagine she would treat my commands any differently?

'How did you happen to come here?' I asked the captain of the bounty hunters. I heard rubble being tossed about inside.

'That's our affair, I'd say.'

'I only ask because I happen to know Claudius Nero is in Sicily.'

'Did you start a fire at the back of the house?'

'It was a bit chilly inside.'

'He's inside,' the captain told his companions.

I stepped toward the horses and swept the blade in my left hand across the noses of three of the animals. Two of these horses had riders, but all three animals jumped back in surprise, colliding with the others and causing a general consternation. In the meantime, I turned to the man closest to me, who was already drawing his sword. Before the blade cleared its scabbard I ran him through. The fellow stared at me in disbelief; then, as I twisted my gladius and pulled it from him, his expression lost all animation.

I took the reins of his horse as it skittered away from its falling rider. With all four riders still struggling to calm their mounts, I leapt upon the horse of the wounded man and turned toward the captain of the squad.

He attempted to evade a collision as I bolted toward him, but that only let me collide into the shoulder of his mount. I blocked a desperate stroke as the animals hit one another, then swung at his head with both of my swords. His animal hurt and his life in jeopardy, the captain threw himself to the ground. I spun my horse now, but the animal was not well trained and turned like a ship on its centre axis.

The man coming at my back reached out with a long blade. Ducking under the thrust of his weapon, I swept my left arm behind me. The blade of my weapon cut into the fellow's arm, though I had not the force to sever it. It was enough for him to drop his weapon. I turned at once toward the other two riders. Only then did I realise I had been cut. It was not a deep wound, but I was hurt.

The two men remaining on horses had pulled back to cover their captain as he caught and tried to mount one of the loose horses. Rather than wait for them to surround me, I galloped as fast as possible toward Hannibal. Scissoring one leg over the neck of the nag I rode, I dismounted on the run. I took up Hannibal's reins and jumped upon him. He spun lightly, his weight perfectly settled over his haunches. I pressed his flanks and he bolted toward a broken wall close to the front gate. Hannibal hurdled the wall easily, bringing us directly into the sun-dappled atrium. But it was hardly the safe haven it had seemed only moments before.

Nero's freedman was down. His body lay over one of the javelins. The corpse of one of the bounty hunters lay next to him, a dagger buried to the hilt in his back. The other two men had cornered Nero. He blocked every thrust with either the cloak wrapped around his arm or the blade of his sword, but with two against one he was failing. Livia came toward their backs with the second javelin.

I saw her moving and shouted for her to stop. All I did was awaken the men to their danger. One of the men turned from Nero and went for her with his sword.

I pushed Hannibal into a gallop. We hurdled the low wall of the empty pool; a stride more and we came out of the pool again, brushing past Livia.

Livia's assailant turned his attention to me and swung his sword at Hannibal. I blocked the attempt and guided Hannibal into him, knocking him down. As soon as the man hit the floor, Livia came forward, thrusting the javelin into his belly. The other man, now alone against us, broke from Nero and jumped through the wall and into the smoky forest. I might have taken him; he was only two strides beyond the house. But Hannibal, fearing the smoke, refused the jump.

I turned and rode to the centre of the atrium. Looking back through the rooms I could see that the forest along the back and both sides of the house had started burning.

XXII
FIRE

Sparta: March, 39 BC

I heard the crackle of dry wood burning fast and saw smoke rolling into the atrium. 'Where is the boy?' I cried.

'Hiding.'

'Get him. We need to move fast!'

I watched Livia pull the dagger from the back of one of the bounty hunters. Only then did I see the blood on her. 'You're hurt!' I said.

She looked down at her bloodstained hands and clothing. 'His,' she said simply, her eyes cutting toward the corpse from which she had pulled the dagger. My gladii in my hands, I rode back through the house, shifting Hannibal around the old piles of charred roof beams cluttering the way. Fearing the smoke and rising heat, Hannibal fought me with nervous protests, whinnying, head-tossing, front legs rearing up slightly. For the sake of control I moved him sideways, pressing his flanks with a single leg and holding his head with the reins. He snorted angrily and trotted in place for a time.

I kept watch for the men who had slipped behind the house, but the fire had spread too quickly for them to get inside. The flames were already licking into the house. Vines and treetops inside the garden had begun to burn. The air was hot, breathing difficult.

When I came back to the atrium I discovered the boy standing beside his father. I rode to the front of the building and saw eight men mounted on horseback. A ninth stood on the ground wrapping a wounded arm. The last of their number lay in the grass a short distance away. Slipping off Hannibal, I told Nero, 'I suggest Livia and the boy mount my horse and wait inside until you and I can engage them. When they have surrounded us, Livia and the boy can break from the house and ride to the city.'

'And what of you two?' Livia asked.

'We'll follow into the town after we've finished with them.'

'You haven't a chance against so many men,' Livia offered. 'Wouldn't it be better to go down to the pavilion?'

'The pavilion? What are you talking about?'

'There's a pavilion under the hill.' She pointed toward the back of the property, 'It ought to be well below the fire. From there we should be able to get away from them.'

'There's no way to get there!' I told her.

'Of course there is. We have a tunnel inside the house that leads to it. I shouldn't think there will be any more fire once we are inside the tunnel.'

Nero put his gladius in its scabbard and picked up both javelins. Livia took the child, and I led Hannibal. When we came to the porticoed garden, which was now thick with smoke, Hannibal began to fight me in earnest, rearing up in terror.

'Here!' Livia called and pointed at a burning pile of rubble blocking the way into a wide stairwell. Beyond was darkness, but the slope of the ceiling promised a rapid descent and refuge from the smoke and fire.

Nero began to knock the burning wood away with his javelins. I took the cloak tied to the back of my saddle and covered Hannibal's head. He could still smell the fire and feel the heat, but with his sight gone he grew calmer. Nero tossed the burning tinder further down the stairwell, spreading the fire and so breaking apart its intensity. That finished, he began swinging his cloak, beating the flames down.

As he worked I stepped around a pile of plaster and stones to have a look at the front of the house. Three men had waded into the smoky atrium. Fearing an ambush they spread out at once, keeping watch on all sides and resisting the temptation to rush through the room.

'We have to hurry,' I whispered. 'They're coming.'

Livia and the boy stepped into the stairwell, but the hem of her skirt caught fire. She gave a yelp of terror, but Nero was there to beat the flames down

I descended the steps after Nero, going slowly so Hannibal could find his footing. The tunnel's walls had been dressed in smooth white stone. There were even brackets set into the masonry to hold torches, though they were now empty. The air stank of fire, but it was otherwise clear of smoke and ash. After descending the stairs, we had no more burning tinder. Close to the stairway, however, the dying embers provided enough light for me to discern shapes and shadows on the stairwell. I called to Nero and gave him the reins of Hannibal. 'I'll wait for them here,' I told him. 'You go on!'

—◁▯▯▯◁▯▯▯▷—

I did not dare look for the bounty hunters; I simply waited beyond the stairway, pressed against the wall and listening for their approach. When they did not come quickly, I thought perhaps the fire now blocked their way. I waited so long I nearly imagined they had given up, but then I heard one of them calling to his companions, 'Down here!'

Another spoke, 'Take care now.'

And the next, 'Don't worry. They're long gone!'

The fellow who said this was closest to me. If my guess was correct he was a step or two above me and I had only to turn the corner to meet him. I swung out, swords at the ready. I saw him stiffen in surprise. I took the stairs, knocking his sword away with one gladius as I thrust my second weapon deep into his guts.

But I had lost the element of surprise with the other two. Nor had I time to pull my weapon free. The other two were beside him, their weapons at hand. Spinning, my back pressing into the wounded man, I brought my left arm in low. I caught the second man's leg just above his ankle and heard the whisper of his sword whipping past my skull.

Using the force of my spin I collided into the third man, getting cut on the arm as I did. My opponent fell back against the wall but not far enough to be out of reach. As he hit the wall he stabbed me. I brought my gladius under his sword arm, cutting him just behind his wrist. I pulled back, feeling the blade of his sword tearing from my belly. Despite my wound, I executed a second pirouette, leveraging my stroke this time. My gladius came up from my knees, the stroke finishing at shoulder height. I heard his sword clattering on the stones even before he screamed. His hand had been severed from his arm. I pulled back a step before running him through.

I went to the second man, who was down and screaming that his foot was gone. I stabbed him through his neck, if only to silence him. Then I grabbed my second gladius from the belly of the first victim. I stepped again behind the wall and waited for the rest of them, but the garden within the house was now thoroughly ablaze and blanketed in thick smoke.

⸻◦⸻

Perhaps three hundred feet below the house I saw a light and followed it as I emerged from the inky darkness of the tunnel. Beyond this I discovered a forested ravine. The pavilion was a bit further down the hill along a stone path.

I looked at my wounds. My arm was cut, but only into the flesh and the bleeding would eventually slow. Pushing my fingers into the wet heat of my guts, I knew this wound was not terribly deep, but it was the sort that will kill a man slowly, especially as the blade had cut through the muscle and gone into the soft inner parts. There was no rush of blood, only a steady, awful leaking. My back had been cut as well, but seemed no worse than my arm. With a surgeon and the proper medicine I might hope to survive all three wounds but of course, at the moment, I had neither.

—⁂—

The forest on the hill above us was bright with fire; treetops were burning like crowns of flame; white smoke roiled thickly toward the heavens. Below at the pavilion the air was clean. As I followed the lane toward Nero and Livia I studied the slope of descent beyond the retaining wall with some trepidation. A creek lay three hundred feet below our position, but the way was unpaved and quite steep. At the pavilion, built for shady summer afternoons, I studied the ground beyond its foundations. Here the slope was guarded by trees all the way to the creek.

I found the safest way and led Hannibal over the retaining wall. We turned together into the descent, as if I meant to lead him down the hill, then, as he started sliding forward, I let him go. He went with his front legs braced, his haunches scooting through the dirt. The danger was he would build speed and begin tumbling out of control, but Hannibal fought the mounting speed and steered himself between the trees, sliding wildly to the bottom of the hill.

I jumped forward after him, aiming my path so that I might catch a tree trunk some feet below. Bracing myself, I turned back and told Livia, 'Send the boy to me!'

Tiberius refused, but once his mother had grabbed him, they jumped together, sliding into my arms. Nero came more slowly, making his own way down. I turned and slid another thirty paces, catching hold of an outcropping of stone and bushes. I looked below and saw Hannibal already in the stream drinking water. 'Look at Hannibal! It's safe, boy! Perfectly safe!' For all my encouragement Tiberius still needed his mother's arms.

We descended slowly, losing some skin here and there but coming finally to the water, where we drank our fill. Afterwards, as we hid behind thick vegetation, Nero looked at my wounds. We hadn't even fire to cauterize the belly wound. So Nero washed the cuts with water and then wrapped my cloak tightly about my waist. The cloth was soon saturated with blood, but this eventually hardened into a kind of plaster. Having no more clothing to spare for bandages, he left the wounds on my back and arm open. While Nero tended me, Livia had kept watch on the pavilion. The bounty hunters, she told us, had apparently abandoned the chase.

—◁▰◁▮▶▰▷—

We were four or five miles beyond the estates that bordered the great plain of Sparta. Half an hour if we could run; an easy gallop on horseback. But all of that assumed a straight way and a good road. We were in mountain country, far from the only road in the region. So we followed the path of the stream. This made for an easy walk during the first hour and gave me some hope of getting to a surgeon quickly, but after an hour we came to a waterfall. Backtracking now, we climbed a steep embankment, which proved nearly impossible for Hannibal. Then we stumbled through a series of hills as the sun faded behind us and the forest shadows grew long. Where it was possible I rode Hannibal with the boy before me, but as the hours passed I had trouble keeping upright and conscious.

We began talking about the estates before we had found one. Nero knew all the owners in the region. Many had been his clients in happier days. Of course now they were obliged to murder him on sight, and Livia and me as well for being in his company. There was always a good chance however that the owner might be gone. In that case a freedman would be directing the business of the farm.

These fellows know a great deal about farming but are not always familiar with the dominant political figures in their region. If Nero assumed the role of a slave, they might not recognise him. That was the hope at least.

But darkness came before we discovered any of the farms. We spent the night buried inside a pit Nero had dug with his gladius; we used leaves for cover against the dew, all four of us huddled close for the sake of heat. As for Hannibal we turned him loose to forage for whatever he could find. We went into the pit exhausted and hungry, but thirst began to set in as the night passed.

At dawn, or actually some hours before, I became acutely aware of my belly wound. I was certain it had become infected. That being the case, it was simply a matter of fading to death over the next few hours.

Departing at first light we moved listlessly. I could not sit upright in the saddle, but I did manage to straddle Hannibal and then lean forward across his neck. I rode by habit, slipping into and out of consciousness as we went. The boy was nearly as weak as I was but too thirsty to complain. He took turns riding his mother's and father's hip.

At midmorning dogs found us. Soon after that the slaves whose herds the dogs guarded arrived. Nero, pretending incompetence with his Greek, explained that his master had been hurt by highwaymen. We had escaped and found shelter in the forest until the fire drove us away. We had stumbled about all night, lost in the hills.

The slaves did not care to question his tale. They could see the stripe on my tunic and the fine horse I rode. This was a matter for the manager of the estate. With one look, the manager saw I was close to death and brought the farm's animal doctor to me; this fellow was a slave with only a rudimentary training in medicine. He drained my belly wound of bile, then washed the cuts on my arm and back with salt and vinegar. He dared not attempt more but put me to bed with instructions that I must promise a sacrifice to Asclepius. Then he added that in his experience it did not hurt to include promises to another deity, especially if I had a favourite.

I told the fool Artemis had special regard for me, and so he insisted that I must make promises of splendid sacrifices to her – a whole pig, if I could afford it; she loved swine more than other sacrifices. 'I will capture a wild boar still living and take it to her altar,' I groaned.

'Yes, if you could manage such a feat, that might save you.'

Fortunately, the vinegar and salt had more potency than Artemis, and sometime the following day I came out of the darkness. Nero and Livia and the child had stayed in my room keeping me warm and watching over me. Another night saw my fever break and, though I was not yet whole again, I was now fully conscious and on the mend. On my fourth morning I had an appetite, but my doctor warned me not to indulge it. Better to keep drinking broth and offering prayers to Asclepius, and I must not forget my promise of a wild boar for Artemis.

On the fifth or sixth morning I was well enough to travel in a wagon and sent a boy to Sparta with a letter to my most senior tribune. As we waited for my men to arrive, the manager of the estate entered my bedroom. He had avoided visiting me until then but thought I might enjoy the latest news: Claudius Nero had been killed by bounty hunters. Nero of course stood at my bedside playing the faithful servant as I heard this news, so I had no worries. I simply feigned surprise. 'I thought Nero was in Sicily with Pompey!'

'It turns out he has been in Sparta for several months. Caught in the same fire that nearly killed you. How is that for a coincidence?'

'Then they have no proof of his death?'

'On the contrary, they got their proof. No head, no money. They waded in after the worst of the fire and took his head, charred as it was. What I hear is they've already presented it to the magistrates in Sparta for their reward.'

———

Twenty horsemen arrived that afternoon. The tribune commanding the party questioned me in private about my servants. Was there something he should know? I thought he recognised Nero or at least suspected that something was up, but I knew if I told him the truth I would invite him into a dangerous conspiracy. So I confessed to having survived an attack by highwaymen. 'These two might have stolen my horse and left me to die,' I told him. 'Instead, they brought me out of the forest at risk to their own health. After such service, I couldn't very well let them go on down the road without a reward. They were hardly in better shape than I was; so I claimed them as my property so that they might be allowed to stay in my room.'

'Shall I give them some money and send them on their way?'

'I mean to give them a proper reward once I'm on my feet,' I answered. 'Until then, keep them close to me.'

'As you wish, Prefect. By the way, did you hear some men brought in the head of Claudius Nero?'

Once we had returned to Sparta I put guards on the room where Nero and his family stayed without explaining my reasons to anyone. Not having to explain one's actions is of course one of the perks of command. Nobody entered their room and nobody was allowed to leave it for any reason. I did, however, provide them with one of the guard's servants, who brought them their meals and emptied the chamber pot.

I was still weak and in need of recovery, but a day or two later I drafted a letter to Antony, which I sent by courier to Athens. The rider would change horses every ten miles; this allowed him to make excellent time on his sixty-mile journey. If Antony gave his immediate attention to the matter, we could expect a return letter before sunset.

In my letter I admitted to having Claudius Nero under house arrest. On Antony's orders I said I would see the man executed, but in the circumstances I thought it best for Antony to decide Nero's fate after speaking with him. He had come, I said, from Pompey's court in Sicily and had news of vital importance to Antony's interests.

I said no more, for I knew Antony's new wife, Octavia, might learn the contents of that letter. I hoped Antony would trust my judgment, but I told Nero I was not sure if he would take my advice. I did not care to play Nero's friend in the morning and bring his executioner to him that evening. 'Once Antony answers my letter,' I told him, 'I will call you to me before I read it.' I meant this as a sort of kindness, but of course there is no such thing when it comes to executing a criminal.

At any time our courier might have returned from Athens with Antony's response: ordering Nero's death or giving him a reprieve. So the hours passed slowly. For Nero it must have been awful. At sunset, when there was still no response I sent a note to Nero informing him that I had no answer from Antony. Should a message now arrive, I promised I would not read it until next morning. In this way I hoped Nero might enjoy one more night in the arms of the woman he loved.

Late next morning a courier brought me the answer we had waited for. I ordered Nero escorted to my court before I broke the seal on the letter. I had armed men standing by should Antony have refused my recommendations. At my signal, they were to take him down with their swords at once.

By my orders, Livia and the boy waited in their room. I certainly did not care for her to witness the murder of her husband; I should add I did not care to see it myself, for I had come to have no small degree of affection for the old fellow. Slow and ponderous he might have been, but Claudius Nero had survived where wiser and swifter men had failed.

I read the letter in silence, fearing the worst, but Antony bid me to bring Nero to him and named him in the letter that I might use the document as a defence, should Caesar's bounty hunters find us on the open road.

Athens: March, 39 BC

I rode in a carriage with Nero and Livia, for I was still not fully recovered from my wounds. We had an escort of twenty of my best men. I did not identify either Nero or Livia to my subordinates, but I did tell them that Antony had ordered the man to his palace for a meeting. I expect some of the men knew Nero on sight; a great many of my best men were Spartan auxiliaries, some from the best families in the Peloponnese, but if they did recognise him, not one of them protested or even bothered asking questions.

As there were too many of us to change horses at the post stations we went slowly, stopping at one of the inns where we stayed overnight. This put us into Athens late next day. Antony was seldom in a hurry, either for business or war, and proved consistent on this occasion. His freedman informed me that I should bring Nero to Antony's court early next morning.

That gave me the chance to get Nero dressed in a clean white tunic, though without any stripe to advertise his former rank. Nero of course would have preferred a toga for the occasion, even a plain one, which would have announced his citizenship; but proscribed men enjoyed none of the rights of a Roman citizen and to wear such clothing might tempt Antony's patience. Better to come humbly before the great man and beg mercy. Humble however did not preclude a haircut and shave; so at least Nero looked the presentable petitioner and not like some bearded Germanic wild man dragged into court.

Uninvited for the hearing, Livia waited with her son in a room inside the great house Antony used as his headquarters. I had told her that Nero would have no appeal; if he was not given amnesty he would likely be executed at once. That she might know her husband's fate, I told her I would come to her if the news was bad. Nero would return to her if Antony had granted him amnesty.

Antony remained seated as Nero and I entered his praetorium. Not a good sign. 'I authorised payment for your head only a few days ago, Nero!' Antony announced cheerfully. 'It is encouraging to see that Death proves unable to hold you.'

'The rumours of my death, sir, have been greatly exaggerated.'

To this Antony roared with laughter, I suppose because it was the first joke he had ever heard Nero utter. 'So tell me, old friend,' he said, still smiling but with cooling eyes, 'what news do you bring from Sextus Pompey?'

'Caesar negotiates with Pompey for a treaty that will allow them to turn their combined armies against you. They will attack your rear the very moment Quintus Labienus brings his Parthian mercenaries against you in Syria.'

Antony held up his hand to stop him. The gesture was an odd one. I certainly had never seen him use it before. I thought he feared spies and did not care for Octavia to know more. I believe now he only meant to stop Nero that he might consider how to respond. Finally, in the judicial tones he might have used in a civil trial, Antony said, 'You offer an interesting theory, Nero, but, if I may ask – with all due respect – where is your proof for such a charge?'

'Caesar asked Pompey to turn over several men for execution before he offered a grant of amnesty for the remainder. These were all assassins of the divine Julius Caesar, but Caesar included my name for the sake of my actions in northern Italy, with Fulvia and your brother Lucius. When I learned of the request I escaped Sicily before Pompey could lay hands on me. The only proof I have of any of it is my willingness to flee the safety of Sicily and risk capture by bounty hunters.'

'You are mistaken about one thing, friend. Caesar and I have kept no secrets from one another. When Pompey approached me about forming an alliance last year, I informed Caesar of the matter at once; now, as he negotiates with Caesar this year, Caesar happily relays to me all that Pompey is willing to give us. That Caesar has asked for certain men to be turned over to him proves nothing more than his determination to execute them. You along with the rest, I'm afraid.'

'Then I have nothing of value to offer you. I apologise for begging this interview.'

'I did not say you bring nothing to me, Nero. On the contrary, you inspire me with an idea.'

'I don't understand.'

'I think it is time Caesar and I began formal negotiations with Pompey. Enough of these backchannel communications! How would you like to arrange a meeting between Pompey and Caesar and me?'

Nero's mouth moved, but he could not utter any words. Finally, clearing his throat, the old fellow remarked,

'I should like nothing better.'

'That's the spirit!'

———

I took Antony at his word that morning. I know Nero did as well. Some years later, however, Antony confessed to me that the news Nero had brought to his court that morning had hit him like a knife in the back. The 'little twit' owed his life to Antony, and this was how he showed his gratitude.

Without really considering the matter, Antony knew that the best way to thwart Caesar's betrayal was to force open negotiations with Pompey. Rome was close to starving, and though Sextus Pompey was the cause of it everyone blamed Caesar for his failure to break the blockade. If Antony sent word to Rome that he and Caesar were in talks with Pompey, the city would rejoice. It would buy time for Caesar, but if the mob was subsequently disappointed Antony knew Caesar could not survive to the end of summer. Nor would Caesar have an answer to Antony's gambit. Antony would join him and together they would proceed to negotiate an end to Pompey's blockade.

All of this Antony decided at the very moment he discovered Caesar's betrayal. Reflection, so dear to so many leaders, only made Antony morose and bitter. Had Antony sought the advice of his closest advisers he almost certainly would have ended up at war with Caesar. This would have happened because it seemed inevitable and because, given enough time to think about it, Antony's anger with Caesar would have spurred him to act. I expect what Antony enjoyed most about his decision was the fact that Caesar would be forced to embrace Antony's lie.

What Caesar's chief adviser, Maecenas, made of all this I cannot say with any certainty. I never spoke with him about these matters, though in later years we were good friends. I expect, after long consideration, Maecenas recommended that Caesar should play along with Antony. Antony might only be about the business of surviving. If that was all it was, so be it. If they did not destroy him at once, Antony, being Antony, would give them opportunity on some future occasion.

At the same time that Antony announced to the public that negotiations were underway with Pompey, he sent word to his commander in Tarsus, Publius Ventidius Bassus. His message declared that he was unavoidably delayed. Ventidius should not advance into Syria, but ought to continue holding the mountain passes between Syria and Asia Minor.

Antony's next move was to wait patiently for Caesar's formal recognition of Nero's appointment as their ambassador to Sicily. This took several letters between the two Triumvirs and cost nearly a month. Once Caesar agreed to it, Nero departed for Italy, where he set about arranging a satisfactory place for a meeting.

—◦—

The night after Nero departed for Italy I returned to my apartment within the palace at my usual hour and discovered Livia waiting for me. And the night after that she was there again. On the third night, following our lovemaking, I proposed marriage. She kissed my neck, whispering in the dark that she would like nothing more. 'We must wait until my husband has finished his work in Italy, Dellius. Then I will ask his permission.'

'He will not give it,' I answered.

'I think he will. If I ask it of him. I think it will break his heart, but he will not force me to st`ay with him if he knows I love you.'

'And do you really love me?'

'I do.'

'Do you promise to ask him?'

'I do.'

'And you will marry me as soon afterwards as possible?'

'I will.'

So our nights passed with whispered promises and kisses of pure fire.

XXIII
BETRAYAL

Misenium, Italy: June – July, 39 BC

Antony's entourage set sail for Brindisi in mid-June. His wife, Octavia, remained in Athens, as did Livia. It took us the better part of a month to make the journey, but this was only because of security concerns. Antony required intelligence on the location of Caesar's legions in Italy, and he intended to bring in at least a legion of his own men. When all was set, he advanced.

The site of Misenium satisfied both sides, or perhaps I should say all three parties. Situated on the northern horn of the Bay of Naples, the land reaches out toward two rather significant islands, Procida and Ischia. These islands allowed Pompey to bring a small fleet safely to anchor.

The Triumvirs had two legions camped opposite Capri, with elements of these extending all the way to the Italian shore opposite Sicily. One of these legions answered to Antony, the other to Caesar. The fear was that Pompey's legions might attempt to cross to Italy and march north against Misenium; alternatively, he might send a fleet of ships to attack Misenium.

Sextus Pompey's essential condition for his personal security was that he always remained on water. Caesar and Antony, in contrast, insisted they never leave land. Nero took credit for the ingenious solution, but it was certainly the brainstorm of a cleverer fellow than he, probably one of the Greek slaves serving him. Two floating islands were constructed off shore. One linked back to the harbour and dry land with a floating pier; the other allowed Pompey's flagship to dock against it. Between these two islands was a channel some ninety feet in width. At this distance the participants might shout to one another quite easily.

Of course no artillery pieces were allowed within range of these wooden islands; Pompey's flagship was stripped of catapults and each side submitted to a daily search of their party members for any weapon that might launch some kind of aerial attack: slings, bows, or even hand-held ballistae. Pompey, Antony and Caesar were all permitted guards who carried shields and swords. Because of these provisions, I remained close to Antony during the negotiations.

On the evening following the first exchange of offers Antony was justifiably frustrated. Caesar had spent the day refusing any compromise. He insisted on crucifying every slave who had left Italy to join Pompey in Sicily; these men had joined Pompey's army either as marines or legionaries and Pompey could not afford to betray them without risking a general uprising.

Caesar created even more discouragement when he refused to agree to return property to anyone who had lost it through the proscriptions. Antony knew Caesar was simply posturing. In his secret negotiations, Caesar had been prepared to accept all of Pompey's conditions. Of course Antony was not especially surprised Caesar refused to cooperate; he rather expected it. What frustrated him was his inability to find a way to stop the posturing. Put simply, Caesar did not seem to understand the risk of failure.

If the negotiations broke down, Rome would remain hostage to Pompey's naval blockade and Syria would languish in Parthian rule indefinitely. As for the chances of the Triumvirs surviving for another year, Antony gave it low odds. What Caesar expected to gain by sabotaging the talks, Antony simply could not fathom.

—‑‑‑—

On the second day, Caesar continued quarrelling without changing any position. He pretended not to understand Pompey's demands. When Pompey promised him riots in Rome if his blockade continued, Caesar answered that the Roman people were both resilient and resourceful.

What that meant no one knew. Pompey was clearly as frustrated as Antony. At one point he complained that the Triumvirs had asked for a meeting but were now unwilling to grant any of Pompey's conditions for a treaty. What was the point of going to all this trouble if the Triumvirs were not prepared to offer any sort of compromise? Caesar admitted he thought the negotiations were a bad idea. 'I went along with Antony's plan in the hope that you might see there was no hope but unconditional surrender.'

That finished the day with an angry verbal assault from Pompey. It also left most people convinced nothing was going to happen with these talks. Having very little hope of a solution, Antony nevertheless asked for a meeting with Caesar before their dinner hour, which they intended to have in separate houses. The meeting required some security arrangements, but Caesar at least cooperated in these matters.

When they finally came together, Antony bluntly accused Caesar of negotiating with Pompey behind his back. Caesar denied it quite credibly, but of course he had known the charge was coming sooner or later. 'Play innocent if you like,' Antony said angrily, 'but we both know Rome is starving, and things will only get worse from here.'

'Rome is not starving, Antony. Why do you insist on being so dramatic?'

'Give Pompey's runaway slaves their freedom. We can settle nothing else with him if we do not agree to that. He is not going to turn them over for execution because he can't. They will destroy him if he even considers it. And mind you, if he does not end his blockade of Rome this summer, you will see riots that will make your troubles on the Camp of Mars last winter seem like a stroll in a garden!'

'If we permit slaves to hope,' Caesar answered, 'we shall soon have another Spartacus to deal with.'

'You don't seem to understand the situation in the least. Someone else will deal with Rome's new Spartacus. You and I will be dead.'

'My father never negotiated with Pompey Magnus, Antony. I don't see why I should do so with the man's son.'

'Are you mad? Caesar spent most of his life negotiating with the old bore!'

'But in the end it came down to a fight.'

'In the end. After thirty years! You cannot make up history because you had rather pout than do something of real value.'

'Are you finished?' Caesar asked.

At his evening meal Antony listened to two generals on his staff as they discussed the many negotiations between the divine Julius Caesar and Pompey Magnus. It was not brilliant conversation but somewhat interesting. Suddenly Antony broke in angrily. 'He really is a *stupid* boy! The little twit. Stupid and stubborn and dangerous. Oh, I know he doesn't look dangerous. He looks like a flower that's about to wilt. But he is. He is! He wants to drive me off in a fury so he can give Pompey all he demands of us and then tell Rome he made the treaty at Misenium.'

'Then let him. Peace is what we need.'

'If I let him strike a private deal with Pompey, I will never be able to sail to Syria. I would not dare, lest they join forces against me.'

'Strike the deal with Pompey yourself,' one of his legates offered.

'At the cost of a war.'

'It is Caesar who wants war. Give it to him if he insists.'

To this Antony had no answer. I think every man in that room expected war between the Triumvirs. Antony was considering it, of course, but he did not want it. He wanted an end to civil war. His entire adult life had seen infighting and fratricide at a cost that had brought Rome close to economic ruin. Worse still, the constant infighting had finally opened the way for the Parthians to steal the finest real estate in the empire, Anthony's real estate no less. More fighting in Italy meant the entire orient would eventually collapse.

<hr />

Before the meal had finished I saw one of my officers reacting to some matter beyond the open doors of the triclinium. A scroll of some kind passed to the guard, who sent one of the servants with it to me. I signalled to one of my men and he came to replace my position behind Antony. The men Antony dined with were old friends, but so were the fellows who had knifed the divine Julius Caesar.

'For Mark Antony, Dominus,' the slave whispered.

I read a rather lengthy correspondence quickly and then took it to Antony at once. Antony was in no mood to read the usual reports, though he was curious at my willingness to interrupt his dinner. 'What is it?' he asked.

'Ventidius has killed Labienus, Imperator,' I answered. 'The Parthians are in full retreat from Syria.'

'Ventidius had orders to sit tight!'

'Imperator,' I repeated, 'your legions have recovered Syria.'

⬥

I knew Maecenas was at Caesar's residence and summoned him with a note declaring I had information I thought he would very much like to share with Caesar. I thought Maecenas might refuse me or send a man to take the message, but within a quarter of an hour of receiving my note Maecenas found me in the shadows where I waited for him. 'Dellius!' he said, signalling his bodyguards to leave us alone, 'What is so urgent it cannot wait until tomorrow? And why are we talking in the shadows instead of inside?'

'Quintus Labienus is dead, sir. Antony's troops are presently driving the last of his army from Syria.'

'That is splendid news,' Maecenas sounded cheerful, but I knew he must be calculating the considerable damage this caused Caesar.

'Splendid for Antony,' I said. 'What victory can Caesar boast?'

'Agrippa is fighting in Gaul. We have very good reports of his success.'

'Maecenas, your man needs victory at once. Without it, Antony and Pompey will sail away. With the East suddenly secure, Antony has a great many legions available to turn against Italy. If he tempts Pompey with a full pardon and even gold, there is no reason for them not to form an alliance against Caesar.'

'He rejected Pompey once.'

'No longer. I heard the matter being discussed just now. Antony resists it because he does not want war. But if Caesar will not cooperate, Antony must take the opportunity Fortune deals him.'

⸻⸻

Next morning, while they waited for Pompey's flagship to dock, Caesar told Antony he had decided to agree to the emancipation of all runaway slaves presently under Pompey's protection. He also proposed to Antony that they return fifty percent of the value of the property families had lost due to the proscriptions.

Antony countered this with a suggestion that they require the new property owners to donate twenty-five percent of the property value to the former owner. The payment might be in cash or land and would be based on current value, not the price paid at the time of the auction. In this way, he said, the Triumvirs could retain some measure of control over each exchange. Some men might receive a token repayment of their losses; others would enjoy significant returns. It went without Antony saying it that the adjudicated amount could be affected by bribes, which of course might accrue to the Triumvirs.

Venal though he was, Caesar was not an especially clever lad and had to retreat with Maecenas to discuss Antony's proposal. Once Maecenas had made it clear to him that they could actually make money by returning property to the men they had robbed, Caesar returned and declared that Antony's proposal was quite fair to all concerned.

These matters settled, the two men waited in silence until Pompey had docked on his island. Once both parties had submitted to a search for missiles, Antony and Caesar approached their island. Pompey and his guard in the meantime disembarked to their own. Antony let Caesar conduct the negotiations for them, though Caesar's shrill voice was easily carried off by the wind. Pompey took the new proffers and retreated to his ship to discuss the terms with his staff. An hour later, Pompey returned to his island and asked Nero's permission to send a slave across the channel.

Nero received permission with a nod of the head from Antony and Caesar and the boy swam to our island, holding a leather tube above the water's surface. This he eventually handed to Nero's slave and then returned to Pompey. I did not see the document but eventually learned its contents.

Pompey asked for an appointment in the college of augurs. This was an honorific that recognised Pompey as one of the city's most prominent men; he was more than a decade away from eligibility for such a position, but of course by then every law concerning the minimum age for a public office holder was thoroughly bent. Pompey also wanted the right to be elected consul in absentia; this was more than a decade sooner than the law permitted, but no one had cared to quibble about such matters when Caesar won his consulship at the age of twenty; so Pompey was confident he would get what he asked for.

Lest anyone imagine Pompey actually considered returning to Rome, Pompey also required a five-year appointment as the Governor of Sicily, Sardinia and the Peloponnese of southern Greece; this amounted to an expansion of his already potent thalassocracy and made Pompey in effect, if not by title, the third Triumvir.

In exchange for these concessions he did not turn over any of his ships. Instead, he simply promised to cease with his blockade. Finally Pompey insisted on amnesty for all the men in Sicily, not just the runaway slaves. This last point was one too many. Caesar agreed to pardon any man so long as he did not have the blood of the divine Julius Caesar on his hands. Amnesty for the assassins, however, was out of the question.

An hour passed, more for show than debate, and Pompey returned, calling across the water that he accepted the accords.

◦───⊶⊷───◦

Over the next three nights Antony and Caesar boarded Pompey's flagship; then Pompey came into the city. There was soon the promise of marriage between certain infant relatives. This is the sort of union that inevitably accompanies new alliances.

Everyone carried daggers – concealed politely – but, for all that, the three men were unusually cheerful. Antony had thwarted a conspiracy; Pompey had at last inherited some piece of his father's fortune and good name; and Caesar had finished taking his revenge on the assassins. On the second night of their party, Antony announced his victory in Syria. The rebel Quintus Labienus was dead; Syria was again under Roman authority.

At this news, finally made public, Maecenas glanced up at me from his table as he lay beside Caesar. I stood at attention against the wall and refused to meet his gaze, however. That was all Maecenas needed in order to believe

I had betrayed Antony. I cannot say if he ever considered the possibility that Antony had sent me on my errand, but this I do know: for the remainder of his life Maecenas always treated me as a close friend.

A day or so later Pompey returned to Sicily, where he proceeded to execute the last of those senators who had murdered the divine Julius Caesar. As for our new Caesar, once he had left the heads of the assassins in the Forum for all to see, he retreated to Gaul, where he might impress Rome with glowing reports of his martial accomplishments. There was, I'm sure, a quite general relief all around when he did not attempt to write a book about it, as his adoptive father had done.

For Antony, the war he had anticipated fighting was now a mopping up operation, something best left to his subordinates. The last thing he needed was to snatch defeat from the jaws of victory – no, he must remain at his court in Athens and let Ventidius recover Syria with the men he presently commanded. Should the Parthians mount a counterattack Antony might then answer with his legions, but only after Ventidius had got in over his head, as he well deserved to do.

Before he departed for Athens, Antony said to me, 'I suppose you might as well join Herod in Judaea, Dellius – if you still desire it.'

Italy, Greece and Cyprus: August, 39 BC

I arranged for my secretary to take Hannibal to the farm of Titus Flavius Petro, a centurion who was then retiring from Antony's Guard. Petro's family possessed no property on the morning Julius Caesar had crossed the Rubicon. Ten years later, having fought for Pompey, then Caesar and finally Antony, Petro had saved up enough fortune to buy a farm at auction. His farm manager was presently breeding horses and had acquired a string of broodmares that he typically bred to three or four of the region's better stallions. With Hannibal at stud we intended to establish a partnership that might earn us both a handsome income.

We had talked about such a venture at some length, but I had no intention of retiring and I was also reluctant to lose Hannibal before a long and dangerous campaign in Syria. Suddenly, however, the idea was quite appealing. I hadn't time to waste but needed to use relays of horses to get to Brindisi as quickly as possible. So I gave Hannibal an early retirement, while still retaining complete ownership. I then rode to Brindisi at full gallop, changing horses at every post station along the Appian Way. I left an hour before dawn and arrived at midnight. I was at sea next morning.

Once I had crossed to the Peloponnese I bought a horse, which I rode to Sparta. Within a matter of days I had gathered three hundred cavalrymen, all of whom had been previously committed to Antony's service. In Athens, with a letter from Antony authorising it, I spent a fortnight recruiting an additional thousand auxiliary infantry. While

I was doing this, I stayed at Antony's palace. I had hoped to see Livia before departing for Judaea, but she had sailed for Brindisi at the news of the Treaty of Misenium.

In fact, I believe she was sailing around the Peloponnese while I was on my way to Athens. At any rate, I missed her by only a matter of days and had not even a note from her when I arrived. I was naturally frustrated but, to be honest, I was confident of her affection. Nor had I any time to worry about Nero giving his permission for her to divorce him. That is not entirely true, come to think of it: there were nights when I awakened in a sweat, imagining Nero had refused to release her from her vows. Of course I would then settle my nerves at once: Livia could get that old boy to do anything she asked; she was going to be my wife and I was a fool to doubt it.

⚔

Once Antony arrived in Athens, he added three cohorts of legionary infantry under the command of one of the legion's prefects, an eques named Poppaedius Silo. Silo had been a client of Livia's father and, though he had drifted by necessity to Antony for patronage, still had an amicable relationship with the Claudii. Antony's appointment of this fellow was for the sake of his debt to Nero.

Silo was nearly a decade older than I and doubtlessly resented being my subordinate. Still, as long as we stood in

Antony's company, he refused to show his colours. As soon as our fleet set sail, Silo approached me. We were in fact still in the harbour. I was looking at golden Athens on its famous hill when I felt his presence. 'I'm taking the legionary and auxiliary cohorts to Ventidius,' he said. 'You can do as you like with the Spartan cavalry, but the rest are mine.'

'Those are not the orders Antony gave,' I answered.

'Of course they are. I was standing right next to you when he gave them.'

I considered taking Silo into custody, but the legionaries were loyal to him. As for my Spartan recruits, they were all still quite new to military protocols. This was not a game I could win. So I acquiesced.

<hr />

We sailed as a fleet as far as Cyprus. Once I had disembarked my men and horses, Silo continued to Tarsus and from there into Syria. Ventidius, after all, had suddenly become a rising star and Silo welcomed the chance to bring him what amounted to half a legion.

Herod's friends in Cyprus sent a carrier pigeon into Galilee with a note attached to its leg. This informed him succinctly that Q. Dellius came with three hundred cavalry. Within hours of sending the message another bird returned with instructions for me to make port at Acre three days hence.

Herod had arrived in Acre early that spring; he too had led some three hundred mercenary cavalrymen. He had then proceeded to recruit the Galilean bandits who operated along the Syrian and Galilean border. These were the very same villains Herod had sought so earnestly to eradicate when he was first procurator and then later Tetrarch of Galilee.

Of course these fellows had no love for Herod, but neither did they care for Antigonus or his Parthian allies. What they did possess was a grudging respect for Herod's fighting talents. So with gold and promises of perfect autonomy in Herod's new kingdom, he turned them into allies. By midsummer Herod's raids on Antigonus's strongholds in Galilee had inspired still more of the bandit gangs to support his cause. He had also negotiated terms with certain of the Samaritan nobility. These men despised the pro-Judaean Antigonus, who, like Herod, now sported the title of king. The Samaritans were not yet willing to provide fighting men for Herod's army, but they were willing to shelter Herod's men on Herod's promise that they would have some limited autonomy in his new government.

Ever since Ventidius had broken into Syria at midsummer, Herod's fortunes had been on the rise. In fact, after months of assaults on Jewish strongholds, which had always included plunder, Herod's Galilean bandits finally agreed to attack the Judaean army besieging Masada. These bandits were extremely tribal in their view of the world.

Early on, they had resisted the idea of going to Masada and insisted on staying in territory they knew. Flush with riches from a profitable summer they might have preferred retiring for an early winter holiday, but Herod begged their help. Without it, he said, he would lose his mother, his wife, his son, his sister and his two younger brothers.

Even bandits love their families, and so they agreed to risk everything for Herod's sake. Of course, there were also deals with certain of the patriarchs of these bandit clans, including promises of high position in Herod's new government, but Herod knew that the rank and file must believe in a cause, especially one that did not offer instant gratification in the form of fresh plunder.

I learned much of this shortly after my arrival, and I must say the news left me uncertain. I had imagined Herod brought several legions of mercenaries into Galilee and then rallied old friends from the area for support. I had not imagined that he had been forced to recruit his former enemies. In fact, he was nothing more than a king of bandit country, boasting at most a thousand fighting men. We had enjoyed a larger force when we fled Jerusalem.

An accomplished general with more than twenty years in the saddle, Herod had shaped his army of mercenaries and bandits into a potent force, but the Galileans were still only bandits at heart. Such men know one thing above all else. In a tight spot, it is always best to run. They were constitutionally incapable of engaging and holding an enemy line for several hours the way legions fight.

Nor did I bring much to the banquet. My recruits were not even blooded. I had made sure they had some training during our brief sojourn in Athens, but afterwards we had no further opportunities. They were all young men who had learned to hunt, but few of them had ever seen mortal combat outside the arenas; I don't think any of them had ever held a knife in anger. Truth is most of them were on their first journey away from their mothers.

⎯⎯⎯⎯

I did not care to confess to Herod that Silo had disobeyed Antony's orders. Instead, I explained that Silo would eventually support Herod's cause but had first wanted to report to Ventidius and coordinate with the legions in Syria. We spent a week sending couriers into Syria to ask for reinforcements. In the end, Herod received much encouragement and with it the promise that Ventidius intended to send Silo into Judaea before winter.

And with that discouraging message Herod told me we had no more time. We had to move at once or lose everyone at Masada.

The Road to Masada: October, 39 BC

The fighting at Masada had been quite desperate the

previous autumn. Antigonus had wanted to kill all of Herod's family and so brought his army to the mountain fortress hoping to overwhelm Masada's defenders.

A month into it Antigonus had finally acknowledged the folly of his plan. Masada was a magnificent fortress and simply could not be taken as long as there were men to defend the only road leading to its high plateau. He could buy off Masada's defenders easier than he could kill them. Which is exactly what he decided to do.

This change in policy left Herod's younger brothers, his sister Salome, and even his mother making desperate promises on Herod's behalf. Any man betraying Herod could count on being hunted down and killed. Any man remaining on the mountain would know Herod's eternal gratitude. It is doubtful such promises meant very much to his veteran mercenaries, and by early winter most of Herod's former army had left the mountain. The only men who remained were the four hundred wounded Spartan cavalrymen I had been forced to leave behind. If they abandoned the fight, they knew Antony would have his revenge on their families in Sparta. No bribe or promise was ever going to bring them off that hill.

During the winter there had been some raids against the mountain's defences, but these had cost the attackers dearly. With spring word came that Herod had come into Galilee with an army. When he did not immediately rescue those at Masada the last of Herod's mercenaries slipped away. But still the Spartans remained; not a single man deserted.

The problem at Masada was the same we had suffered in the citadel at Jerusalem. The water reservoirs were insufficient for the population. In fact, if not for the desertions, Herod's family could not have survived through the summer. Some unexpected rainfall in late summer had extended the days remaining before the water was gone, but after that there would be no choice but to break out and make a run for Arabian Nabataea; this of course would include only those civilians capable of such a desperate journey. The rest must either be killed or abandoned to torture and crucifixion.

Before leaving Acre, Herod sent a carrier pigeon to friends in Jericho, who then forwarded birds to Masada and certain friendly Idumaeans in the south. We then packed our supplies on some fifty spare horses and departed Acre two hours before sunrise. This brought us down the coastal road as far as Strabo's Tower by midday. Here we made camp and rested for three hours. These days Strabo's Tower is the famous harbour town of Caesarea; in those days it was nothing more than a post station along the coastal road without even a cove for ships to take shelter.

We departed late that afternoon and rode until nearly midnight before our second rest. This camp was five miles north of Ashkelon, where twenty-five hundred infantry and cavalry were set to stop Herod's advance on Masada. Outnumbered two-to-one, we ought to have abandoned all hope, but Herod had arranged for the men we had left in Egypt to join us. Two hours before dawn, according to their orders, these cohorts brought artillery forward and began lobbing fire into the city. When the garrison responded by sending cavalry against them, they retreated quickly to some makeshift fortifications. The Judaean cavalry, seeing the chance to destroy the entire force, called for infantry reinforcements.

Our scouts were watching for just this moment and we were soon riding through the darkness and into the rear of the Judaean infantry. The moment we hit them, our Egyptian cohorts attacked as well. With the enemy trapped between us, the slaughter that followed left a thousand dead or wounded; as for the rest of them, they hadn't the courage to keep on fighting and ran into the sea.

We had no time for happy reunions. We gathered what extra horses we could find and rode double for the rest. Masada lay fifty miles due east and Herod wanted to cover as much ground as he could lest the remnants of the force at Ashkelon regroup and give chase. We took thirty miles by midday and then called for a rest. Next morning, four hours before dawn, we rode the last leg of the journey.

Masada: October, 39 BC

An army the size of a legion waited for us, but their singular duty was to guard the path leading to the top of the mountain. As that road lay on Masada's eastern flank, the army's camp was located there too. This was not far from the waters of the Dead Sea. We came out of the west using the cover of the hills. Still in darkness, we broke into the open and raced toward the mountain. Judaean sentries raised the alarm then retreated hurriedly.

Herod took twelve hundred riders along the northern route; I went south with my six hundred Spartans, all of whom by this point had seen battle. Herod came into the fight a quarter of an hour before we did. The Judaeans were still coming awake when he hit them, and for a time Herod's men ran down squads as they tried desperately to organise a defence. Once the Judaean commanders had called their men to order, Herod sounded the retreat. The Judaean infantry, now well positioned to repulse Herod's second attack, suddenly discovered my Spartan cavalry coming at their camp from the south.

Herod gave their generals no time to organise a second line, but reversed course and charged with his entire cavalry once more. I hit the Judaeans from the opposite side simultaneously, using a combination of horse and infantry.

Once the dust had blinded everyone, Herod's Galilean bandits pretended panic. Giving a cry of terror, they broke and ran, as bandits are known to do. Seeing an easy victory there for the asking, the Judaean commander ordered an attack against Herod's exposed flank.

The Galilean bandits, however, quickly reversed direction and came crashing into those Judaeans furthest in advance. Before the Judaeans could pull themselves back into formation, my Spartan auxiliaries on the mountaintop came down on foot and drove into the enemy at its western flank. With enemy forces now on four sides and no hope of forming any kind of defensive line, the Judaeans threw down their weapons and begged for mercy.

Those who had abandoned Masada to join the enemy were sorted out and executed in the aftermath of the battle. The rest were given the opportunity to return to Antigonus in Jerusalem or join Herod's army. Some few men left, but those with no political stake were happy to swear allegiance to Herod, upon whom it seemed Fortune now smiled.

⸺⸺

Afterwards, Herod and I ascended the long road to the mountaintop and greeted those of his family and friends whom we had not seen for sixteen months. I found Salome beyond the press of bodies, her eyes bright but tearless. 'I must tell you, sir,' she said, 'I was beginning to think you'd forgotten us.'

Jericho: Winter, 39 – 38 BC

Following his victory at Masada, Herod advanced on Jericho. His numbers now exceeded three thousand fighting men. There was some resistance at the walls of Jericho but friends in the city opened the gates on the very day we attacked. At that point, Antigonus's garrison threw down their weapons. Once again, Herod gave the captured men the choice of joining him or returning to Antigonus and once more his numbers swelled. As for the rest of us, we were soon installed inside the walls of that most ancient and splendid city. Once we had taken Jericho, Silo marched into Judaea with nearly a full legion under his authority. These included the three cohorts Antony had sent, plus auxiliaries and some mercenaries provided by Ventidius. We imagined the war would soon come to a conclusion. Instead, Silo negotiated a treaty with King Antigonus.

This amounted to Antigonus providing Silo with Judaean gold. With these matters settled, Silo retreated with his army back across the Syrian border, claiming yet another Roman victory for Ventidius.

———⬥———

Jericho is an oasis town at the base of the Judaean mountains. It is rich in produce of every variety but most famous for balsam. Due largely to the wealth of its population, Herod had enjoyed a great many contacts in this city when his father served as a Roman procurator. Despite the city's close proximity to Jerusalem, Herod elected to winter his troops here. Antigonus sent a force down the mountain to hold us in place, but there was otherwise very little contact between the two armies that winter.

With the seas closed for the season, I had no choice but to spend my winter in Jericho with Herod. With the coming of spring Herod's army broke out of Jericho and fought its way north along the Jordan valley. In the wake of his victories at Ashkelon and Masada and Jericho, he found fresh recruits in Galilee. The Samaritan lords eventually provided him over two thousand additional cavalry. For my part, I had fulfilled my promise to those Spartans I had left behind and sailed with them to Greece with the help of Herod's friends in Cyprus.

I learned of Caesar's marriage to Livia during the journey.

XXIV
THE BEAUTIFUL EXILE

Athens: April, 38 BC

I could not comprehend the news at first. Caesar had been married to some relative of Sextus Pompey; breaking off that marriage risked the treaty Caesar had just signed. And how had he even met Livia? I was sure it was only a botched rumour and would not believe it until I came to Athens. Once there, I talked to men who were better informed. They gave me full assurance it was true: Livia, nine months pregnant on her wedding day, had married Caesar in the first days of the new year.

By all accounts, the two had fallen in love on the very day they met. I didn't believe it, because I did not want to believe it, but I was not really sure what else I could believe. Brooding on the matter, I finally recalled that Octavia had been at the palace with Livia for several weeks in Athens. Livia had, I was sure, impressed Caesar's sister, and she had decided Livia would make the perfect consort for her brother. Caesar, looking for any excuse to wreck the peace with Pompey, was only too happy to rid himself of Pompey's relative. All the better that he could do it and also have his revenge against Claudius Nero in the process. Adding insult to injury, Caesar obliged Nero to act as Livia's father during the wedding ceremony and give her away to her new husband.

~•~

On my second morning in Athens and much hung over from a futile attempt to drown my sorrows, I went to report to Antony. I was not thinking about Livia's betrayal. I had outrage enough over Silo's mutiny and reported the facts of the case simply and plainly: Silo had disobeyed Antony's orders.

Antony knew I wanted retribution, but he did not seem especially offended by Silo's disobedience. In fact, he told me he had half expected something like that. I decided, quite suddenly, to offer my resignation. Up to that moment, I had been content in Antony's service, but without a moment of reflection I resigned my commission.

I have no doubt Livia's marriage to Caesar was working on me, though it did not seem so when I announced my intentions. What I told myself was this: I was sick to death of Antony's apathy. Insubordination and taking bribes from the enemy ought to have meant Silo's death, but Antony took no notice of the matter. In fact, his only irritation seemed to be with me, that I complained to him about it. After all these years, I have a better understanding of the situation. I am sure Antony believed me; the problem for him was Ventidius. Ventidius had also disobeyed orders and he was suddenly Rome's new hero. Caesar had already encouraged the senate to vote the man a Triumph for his victory in Syria. We had not had a Triumph since the one I had walked in with the divine Julius Caesar; so this was no small matter and would make Ventidius a powerful rival to Antony. In my fury, however, I saw none of these issues. I had no idea Antony was struggling just to stay alive. No, I wanted the world made right for my sake, and I wanted it at once.

'Resignation?' Antony asked in surprise. 'For what reason?'

'I mean to claim my patrimony,' I answered. 'I will then buy some land. I'm not sure exactly where. Perhaps Spain.' *Far from Rome*, I added but only in my thoughts.

'Don't be a fool, Dellius. At the moment, you are an important man. Will you give that up to be a farmer in Spain?'

I did not care to be called a fool on top of the rest and my anger went icy; my resolve became quite fixed. 'I will,' I told him.

'Haven't I always given you exactly what you asked of me?'

'You have. Mostly. Eventually, I mean.'

'But you are not happy serving me?'

'In the six years since Julius Caesar's murder I have not

had more than a day or two of luxury, and even then it was only luxury. I have not had the chance to marry or think about the patrimony I have lost.'

'Then take the remainder of the year off. Report back next spring, and we shall march on the Parthians together.'

'I require more than a few months.'

'I won't beg you to stay, Dellius. Go, if that is what you desire, but on your life do not come asking favours of me again.' I was walking for the door. 'Do you hear me, Dellius? I won't take you back. Not if you beg it of me!'

Italy: April, 38 BC

A free man, I took only those belongings that mattered and left the palace at once. I found a public room that evening and then joined up with the first merchant ship sailing for Italy.

I had no clear idea what I intended, but there were matters in Rome I needed to settle before I considered my options. The first order of business was my patrimony. Twenty-five percent of my father's great estate was a fortune by my reckoning, but of course I knew there were difficulties in making a claim of that sort. In fact, with the prospect of bribing officials for a fair ruling, I was not at all sure how much money I would have in the end. I decided therefore to contact Maecenas the moment I arrived in the city.

I actually approached him with a letter. In return, I also received a letter with the name of a lawyer I should visit. This was a day or so after writing to him. I met with the lawyer, explained my circumstances and then agreed to give him some weeks to arrange my payout. 'As easy as that?' I asked. I had heard stories about settlements that were being fought in the courts and payments that the new owners simply refused to make. No one, so far as I knew, got his money simply by asking for it.

The fellow's smile was a bit sly, but it was friendly enough. 'It's a simple matter for the man Cilnius Maecenas calls his friend.'

After that, I sought an audience with Claudius Nero. Nero had settled in his former house on the Palatine and was enrolled again as a member of the senate. He admitted me before all the others in his vestibule on the first morning I went to see him. I was not confident this would happen, but I thought, in the circumstances, it was only proper.

When I was standing before him, I offered my hand, but Nero pretended not to see it. Instead of greeting me, he told his attendants to leave the room. When we were alone, he said, 'I have sacrificed often to various of the gods, Dellius. I prayed to them that you and I might speak to one another soon.'

'There are no gods, Excellency.'

'And yet here you are.'

'I have need of your assistance.'

'Let me guess. You want to speak with Livia?'

'I do.'

'I know the truth about the two of you, Dellius.' When I did not answer him at once, he continued. 'Livia told me about your love affair. I came to her with Caesar's proposal of marriage last autumn, and she refused it. Not for my sake, mind you, but because she said she wanted to marry Quintus Dellius. Quintus Dellius, not Caesar! Do you know what I did? I slapped her pretty face. I told her I would not permit it. I would kill her before I would let her debase herself with a marriage to the likes of you. She took her belly in her hands, Dellius. She told me the child she carried was yours.

'Oh, yes! I know the truth about my new son! My son, not hers and not yours. By right of ancient Roman law the boy is mine. He shall be raised with Tiberius as his full brother. As a Claudian!

'I hope you live a long life, Dellius,' he continued. 'I hope when you are my age some pretty boy steals your wife for an afternoon or two. Just enough to take her heart from you. Perhaps she might even give you his son to raise afterwards, though all and sundry know he is not of your blood.

'Look at me, lad! You were brave enough to face down Caesar's bounty hunters. Let me see that courage now.'

'I am sorry,' I muttered.

'Sorry? Sorry for what? Being caught in your lies? I know you are not sorry you fucked her!'

I could not answer him, but stood there as dumb and astonished as dreary old Claudius Nero before Dolabella.

'You know what I am tempted to do? I am tempted to arrange a meeting for you and Livia. I would do it too, but it is bound to get you both killed. Bad business for the mother of my sons. So I will do what is best for you, if only to save Livia. I will tell you what you must do. You must go as far from Rome as you can get and never come back. If you do not exile yourself, if you attempt to slip away and then come back in a year or two, I will send men to kill you. Far away, Dellius. Far from my child and from the woman whose heart you stole from me. And if you are not sure it is far enough, go even farther.'

—⚏⚏—

Once threatened, I made sure to linger in Rome and visit old friends. I actually hoped Nero would keep his word. I kept my swords handy, but otherwise I was not especially worried. To be honest, I hardly cared whether I lived or died.

The lawyer to whom I had spoken eventually sent a small fortune to me. As per the custom, some of the money came in coins; the bulk of it was a letter of credit.

In addition to the money, the lawyer handed me a letter without any mark on the seal.

There was no signature at the bottom of the letter but I knew it was from Livia. She asked to meet me at her former husband's house. She named the day and hour when she would next visit her children. Servants would be present, she wrote, but we could at least hope to talk to one another.

Nero's steward led me through the house to Livia, who waited in the porticoed garden at the back of the house. She held her infant son in her arms; young Tiberius was in a room nearby under the care of a slave. 'I thought you might like to see your son,' she told me.

I stood before her, wanting her touch but forced to stand apart. Nor did she offer to let me hold the child.

'What is his name?'

'Drusus. After my father. I only wish I could have given him your name, instead.' Her gaze met mine as she said this and I knew she had not betrayed me, that she wanted my touch as much as I wanted hers. But that would not happen. She would not give Nero's slaves power over her. They would have nothing to tell the dominus except that Livia had a visit from Quintus Dellius, who spoke with her briefly and then left.

'He is a handsome child,' I said.

'If Nero had his way,' Livia told me, 'I would never see either of my sons again. As it is, I am permitted an hour with them every fortnight.'

'Nero is angry because of our love affair.'

'The permission to visit them comes from Caesar. He tells me the boys must stay with their father and that I am fortunate to see them as often as I do.' There seemed nothing to say to this. I could certainly do nothing to help her. 'I am a prisoner, Dellius. There is no other way to put it. I cannot come to you again. I risked everything for this meeting. Nero will find out about it, of course. I can't very well pretend he won't, but I don't think he will tell Caesar.'

'But surely we can meet again?'

'Not alone, not even like this.' By this she meant standing in the open with all of Nero's servants observing us.

'In a year or two Caesar will probably want to marry someone else,' I said.

'I will not give him cause for it. Besides, if he does, it won't help us. I am sure he will only pass me on to someone else, certainly not someone I might choose.'

'I suppose we were fools to imagine it could be otherwise.'

'You should marry someone, Dellius. Start a family.'

'I was hoping to marry you.'

'We have a child, at least.'

'Nero has him.'

'Not for long.' At my look of surprise, she added, 'I will not lose my sons, Dellius. They will be living with me before the year has ended. That I have promised myself.'

I did not doubt her, though I imagined she meant that she would persuade Caesar to bring them into his house. In fact, Caesar had nothing to do with it. Nero took ill not long after the first frost that autumn. He was dead within a matter of days. After that, Caesar had no choice but to let Livia's children live with their mother.

We did not kiss goodbye, nor even touch hands. A servant came to her with Tiberius, and Livia wished me happiness. And that was it. A slave escorted me to Nero's front gate, and I was soon beyond the walls of the house.

After that, there was nothing in Rome to hold me, and I went off to find my secretary, who had stayed with Hannibal on Flavius Petro's farm. While I was in Judaea Petro had been offered work in the city as a tax collector and had hired a manager to look after the breeding project. I did not care for the situation; for one thing it was too close to Rome, but I thought the broodmares were all fine animals; so I returned to Rome and made an offer to Petro to buy the broodmares. Petro, now committed to a political life in Rome, was happy for an infusion of cash to finance his new lifestyle and I became the sole owner of our enterprise. I hired a few of Petro's slaves to help take the horses as far as Ostia.

Once there it took me nearly a week to find someone willing to sail to Spain with twenty-five horses for cargo.

Seville, Spain: Summer, 38 BC

I found Trajan at the house where I had recuperated following the battle at Ronda. After explaining my situation to him, Trajan said he would be happy to lease me whatever property I desired for my stud farm, but if I cared to be his son-in-law he would provide the land as a dowry instead. After some negotiations, I married his eldest son's daughter, Ulpia, the very girl who had nursed me back to health in the days when the divine Julius Caesar still walked this earth. In those early days of my career she had been a mere child, seven or eight years old; even so she had been eager to see me whole and healthy again. As a young wife she came into my life again and healed me of a broken spirit.

⚬

A few months after our wedding, I looked up one morning and saw my land stretching out for as far as I could see. The broodmares had foaled and the offspring were grazing with their mothers. Ulpia was standing a short distance from me. She was soon to give us our first child, and I knew that I was content. Recalling that my father had encouraged me to believe that contentment was a worthy aim in life I suddenly found myself smiling at the memory. At the time my father had given his opinion I was too young to appreciate the wisdom of it. The years, however, had changed me. I could now see my life taking a new direction and I knew I need never touch my swords again, not for the sake of Rome, at least. My ties to the past, to Antony and Caesar and Herod and Livia seemed perfectly severed that day and I could almost imagine that nothing could ever pull me back.

I was mistaken of course. I was to spend several more years in the service of the empire. There were differing reasons each time I returned, but gone was the savage ambition of my youth; gone, too, the young fool's lust for the glory that one buys with the blood of other young fools. What mattered in my life waited for me in Spain, and to Spain and my family I would always return.

EPILOGUE

Spain and Italy: Autumn, 8 BC

The story of a man's youth is sometimes not entirely finished with the advancement of years. There are threads that haven't been cut, answers to riddles that have long remained obscure.

I was in my fifty-seventh year when a traveller came through Seville carrying a letter for me. I did not know the man, but he was a legionary freshly retired from service in the north. He was on his way to Cadiz, where he had friends and hoped to marry a girl and start a family. The letter he carried was from my old friend Horace. For taking the trouble to deliver it, I gave the man a couple of nights in my house and the best food and wine my estate could offer.

Only after my guest had departed did I instruct my secretary to open Horace's letter and read it to me. The letter was mostly an introduction to a poem Horace had written, called *Ode to Dellius*. I attach it at the end of this manuscript for anyone curious about its details, though of course it is now published everywhere. I expect one may find a copy of it in almost any decent city bath, though it is much altered from the draft I possess.

I listened eagerly to the poem, but to be honest I did not recognise myself. There was no reference in it to our youth together, nothing at all of those inglorious days we had spent huddled in Antony's prison at the edge of the marsh at Philippi. Nothing of my duel with a Celtic gladiator or the fortune we both won in its aftermath. Not even a poetic allusion to my fondness for fighting with two swords.

No, Horace had left those memories for the wind. He chose instead to chide me, poetically, for my contentment. And then of course, because he was Horace, he brought me face-to-face with the prospect of my death. This was more chilling than cruel, but I reacted defensively. Yes, I thought, life is short for the rich man and the poor, Horace, but what can any of us do about it?

Then I poured myself a cup of my good Spanish wine – not the Falernian vintage so many Romans worship that tastes to me like beetle piss – and as I sipped pure ambrosia I told my secretary, Judah's predecessor, 'We all have to die, but this I can tell you from personal experience: while we live it is far better to be rich and loved than poor and forgotten!' That was my answer to Horace's pretty poem.

Trained to please his master, my secretary answered crisply, 'Yes, Dominus.'

And then, as I listened to the poem once more, I finally understood what it was really about. Horace was chiding the poetic Dellius for the very things Horace had always loved. And that could only be for one reason.

I took all my sons and one of my grandsons on the journey to Italy. My grandson was then of an age to put on his toga virilis and sign his name into the immortal list of Roman citizens; so that was our excuse. I took as well two of my dogs, since at least on part of my trip I expected to be travelling with only my secretary. He was a fair hand with a sword, not nearly the equal of Judah, but not a disappointment like the secretary Horace had given me either. I still carried my two swords of course and could hold my own with most men, but dogs are keener than soldiers during a night watch and mine are trained to fight at the flanks like good cavalry. They are also fine companions for a long journey. Better than sons in some respects.

Once my progeny had settled with my old friend Petro and his family, I left them to their gaudy pleasures in the city and made my way by hired carriage to the estate Maecenas had bought for Horace.

I was glad I had made the long journey when I saw Horace. He had gone for years always looking the same: sleek, short, fat, and happy. Quite suddenly he had turned grey and old and looked somehow sunken in. Horace was my age, of course, which is to say aging but not yet ancient, but something had hooked into him. A worm or the black rot that gets so many of us. Bribe any god you like, throw a living wild boar on the altar of Artemis if you can; it is all for nothing. Once a hard illness takes hold, Death is coming and there is no escape.

When I asked about his health, as old friends do, Horace sighed. 'Tired lately. Always tired it seems.'

I had my secretary unpack some of my Spanish wine and promised Horace his weariness would soon vanish. And it did for the course of an hour or two.

'Maecenas is dead. I suppose you heard?' Horace announced this not long after our first cup. I had only learned of his death when I arrived in Rome and admitted as much. 'Caesar had a great celebration for him, full honours at public expense,' Horace told me. 'I thought that by now everyone in the world would have heard about it.'

'I know that Livia's second son perished in the north last year,' I answered, 'but I had heard nothing about Maecenas until a few days ago.'

'Poor Drusus. There is a tragedy for one to contemplate. A prince of the empire cut down in the prime of life. You know, they say Livia has not left her house since his funeral. That is almost a year. Most believe the loss will kill her.'

'She loved the boy dearly. I know that.' Then, rather desperate to change the subject of my son's demise, I added, 'I came to visit you because of that awful poem you dedicated to me.'

'You didn't like it?' Horace smiled, but I could see he was hurt or at least disappointed.

'We are too old to be melancholy about death, Horace. I hoped you would write about my two gladii flashing in the bright sunlight of my youth. Or a paean to our race through the marsh at Philippi that we might burn a few of Antony's tents.'

'As I have grown older, Dellius, I have tried to write about what matters.'

'You think death is what matters?'

'The prospect of our death ought to teach us the difference between what is true and what is only vanity.'

'Death is a wolf slinking about in the shadows, my friend. There is nothing to learn from such a beast.'

'The prospect of death is what gives life its urgency.'

'You should write a poem about our Caesar Augustus, who used to die a little before every battle.'

'I enjoy life too much to risk what remains of it so foolishly.'

'An ode to Caesar's battle terrors and how his fear gave his life a sense of urgency. That would work for me!'

'I could write a more dangerous poem than that if I wanted.'

'*You* know some secret the rest of us don't?'

'Let us say what I know I ought never to mention.'

'Horace, Caesar murdered his friends that he might have their money. As a boy, he ran from every battle he ever faced. The man is a thief and a coward of the first order. *You* are not going to tell me he was Maecenas's girl, as well, are *you*? I'm afraid that secret is already out and fairly well confirmed.'

'It is nothing like that, but it involves Maecenas.'

'*You* have me curious.'

'I don't dare say it, Dellius. It is the sort of secret to get a man killed if he speaks it.'

'Tell it to me, or I will never forgive *you*.'

'*You* mustn't repeat it to anyone.'

'Not even to my dogs.'

'I am serious, Dellius. It is too dangerous even to joke about.'

'I will keep silent for as long as you live.'

'Better be silent for as long as *you* live.'

'I will not make that promise. I'm thinking about writing my autobiography one of these days. I only lack the ambition at the moment. But I will say nothing about this matter until *you* are safely beyond the reach of all that is mortal.'

'That will have to do, I suppose. It is your skin after all. *You* know, I expect, that Maecenas always had a great talent for forgery?'

'Maecenas had many talents,' I answered. 'I wasn't aware forgery was among them.'

'Oh, he was a prodigy. I saw him do it several times with different friends. He would show them some letter in

421

their own handwriting that they had sent to a friend. In it would be some terrible remark about Maecenas, insulting his dinner parties, his poetry, his lack of manliness. And showing it to them, Maecenas would ask them why they hated him. Of course they were terrified and denied writing it and claimed some terrible conspiracy to ruin a perfectly wonderful friendship. At that point Maecenas would laugh and take credit for the forgery himself. It always seemed to be a parlour trick and nothing more, but I often wondered if he had ever used his talent for some more sinister purpose.'

'Letters of credit?'

'I was thinking more along the lines of promoting a friend's career.'

'You're talking about his friend Caesar?'

'To tell you the truth, I had frankly always wondered if Maecenas had forged Julius Caesar's will.'

I laughed at this. 'That's mad! Had he even the opportunity?'

'He did. And with Octavian's help he could have done it.'

'But if you're right…'

I stopped as I realised quite suddenly the full implications of such a crime. With Julius Caesar's will written by Maecenas and Octavian, those two boys had stolen more than Caesar's name and fortune. They had taken fire from heaven! Without that document Octavian would have enjoyed no following, no claim for justice and no reason to be elected a consul while he was yet a boy. This was more than a purloined fortune and a pretty name; this was the theft of an empire.

I cast a glance back across the room. My secretary was reading one of the books from Horace's library. I did not think he could hear us, we were actually whispering, but I did not care to trust him to listen to such treasonous talk and sent him from the house on some errand. When we were alone I asked Horace in a softer whisper still, 'Had they really the opportunity to do such a thing?'

'Did you know that the summer before Caesar's assassination, after his campaign in Andalusia, Caesar entertained Octavian and Maecenas at his house outside of Rome?'

'No. I was recuperating in Spain.'

'It's well documented. There were others at the house, coming and going, but Octavian and Maecenas were there for several weeks. Enough time to get comfortable with the routines of the servants and to learn Caesar's habits. And it was just at that time Caesar rewrote his will for the last time.'

'But you have no proof!'

'As I say, I had always known it was possible – even likely, knowing those two. But that's all it was until one evening, when we were drunk – this must have been two or three years ago. I asked Maecenas outright if he had forged Caesar's will.'

'What did he say?'

'He seemed startled at first. Then he smiled and said it would have been a neat trick if he had.'

'He didn't deny it?'

'I think he wanted me to know he was the one who changed our world, Dellius.'

'But what if they had been caught?'

'That was the beauty of it. They had handwriting samples of the secretary available to study; they may even have listened to Caesar dictating his will. They knew his style of composition, and they could create the document in secret, then exchange theirs for the real one when the opportunity presented itself.'

'But the seal?'

'A simple matter of distracting Caesar's secretary. You know how clever boys can be when it comes to that kind of thing.'

'But when the will was read, the secretary would know the truth.'

'Of course he knew the truth. He knew as well to keep quiet.'

'They would have been mad to attempt such a thing!'

'They were boys. It probably seemed nothing more than a clever prank when they did it.'

'A prank on all of us. What if Caesar had lived and discovered their crime some years afterwards?'

'That's the beauty of it. Once Caesar put his seal in the wax, his will would not be opened until after his death. When he finally entered Rome later that summer, he intended to deposit it in the house of the Vestal Virgins. Should he ever want to revise his will, he would submit a new will and the caretakers would destroy the old one, unopened and unread. By law the crime simply could not be discovered.'

'And Maecenas didn't even attempt to deny it?'

'Maecenas forged Caesar's will, Dellius. I could see it in his eyes.'

'So we add to the long list of our Caesar's iniquities the charge of imposter and fraud. Why am I not more surprised?'

'Not a word, Dellius. If he hears of it, Caesar will know where the rumour began.'

'Not a word, I promise.' And to myself I added, *Until you are gone, my friend.*

⬥

A day or two after that first drunken afternoon, Horace called me to his room and admitted that he could not leave his bed. I made some joke about a hangover, but he would not pretend any longer. 'I am dying,' he whispered. 'Why don't you leave while I am still conscious and can give you a proper farewell? These things are never pretty.'

Bachelor that he was, Horace had friends by the thousand in the city and of course several faithful servants in his house. But that is not family, and so I told him I had come prepared for this. Hoping otherwise but ready for the worst if my premonitions proved true. 'I mean to fight all the gods in heaven to keep you in the light, Horace! Summon the heartless bastards, and I will take them on in turn or all at once! Whatever way they like it!'

Horace shook his head. 'I see an old man before me, Dellius, but I still hear the young tribune who thought we ought to burn Antony's camp just because he had burned ours.'

'It seemed a good idea at the time.'

He shook his head in mock sadness. 'Youth is a beautiful country.'

'Youth is a country, is it?'

'A land without shadows, where everything is clear and unambiguous, and we will live forever. And what we want to be the truth is the only truth we know.'

'If youth is a country, Horace, you and I are exiles.'

'I think not. You with your swords, I with my poetry – we have not changed. Not really. We are slower in our movements and never miss the chance to complain, but when I write I am still the young god who never grows old, and I expect it is no different with you. Touch a sword and you are immortal, or at least imagine it. We may travel away from it, but I tell you this: we always return to the country of endless sunlight. It is why, in the end, we are all such fools.'

My friend did not die in his next breath, not for many days more. I stayed to the end, and we talked about the old days, mostly about Antony as it happened, for we both had long and complex relationships with him, and because, despite all the complaints against him in recent years, Antony really defined the age far better than the boy who stole Caesar's name.

When Horace had faded and there was no more talk, he lasted another few days in perfect silence, and then he was gone. I travelled with his corpse to Rome and stood with a great many old friends. In fact, I stood not far from Caesar and his adopted son, Tiberius, that same Tiberius who owed his life to me, though he could not remember it.

We had all become old men, even Tiberius. And so we burned the remains of Horace without a tear shed, then consecrated his ashes to gods that do not exist; I don't think any of us in that circle believed in the Olympians, though I was the only one ever to admit it openly and certainly the only one with the courage to taunt the empty skies.

At any rate, we gave up the ashes of our friend to something, and looking at the men I had fought with and against through all our long years, looking at Caesar even, I wondered if Horace was right.

I have never believed we remain one being inside our aging bodies; it is a principle of my faith that I am something more than flesh; my mind and my spirit wax large even as my body fails. But I must say Horace had given me pause. Perhaps, as we stumble along toward what will ultimately be our grave, nothing at all really changes, not the essentials, anyway; perhaps we are all still the young fools we were at the very beginning.

There is something beautiful in that, I suppose, something immortal even. And though it ought not to be, perhaps it is even true.

HORACE'S ODE TO DELLIUS

In travail
remain steadfast;
in joy temper your pride.
You will die, Dellius.

Whether you waste your days in sorrow
or recline on the grass drinking
Falernian wine at every festival:
it is the same.

Why do the tall pine
and white poplar
offer shade?
Why does the river run?

While the fates let the black thread of your life
spin out uncut,
enjoy the wine, walk serenely
in your garden, bathe with sweet oils.

Your house and fields
and all your wealth
your heirs will come to own
once you leave.

Born of a king
or the lowest field slave
it doesn't matter:
your last road is always the same.

And you will follow it until,
almost by chance, you come upon
a certain ferryman who will take you
into the eternal exile.

HISTORICAL NOTE

With few exceptions I have substituted modern place names for the ancient ones. With respect to proper names, I have employed the Roman name and spelling unless the individual is better known by the anglicised version. With Octavian, I have broken with a long tradition of calling him Octavian in the aftermath of Julius Caesar's assassination. My choice fits with the historical facts, he was emphatically called Caesar, but I made the decision so that the reader might more perfectly appreciate the power of the name.

In the ancient histories Quintus Dellius shows up in the oddest places and often for no very clear reason. There is no evidence he was ever elected to public office, nor is his military rank ever mentioned. The only safe bet is that he was an eques, which is to say his father was a Roman citizen in possession of at least 100,000 denarii. We know Dellius served Dolabella and that he was probably with Dolabella in Spain for Julius Caesar's last military campaign. Circumstances suggest that he might also have been present for the murder of Gaius Trebonius. Dellius is not mentioned as leading an army into Judaea. Nor is there any record of his imprisonment in Samaria. A Roman army of four legions did arrive in Judaea commanded by Aulus Allienus, but that is all we know. Josephus credits Malichus with the assassination of Antipater.

It is possible Dellius met Horace at Philippi. We know Brutus recruited Horace in Athens, where Horace was studying. Horace himself confesses to being an incompetent officer. Dellius and Antony may or may not have known each other before Philippi. What is clear is that Antony very quickly promoted Dellius to a position of prominence in his court. Dellius famously led a delegation to the royal court of Egypt only a year after joining Antony. Dellius essentially vanishes from history after he leaves Antony's service and joins Caesar's staff at Actium in 31 BC. In fact, all that we know about him after this final change of patrons is that his new circle of acquaintances dubbed him 'The Horse Changer'. This sobriquet compares Dellius's adroit shifts from one patron to the next with a rider who comes galloping into a post station and changes to a fresh mount.

Virtually every public scene in this novel occurred as I have described it; some details are at variance with the historical accounts, but I usually made adjustments because the histories either left inviting gaps or they were not entirely credible. Where there are private exchanges beyond the scope of the historical record, I have asserted my rights as a storyteller. Everyone named in this novel existed, except for Livia's horse, Artemis. There actually was a tall red horse originally owned by an eques named Seius. Dolabella possessed this horse in Syria, Cassius took ownership of it after Dolabella's death, and finally Antony won the horse with the death of Cassius; nobody ever recorded the ultimate fate of the animal or bothered to mention its name. Judah, the secretary, entered history in the same year that Dellius completed his autobiography. More about that I hope to present at a later date.

Livia and Nero were chased by bounty hunters and nearly burned to death in a forest fire close to Sparta, but there is no record of anyone assisting them. Likewise, Herod escaped with his entire family from Jerusalem and then left them at Masada for nearly sixteen months. Whether or not his Roman allies included a cohort of Spartans led by Q. Dellius, we cannot say, but elsewhere Dellius is mentioned by Josephus as helping Herod storm the walls of Jerusalem in Herod's decisive battle against prince Antigonus.

ACKNOWLEDGEMENTS

For their close reading of an early draft of this novel I owe a debt of gratitude to Donald Jennermann, Frederick Williams, Harriet McNeal, Burdette Palmberg, Tim Murgatroyd, Ben Haymond, and my mother, Shirley Underwood.

As always, a sincere thanks to my agent, Jeffrey Simmons, and my editor, Ed Handyside.

The continued encouragement from my brother Doug and his wife Maria keeps me going in ways they cannot begin to imagine. Most of all I am indebted to my wife, Martha Ineichen-Smith, for her support, encouragement, and love.

MORE GREAT WRITING FROM CRAIG SMITH
THE PAINTED MESSIAH

Legend persists that, after the scourging of Christ, Pilate commanded that his victim be painted from life. Somewhere, the portrait survives, the only true image of the Messiah, granting everlasting life to those who possess it.

Wealthy young English widow, Kate Kenyon, and antique bookseller, Ethan Brand, get their thrills from armed robbery. Their latest target is a priceless 'Byzantine' icon. Until now, they've never had to shoot anyone. This time things will be different.

Retired CIA man, TK Malloy, is hired by a rich but ailing televangelist to courier his newly acquired painting from a Zurich bank to the local airport. Malloy anticipates trouble, but not the maelstrom of bullets and betrayal that threatens to pull him under.

Sir Julian Corbeau is an international criminal holed up in Switzerland to avoid US extradition. He is also the sadistic head of the modern Knights Templar. He had the painting and now he seeks bloody revenge on those who stole it.

As the contenders vie for possession and the body count rises, the secrets of the painting gradually unfold to reveal how an object depicting the Light of the World could exert so malignant an influence on all who possess it.

"I got paper friction burns on my fingers and pressure sores elsewhere because I could barely move until I'd finished it. Things were so tense that at several points I had to remind myself to breathe."

Dovegreyreader

"A marvellously thrilling book... the distinction between villain and hero is constantly blurred... a most enthralling story."
Paul Docherty, author of the Hugh Corbett mysteries

£7.99   978-1-905802-15-9

THE BLOOD LANCE

KUFSTEIN, AUSTRIA 1939

At the foot of a mountain lies the body of an SS officer, his neck broken, his face a picture of bliss and serenity. Known to history as Otto Rahn, Himmler's personal Grail hunter, his quest for the legendary Blood Lance of the Cathars has set in motion a vicious cycle of violence that will last for seventy years.

THE SWISS ALPS, 1997

Lady Katherine Kenyon celebrates her honeymoon on the perilous slopes of the Eiger with her husband Lord Robert Kenyon, financier and influential member of the philanthropic Knights of the Holy Lance. Attacked by unknown assailants, Kate is left for dead, widowed and with a burning thirst for vengeance.

HAMBURG, GERMANY 2008

When a billionaire fraudster cuts loose from the US, former CIA agent TK Malloy is assigned to hunt him down. The trail leads to the mysterious Knights of the Holy Lance. With his friends, Kate and Ethan Brand, Malloy sets out to uncover its secrets. Malloy must find his man; Kate still seeks her former husband's killer. Their first step is to kidnap a corrupt Hamburg lawyer from his home. Things don't quite run to plan and then all hell breaks loose...

"Seamlessly mixing history, legend and fiction, Smith's writing is both intelligent and exhilarating. His characters are alive, and the twists and turns of the several plots will keep readers breathless."

Historical Novels Review

£7.99   978-1-905802-29-6

COLD RAIN

"I turned thirty-seven that summer, older than Dante when he toured Hell, but only by a couple of years..."

Life couldn't be better for David Albo, an associate professor of English at a small mid-western university. He lives in an idyllic, out-of-town, plantation-style mansion with a beautiful and intelligent wife and an adoring teenage stepdaughter. As he returns to the university after a long and relaxing sabbatical, there's a full professorship in the offing – and, what's more, he's managed to stay off the booze for two whole years.

But, once term begins, things deteriorate rapidly. The damning evidence that he has sexually harassed his students is just the beginning as Dave finds himself sucked into a vortex of conspiracy, betrayal, jealousy and murder. Unless he can discover quickly who is out to destroy him, all that he is and loves is about to be stripped away.

"... an absolute gem of a surprise. This is good, solid writing, piled with suspense and tension." *It's a crime! (or a mystery...)*

SHORTLISTED FOR THE CWA IAN FLEMING STEEL
DAGGER FOR BEST THRILLER 2011

£7.99   978-1-905802-34-0

EVERY DARK PLACE

Ten years ago, sleepy Shiloh Springs was shaken as five teenagers were clubbed and shot to death...

But now Will Booker's conviction for the crime has been overturned after allegations that his rights were violated on arrest.

Rick Trueblood, careworn private investigator working for the county prosecutor's office, still grieves for a daughter murdered in a crime he has never been able to solve. The judge has allowed just sixty days to find enough evidence to retry the Booker case. But as Rick struggles to re-investigate a trail long gone cold he uncovers a rat's nest of intrigue and duplicity far closer to home than he could have possibly imagined.

Out on bail, Booker plots the kidnap and murder of two adolescent girls while the local authorities follow procedures and file reports. Rick, on the other hand, has learned something about the way Booker thinks. In the desperate hours that follow, Rick must recover both his instinct for the hunt and a renewed passion for life.

A terrifying tale of search and rescue, madness and redemption.

£7.99 978-1-905802-53-1